The Search

For The

King James

Bible

Anne-Marie Price

This novel is entirely a work of fiction.
The names, characters and incidents portrayed in it
are the work of the author's imagination.
Any resemblance to actual persons, living or dead,
events or localities is entirely coincidental

ISBN: 987-0-9942761-0-0
ISBN-13 987-0-9942761-0-0:

DEDICATION

To Margaret and Laurence Price,
who fight the black dog
with me each and every day.

ACKNOWLEDGMENTS

My sincere thanks to Wendy Stackhouse
for her expertise and technical support
in getting this book finally published.

A big thank you also to my Beta readers
Lynne Doyle and June Earle.

Finally to Evanescence
and the beautifully haunting music
of their Fallen CD.

THURSDAY

A Spirit Healer

Amongst the ruins of Theobalds Palace, Jenny Weston stood motionless, warmly enveloped in a long black trench coat, as she took in the atmosphere that surrounded her. The morning mist slowly began to rise as the first shards of the dawn's light appeared through the trees, dancing merrily amongst the leaves as it was partnered by a cool, cool breeze. Her wavy long blonde hair was ruffled in the breeze, and her coat did little to conceal the voluptuous figure in the fairy like dress that lay beneath it.

Time slips flashed before Jenny, giving her a pretty accurate picture of life at the Palace during the reign of King James the First. As people of that century went about the daily routine of life, Jenny made no attempt to reach out to any of them, as they weren't real ghosts. These people had nothing to keep them earth bound; they were just imprints that could occasionally be seen by gifted mortals.

Walking through the ruins, the occasional image of spectacular and ornate rooms came to Jenny, retaining her complete attention so that when there was a loud 'Oy!' right behind her; she nearly jumped out of her skin.

'Whatcha doin' 'ere?' The ghost of a little Scotsman with the remnants of a shock of red hair with his hands upon his hips, his bushy brows drawn in a fierce scowl, stood behind her. He wore not a kilt but trousers in the McGregor tartan and a jacket that had been the fashion fifty years ago.

'Hello,' Jenny said, not disturbed by his glare.

'Y're not a child! Yet ya can see and communicate with me! How is tha' possible?'

'Not all adults are blind to the supernatural. I assist ghosts who have unresolved issues that keep them from finding peace.'

Jenny pulled a business card out of the pocket of her coat and handed it to the ghost. He stared at it, then back at Jenny with a look of suspicion.

'Spirit Healer? So ya not 'ere to look for the book?'

'What book?' A blank look answered him. 'Oh, are you referring to the original King James' Bible?'

'Aye! I'd searched for 30 years for tha' book. I wanna know what the person, who does find it, plans to do with the rare tome.'

'But there is little you could do if they don't do with it what you want them to.' Jenny placed her hands into the pockets of her trench coat to keep them warm as her eyebrows rose in enquiry.

The Scotsman gave a wicked laugh, 'Nay lass! I'd haunt the bastard if he were to displease me! What would ya do if ya found the bible?'

Jenny took time to consider the question seriously. 'My main concern is finding the King and releasing his disturbed spirit. I suppose the first thing I'd do if I found the King's bible would be to return it to him.'

The Scotsman nodded. 'But he canna take it with him.'

Jenny shrugged. 'Then the British museum?' She suddenly frowned. 'Or should it actually be given to our current monarch?'

A crooked, satisfied smile covered the Scot's features and he finally extended his hand towards her. 'Ian Andrew McGregor, at y'r service.' Jenny took his hand, willingly shaking it, surprising the ghost when her hand firmly gripped his and didn't simply pass through. 'Now how is tha' possible?'

'I'm a genuine mystic, Ian; I have the ability to make you feel almost alive again.' Jenny indicated her card still in his other hand. 'Have you seen or met King James?'

'Aye, I'm very wary about approachin' his Majesty; he can be a mite queer at times. Rambling like a mad man, ya know!'

Jenny nodded. 'Like King George the Third, King James suffered from Porphyria which caused mental disturbance as well as a few other uncomfortable symptoms.'

'Poor Sod!'

A young woman in a 17th century maid's uniform suddenly materialised. She was short and plump but very pretty and had the most fascinating puppy dog eyes. 'Is it all right, Ian?' The young woman cringed submissively behind Ian as she glanced shyly at Jenny.

'All's grand Mandy.' The Scotsman smiled reassuringly as he put an arm around the girl and drew her forward. 'Tis Jennifer Weston, she's 'ere to help us.'

'Oh!' Mandy dropped into a curtsy. 'How do you do Miss?'

'I'm fine, thank you, Mandy. Why are you still earth bound?'

Mandy glanced nervously about before dropping her voice to a whisper to answer, 'Me brother, Richard was a follower of Cromwell and when Richard was wounded he came to me for help. I got him away to safety but the Palace was in a blaze by the time I returned. All the other staff died in the fire.'

'Ya had to do yer duty to yer brother luv,' Ian said as he squeezed her shoulders.

Jenny nodded in agreement. 'You've nothing to be ashamed of Mandy, especially nothing to keep you here three hundred years. If it wasn't for a certain fiery Scotsman, I'd send you on to your after life now.' The maid blushed as Ian shuffled his feet self-consciously. Their eyes met guiltily but Jenny only smiled in amusement.

Sean Hanson

'Excuse me Miss! Excuse me!'

Mandy immediately vanished as a male mortal strode towards them through the Park. Tall, rugged and fairly handsome, the man in his 30's wore the uniform of Cedar Park and in his hands was a shovel. As Jenny turned to greet this new arrival, Ian became more transparent as he drew less upon Jenny's energy.

'Lovely sunrise isn't it?' greeted Jenny.

The workman doffed his cap. 'There are specific hours for visiting the park Miss.'

From another pocket in her coat, Jenny withdrew a letter from the Borough of Broxbourne Council, which gave her permission to enter anywhere within Cedar Park at any time and handed it across to the workman. He perused the letter before handing it back.

'Sorry about that, Miss Weston. With the recent spate of vandalism, we have to be careful.'

'I understand completely.' Jenny put the letter back into her bag, smiling. 'Have you seen anything unusual, Mr…?'

'Hanson, Sean Hanson.' The workman interjected, stroking his chin as he considered Jenny's question.

Ian crossed his arms in an arrogant manner as he sneered. 'If this bloke thinks too long he'll hurt himself!' Jenny looked around to glare at him, but Ian only grinned mischievously. 'Wait! Wait! Watch out Lass, here comes the thought!' Ian McGregor threw up his hands as if to protect himself.

'Ian, be quiet!' Jenny looked reproachfully at the ghost.

Sean Hanson stared at Jenny in surprise. 'My name is Sean and not Ian, Miss Weston and you did ask me a question!'

'Sorry Sean,' Jenny thumped Ian's arm. 'Ian McGregor is being a little childish. You don't see him standing behind me?'

The workman shook his head, 'No Miss. My dad knew him when he was alive though. He was on a mad crusade to find King James' personal Bible. I and some of the lads have seen Jamie wandering around the ruins but we've never tried to approach him.'

'Jamie?' Jenny's eyebrows rose in a question.

Ian McGregor snorted in disgust, 'This turd is referring to his Royal Highness King James the First of England and the Sixth of Scotland! Let me deal with this disrespectful bastard!' exploded the ghost's temper.

Jenny shook her head. 'Simmer down Ian.' As she checked her watch, tiredness suddenly washed over her and knew that she had to wrap up this meeting. 'Ian, see if the King will agree to see me. Mr Hanson, I'd appreciate it if you could inform the other staff in the park of my presence. I may only get one chance to speak to the King.'

Before his eyes, Sean saw Jenny wilt and he reached out to support her but Ian reacted faster, placing an arm about her waist and leading her to a bench to sit down on.

'Are ya all right Lass?'

Smiling wearily, Jenny pressed a hand against her forehead. 'I'll be fine, Ian. Your anger is just a little draining upon my energy. When does the King normally materialise?' Jenny looked from one man to the other and Sean carelessly shrugged his shoulders.

'About twilight, early evening,' Sean said. Ian nodded and continued to fade from her sight as Jenny rose to her feet.

'I'll return later then. Thank you both.' Jenny paused and turned back to where Ian was vanishing and Sean was heading to his truck.

Lord Death

Amongst the nearby trees, Jenny saw a cloaked figure with a hood pulled down to conceal their features. A gasp was drawn from her as the hood was flung back to reveal beneath a skeletal figure that grinned wickedly at her. As a chill swept down her back, as it always did, Jenny was left in no doubt as to his identity and respectfully sank into a curtsy before Lord Death. When he gestured for Jenny to come to him, she resolvedly shook her head.

'No! There are still so many people that I can help. Isn't that what I'm supposed to do for you?' Slowly the skeletal figure lowered his hand and the smile changed to one that was more affectionate.

When Jenny had cried out, Sean Hanson had turned back to see her talking to thin air again. Thinking that she was in trouble Sean ran back towards her with his shovel raised as if to use it as a weapon. 'Miss Weston? Is there a ghost threatening you?'

Both Jenny and Lord Death looked at Sean and as Death raised his hand, Jenny cried out, 'No! He knows you not! If you must take someone, then take me!'

Again Death lowered his hand and slowly shook his head. Turning, the cloaked skeleton gestured to an open space where Mandy hesitantly materialised. The plump maid shook all over as she obeyed the command for her to approach His Lordship. *I know that Mandy is well passed the time to cross over, but also know why she stayed*, mused Jenny.

'It is time!' The voice boomed through the subtle morning noises, frightening Mandy even more. Lord Death's words had only been heard by the two women.

Ignoring Sean's attempts to get her attention, Jenny rushed forward to stop Mandy taking Death's hand. She glared up at the cloaked figure. 'There is no need to frighten her, my Lord!

When the book of King James is found, Mandy and Ian will both willingly come to you.'

Sean Hanson grabbed hold of Jenny's arms and pulled her around to face him. 'Are you in trouble, Miss Weston? Should I call the Police?'

The stupidity of the question made Jenny laugh, as she disengaged his hands. 'What could they do, Mr Hanson? The Supernatural being I'm arguing with could kill us all with the touch of a finger.' Jenny turned her attention back to His Lordship who was patiently waiting. 'Please my Lord, what can a few more days matter to you? You get us all anyway in the end!'

A wicked grin covered Death's bony features as he reached out to take Jenny's hand and gallantly raised it to his lips. 'It is always an honour doing business with you, Jennifer Weston. I shall see you again... soon.' Releasing her hand, the cloaked figure vanished. Mandy rushed forward and grasped hold of Jenny's hand and also kissed it.

'Thank you Miss!' It was all the girl could manage before she also disappeared.

Sean stood, open mouth as he had seen and heard Jenny's actions and words but not those of the people she had been talking to. 'I don't understand any of this!'

'You don't have to Mr Hanson.' Jenny reassuringly squeezed his arm. 'After an encounter with Death, I think I need a cup of tea!' As she headed slowly to her car, Sean went back to his work truck. Halfway there he suddenly turned and stared at Jenny's back. His glance was puzzling as he looked from her to the ruins and then back again. Having reassured himself that he could see no unearthly creatures, Sean continued on his way. Unbeknown to him, he was being watched and not all eyes belonged to the dead.

The Roberts Family

The Dog and Bone Pub in Waltham Cross had been a well-run and very popular watering hole during the long ownership of Jeff McBride. When he died, three years ago and his daughter Cheryl Roberts took over the pub, she had bought the café next door. A few major structural renovations later and the Dog and Bone became a first class establishment.

The café, now a restaurant and attached to the pub, did smashing business for lunch and dinner, but the cheap prices and the large portions offered for breakfast were very popular with the locals and visitors alike. Cheryl had worked very hard to improve her father's business, keep her family fed, clothed and educated and attempt to keep her marriage together.

The marriage had unfortunately failed but the business had thrived and her son, Peter, now had an apprenticeship with the Bakery in Waltham Cross. Cheryl's daughter was a source of concern, Amy, or as she preferred to be now called, Carmen, was 18 and worked in the Restaurant. She was also a witch, well; she would have liked to be. Her long brown hair, she had dyed jet-black, she wore very heavy white makeup, red lipsticks and long flowing clothes that covered her arms and feet that nearly always was black. Carmen had been seriously affected by her father leaving them for a girl her own age and had lost herself in her study of the Craft.

What Baloney!

Both Cheryl and Carmen were assisting in serving breakfast when Jenny Weston entered the packed restaurant. Jenny looked around at the full tables and deciding on foregoing food, had started towards the double doors which lead through the saloon to the stairs that lead up to a dozen guest rooms. Carmen had been closely watching Jenny and correctly interpreting her train of thought; she called out to her mother and directed her attention to Jenny with a jerk of her head.

'Miss Weston, I'd be happy to bring a tray up to your room,' called out Cheryl Roberts.

'Thank you, Mrs Roberts, I would greatly appreciate that.' Jenny felt a little bit brighter as she continued upstairs.

Carmen put in a full breakfast order with a pot of tea, to the kitchen. It was no secret in the village as to why Jenny was there and it wasn't surprising that it was the topic of conversation in the restaurant.

'Imagine! All these dead people just walking around and we don't know it!'

'I'd rather not know!'

'I think she must be very brave.'

'Yeah, I wouldn't do it for a million pounds!'

'You would for a million pounds!'

'What baloney!' At this loud harsh exclamation, the restaurant patrons fell silent. Cheryl had just finished putting a hot teapot on a tray beside a plate of sausages, bacon and eggs and a rack of toast when she angrily slammed a cup into its saucer. She opened her mouth to speak, but her daughter got in first.

'Mum. don't let Miss Weston's tea get cold.'

'Keep things down to a small riot,' begged Cheryl.

As soon as Cheryl headed out of the restaurant with the tray, Carmen turned a deceptive smiling countenance upon the old relic who had uttered the silence inducing statement.

'Why baloney, Mr Daglish?' Her tone was sweet and inviting but those who knew her well were not deceived by it.

The old relic didn't know her well. 'Counsellor to the dead! Just another charlatan way to get money out of misguided fools!'

What the people who knew Carmen had been waiting for finally happened as she exploded. 'You pompous, ill-informed old fool! How can you dismiss something just because you've never seen it or experienced it? Have you ever seen God? Or an angel? What about the other things we cannot see but know to be real?'

Mr Daglish spluttered and flushed deep red and a giggle rose amongst the patrons but Carmen wasn't quite finished.

'She's here to harm none! So if anyone interferes with Miss Weston, they'll have me to answer to!'

There was a disbelieving laugh from a large youth of 19, 'you and what army?' He demanded as he towered over Carmen.

Sergeant Lucas Greenaway

A deep, rich masculine voice came from the open door, 'I'd be very unhappy with any trouble makers, period!' Senior Sergeant Lucas Greenaway came further into the restaurant and laid a meaningful hand upon the thug's shoulder.

The Sergeant was a large man, well over six-foot and built on solid, muscular lines. He was nearly 40 and was very much a force to be reckoned with. Having stared up at the police officer in surprise, the youth turned his head to glare at Carmen. She only smiled sweetly back at him, as she called out into the kitchen behind her.

'Penny! The Sarg is here for his breakfast!'

From the kitchen came a comely, plump woman in her late 30's with a sterile cap covering her short wavy blonde hair. She wrapped her arms around the Sergeant's neck and planted a very passionate kiss on his lips. 'Did you sleep all right last night?'

'With you beside me, how else would I sleep, but like a baby.' Lucas Greenaway wrapped his arms around Penny's waist and affectionately squeezed his wife's backside.

The prudish looked away at this show of affection but Carmen smiled, pleased that after 19 years of marriage they could still be so much in love. It wasn't that Lucas was a chauvinist and wouldn't fix his own meals but Penny was such a fabulous cook and she loved to cook for him. Besides which Cheryl was more than happy to have the daily friendly police presence, it helped to keep trouble down to a minimum.

The Rumours Begin

The mystery that surrounded Jenny and her unusual occupation continued to grow as speculation and rumours fuelled the gossip hungry residents of the village. A few people had actually glimpsed the ghost of the King; others had heard his voice through the ruins of the Palace. These people became overnight celebrities, other villagers wishing to know every detail of their encounter (that may have lasted only seconds), if told right could be dragged out to cover a couple of pints, hopefully bought by someone else.

So while Jenny was restoring her energy up in her room, the stories grew and took on a life of their own. As she ate her breakfast Jenny read through the notes she had collected from the internet about Theobalds Palace and the surrounding park of Cedar.

Theobalds Palace

The ruins of Theobalds Palace lay within Cedar Park, just north of Waltham Cross a part of the Borough of Broxbourne within the county of Hertfordshire about 10 miles from London. In 1607 Robert Cecil exchanged with the Monarch, Theobalds for Hatfield Palace nearby and Theobalds became the favourite country residence of King James where he died on the 27th March 1625. Like so many other royal residences, Theobalds was disposed of by the Commonwealth and by the end of 1650 was largely demolished.

Although rebuilt after the Restoration of the Monarchy, in 1763 it was purchased by George Prescott and the new manor, now called Cedars, was erected about a mile to the north west of the original Palace. From the Prescotts, Cedars passed to the Meux family who made alterations and extensions during the 19th century and in 1919 Cedars was given to the Borough of Broxbourne Council. Cedars became a hotel, was used by the Royal Artillery during WWII, a riding school by the Metropolitan Police, in 1950 became a secondary school and after 1969 an adult education centre.

In 1995 Cedars was transformed into a conference venue but under the name Theobalds Park, it became a hotel run by the De Vere Group. The park retained the name of Cedars and was still the property of the Borough of Broxbourne of which Waltham Cross was a part.

Carmen's Fears

It wasn't surprising then with all the stories of ghostly accounts being told in the restaurant that Carmen was a little hesitant in going upstairs to collect Jenny's breakfast tray when the morning rush had died down. Not that she was afraid of Jenny, but was concerned that she might be asleep.

The answer Carmen received when she knocked upon Jenny's door was far from being sleepy and she cautiously entered. Although she had removed her overcoat and boots, Jenny was still dressed as she lay on top of the bed spread. Seeing Carmen, Jenny sat up and swung her legs over the side of the bed.

'Thank you for breakfast. I wish I could cook as well as Penny does.'

Carmen gave a nervous laugh, 'Don't we all!' She picked up the tray from the desk and catching a glimpse of herself in the mirror, the pale makeup with heavy mascara and blood red lipstick, put the tray down again as she turned back to stare at Jenny. Without her long overcoat, Jenny looked even younger and more like a mischievous fairy with only the delicate touch of makeup, her long blonde hair was slightly tousled by the wind and the soft floral colours and breezy georgette material of her light summer dress made Carmen feel old and dowdy.

'How do you know…? What is the difference between a gift and insanity?   What do the voices mean?' Carmen's words tumbled out in a rush, as she was desperate to try and explain herself.

'Come and sit down and tell me exactly what's on your mind.' Smiling, Jenny invitingly patted the bed beside her.

Taking a deep breath, Carmen plonked herself down on the edge of the bed and her hands fiddled constantly with the edges of her long sleeves. 'Since I was eight, I have heard… voices. Sometimes I can see people that no one else is aware of. When I mentioned this to my mother, I was sent on a roller coaster of Doctors and psychiatrists to determine if I was mad.'

Jenny laid a reassuring hand over Carmen's. 'Schizophrenia? Yes, that is a common accusation. What did the Doctors say?'

Carmen shrugged her shoulders, trying to not think about that part of her life as it held very painful memories for her. 'It wasn't madness but they couldn't tell me what was wrong with me. Since then, I've never again mentioned what I hear or see.'

'Come downstairs and we'll start your first test.' Pressing the girl's hand before she finally released it and Jenny pulled on her boots before rising to her feet. She straitened her hair and linked her arm through Carmen's and drew her off the bed.

Carmen grabbed the tray on the way out but Jenny's words made her pause, 'Test?'

Smiling, her eyes twinkling as Jenny opened the door, she looked back mischievously. 'I wasn't just sent here for King James, I was informed of your presence and your gifts. You're not alone and if you want to develop your skills then I'll begin your training.' Jenny closed the door and locked it before following Carmen down the stairs that lead into the main saloon of the Pub.

'What if I don't want to be like you?' Realising how rude that sounded Carmen gasped and the tray shook in her hands. 'Oh! I'm sorry! I didn't mean it that way.'

Jenny reached out and steadied the tray. 'If you don't want to follow this path, then I can teach you to block the voices.'

'What voices would these be?' Behind the bar, polishing a glass, Cheryl glanced nervously from Carmen to Jenny. She attempted to keep her voice light and cheerful but there was a hint of fear. They weren't alone in the saloon, as the pre-lunch crowd had already begun to trickle in. As the girls were drawing quite a lot of attention Cheryl slipped from behind the bar and drew them to one side.

'Not here! I thought that all that nonsense had finished years ago.'

Carmen shook her head as she put Jenny's tray on a nearby table and her lips thinned. 'No Mum. I just never mentioned it again.'

Taking one hand of the mother's and one of the daughter's, Jenny held them reassuringly. 'Your daughter isn't mad, but gifted. I won't persist if you honestly disapprove.'

Cheryl hesitated, but the call for service at the bar meant that she couldn't hesitate for long. 'It's just... I don't want my daughter to be any more of an outcast.' She hurried back to the bar to serve her customers.

The First Test

'There is a presence here,' Jenny stated, a silence falling over all those assembled. 'It's not a ghost though.' The room breathed a collective sigh of relief. 'Tell me what you hear Carmen?'

Carmen looked self-consciously around the room. *If I answer honestly will I be burning my bridges from ever being considered normal?* Carmen sighed and began to walk around the saloon. She stepped behind the bar, turned around and took only a single step forward. Jenny sat down at one of the tables maintaining a distance from the time slip.

'Just here,' stated Carmen. Jenny ignored the speculative chatter, remaining focused on Carmen who continued to speak, 'I'm not certain, but I think that it's Grandad. It's a man, and he's talking about the first time they showed boxing on the television. Also a royal wedding,' Carmen frowned in concentration. 'Andrew and Sarah, I think, but then he goes on about the names of their daughters.'

Cheryl burst out laughing which brought a look of surprise from her daughter. 'That's your Grandad all right! He never could stick to one subject for more than ten seconds!' There was a murmur of agreement from some of the older drinkers who had known Jeff McBride.

Jenny nodded solemnly. 'Close your eyes, take a deep breath and picture in your mind what your Grandfather looked like.' She waited a moment or two and then added, 'Now open your eyes and tell me what you see.'

Carmen gave a gasp and stepped back warily, her hand shaking slightly as she reached out to try to touch the image before her. The image of Jeff McBride continued with his story telling to a long gone public, unaware of current people or surroundings. Lowering her hand again, Carmen took a more serious look at the image.

'It's not exactly as I imagined,' she said. 'I visualised him in his tweed jacket, but here he's in his shirt sleeves which are rolled up to the elbow. Mum, did he really have a tattoo on his forearm? I don't remember it at all.'

With eyes misting over, Cheryl nodded in memory. 'Oh yes, from when he was in the Navy.'

'Is that the end of the test?' Carmen looked suspiciously across at Jenny.

The Spirit Healer shook her head, her eyes twinkling although her expression remained unreadable. 'See if you can make the image fly around the room.'

Conjecture and words of wonder swept around the room as the patrons took in every delicious moment of Carmen's test. Cheryl shushed the drinkers as her daughter concentrated hard upon the image in front of her. Sweat beaded her brow and Carmen chewed her bottom lip in a desperate effort to perform the act expected.

Finally gasping for breath, she collapsed against the bar. Cheryl slammed down a tankard of beer she had been pouring onto the top of the bar, as she reached across to take a tearful Carmen into her arms.

'I'm sorry! I can't do it! I've failed!' The muffled words could be heard from where Carmen pressed her face into her mother's shoulder.

'No Carmen, you didn't fail,' Jenny smiled as she shook her head. 'This was a different type of test. You can't move or shift the time projection, as it contains no actual substance. I had to test your ability to accept that there are some things that are not humanly possible. Even for us.'

Carmen raised her head from her mother's shoulder, tears streaking her mascara and make up, and she gave an unladylike sniff. Cheryl pulled out a tissue from her pocket and pressed it into her daughter's hand.

'What does all this mean, Miss Weston?'

Pausing while Carmen discreetly blew her nose, Jenny said, 'The talent is there Mrs Roberts, but it is up to Carmen, if she wishes to pursue such a career.'

'What if I do?' Wiping some of the smeared makeup from her face, Carmen found her voice.

'You may require additional training to overcome a few confidence problems you have.' Jenny rose to her feet and as Carmen began to protest Jenny waved this away. 'You'll have to deal with sceptics and ridicule for the rest of your life. Dealing with ghosts is also mentally and physically draining. Finally, some ghosts can be very violent and unreceptive to your attempts to help them. You need to be complete within yourself before you can attempt to deal with other people's problems.'

Return To Normal

An interruption came from the doorway that led into the restaurant where Penny popped her head through. 'I don't wish to nag, Carmen dear, but the morning tea customers have begun to file in.'

Carmen gave another sniff and wiped away a stray tear. 'Just give me a minute to wash my face and I'll be right there.' Penny disappeared back into her kitchen and Carmen emerged from behind the bar to stand opposite Jenny. 'Is it all right for me to go now?'

'Of course.' Jenny smiled, 'Think about your options and if you wish to become serious about witchcraft, I know a few people you can get in touch with.'

'Really?' Surprise was written all over Carmen's face.

'Yes really. Later I think we can talk about your appearance. You're much too young and pretty to be completely shrouded in black.'

'Another confidence problem?' A flush crept across Carmen's cheeks.

Jenny nodded, 'Just a little one! You'd better go, we'll talk later.' Hearing the bell of the outer door of the restaurant tinkle open again, Carmen hurried off to tidy herself up before returning to the restaurant.

Talk ran merrily through the Saloon about all they had just seen and heard which gave Cheryl the chance to approach Jenny.

'Miss Weston, I'm worried. What does Carmen have to prepare herself for?'

Studying the concerned mother, Jenny didn't immediately answer, 'I think I should talk to you both when you're less busy.'

'We're usually pretty quiet about three in the afternoon.' Cheryl's frown lifted a little, but didn't completely disappear.

'That'll be fine. I'm just going to visit a few contacts in this area.' Jenny ran one hand through her hair. Cheryl returned to the bar, as Jenny collected her overcoat from her room upstairs, before she left the pub. The clientele's chatter continued to wash over Cheryl as she worried about what the future held in store for her daughter.

The Local Witch

In a cosy old-fashioned parlour in a small cottage, an elderly, deceptively fluffy woman suddenly sat up in her crochet covered easy chair with a look of horror on her face. Instinctively she reached out with trembling fingers to grasp the pendant on her necklace. The points of the pentagram pressed sharply into the palm of her hand and although it didn't draw blood, the symbol left its imprint on her frail skin.

'So you've finally come child!' With an agility that was surprising for a woman her age, Kathleen May rose out of her chair and crossed to the window. Pulling back the lace curtains, she looked out into the street and saw Jenny Weston walking past. As if she could feel that she was being watched, Jenny looked straight at the old woman and with a smile Jenny inclined her head in greeting but she didn't stop. The old woman raised her hand in reply.

'Be careful child,' murmured Kathleen as she watched Jenny disappear out of sight. 'All is not as it seems!' With a sigh, the old woman released the curtains and headed out to her kitchen as she contemplated sardines on toast for lunch.

I Want That Book!

Food was also on the mind of one of the three men who were lounging around an empty warehouse, waiting for the fourth member of their team. They were a rough looking lot, as Nigel Baines grumbled about the rumblings in his empty stomach as he had missed breakfast, Lenny Carter was intent upon flicking through a pornographic magazine of young men, and Simeon Masters spent his time chain smoking.

'Where the hell is he? Does he think we have all day to wait for him?' complained Nigel, taking a swig of beer before belching artistically. Lenny, a thin reed of a man, merely shrugged his shoulders, as he was more interested in his magazine.

'He's the brains, mate,' Simeon butted out his current cigarette and paused for a moment before lighting another. 'You know you can leave anytime you like!'

A burp was cut short by a snort from Nigel, 'with a bullet between me eyes, oh yeah!'

An attractive masculine voice answered from the doorway, 'That might even be an improvement for you. Put that away Lenny before you go blind!' The Boss remained standing, which meant that he wasn't there for idle chatter. 'What have you found out?'

Three 'Nothings!' wasn't what the Boss had wanted to hear.

'We should have found that book before that pretty little elfin of a ghost whisperer even turned up in Waltham Cross!' The Boss took a sharp turn around the floor.

'Could always bonk the whereabouts out of her,' suggested Simeon, the chain smoker finally butted out his last cigarette.

Nigel snorted with laughter. 'Do we draw straws?'

'Count me out. She's not my type.' Lenny pulled a disgusted face.

Another snort came from Nigel. 'If only they'd sent a young male psychic.' Lenny thumped him and it looked like they were about to come to serious blows.

'Knock it off you two!' ordered the Boss. 'Anyone harassing the elfin and I'll castrate you myself. I want something a little more solid next time we meet.' Not waiting for a reply, the Boss marched out of the warehouse. Lenny's eyes returned to his magazine as Simeon lit up a cigarette from a new packet.

'Whatcha think? The Boss wants the girl for himself?' The question came through a cloud of smoke.

'Probably; still wouldn't mind trying for a poke, she's an attractive little thing.' Nigel got to his feet, 'How about lunch then?'

Simeon glanced at his watch, 'Nah, gotta get back to work.' They left the warehouse separately, taking different routes so that it was less likely that they would be seen together. The Boss wanted results, and they needed to produce them fast.

The Local Constables

'Yes Sir,' Constable Dave Hedley rolled his eyes and pulled a pained face across the police station at Constable Lisa McGraw as he spoke respectfully into the telephone, 'Of course Mr James. Are you certain that you're not possibly mistaken?' Dave held the telephone receiver away from his ear as he was bombarded by loud and colourful language. This time Lisa grimaced but continued to type away upon her computer.

'We'll look into it as soon as possible.' It was with a great sigh of relief that Dave put the receiver down. 'Silly old bugger!' He picked up his hat and notebook and was about to grab a set of car keys, when there was a voice behind him.

'Who's a silly old bugger, Hedley?' The deep resonating voice of Senior Sergeant Lucas Greenaway, although was amicable, still made the Constable jump.

'Charlie James, Boss. He's claiming that he saw Mrs May running naked amongst his cows last night, and they're refusing to be milked today.'

Lucas closed his eyes as he shook his head and sighed. 'How hung over did he sound?'

'Paralytic Boss, but he wouldn't take no for an answer.' A grin covered the young Constable's features, making him look quite boyish.

'Stay there.' Lucas laid his hand upon Dave's shoulder to keep him from rising to his feet. 'I'll go and have a chat with Kathleen. Something odd happens and the local witch is usually blamed.' Lucas pulled on his jacket and took the car keys from Dave. 'There's a need for some tact with Kathleen.'

Dave Hedley pulled a face, but quickly reverted to his amicable expression when he realised that Lucas was still watching him. 'Yes Boss.'

'Oh Boss…' Lucas was almost out the door when Lisa McGraw called out. 'Can you ask Mrs May for some of her delicious scones? I need a pressie for Mum.'

A devilish gleam entered Lucas' eyes, 'Are you in trouble again Mac?'

'Never out of it, Boss!' Lisa McGraw grinned, 'I've had to move back home while my flat is being painted and mum is sick of all my boyfriends calling all the time.'

Thinking about this made Lucas smile as he drove around to Kathleen May's place. *Lisa's popularity has always surprised and confused Dave*, mused Lucas. *A bit of a cocky upstart, Dave's tall, lean figure and boyish good looks makes it easy for him to get any girl, but he never succeeded to seduce his co-worker. What Dave doesn't know, but I do, is the fact that none of Lisa's dates ever "got their leg over" as Dave would crudely put it. Lisa is fun and a great dancer, but as most of her escorts consider her like a sister, even jealous wives are happy enough to allow their husbands out for a bit of freedom with Lisa, especially if it is a function they couldn't or didn't want to attend.*

What Have I Done This Time?

Pulling into Kathleen May's driveway Lucas' thoughts returned to the matter that he wasn't even half-heartedly investigating. *Charlie James is hardly a reliable witness, especially when he has been hitting the bottle.* The front door was already open as Lucas swaggered up the pathway and he fixed a rueful grin upon his face. Kathleen May stood in the doorway, leaning upon her walking stick as her eyes twinkled mischievously.

'Blessed Be Lucas. Is this a social call or have I been up to mischief again?'

'Oh Aunty Kath, you're a wicked old woman! Can't a copper simply drop in for a cup of tea?' Kathleen was no relative of the Sergeant but like many of the locals had been baby-sat by the witch. She linked her arm through Lucas' as he led her into the kitchen where the magnificent scents of cooking wafted through the cottage.

'You radiate your thoughts as if you had spoken them. So who has made a complaint?' Kathleen released his arm and put the kettle upon the stove to boil. Removing his hat, Lucas fell into a chair and breathed in deeply and his taste buds were tantalised. *I have a job to do first, though.*

'Charlie James is saying his cows won't cooperate as you were doing a midnight cavort in his fields.'

A twitter of a laugh answered him, 'would that be sky clad Lucas?'

His fingers were slapped as he reached for a biscuit, and he grinned ruefully. 'I'm surprised that you're still not blue from the chill! Was it a full moon last night, my dear?'

Having brought down a pair of mugs and filled them with a couple of tea bags, Kathleen didn't even need to consult the calendar on the wall before she answered, 'No it's still several days off.'

What Do You Make Of All This?

Becoming serious, the elderly lady sat down opposite Lucas and placed her hand over his. 'My dear boy, does it make considerable difficulties for you the way I live?'

'Life would be pretty boring if we were all the same.' A look of amusement crossed his features and his fingers tightened around hers. 'Besides it adds a bit of prestige to the village to have a local witch.'

'You may have another witch soon.' Kathleen rose to her feet to pour the tea.

This time Lucas managed to get hold of a biscuit without getting his hand slapped again. 'Do you mean Carmen?' As Kathleen nodded in agreement, he continued, 'That's one confused child. All that heavy makeup and black clothing is very depressing for one so young.'

'That'll soon change.' Placing a cup in front of Lucas, Kathleen returned to her seat. 'Life is for the living, and must be experienced and not just endured.'

Sipping his tea in deep appreciation, Lucas murmured in agreement. 'What do you think of the lass everyone is talking about?'

'Jenny Weston?' Kathleen hesitated as she absent-mindedly broke up a biscuit and dunked a piece into her tea. 'I'm concerned about her, Lucas. Her job should be straightforward if she's here about King James, but there's his book to consider. It would be priceless, and that makes it worth killing for.'

'We'll keep an eye on Cedars Park while the ghost girl is here.' Lucas pilfered another biscuit as he gulped down his tea.

'Anyway, Aunty Kath, how's Evelyn doing?' His words were slightly muffled by biscuit, which caused a laugh from a bedroom door behind him.

Evelyn May

Glancing around Lucas smiled as his eyes enlightened upon a good looking youth with shoulder length blonde hair and twinkling blue eyes. Several scars that were healing on his face and the arm crutches that he leant heavily upon marred this picture of youthful masculinity.

'You never could resist Gran's biscuits could you, Sarg?' Awkwardly Evelyn May extended his hand to Lucas, which the policeman shook.

'It must be the fairy dust she adds to them. How are you Evelyn?' Lucas was aware of the concern in Kathleen's eyes as her grandson painfully lowered himself into a chair.

'I'm alive, Senior Sergeant that is the main thing!' Tears entered Kathleen's eyes, causing Evelyn to reach across and press her hand. 'It's all right Gran, I'm not going to brood. I think I'll try to walk to the Village Square today. Doctor Shepherd said to extend the distance I walk more each week.'

There was another great effort as Evelyn pulled himself back up to his feet. Kathleen's look of concern increased and Lucas also rose to his feet.

'Do you mind if I join you Evelyn? I may have some work for you.'

A stunned Evelyn burst into unbelieving laughter. 'What kind of work could a cripple do?'

'Eve...' Kathleen cut short her protest at the acute pain in her grandson's eyes.

Lucas launched into speech to prevent an argument. 'I know from past experience that you have two very sharp eyes and an intelligent brain! I'll explain on the way.' Lucas picked up his hat and led the way to the front door, pausing to assist Evelyn into a jacket before they left the house. They had barely stepped out of the front door when Kathleen called out, 'Oh Lucas, tell Lisa to pop round later for the scones she wants.'

'Righto!' Lucas waved his hand.

He continued passed his car, but stopped suddenly when he realised that at no time during his conversation with Kathleen had he mentioned the Constable's request. *To be honest I had forgotten all about it.* A twinkle of mischief entered Evelyn's eyes.

'Gran received a call from Lisa just before you arrived as she didn't think you'd remember. From your expression I presume you thought that Gran had read your thoughts or something.' Lucas threw back his head and laughed heartily. He had honestly thought it had been some kind of trick.

Evelyn's Slow Progress

They settled into a slow, and in Evelyn's case, painful progress on the way down to the village square. While Evelyn struggled to overcome his pain and weariness, they continued in companionable silence. During this time the Senior Sergeant considered his companion. *Evelyn May should be in his third year at University studying Architecture, but a car accident eight months ago had nearly cost him his life. Evelyn and a few of his mates had been celebrating the end of their second year exams at a pub, and Evelyn had nominated himself skipper as he didn't really drink.*

Evelyn was driving them home at about one in the morning, when they were hit head on. Evelyn was crushed and mangled behind the steering wheel and the Doctors had thought he would not live through the night. The other boys ended up with only cuts and bruises. If by some miracle Evelyn did live, the Doctors could not promise that he would not be completely paralysed.

Upon hearing of her grandson's accident, Kathleen May went straight down to the hospital and began to work immediately. The Doctors were sceptical about Kathleen's potions, lotions, spells and tonics, but when they tried to have her removed, they ran up against June, Evelyn's mother, and Kathleen's daughter-in-law. June had always been rather nonchalant about her mother-in-law's witchcraft, but as her eldest son lay dying, she was prepared to do anything with the faintest hope of keeping him alive.

It was touch and go, but Evelyn survived that night, and many more to follow. Upon being discharged from the hospital, Evelyn was brought to Kathleen's cottage in the hope that the peace and quiet would be better suited to his recovery, than a house with three teenage siblings. For the first month, neither his mother, nor grandmother left his side.

So amazed was Lucas by this momentous courage, that he put his arm around Evelyn's shoulders and smiled warmly down at him. 'My God, you're amazing!'

'I don't think so,' he mumbled and colour tinted Evelyn's pale cheeks as he looked up startled and embarrassed.

Lucas didn't agree. 'The odds were clearly stacked against you. It would've been so easy just to give up.'

'I nearly did a couple of times. Then I saw her.' Nodding, Evelyn's colour deepened.

'Ah,' The image of pretty Carmen immediately sprang into both their minds.

'A couple of months ago Gran had to go to see the Doctor, and I wasn't up to going with her.' Evelyn saw Lucas' eyebrows go up and grinned. 'What? Do you think that just because Gran's a witch she doesn't need a Doctor? "Witch heal thyself?" Sometimes science just needs to step in and help.'

'Okay,' Lucas threw his hands up in defeat. 'I take it Carmen volunteered to baby-sit you while Kathleen was out.'

Cheekily Evelyn shook his head. 'Actually Mrs Roberts offered, but at the last minute she was needed at the pub, so Carmen came instead.'

'So that is what got you back on your feet so quickly?' Lucas smiled; he wasn't too old to remember the first time he had felt that special bond with a young woman.

A deeper flush covered Evelyn's cheeks. 'Don't let Gran hear you say that!'

Lucas chuckled wickedly. 'Oh! So you don't intend to drop in to see Carmen on the way into the village?'

'You gotta be joking.' Grinning, Evelyn shook his head. 'You don't think I'd come this far without some sort of reward do you?'

A Review Of Carmen's Wardrobe

Later that afternoon Carmen had a quick shower while Jenny was having a sticky beak through Carmen's wardrobe, with her permission of course, and what she saw was rather depressing. If it wasn't black or dark and completely neck to floor, then it wasn't there. With a thoughtful sigh, Jenny sank down onto Carmen's made bed, and considered her options.

The room she was in was a part of a flat over the Restaurant that had been remodelled when the rebuilding had taken place. There were three small bedrooms, a nice little kitchen/dining area, and a decent living room with not only a 61 cm screen television, but also a DVD player and computer.

The computer and its games were largely Peter's, Carmen's brother's domain, but the normal animosity that usually existed between siblings was lessened when Carmen showed interest in the Internet to keep up with the latest Craft and Wicca web pages and chat rooms and Peter was happy to instruct his sister. These caused considerable arguments, but they were basically good-natured, and even strengthened their relationship.

Carmen's bedroom was what Jenny had expected, being quite bare, with the exception of a few crystals, and the gothic art work of Anne Stokes and Lisa Parker. There was not even one stuffed toy sat on the bed. This Jenny found a little sad, as she never went anywhere without her toy black panther. He was sitting on her bed now, in her room over the pub. With this in mind, Jenny jumped to her feet and knocked lightly on the bathroom door.

'I'll just be a minute Carmen, don't get dressed until I get back.' Jenny heard a watery 'Okay' before she slipped out of the flat and across to her own room.

Less than five minutes later, Jenny was back in Carmen's room, where the younger girl stood in front of the mirror of the dressing table, wrapped in a towel and briskly brushing her long black hair. Across Jenny's arm was another light weight georgette floral dress, no sleeves only thin spaghetti straps and a knee length circular skirt. Carmen looked surprised as Jenny held the dress out to her.

'Try this on, I'm a little bigger in the bust than you, but it should be all right.'

Carmen's surprise turned suspicion. 'Why?'

With her hand on the door handle, prepared to leave Carmen to dress alone, Jenny turned and smiled. 'A change Carmen! If you honestly don't like it, you can go back to your funeral blacks. Let's see if we can surprise your mother.' Without waiting for a reply, Jenny closed the door behind her as she left, and ambled over to the window in the living room overlooking the main street.

She didn't turn when Carmen's door opened and a nervous girl, with her hair hanging loose down her back and a decent amount of pale but shapely arms and legs showing and no make-up on, stepped out.

'Well?' Carmen cautiously pushed a strand of hair out of her eyes. Jenny finally turned, her eyes resting upon the younger woman's face, as she had already scanned her using the window as a reflection.

'How do you feel?'

Carmen looked sceptically down at herself. 'Exposed! And yet...' Jenny waited as Carmen looked at herself from different angles and had a little spin around. 'You don't think that my legs should be covered up?' A short stubble of dark hair covered Carmen's legs.

'Waxing would mean that you wouldn't have to shave as often. If you're unhappy about being so pale, wear stockings or get out in the sun while it lasts during summer, otherwise if you've got it girl, flaunt it! These should be some of the best years of your life.'

'Are you sure?' The look of concern did not leave Carmen.

Smiling, Jenny shrugged her shoulders. 'Do you see the fairies prancing around in black or neck to ankle attire?'

That statement made Carmen stop and think. 'All right then, what about make-up?'

Jenny came forward and placing a hand under Carmen's chin lifted her face towards a natural light.

'You have such lovely skin; you shouldn't try to clog up your pores with heavy applications. Pull your hair back into a pony tail for the moment, and I'll show you a style that might suit you.'

A smile spread across Carmen's features before she turned and headed back to her bedroom to finish her transformation.

A Spirit Healer's Life

When Cheryl walked into their private lounge room, half an hour later, she drew in a stunned breath, 'Oh my lord!'

Carmen blushed furiously as she rose to her feet and approached her mother. 'Well?' Her question was a nervous enquiry.

'Oh Darling! You look stunning!' Indeed Cheryl's praise was justified. Carmen had found a pair of tan stockings in the back of a drawer and with the lighter style of makeup applied by Jenny, and her hair plaited back off her face; she did indeed look totally different. 'The important thing is, Love, are you comfortable with how you look? I think you look smashing, but if you aren't happy, then I wouldn't want you to live a lie.'

Carmen took a new look at herself and finally smiled shyly. 'I think I like it! But you know what this means, don't you Mum?' She was suddenly very serious again.

A look of concern crossed Cheryl's face, 'What?'

Carmen's suddenly smiled. 'I'll have to do something about replenishing my wardrobe.'

A laugh rushed out of Cheryl in a breath of relief. 'Well then, we can pop up to London sometime next week.'

They both sat down opposite Jenny, who had been patiently waiting. 'The first thing to realise is that you do have a choice. Now and at any time in the future you can decide to give up to lead a normal life.'

'Normal?' Carmen gave a nervous laugh.

Jenny was serious though. 'Well, it does depend upon what you consider normal, but counselling ghosts is like nothing you have ever experienced before.' A scared look was exchanged between mother and daughter. Jenny wasn't surprised by their concern. 'Don't panic, it's like anything you've never tried before. It's just that very few people experience what you can do, so it's hard for others to understand what you may go through.' There was a sigh of relief as they digested this piece of information.

'There are varying types of Spirit Healers; some can only hear ghosts, others sense their presence. Some get visions or dreams from the departed and unfortunately there are charlatans and fakes giving real Healers a bad name.'

'One of the things I recommend to other novice Spirit Healers is attaining qualifications. It isn't essential but it can help. There are plenty of books that you can read and other Healers that you can talk to but you can't beat a university degree. I'll provide you a start-up kit and while I'm in Waltham Cross you'll shadow me while I deal with any supernatural phenomenon that turns up.' Jenny took a break for a deep, cleansing breath.

'Now, the bit that may scare you,' Jenny leant forward to take Carmen's hand between her own. 'The life of a Spirit Healer isn't always a very long one. Most Spirit Healers cannot make ghosts fully visible to non-Healers like I can. While they're in my presence the ghost becomes as close to being alive again as possible. Every counselling session, or meeting with a ghost, drains upon your mortal energy. Very few healers can actually regain that lost energy.'

Carmen swallowed several times, and seemed about to speak, but no words came out. It was Cheryl who voiced her concerns, 'Does that mean a limited life expectancy or continuous pain or…?'

Jenny nodded slowly. 'There's no pain involved, but some of us won't see 70. It depends upon how many spirits you try and send on during a given time. When my mentor Allan found me it was thought with my fragile constitution that I should not try to follow this path. Although I'm only 32, working full time, and having come across a few poltergeists, I won't live beyond 40 or 50.' Pity and sadness reflected in Cheryl's eyes, but Jenny only smiled.

'Doesn't that scare you?' Carmen had found her voice.

The question was obviously one that Jenny had expected, as she showed no surprise. 'Death holds no fear for me. How I die, is what worries me. Slowly, painfully, prolonged, that would scare me, but for most Healers it would be going to sleep, and not waking up again in this world. We have to believe that where we go to after that is a wondrous place, or why would we be helping troubled spirits to cross over to the afterlife?'

Jenny paused to ensure that her words had sunk in before continuing, 'I have a young ghost working for me, Tommy. He's a London boy of 13 from the early 1800's. He refuses to cross over until he feels that he has atoned for a mistake he made which caused the death of everyone in his apartment block. Each Healer is assigned a particular spirit who is willing to work off their purgatory sentence, to allow them to cross over. They become like your little finger, not with you always, but never far away. So where ever you are, they can appear. If someone crosses over from the afterlife back to the present life, they must cross the River of Unrest. It is this that keeps the spirits from going to their afterlife. It isn't so easy to go back across the river once you've left to come back here to this present realm. That is why I use a guide to see that they can get back safely.'

'Am I likely to become a ghost myself?'

Jenny shook her head, 'only if you have unfinished business, or unresolved problems. Most of us go straight over.'

'Over what?'

Releasing Carmen's hand, Jenny reached for a piece of paper and a pen. 'I'll go into more detail later, but for the moment this is what happens.' Jenny laid the paper in front of Carmen and began to draw as she explained.

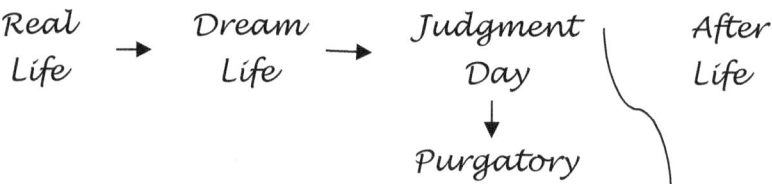

'This side of this line is the Present or Real Life. Through the Dream Life is a door which Lord Death passes through to collect the recently deceased. They are led to a Judge's panel where their life is reviewed and those who are ready receive coins and are escorted to the ferry that crosses The River of Unrest. The coins are to pay the ferryman and without it he won't let you on the boat. On the other side of the river you're met by family and loved ones. This is true regardless of what religion you believe in. With the exception of Hindus as they are reborn rather than travelling to the afterlife.'

'What about those who don't get a coin? What happens to them?' asked Cheryl.

'Those souls who refuse to go with Lord Death wander the earth looking for answers, these ghosts we can sometimes help. Those not given coins are trapped in a judgement area; forced to pay a penance in Purgatory for whatever reason they're not allowed to cross over. These people we can't help, they have to pay a price before they can continue. Poltergeists are also impossible to help. They just drain you and don't answer to logic or reason. The couple I've seen I've had to hand over to the local Catholic Priest. Exorcism stops the gremlin from coming back and forth through the door between this life and the judgement sector and sometimes inhabiting another's body.'

There was a brief moment of silence, which Jenny allowed to continue for a while as mother and daughter took in what they had just heard. Finally, Jenny rose to her feet.

'It is a lot to consider, so I'll leave you now so you can discuss this. Note down any questions you may have and we can talk them through later.' Stepping back to the window, Jenny glanced down into the street and a smile gently touched her lips. 'Although it would appear that you have a visitor,' she added.

Forgetting for a moment the momentous future before her, Carmen jumped up and rushed over to stand beside Jenny. 'Oh! It's Evelyn! He must have walked all the way from his Gran's!' With difficulty, Carmen tried to hide her excitement as she looked back at her mother, who only smiled in return.

'Go on love. That brave young man has come all this way to see you. We can talk later. I have to return to the bar anyway.'

Cheryl's Concerns

With brief thanks, Carmen trotted down the stairs to the restaurant where Evelyn May and Senior Sergeant Lucas

Greenaway were just entering by the outer door. Upstairs Cheryl turned a concerned countenance towards Jenny.

'Honestly Miss Weston, do you recommend your way of life?'

Smiling sympathetically, Jenny came across to place an arm around Cheryl's shoulders. 'My mother was just as concerned when I was first approached by my mentor. I can give you a few names of other parents in your position, as you're not alone with your concerns. A few of the best Spirit Healers have been people who have only tuned into their abilities very late in life. With age, you see, comes a wisdom that we younger people can't possess.'

The concerned look lessened, but didn't disappear from Cheryl's features. Together they headed out of the flat and downstairs. 'A decision doesn't have to be made immediately, or even in the near future. Advise Carmen, discuss this over with her, but in the end, the decision must be hers.'

They paused in the doorway of the saloon, about to go separate ways; Cheryl once again behind the bar, and Jenny into the Restaurant.

'I know,' Cheryl sighed. 'But it is still a little hard to let your child go down a road that will make her more of an outcast.'

Carmen's New Look

The stir that had been caused by Jenny's arrival in the village was nothing compared to the commotion that occurred when Carmen entered the Restaurant that afternoon. Conversation ceased and all eyes were centred on Carmen as she came forward to meet Evelyn and Lucas.

Slipping into the Restaurant basically unnoticed, Jenny watched amused as Evelyn's jaw dropped and Lucas' eyes opened wide in surprise. Carmen's fingers twisted together nervously as she waited with trepidation for Evelyn to say something. Having looked her over from head to toe, Evelyn screwed up his nose.

'I dunno if I like having so much of my girl on view for all other guys to see.' Carmen was torn between disappointment at his disapproval and giddy delight at being called, "his girl", but Evelyn hadn't finished. He unscrewed his face as he smiled. 'But I could grow to live with it if what is displayed is still restricted access!'

'What sort of girl do you think I am?' Carmen bridled in defence.

Evelyn's expression softened. 'I don't want every guy in town trying to make me look too pathetic to you so as to win you from me.'

'Oh!' Carmen's anger dissolved instantly, 'As if anyone would dare!' She wrapped her arms around his neck and their lips met in a tender kiss.

The Restaurant burst into applause and the embracing couple pulled apart as Olivia, the evening waitress approached. 'Why don't you go and find a quiet spot!'

The gathered diners quietened down as Carmen assisted Evelyn through to the unoccupied function room. Lucas nodded amicably across at Jenny before heading back out of the Restaurant and ambled back to his car, deep in thought.

Nigel's Seductive Style

Cheryl was once more efficiency itself behind the bar. Her ready smile in place and she was chatting happily to an ancient local who was nursing a glass of whiskey. Seeing Jenny caused Cheryl's smile to disappear as their recent conversation came back to her. It took a minute for Cheryl's usual good humour to return. 'What can I get you, Miss Weston?'

Jenny slid onto a stool at the bar beside an old timer, Alf Baines. 'A cup of coffee would be lovely, Cheryl.'

A medium built man in his late 30's strode arrogantly into the Pub. 'You drinking still Grandad? Gran's tea will have gotten cold.'

Alfred Baines flinched as the younger man slapped him on the back. 'Here for a reason Nigel, or are you just taking up space?'

Nigel Baines's hands tightened momentarily as his lips thinned in displeasure. 'Gran was wondering if you're coming home for supper then she needs a few things.'

Finishing his whiskey, Alfred raised a quizzical eyebrow. 'And like a good dutiful Grandson, you offered to help your Gran with her shopping?' His jibe caused the colour to rush up Nigel's cheeks.

'Looking after Gran is your problem and not mine.' His sarcasm was somewhat lost under the fierce rumblings from Nigel's stomach. Alfred slid off his stool and stared silently at his Grandson before turning calmly back to Cheryl.

'My dear, could you call Mabel and ask her to put on her glad rags as I'm taking her out to dinner!'

Cheryl chewed on her bottom lip to hide her smile, 'Of course Alfred.'

With a brief nod at Jenny, and a cheery wave to a couple of drinking mates, Alfred strolled out without a word, or even a look at his Grandson. Nigel shoved his hands deep into his trouser pockets, a wry grin on his face as he watched the old man go. Jenny ignored Nigel as Cheryl turned away to use the landline telephone as Alfred had requested. The rumbling of Nigel's stomach made him laugh.

'You wouldn't think I'd already had a big lunch,' He said in Jenny's general direction. She continued to ignore him, sliding off her stool and walking past him. Nigel, though, wasn't prepared to allow her walk away. 'Hey, there lovely lady, I don't think we've been properly introduced.' He had hold of Jenny's arm, and when she tried to pull it away, he refused to let go.

Jenny glanced down at his hand and then up into his arrogant face.

'Unless your manners improve towards your elders, we never shall!'

Nigel's fingers tightened like a vice, causing Jenny to wince in pain. 'That's not very nice, for one so small. We're a pretty friendly lot in this neck of the woods, and we can do without cold London manners!'

'I am neither a Londoner, nor cool to those who deserve friendliness.' She managed to keep her voice cool and calm. 'Release me or I'll be forced to hurt you.'

Nigel threw back his head and roared with laughter. 'You couldn't hurt a grasshopper! Come now, a little kiss.' He pulled Jenny hard against him.

Cheryl turned around from the telephone and frowned in displeasure. 'Nigel, grow up!'

Ignoring Cheryl, he lowered his head towards Jenny's but she was no weak and mild woman. With her free hand, she reached out to grasp hold of Nigel's ear and twisted hard. He cried out in pain, releasing Jenny long enough to backhand her across the face. She fell back against the stool, grabbing hold of the bar to prevent herself from falling to the ground.

'Nigel Baines get out of my pub and don't come back until you have learnt some manners!' Cheryl slapped her hand against the bar.

A snarl twisted Nigel's lip. 'Make me!'

Not So Helpless

Before Cheryl could come out from behind the bar, Nigel felt a savage pain in the back of one knee as he received a swift blow from behind. He collapsed to the ground, a foul oath streaming from his lips. Behind him, Evelyn's eyes blazed in anger as he returned his full weight to his two crutches. Carmen wasn't with him.

'You were asked to leave, Nigel. Don't make this harder than it has to be.' It would have been comical to watch the crippled youth stand over the bulkier man, except that Evelyn was deadly serious. Nigel, though, was too cocksure about his own strength and picked himself up in an angry burst of energy. 'I'll break both your legs for that!' Nigel reached out to grab Evelyn, but before he could touch him, Nigel suddenly clutched his chest in pain.

Taking a step backwards the pain disappeared, but when Nigel tried to grab Evelyn again, the pain returned. Evelyn grinned mischievously as he thrust one of his crutches into Nigel's chest again.

'Sorry Nigel, didn't you know I was once a hockey champion?'

Before Nigel could try again, he was seized from behind; his right arm pinned back and he was forcefully being propelled towards the outer door. Virtually hurled onto the pavement outside, he landed on his hand and knees. Looking up, to his horror, Nigel discovered not some hefty man, but the slender figure of Jenny standing over him, her hands on her hips.

'You were warned, Mr Baines,' she said cheerfully. As Nigel picked himself up off the pavement and dusted himself down, a deadly gleam entered his eyes. Jenny wasn't blind to his thoughts of revenge.

'I shall be informing the police of your harassment, although I'll press no charges. If anything was to happen to me, you'd be the first suspect the police would round up.' Jenny could feel the curious witnesses from the Pub follow them out into the street. Cheryl was standing close behind Jenny in a very supportive manner.

'Go home Nigel, and think yourself lucky Miss Weston won't have you charged with assault.'

Looking around at the obvious 'Jenny supporting' crowd, Nigel swore and strode angrily away. With the excitement over, the crowd filed back into the pub and business returned to normal. Although she appeared cool and calm, Jenny jumped slightly when Cheryl laid her hand on her shoulder.

'I'm sorry you were subjected to that Miss Weston. I'll get some ice to take care of the swelling on your cheek.'

Jenny smiled her thanks. 'Really, I do think that you should start calling me Jenny.'

Quietly all this time, Evelyn had been watching Jenny, and now as she turned to thank him for his assistance, he suddenly blushed furiously.

'It was a lot less than I'd have liked to have done.' He wavered slightly on his feet, and Jenny immediately pulled up a stool for him. Gratefully he perched on it.

'It was more than some people would have done and I am thankful.'

What Did I Miss?

With the intention of heading up to her room with her sachet of ice, Jenny met Carmen in the doorway as she was looking for Evelyn. Carmen looked from her boyfriend to Jenny and sighed.

'I missed something again haven't I?'

Jenny glanced across at Evelyn and he smirked back. They both started laughing. Carmen was a little taken back by their response but Evelyn immediately said, 'We're not laughing at you. I'll explain on the way home.' With Carmen's hand firmly clasped between his, Evelyn looked over his shoulder at Cheryl, 'If you can spare your daughter?'

This time Cheryl looked surprised. 'But of course, Evelyn, I don't expect Carmen to work all hours of the day.'

'Then you could stay and have dinner with me and Gran.' Evelyn grinned as he squeezed Carmen's hand. 'It would give you a chance to talk to her about the Craft.'

Carmen's eyes lit up in delight, but then suddenly grew serious as she glanced at Jenny. 'I would love to, but did Miss Weston wish to start instructions this evening?'

'Not tonight, Carmen.' Jenny said as she shook her head. 'I hope to have a word with King James, and that may be a little too frightening for your first ghost visit.'

Carmen accepted this explanation, but Evelyn was curious. 'Why?'

Jenny hesitated, knowing that there were quite a few others listening to their conversation. 'When King James died, he would have been completely insane due to the disease Porphyria. I don't know in what state his ghost will be, or how coherent or passive the interview may be.'

Evelyn nodded in acceptance, allowing Carmen to ease him off the stool.

'Will you need me before closing time, Mum?'

Cheryl had been distracted by the need to serve a customer, now turned back to her daughter. 'You go and enjoy yourself. Just remember what I've always told you.'

'Yes mum,' Carmen blushed but managed a wry smile. 'If it's not on then it's not on.'

Evelyn looked blank as he glanced from mother to daughter, but when a wicked little laugh escaped from Jenny, he also went crimson.

'No, no, no! You don't have to worry about that Mrs Roberts. I'm not physically capable to... Well, at the moment.' As he wavered slightly on his feet, he added, 'I'm not even sure I'm capable of walking home.'

Carmen reached out to support him and glanced quickly back at her mother for advice. Cheryl was already one step ahead of her, taking her car keys off the hook beside the cash register.

'See Evelyn safely home dear. I won't need the car.'

Gratefully Carmen took the keys and with a word of thanks from both youngsters; she led Evelyn out of the pub and into her Mum's station wagon. With the ice having numbered her battered cheek, Jenny bid Cheryl adieu, before heading up to her room to prepare for the big spiritual meeting that evening.

Simeon Reflects

Sitting at one of the tables outside the pub was a man in his early forties, an ashtray filled with butts in front of him as he puffed deep in thought on a new cigarette. He had witnessed the attempt of his colleague to get close to Jenny, and been very amused by the result. *I'm a little concerned that Nigel's stupidity will ruin the boss' plans, but that isn't my headache. I'll certainly enjoy watching the Boss tear strips off Nigel for not only sleazing on but also striking the girl, but all that is for later, as at this moment I've other fish to fry.* Draining the remainder of his ale and extinguishing his latest cigarette, Simeon rose languidly to his feet and left the pub.

The Loving Home

A mouth-watering aroma rushed forward to greet Lucas Greenaway as he entered through his front door. He paused in shutting the door behind him, closing his eyes as he breathed in deeply.

'Oh heaven!' The sound of his voice, although barely raised, carried through to the kitchen.

'Is that my Bear?' Penny poked her head around the doorway into the hall as she wiped her hands upon a tea towel. The use of an old nickname brought a smile to Lucas' face as he finally closed the front door.

'Certainly is, Goldilocks! What is that divine smell?'

Penny melted into her husband's arms and they kissed passionately. 'We're having Sauté de Boeuf Stroganoff with Pomes Dauphine and Champignons farcies.'

The French was lost on Lucas but he raised his eyebrows and grinned, 'Sounds wonderful!'

A chuckle from the living room came from their teenage son. 'In case you're wondering Dad, we're having Beef stew with mashed potatoes and stuffed mushrooms.'

Disengaging himself from his wife, Lucas entered the living room amicably shaking his head. 'Now you have spoilt the surprise of not knowing what your mother was going to present at the dinner table.'

Lucas was about to leave the room to change out of his uniform, when his son, Tim called him back. 'Dad, what do you know about this Ghost Healer?' His question caused Penny to also enter the room, and when Lucas sat down on the lounge, Penny perched herself upon his knee.

Tim added, 'There are all sorts of rumours, gossip and here-say about this ghost girl going around school.' *I'm accustomed to my parents' open display of affection, so long as it isn't in public when I am around. I actually like the fact that they're still very much in love.* So when Lucas tenderly kissed Penny's neck and shoulder, Tim accepted it without a blink of an eye, or a blush.

'What rumours have you heard?' Always the police officer, Lucas was particularly closed with giving information, but not impartial about gathering it.

'How tame or wild do you want to go? How about drug dealer, sex worker, a witch wanting to start up her own coven, a Russian spy, a movie star drying out. It just seems incredible that someone can actually survive counselling ghosts. I mean, who pays the bills?'

'What imaginations you kids have. I suppose too many of you watch the TV programs "Supernatural", "The Ghost Whisperer" or "Medium".' Penny shook her head as she laughed. 'So how are the other kids going to satisfy their curiosity?'

Tim looked cautiously at his father. 'Most of them have dared each other to spend the night at Cedars Park for a spot of ghost hunting.' The teenager frowned in thought. 'They're going to be a pain, aren't they? To Miss Weston I mean.'

'That is an understatement, my boy,' Lucas said with a groan. 'I'll have to arrange for a patrol of the park. The last thing I need is the Borough of Broxbourne Council breathing down my neck about allowing Miss Weston to do her job without hindrance. It's the Council who are paying her wages, so they want a result.'

Patting his wife on the backside, Lucas brought them both to their feet, 'How long before supper?'

Penny glanced at the clock on the fireplace before replying, 'Oh enough time to make a phone call, change out of your uniform and maybe a quick snuggle with your wife.'

Tim rammed his hands against his ears, 'No images please! You can't afford the psychiatrist fees!' He was on his way out of the room when his mother called out after him.

'Keep an eye on dinner, Tim, don't let it burn.'

'Okay, okay, just let me channel my thoughts in other directions.'

Lucas grinned at his son's reaction. As they headed upstairs to the bedroom, pausing only for a minute as Lucas made a phone call to his night duty officers. *I hope that our frankness and openness aren't a serious problem for our children; Tim is 16 and Jayne is 13. I'd grown up in an emotional suppressed household. I had sworn to myself that my family would always know how much I love them, but being a teenager is such a tough age.*

As if understanding his musings from his silence, Penny gave her husband an exaggerated wink as she ripped off his tie and began on his shirt buttons.

'Don't worry Bear; in a couple of years that boy will be turning to you for prowess advice.'

A look of concern crossed the policeman's features. 'Do you think I'm sufficiently qualified to give that advice?' A wicked twinkle danced in his eyes as Penny removed her own clothing.

'Your ego would be sadly deflated if I said no, now wouldn't it?' She paused, as if considering a particularly sticky situation. 'Mind you, they do say practice make perfect!'

Lucas gave a mock growl as he pulled his wife into his arms. 'Then let's practise.'

Kathleen May's Question

Entering the May house was like coming home and Carmen felt immediately comfortable, assisting Evelyn to his bed, before offering to help Kathleen with dinner. While she peeled and chopped vegetables, Carmen was half expecting either a comment about her new look, or about her developing relationship with Evelyn. Kathleen, softly humming to herself as she seasoned and prepared several fillets of fish, allowed those questions to go unasked. They weren't the issues that the elderly woman wished to discuss as she had more worldly concepts on her mind.

'Tell me Carmen, why do you want to be a witch?'

The question was so unexpected that Carmen could only stare at Kathleen for a minute. 'I found no joy, no comfort from mainstream religion. I'm not happy with being one of a crowd. After all the Doctors I was dragged to as a child, to make it stop I had to suppress what Jenny said was my gift. My natural calling I suppose. So to me, Wicca was more down to earth, back to basics, and different.' Carmen gave a rueful laugh. 'I suppose that's just it! I want to be different, unique. If I am a Ghost Healer then I am already unique but I wasn't allowed to keep that was I? That's how it started, but as I continued to read about the Craft, the more I wanted to find peace in my life.'

'When did the need for the physical change start? The heavy makeup, the completely black clothes, the black hair and the change of your name from Amy to Carmen.'

Carmen screwed up her nose as she tried to think. 'I must have been about 14 or 15.'

Kathleen nodded knowledgeably. 'When your father took up with that young woman before your parents divorced?' Carmen looked momentarily surprised before she finally nodded and Kathleen continued, 'so to get any sort of attention, you felt that you needed to be different, a rebellion, and yet you never went the whole way. Why?'

'What do you mean? What could I have done?'

'Oh my dear!' The witch smiled at the other's innocence, 'you barely scratched the surface of rebellion; drugs, sex, nightclubs, rowdy behaviour, in trouble with the police, alcohol. Something happened didn't it? Something stopped you from carrying the rebellion on to its full possibility.'

'Is there anything you don't know?' Colour rushed across Carmen's cheeks.

Kathleen gave a very old lady-like laugh. 'Does that really surprise you child?'

Carmen also laughed, 'No, not really. I had the most unusual dream. When I awoke... The need for attention was gone, the anger was gone, and there was a sense of peace. I didn't care any more about trying to get people's attention. I was finally happy enough to just be me. Well the me that I was allowed to be for now.'

Satisfied, Kathleen patted Carmen on the shoulder, 'Good, very good. Focus upon that peace my dear, and ignore the stereotype.' She hesitated with her hand resting on the younger woman. 'I understand Jenny Weston has shown interest in you. Does her way of life compromise your ideas of the Craft?'

Carmen scratched her head as she considered. 'I don't think so. The way Jenny described passing over, it could really apply to any religion.' She paused, chewing on her bottom lip. 'Do you see it as a problem?' She asked.

'Not at all child, but you do need to be clear in your own mind.' Kathleen smiled, finally releasing Carmen's shoulder. 'Now, if you wouldn't mind seeing if Evelyn needs a hand while I set the table.'

Carmen jumped to her feet, eager to help and as she headed up to Evelyn's room, Kathleen wondered, *Do those youngsters realise the years of difficulties that are ahead of them from the car accident. I hope that Carmen has the stamina if she means to stand by Evelyn, for she is certainly going to need it.*

Offer You A Drink?

Upon entering the Dog and Bone Pub Sean Hanson found the drinking establishment packed to the rafters. The news had spread throughout Waltham Cross that something big was going to happen that evening, and no one wanted to miss any of the action. Having greeted Marcus, Cheryl's evening bar tender, Sean sat down at the bar and silently sipped his half-pint. He nodded to several people he knew, but on the whole he remained his usual taciturn.

This made it easier for him to watch and listen, and there was plenty to hear, some of it nonsense, but there was the occasional spark of intelligence. The rare moment made Sean smile, but he couldn't be drawn into making any statements.

A silence suddenly descended over the assembled crowd, and Sean looked up and dragged in a sharp breath. Dressed in a teal full length ball gown, with a cape thrown over her arm, and wearing a diamond necklace that would make any jeweller drool, Jenny Weston glanced around the pub with an amused expression. The bruise, that was developing upon her cheek from being struck by Nigel, was cleverly concealed by foundation. Her eyes met Sean's and nodding amicably, he raised his eyebrows and his glass.

'Can I offer you a drink Miss Weston?' The sound of Sean's voice surprised the assembled group and whispers began as Jenny moved cautiously with her expensive dress through the tables towards him.

'I'd love one, Mr Hanson, but it'll have to be a soft drink, as I'll need all my wits about me tonight.'

Sean rose to his feet and assisted Jenny with her dress on to a stool before reseating himself and signalling to Marcus for Jenny's order.

'Will Ian McGregor be able to convince the King to talk to you?' Although they were the centre of attention, Sean acted as if they were alone. Jenny thanked Marcus as he handed her a tall glass of lemonade before she answered Sean.

'I hope so. I don't want to wear this dress too many evenings in a row.' Jenny pulled a face as she slightly adjusted the tight fitting bodice that felt like it was strangling her ample bosom.

Sean grinned as he quickly glanced over her. 'I have to admit you look mighty fine. Protocol, I suppose, really does prevent you from meeting a King in jeans and tee shirt, even if he's dead!'

Dean Schofields

A sardonic laugh came from the doorway that led into the Restaurant, causing colour to rush across Sean's cheeks as all heads turned towards the sound. 'You always were the master of the understatement, weren't you Sean?' Although the man's voice was sarcastic, it wasn't malicious, even so Sean clammed up. People moved back automatically, so that the tall dark haired gentleman in his 30's could easily make his way towards the bar.

'Well, well, Dean Schofields!' Jenny had managed to swing herself around on her stool. When the Millionaire newspaper magnate smiled warmly at Jenny, she extended her hand. 'I'm glad to see you got out of Nepal alive. Your mother is well I hope?'

Dean grasped her hand between both of his and he laughed in memory. 'Very well, thank you Jenny. Although Mother was prepared to kick up a fuss about the artefacts she wanted to bring home, and the officials weren't going to let her. I'm still surprised that we didn't end up in a prison cell.'

'What brings you to this little corner of the world Dean? I expected you to be London enjoying the high life.'

He easily slipped onto the vacant chair beside her and ordered a martini. 'I'm here because of you, Jenny. I'd heard on the grapevine that you were in my home town, and couldn't pass up the opportunity to see you again.'

Sean coughed violently and Jenny cast him a suspicious glance. Their eyes met and Jenny stifled a giggle.

'I would be flattered Dean, if I wasn't suspicious about your motives. The last time you suggested an expose of my profession, I ended up looking like a freak. No articles or I'll tell your mother about that night in Kathmandu.'

Dean threw up his hands in surrender. 'No need for blackmail Jen. I'm not here on newspaper business. I'm here to see you.'

Placing a hand against her breast Jenny said, in mock seriousness, 'Be still my beating heart. Unfortunately I have to put a crimp in your amore, as I have a date with a King.' With Sean's assistance Jenny slid off her stool and she shook out her skirt to remove any wrinkles and creases. Sean opened his mouth, about to offer to escort Jenny down to Cedars Park, when Dean beat him to it.

'Allow me to drive you, Jen. I know how tired you usually are after a ghost meeting.'

She hesitated, still slightly suspicious of Dean's motives, but finally she gave in. 'Thank you. I wasn't sure how I'd drive with all this material.' Glancing back at Sean and noticing that he looked put out, Jenny smiled at him and laid her hand upon his arm. 'Thank you for the drink Sean. I look forward to having a proper one with you some time.'

'I'd like that.' His expression brightened and he smiled happily.

The look of two tomcats eyeing each other off passed between Sean and Dean as the latter tossed off his drink and offered his arm to Jenny. The newspaperman's look of wariness became one of smugness as he regally led Jenny through the tables and out of the pub, all eyes watching their progress. As they stepped out into the cool night air, Jenny slipped her cape on but left the hood pushed back.

What wasn't seen by the patrons, as they submerged themselves in gossip and speculation about the relationship between Dean and Jenny was that the lady in question, once outside, pulled her hand away from Dean to punch his arm. A look of displeasure crossed her pretty countenance and he looked stunned at the sudden attack.

'Don't ever do that again, Dean! You can't afford to make enemies!'

'You've lost me, Honey.' He shook his head in confusion.

She threw her hands up in despair. 'You don't even know you're doing it, do you? You swan in like the Lord of the Manor and everyone else is just your insignificant servant!' She strode away from him, towards her own car, but grabbing her hand, Dean turned her back to face him.

'Where are you going? I thought I was driving you to the park?' He gestured to where his Jaguar was parked, not far away.

'How would it have looked if I had turned you down in front of all those people?'

'Don't be like that Jen.' Dean brushed his thumb down Jenny's cheek, his expression softened in affection. 'How else was I supposed to get you to myself? I didn't know how many boyfriends I'd be fighting off!' Briefly and gently, Dean kissed her lips. She didn't resist, but didn't actually respond either, although her attitude toward him had softened. A little.

'Now you're just being silly.'

'I know, but at least you're not mad at me anymore.' He grinned, rather boyishly. 'Come on Jen. You still love me don't you?'

The thoughtful look Jenny cast him wiped the grin from his face. When she shook her head, he was frowning. 'I don't know that I ever did, Dean. Oh don't get me wrong, you're fun to be with and at times dangerous, but neither you nor I are the settling down type. Don't get sentimental about the fun we've had, as you know as well as I do, I won't be here long enough for a long term relationship.'

'Don't Jen!' Dean wrapped one arm around her waist as he pressed a finger against her lips. 'You know I don't like you talking like that. Let's just enjoy what time we do have!'

Jenny smiled as she moved his hand away from her face. 'That's what I've been trying to say to you. Not that I actually think you've been pinning away for me! What is the name of the redhead you were reported dating last week?'

Dean had the grace to look uncomfortable. 'Angie, but that's not the point.'

'It is the point. Please don't put unnecessary pressures on me at the moment. There are too many people watching my every move and you know how I like to go in, get the job done and get out again without a lot of public scrutiny. Carmen Roberts isn't the only one who has spent her whole life being called a freak!'

'I'm sorry Jen, I always thought that since you so deeply loved what you do that you never took any notice to the name calling.' Dean kissed her again and gave her a quick hug before opening the passenger door for Jenny. He assisted her into the car, piling up the extensive skirt around her before he could close the door.

Moving around the Jaguar, Dean hesitated getting behind the wheel as he thought he heard someone call out his name. Glancing around the car park his eyes narrowed as he searched for the caller. Not able to see anyone, Dean slipped into the car and although he appeared quite calm, he locked the car doors, just the same, before driving out of the pub car park.

Bobby Michaels

Constable Robert Michaels, known far and wide as Bobby, for not only his name, but also his job, was feeling rather frustrated as he attempted to keep control over the growing crowd that was converging upon Cedars Park and the ruins of Theobalds Palace. *I can't see the attraction of waiting around in the twilight in the hope to see something that might scare your socks off. I'd volunteered for this duty not on the chance I might see a ghost but because I've a fondness for Cedars Park, having spent many summers of my childhood exploring its borders.*

The Park covered over 40 acres and there was something for all tastes, woodland walks, 18th century domed summer houses, formal gardens, the ornamental pond, a maze and tea rooms. In 2002 new gates were added to commemorate the Golden Jubilee of Queen Elizabeth II which contained a time line of historical events at Cedars Park, archaeological digs occurred on a regular basis and parts of Theobalds Palace garden walls could still be seen.

While there was no appearance of Jenny Weston, the crowd was happy enough to heed Bobby and keep to the car park, but as soon as Dean's Jaguar pulled up in a spray of gravel, they surged forward in excited anticipation. Dean tried to push their way through the crowd, as Bobby forced his way towards them.

'Come on people, give the lady some air! Back off will you!' The policeman was becoming seriously irritated as he was being ignored. Jenny threw up her hands for silence.

'Ladies and Gentlemen!' She waited until the crowd became quieter, before continuing, 'Ladies and Gentlemen, I do understand your interest. It's not every day you get the chance of seeing a ghost, but I must beg you to let me do my job. If a large group of people invade their territory, it could frighten the King away, and I may never again be able to contact him, let alone help him. I'm not a charlatan; I don't make a fortune from guileless victims. I'm here to help.'

Jenny felt that the crowd was on her side, or at least willing to listen. 'If you want a sighting of a ghost it may be possible to arrange that. I must ask, though, that you stay away from the ruins. Do you agree?' There was a general murmur of agreement from the assembly and they moved back to give her more room. 'Wait here, I won't be long,' Jenny turned to Dean and added, 'you'll have to remain also, I'm sorry.'

Dean perched himself upon the bonnet of his car. 'No problem. Call out if you need any help, Jen.' She smiled her thanks and picking up her skirt a little to keep it off the damp grass; she headed into the park towards the remains of Theobalds Palace.

Tommy

Twilight had settled over the park, a peaceful unreal half existence was felt by all gathered in the car park. Some were believers, other sceptics, and many just not knowing what to believe. As she made her way towards the ruins, Jenny had doubts, *Ghosts like normal people, don't like to be put on display. If I ask Ian McGregor, I know that he would more than likely be rude to the crowd.*

Tommy would do it willingly, he's a bit of a ham, but I'm hesitant to contact him. I don't want to rely upon Tommy, as I honestly feel that it is well and truly time for him to cross over. Jenny checked her watch and perched on the bench, wrapping her cape closely around her.

When a glow of light announced the arrival of Ian McGregor, the Scotsman was frowning and looking distinctly unhappy.

'Won't the King come?' She couldn't hide her disappointment.

'Oh aye, but I canna guarantee he'll make a whole lot of sense.' Ian waved his hand in an agitated manner.

'Half the battle is won if I can just talk to him.' Jenny relaxed in relief.

'Coo Mistress, you do look smashing!' Tommy's voice startled Jenny as he suddenly materialised beside them.

'Hello Tommy. It's nice to see you, but what are you doing here?'

'Thought you might need me help.'

Jenny smiled as she linked her arm through his. 'Indeed, I could do with your assistance.' She quickly outlined the situation with the car park crowd.

'Scare them silly, or just an appearance?'

Jenny laughed, delighted by his youthful, ghoulish intent upon a little haunting. 'Just an appearance, Tommy, I don't want to alienate these people just yet.'

Tommy began to evaporate as he said; 'I'll see you there.' Jenny was about to head back to the car park when Ian touched her arm.

'Don't be too long, the King doesn't like to be kept waiting.'

Jenny nodded. 'Only a couple of minutes Ian. We must be left alone.'

A Little Ghostly Visit

The crowd in the car park had grown considerably in numbers. There were even a couple of photographers, when Jenny returned to the car park and although an expectant hush fell over the assembly, Bobby Michaels was still struggling to keep them under control. There was a sigh of relief and a look of appeal from the policeman as Jenny joined him.

'The natives are getting restless Doctor Livingstone.'

Jenny shook her head as she laughed. 'About an hour, Constable Michaels, then it'll be over for tonight.' She looked around as she called out, 'Tommy, we don't have much time.'

The crowd fell into a hushed silence as their expectation grew and excitement rose. A look of reproach covered Jenny's features as Tommy began to materialise beside a young woman with a plunging neckline, which exposed a considerable amount of bosom.

'Tommy!' Jenny was exasperated.

'Coo Mistress!' The ghost grinned mischievously as he became more visible to the average mortal, 'These girls don't 'alf show off their assets!' The girl, Tommy had been leering at, screamed and started to go into hysterics. Jenny made her way through the crowd and slapped the girl lightly across the face.

'Get a hold of yourself! Really Tommy I did say an appearance and not scaring anyone.'

Tommy giggled. 'Sorry Mistress, I couldn't help meself.'

The crowd burst into noise and movement. The sudden rise of pandemonium meant that the situation was rapidly becoming out of control. As people rushed forward reaching out to touch him, yelling, Tommy's eyes widened in fear and he clung to Jenny for protection.

Bobby jumped up onto the bonnet of his car and blew his whistle, long and loud. 'People, please! Contain yourself. Dead or alive, this is still just a young lad. Settle down or I'll call this whole thing off.'

An uproar of protest arose from the gathered crowd, but Bobby wasn't prepared to put up with any nonsense. 'Either settle down or you can all go home right now!' The policeman jumped down off his car and as the noise level dropped, Tommy hesitantly raised his head from where it was pressed against Jenny's shoulder.

'What do I need to do for this lot?' Growing in confidence, Tommy left the shelter of her arm and took a look at the faces around them.

'Constable Michaels, do you believe in ghosts?' asked Jenny.

Bobby scratched his head thoughtfully, a little doubtful about showing his ignorance. 'Well, to be honest Miss, if I hadn't seen the lad materialise before my eyes, I would've been more sceptical about what you do.'

'Good!' Jenny nodded, satisfied. 'You're a reliable witness, and you'll look after him. I must be on time for my meeting with King James.'

Tommy's eyes returned to fear, 'Mistress! You're not leaving me?' He reached out to grab her hand.

'The Constable will look after you. When you're finished, you can re-join us.'

Jenny transferred the youth's hand to Bobby's, and the policeman started at the cold, solid feel of Tommy's hand. With Jenny moving out of sight, Tommy's hand passed through Bobby's arm. He was still visible, but no longer a solid form. Amazed, Bobby reached out to grasp hold of the ghost's hand, but he kept passing through Tommy.

'Unbelievable! You were so real a moment ago, now I can barely see you! Is this what Miss Weston meant when she said you draw upon her energy?'

Tommy nodded. 'At the moment you could pass right through me.'

'Why are you still a ghost?' The crowd seemed to fade away to Bobby as he became completely focussed on the youth. This was a sore point for Tommy, and he awkwardly shrugged his shoulders.

'I made a mistake. An ancient boiler that was constantly breaking down heated the building we lived in, in London. I woke at three in the morning frozen to the bone and headed down to the basement to try and get the boiler working again. I'd seen the Superintendent fix that boiler a hundred times so I thought I knew how to fix it myself. The boiler blew up and basically destroyed the building and everyone inside it. I killed over a hundred people.'

There was a tut-tut from a woman close by, who added, 'How terrible! You wicked boy!' Tommy's face reflected his own feeling of grief and distress.

Bobby frowned, as he snapped at the woman, 'Don't be stupid! It was an accident; he didn't mean to do it.' He tried to pat the lad on the shoulder, but his hand went straight through him. 'I know you want to get back to Miss Weston, so if you'll trust me, we'll walk through this mob so that they can see that you're the real thing. Okay?'

The ghost looked around at the surrounding faces and decided that they were no longer hostile, he agreed.

Tommy continued to look wary as he and the policeman walked through the crowd. Hesitant, searching and cautious hands reached out to try and touch Tommy, all attempts sending fingers straight through him. When a pretty young girl about his own age, hesitantly reached out to touch Tommy's chest, he suddenly giggled. 'That tickles!'

'Oh, I'm sorry.' The girl withdrew her hand with the speed of lightning.

Tommy took pity on her. 'It's all right, I can't actually feel anything.' He allowed his eyes to travel down her figure and grinned. 'Mind you I wish I could.'

'Oh, you cheeky beggar!' The girl's cheeks suddenly flamed.

Tommy eventually turning to Bobby said, 'Will this lot be all right now? I must get back to the Mistress.'

Bobby nodded. 'I'll get rid of this crowd. It's … it's been nice meeting you Tommy.' The young ghost gave a casual salute before he faded away completely. Pulling himself together he once more became a competent police officer. 'The show's over, the ghost has been and gone, and its time these kids were in bed, so off you go now!'

Like bemused sheep most of the crowd began to wander back towards the village and into their own homes. Soon, nearly only Bobby Michaels was left with Dean Schofields, both with the feeling that what had happened there had not been real.

King James

'Sorted the chumps out, then?' Ian McGregor was pacing up and down when Jenny returned to the palace ruins.

'Tommy is taking care of the crowd.' She looked around as her eyes readjusted to the moonlight now that she was away from the lit car park. 'Are we ready?' A sudden glow began to develop behind Jenny as she turned round; she dropped into a low curtsy.

'Why Ian, you didn't tell me the Healer was so young and pretty,' said the King.

'Didn't see tha' mattered, Your Majesty.' Ian bowed respectfully.

Straightening again, Jenny agreed with Ian. 'It is what I can do for you that matters your Highness. You want peace and release, and I can help you.'

'Damn that book, it is the root of all my problems, but it had to be done.' King James wrung his hands as he began to pace. 'There were enemies everywhere; few people that I could trust. I had to hide the damn thing, had to get my most trusted

Knight to guard it.' He broke off, rambling incoherently as he continued to pace. Ian looked inquiringly Jenny, but they both remained respectfully silent.

'I had no idea I was ill, I thought he would be guarding the book for only a day. No one knew that he was there and I couldn't make anyone understand.' The King was become more and more upset; his hands began to fly about him. 'Sir Rupert Steele will have died down there and there was nothing I could do to save him. Have I condemned Rupert to be forever trapped in the secret room?'

Sadly Jenny nodded. 'I fear so, your Majesty. If he's the sort of Knight that I think he is, he'll still be guarding your bible.'

The King began to mumble again, his words lost to his audience as he faded in and out of vision. During their wait for the King to return to some form of sanity, Tommy appeared and cast a searching glance at Jenny in concern.

'All dapper Mistress?'

Jenny nodded, 'We need to know where to start looking for the secret room though. It is under the palace here isn't it?'

King James stared at her, open mouthed for several minutes before his face crumbled in despair. 'I don't know! I can't remember! Was it in the study? Or the cupboard under the stairs? I don't know, I just don't remember!'

Ian shook his head as he patted the King on the back, 'Never mind Sire. We'll ask Mandy about the location of either site. What we need is any password you may have given Sir Rupert to indicate that someone came from you and were all right.'

'You clever old thing!' Jenny smiled in amazement, 'I wouldn't have thought to ask about a password. Did you have one, your Majesty?' She turned her attention back to King James.

Like a guilty schoolboy, the King nodded his head, 'Isadore.'

'Excuse me?' For a moment Jenny looked completely blank.

'Isadore; she's Rupert's younger sister. That was the password.' The King's eyes glazed over as he contemplated the girl in question.

As Jenny began to collapse to the ground, Tommy put a supportive arm around her. 'Bear up Mistress. There's naught more we can find out here.'

Sadly Jenny agreed. 'Yes Tommy. Three ghosts at one time are a little much.' She glanced back up at the King. 'Thank you for your assistance your Highness. I'll be in contact just as soon as I have any news.'

For a moment the King could only stare at Jenny as never before had he been the one to be dismissed from an interview. Seeing his dilemma, Ian gestured with his head towards Jenny. 'We're a bit of a drain on the lass. We're using up her energy.'

The King continued to look blank for several more minutes, but the penny finally dropped, and he understood what the Scotsman was trying to tell him. 'You should have told me you had a time limit.'

With Tommy's arm firmly entrenched around her waist, the only thing keeping her on her feet, Jenny found the energy somewhere to smile. 'No need for apologies your Majesty. It was necessary to get as much information from you as we could.'

The King nodded solemnly. 'About Rupert, be gentle with him. As I have wandered through these ruins, I have been aware of the changes of time. He has not.'

'I understand Sire.' Summoning up her last strength of will, Jenny dropped a respectful and remarkably graceful curtsy to the King.

With a satisfied nod and a wave of his hand, King James evaporated into the darkness. Jenny finally able to give into exhaustion, crumbled to the bench, only the support of Tommy stopped the descent being too ungraceful. Ian looked on, doubtful about what he should do, as the boy tenderly cradled Jenny in his arms. Tommy though, had no doubts.

'In the car park you'll find a Copper. We'll need someone mortal to see her back to her Inn.'

'What if I only scare them away?' Ian hesitated.

Tommy looked up and grinned. 'Not he! Now hurry before the Mistress becomes unconscious.' Normally not one to take orders from anyone let alone a youth; Ian didn't even stop to think of arguing, as he vanished.

Shake A Leg

Apart from Bobby and Dean, only half a dozen people would not be sent home. Two of them were local reporters with cameras. They hoped for not only further picture (that is if they turned out) of ghosts, but a finale to Jenny's meeting with King James. The sudden materialisation of Ian, though, was enough to weaken anyone's resolve to stick it out, and understandably several people took a hasty step backwards. Ian looked around him contemptuously, his gaze resting briefly upon Dean before fixing upon Bobby in his uniform.

'Miss Jenny needs help!' When they continued to just stare at him, Ian's temper snapped. 'Well what ye gaping at? Are ye lot not man enough to jump to, when a lady needs assistance?' Ian was pointing at Dean, 'Ye're a big strong lad, and Miss Jenny may need to be carried.' Ian turned on his heels and without waiting to see if anyone followed, headed back to the Palace site.

Bobby was the first to pull himself together, wiping a handkerchief across his brow. 'If I never see another ghost in all my life, it'll be too soon!' He cast a quick, authoritative glance at the remaining crowd. 'Stay here, all right?' He needn't have worried, there was no way anyone else was prepared to follow the fiery ghost. So he and Dean were quite alone as they headed into the heart of the historical park.

Seeing Jenny lying prostrate upon the bench, Dean broke into a run, passing Ian and sat down to take her into his arms.

'Jen? Are you still with us? Can you hear me?' Without opening her eyes, Jenny smiled slightly, her fingers lacing through Dean's.

'Loud and clear, Commander, time to go home, I think.' Her words were barely audible, but the message was clear enough. Dean scooped her up in his arms, and with a little more than a nod to Tommy, and Ian, he strode back to the parking lot and his car.

Bobby, bemused, watched him leave, before turning back to the two ghosts. 'Eh, thanks for that. Um, you don't stick around now do you?'

Tommy shook his head, rising to his feet, and Ian said, 'Nay, we've work to do.' Tommy looked back to where Dean had disappeared with Jenny. 'Watch him, Copper. I don't trust him!'

'You may be right.' Slowly, Bobby nodded. 'Night.' The two ghosts raised a hand in farewell as the Police Officer checked the grounds for mortal trespassers, before returning to his vehicle.

There was a moment's silence as the two ghosts finally had the opportunity to size up one another. Neither was entirely satisfied with what they saw, but were happy enough to get along to help Jenny.

'So, you'll question this serving maid about the lay out of the palace ruins?' Tommy's tone was pleasant enough, but there was a hint of authority.

'Aye, I'll do that laddie. What will ya be up to then?' Ian wasn't about to be intimidated.

'There's someone here; someone with power.' Tommy appeared to be sniffing the air around him. 'I'd better have a look around.'

Ian McGregor's bushy eyebrows rose in interest, 'Anything to be worried about?'

'Dunno.' The youth shrugged his shoulders. 'Tell you when I've found them. Wanna stick around? Might be interesting,' this was obviously an olive branch, so Ian took it with reasonably good grace.

'I'd like that laddie.' The uneasy alliance had begun.

Tree Vigil

Within Cedars Park, not far from the ruins, Carmen carefully eased herself out of the tree she had been perched in. Beneath the tree sat Evelyn May, upon the ground with his crutches lying in front of him. He used the trunk of the tree as a back support and was glad when Carmen dropped down to the ground beside him.

'Well?' His tone was just a little cautious.

'I've never seen a King before.' Carmen pulled a face. 'His costume was what I expected though.'

Evelyn waited for Carmen to continue, but when she didn't, he asked, 'Did you feel anything?'

'Hum? Not really, but then again, I don't know what I'm supposed to feel. Of course I saw it all, but then so did you,' for a moment Carmen chewed on her bottom lip. 'I'm going over to have a look. Two of the ghosts have returned. I'll come back for you if it's too far for you to walk.'

'No, no. I'm coming.' Evelyn struggled to his feet. 'I may need protection.'

Carmen opened her mouth to protest, thinking that he had said, that she would need protection, but when she realised what he had actually said; she closed her mouth again on the biting retort in mind.

'That's silly, Evelyn.' She reached out to steady him on his feet; watching him cautiously. It wasn't until Evelyn was resting completely upon his crutches that Carmen started towards the ruins.

To Go A Scaring

Unable to see the ghosts that had remained in the ruins, Simeon Masters strode purposefully across the open ground, a metal detector slung over his left shoulder. He was busy cupping his hands to light a cigarette and was therefore unaware of Carmen and Evelyn also approaching. Tommy and Ian, though, were more than acutely aware of him.

'Him?' Ian screwed up his face in disbelief.

Tommy shook his head. 'Nay, but this one we can scare.' A diabolical laugh escaped from Ian. They advanced towards Simeon, quickly closing the gap that lay between them.

With the cigarette hanging from his mouth, Simeon unhitched the metal detector and concentrating upon switching on the equipment, didn't see the approaching danger. As Carmen and Evelyn drew closer, the ghosts were able to feed off her energy and become more solid in appearance. Carmen stopped with a gasp, unused to the sudden drain of energy, but being young made an instant recovery. Evelyn reached out for her arm, but she shook her head.

'It's okay,' she reassured him before they continued to approach.

While they were still virtually invisible, Tommy snuck around behind Simeon and the boy loosened the strap that held the metal detector on the mortal's shoulder, while Ian yanked out the cigarette and stubbed it out on the back of Simeon's hand. Simeon swore quite fluently and as Tommy and Ian became visible to him, Simeon swore even more colourfully.

'Now that's what I call knowing ya mother tongue!' Ian grinned in appreciation.

'Fuck off!' exploded Simeon.

Tommy sadly shook his head. 'Now that's not very neighbourly.'

'Shame that. Perhaps we should punish him?' laughed Ian.

Simeon began backing away from the two ghosts, who were enjoying themselves immensely. 'Bloody Hell! You must be joking! You can't touch me!'

Ian forcefully grasped his arm, proving Simeon wrong. 'Aye we can and we can inflict pain too.' Ian turned to Tommy. 'Which part do you wanna start with laddie?'

'Hum, I always wanted to know what it would be like to slowly carve a person up alive, piece by piece, until they are begging for death.'

'That could take quite some time laddie.' An evil grin spread across Ian's features.

'What is time to us?' laughed Tommy.

'Aye laddie, that be true.' They turned their attention back to Simeon Masters, who was now trembling in fright.

'You're mad!' Having dropped the metal detector, Simeon began to back away.

Tommy grinned, 'All the more reason to fear us.' A strange stench pervaded through the atmosphere as Simeon lost control of his bowels. He turned on his heels and ran for his life. Neither Ian nor Tommy took after him; they just looked at each other and burst into laughter.

Tommy's Lesson

As Simeon disappeared into the darkness, Evelyn and Carmen entered the ruins and easy speaking distance.

'That was a little rough guys! Did you have to make the man shit himself?' asked Carmen.

The two ghosts continued to giggle as Evelyn settled himself onto a bench and Carmen studied the ghosts as they drew further upon her energy and became more solid.

'Working with the Mistress is usually pretty serious stuff; we don't get to have fun like that.'

With a nod of her head, Carmen conceded this point. 'Are you going to try scaring us?'

'You're the Mistress' protégé aren't you?' Tommy question came out of nowhere.

'Is it that obvious I'm a novice?' Surprise was written all over Carmen's face. 'I mean, it must be obvious I'm like her, or you wouldn't be visible, but it's something else isn't it?'

Tommy sniffed the air. 'There's freshness about your energy that has nothing to do with your age. It's how often your energy is recycled.'

It was obvious that neither Evelyn nor Carmen were a threat, Ian was getting impatient to get some work done, 'If ya don't need me laddie.'

Tommy turned respectfully back to the older ghost, 'Of course. We'll only be talking.' He waited until Ian had dissipated before returning to Carmen. 'You have doubts don't ya? All the Healers I have met through the Mistress have had some form of doubts.'

'Are the doubts justified though?'

Tommy shrugged his shoulders. 'That's a personal matter, but do you want a really negative view of the business?'

Carmen frowned. 'Not really, but I suppose I should see the worst possibility.' Evelyn took her hand and held it to show support.

'There's an Institution not far from here, north a bit, where you'll find a young boy.' Tommy broke off as he gave a harsh laugh. 'I say young, but he was 10 when I first met him with the Mistress, and that was nearly 10 years ago. His name is Zachariah and his story isn't one of the successful ones.'

'What's wrong with him?' Carmen's reservations were plain to all as she looked from one male to the other. 'Has he gone insane? Why can't you tell me his story?'

Tommy screwed up his nose, thrusting his hands into the pockets of his pants. 'Best you speak to him, and his parents. Are you up to trying something?'

'It won't hurt will it?' Carmen nodded nervously.

Smiling reassuringly, Tommy shook his head. 'Not really. You may feel tired though.'

'Okay, then.'

'I want you to make me disappear, and then reappear somewhere else.'

A look of suspicion crossed Carmen's features. 'Is this another reverse test?'

Tommy grinned. 'Nay. You can do it, but don't send me too far, as you may not have the energy the first time to get me back. The other side of that stone wall will do.'

'I'll try.' Carmen didn't sound too optimistic mainly because she didn't feel optimistic.

Chewing on her lip, Carmen stared straight at Tommy, thinking about him as an entity, and the place he wanted to go to. Slowly, very slowly, Tommy began to disappear and as Carmen's confidence grew, he suddenly vanished.

Both Evelyn and Carmen gasped in surprise, looking around to where Tommy was materialising again. When he was once again solid, Carmen rushed across to touch his arm.

'You're all there aren't you? I did it?'

Tommy laughed, taking her hand and squeezing it. 'Aye, you did. How do you feel?'

To everyone's surprise Carmen let out a huge, 'Whoopee! I feel great! What a buzz! Can I transport you anywhere, or did you actually do that?'

Tommy shook his head. 'No, you moved me. Don't you feel even a little tired?'

'Not a jolt!' Carmen started to dance around.

Evelyn's eyebrow rose as he saw the perplexing look on Tommy's face. 'Not in the game plan?'

'Excuse me?' Tommy frowned in confusion.

'Sorry, forgot you're not from our century. Carmen's reaction is not what you expected.'

The ghost's frown lifted, as he comprehended. 'Not in the least. Your lady should be quite exhausted on her first attempt.'

'So what does that mean?' This time it was Evelyn who frowned.

Carmen came back to reality, plonking herself onto the bench beside Evelyn, worried about what Tommy was going to say next.

'Once in a blue moon, as the saying goes, a Spirit Healer has the ability to regain all their energy. Nothing is ever lost permanently. In fact when you've released a ghost apparently you gain what little life force that they have left. You could end up living to 200 or even still looking like a teenager when you're 50!'

Carmen's jaw dropped as her eyes lit up. 'Really?'

Tommy shrugged. 'Don't really know, as it has been some time since anyone's had that gift. Don't get too worked up though. You may be simply living on adrenalin, and when the 'Buzz' as you called it wears off, the tiredness will set in.'

'Oh!' Carmen did not like that idea as much, but had to face the possibility of it being true. Tommy began to fade out of the picture.

'Go and see Zachariah, but don't go alone. A little moral support, you know.'

Jumping to her feet, Carmen reached out her hand to him as he continued to grow fainter. 'Will I see you again?'

Tommy's disappearance halted a moment. 'This is an important case for the Mistress, and I think she'll need all the help she can get.' With a wave he was gone.

Shall We Go Home?

Carmen continued to stare at the place he had once been. Evelyn silently watched her, wondering, *what is she thinking, and worse, if she is suddenly hit by fatigue, how am I going to get her home?*. When Carmen turned to face him, a smile a mile wide was spread across her features and Evelyn was nearly swept off his perch as she suddenly hugged him.

'What an unreal experience! I can't believe I've just been chatting with a ghost!'

Using one hand to steady himself, Evelyn laughed at her enthusiasm. 'How do you feel though?'

Releasing him, Carmen thought about it as she sat back down. 'Not tired at all. I think I should wait 'till tomorrow before deciding if I'll live to 200.' The thoughtful look was replaced by an answering smile as Carmen linked her arm through his. With her assistance Evelyn hauled himself onto his feet, adjusted his crutches before he finally spoke.

'Fair enough, do you feel like a pizza?'

Carmen was so stunned that she stopped walking. 'Evelyn! You've just had a huge meal at your Gran's. You can't still be hungry.'

'Not really, but I would like to spend some time alone with you.' Shaking his head, he looked just a little guilty.

Carmen's expression softened. 'You don't find your Gran's place too inhibiting do you?'

'No, it's just that...'

A devilish twinkle entered Carmen's eyes. 'You're not afraid to be **that** alone with me are you? I mean the things we could get up to in the privacy of the living room, compared to a crowded Pizzeria. No wonder you're concerned.'

Even in the moonlight Carmen knew that he had gone bright red, 'Hardly, in my condition! I just wanted you to feel comfortable that's all.'

Carmen kissed him lightly and they continued to the car park. 'I'd feel more comfortable at your Gran's than anywhere else! Come on; let's just see how much snuggling your condition will take.'

A rueful grin swept all previous concerns away as other; more interesting possibilities were now all Evelyn could think about.

Let's Get Her To Bed

It was rather a dramatic scene that caused Cheryl to gasp in surprise when Dean burst into the pub, Jenny carried in his arms, and he called out to the publican as he headed for the stairs.

'I'll need a hand Cheryl, if you wouldn't mind.' He didn't wait to see if she did or didn't mind, but forged ahead up the stairs. Cheryl cast a quick searching glance at Marcus to see if he could cope without her, before making her way around the bar and up the stairs after the dramatic pair.

Not having a key, and unable to try and find it on Jenny, Dean was forced to wait outside Jenny's room until Cheryl had caught up to let them in with her master key. With a brief grunt of thanks, he swept into the room and laid Jenny gently down on the bed. Cheryl hesitantly followed, turning the light on and shutting the door behind her for privacy. *I'm not really sure what I'm meant to do.*

Dean, though, had no doubts. 'She can't sleep in that dress, so I'll need your help to get her into a nightie.'

Managing to raise herself up onto her elbow, Jenny got out a feeble protest, 'I'll be all right Dean, don't fuss.' With considerable effort she sat up, but only managed to remain up right with Dean's assistance.

'Sure! Let's just see how you go.' His tone would have been patronising if Cheryl didn't realise the truth of his words. As

Dean managed to drag Jenny up onto her feet and kept her upright, Cheryl quickly unzipped the ball dress and allowed it to fall to the floor before hesitating upon undoing Jenny's bra. She looked doubtfully at Dean, but he only smiled and shook his head.

'It's all right, Jen hasn't got anything I haven't seen before. On the word of a disreputable gentleman, I'll behave!'

Cheryl laughed at his rueful grin, and Jenny raised her head from Dean's shoulder to add, 'It's all right Cheryl, we're old friends.'

'Oh, I see.' Not quite sure whether that actually meant that they had been lovers or not, Cheryl helped Jenny to remove her bra and extracting a nightie from under the pillow, slipped it over Jenny's head, and settled it into place. This done, Dean lowered Jenny back onto the bed. She tried to remove her shoes, but being unable to reach down, could only kick them off.

With deft skill that Cheryl felt he definitely should not have, Dean removed Jenny's stockings while Cheryl picked up Jenny's dress, shaking it out before laying it over the back of a chair. The diamond necklace was removed and placed on to the dressing table.

Jenny slipped under the sheets and smiled up at Cheryl. 'Thank you Cheryl. Sorry to be so much bother.'

Cheryl blushed in delight. 'Can't have your reputation sullied by something so innocent. Goodnight.' She opened the door, and stood with it ajar, looking expectantly at Dean.

The millionaire grinned at Jenny and winked. 'Call me when you're human again love.' He briefly kissed her on the lips before turning off the light and followed Cheryl out of the room.

Cheryl's main reason for doing this was obvious, as indicated by her previous words, but she had another reason for wanting Dean to accompany her, as she had several questions for him. They descended the stairs together, and asking for a moment in private, she followed him out to his car.

'Is that what usually happens when Jenny meets a ghost? Is she normally that exhausted?'

Dean leant against the driver's door of his car as he absently fiddled with the keys. 'There were three ghosts, rather than just one, and one of them may have been pretty difficult.'

'Do you approve of what she does?' Cheryl paced a little, still confused and worried.

He shrugged his shoulders. 'Our relationship isn't that sort. On the whole I admire Jen for what she does. It can't be easy knowing that you may never live to a ripe old age, but so long as you enjoy yourself while you can, well live it up.' Dean unlocked his door, and then paused as a thought struck him. 'If Jen mentions Kathmandu, don't believe a word of it!' With that, Dean slipped behind the wheel of his car, and with a friendly wave drove off.

FRIDAY

Absolutely Super!

Carmen, after a good night's sleep, got up the next day feeling happier and brighter than she had in a long time. Not wishing to slip back into her long black dress habit, she raided her mother's wardrobe for some things less sober. Having taken a cup of tea and a plate of toast into Cheryl, Carmen stood in underpants and bra and she chatted away happily as she rifled through her mother's clothes. They were roughly the same size, although Cheryl was no longer as slim as she had been at Carmen's age.

Finally finding a skirt and top that didn't make her look middle aged, Carmen plonked herself down on the bed beside her mother and took one of her hands between her own. Her eyes sparkled in memory of the previous evening.

'Oh Mum! Last night was the wildest experience I have ever had!'

Cheryl's face fell at her daughter's look of rapture. 'Oh love, I'd hoped that you and Evelyn would wait until he was better.'

'Mum!' A deep crimson swept across Carmen's features. 'We didn't! We went to the Theobalds Palace last night and watched Jenny talk to the King.' As one concerned look replaced another, Cheryl listened as Carmen described her discussion with Tommy.

'So how do you feel this morning?' Unconsciously Cheryl had her fingers crossed, but needn't have worried as Carmen jumped to her feet and danced around the room.

'Great! Absolutely super! If I could sing at all in tune, I would.'

'Nonsense dear, you sing very well.'

Suddenly plonking herself back down on the bed, Carmen became serious. 'I do feel guilty though mum. I mean, Jenny is so dedicated, so... oh I don't know. She's the sort of person who deserves longevity. And what if I decide I don't want to help ghosts, won't that gift then be wasted? I'd feel even guiltier.'

Cheryl nodded sympathetically as she put her cup and plate on the bedside table. 'A mother never likes to lose a child. You've been blessed, but you have to feel comfortable with that gift.' Cheryl took both Carmen's hands between her own. 'I want only what is best for you, and having assisted Jenny to bed last night, I can honestly say, I'm relieved I wouldn't have to go through that with you.'

'Is she all right? Is there anything I can do?'

Cheryl was touched by her daughter's concern for her mentor. 'I think she just needed to sleep. Although a good breakfast when she wakes won't hurt,'

'I'll organise a tray about mid-morning,' Carmen squeezed her mum's fingers. 'I'd better get a move on or Peggy will be beating down the door to get in.' She flitted out of the room.

The smile on her face wasn't just as a result of the ghostly meeting the previous evening. *After a sweet cup of tea and a couple of painkillers, Evelyn had been more than up to a little tender making out in his Gran's lounge room. Not sex; Evelyn isn't up to it and I'm not ready for such a commitment. I'd never hold back from Evelyn, but I do want to make sure it was the right time for both of us.*

The morning passed quickly for her, but Carmen didn't forget her promise to take a tray of breakfast up to Jenny about 11 a.m. Jenny was awake and almost her normal self, but was grateful to stay in bed to eat, and would get up later. A large bruise had developed on her cheek where Nigel had struck her. Briefly Carmen filled the older healer in on her meeting with

Tommy, and Jenny agreed that it seemed like Carmen had been blessed and also offered to go the Institution with her. Carmen gratefully accepted and they arranged a time later that afternoon.

Dean Keeps Watch

By the time Jenny had eaten breakfast, showered and dressed; Dean Schofields was on her doorstep.

'Well my dear girl, you're looking much better than when I last saw you.' He leant down to kiss her on both cheeks as she let him into her room.

'You don't get any Brownie Points for diplomacy Dean! You can redeem yourself though.'

'And what would that be my sweet?' A wicked gleam entered the media tycoon's eyes.

Laughing, Jenny punched his arm. 'Not that, you sex fiend! I may need you to sponsor someone through University.'

'What's in it for me?' He wrapped his arms around her waist. Jenny drew his head down and whispered in his ear. It wasn't what he had hoped or expected. 'So this Carmen is blessed with rejuvenation, and could be the greatest healer of the century. I repeat, what's in it for me?'

'You can really be a bastard sometimes.' She pulled away from him, and this time when she thumped him; it was done to hurt.

He raised his hands in defeat. 'A little appreciation wouldn't go a miss.' He pointed to his cheek, with a look of a pleading puppy dog. Jenny laughed, wrapped one of her arms around his neck and with her other hand turned his face, so that she kissed him not on the cheek, but full on the lips.

Not one to miss an opportunity; Dean deepened the kiss, his arms enclosing around her waist and pressed her hard against him. His hands carried lower to cover Jenny's backside, and he would have led her down on to the bed, but she broke off the kiss and succeeded in extricating herself from his grip.

'Are you ever not in the mood for sex?'

Dean's eyes opened wide in surprise. 'Do you mean that you have to be in a particular mood?'

'You're unbelievable!' Throwing up her hands, Jenny donned her overcoat and pushed Dean towards the door. 'I'm going out for fresh air. You, I think, need a cold, icy cold shower.' He put on his hurt and injured look, but she knew him too well and couldn't miss the dance of devilry that crept into his eyes. 'One day Dean Schofields, you'll get everything that you deserve.'

The millionaire's eyebrows rose. 'Is that a threat or a promise Jen?'

'Which do you deserve?' Her answering smile was mischievous.

She locked the door and led the way downstairs. There was a cool breeze blowing outside, but the sun was out and as Jenny stretched like a cat, she felt glad to be alive.

'So where are we going?' Dean's hands sank into his trouser pockets to keep them warm, and to himself.

'Where else but the ruins.'

'Oh! I was hoping for a wooded area.' His eyebrows suggestively rose up and down several times.

'One day Dean. One day!' With a sigh Jenny linked her arm through his.

He threw his head back and laughed, 'Promises, promises!' They walked on together in companionable silence.

Dog Reports

When Lucas Greenaway looked up from the pile of papers on his desk, he caught the rueful glance that was exchanged between Lisa McGraw and Dave Hedley, and the smirk upon the latter's face.

'This isn't some sort of practical joke is it Constable?'

The smile was immediately wiped from Dave's features. 'Of course not Boss! Can you honestly see me wasting time filling out a dozen bogus reports?'

The Sergeant's 'Hum!' was less than convinced. 'Twelve or so houses, empty due to the ghost watching, are burgled or attempted, but the burglar is attacked in each case by a very large dog!'

'Basically Boss,' Dave nodded. 'But some of these houses don't have a large dog or even a dog at all! Yet the dogs were heard barking, and felt, if the hospital is correct about the number of back sides with dog bites they attended last night.'

Lisa took a deep gulp of her tea before piping up, 'No sign of any dog when the residents returned home; nothing taken either, just the occasional broken door or window. Is it connected to Miss Weston's visit?'

Flicking through the report sheets, Lucas shrugged his shoulders. 'Don't know, possible, even probable. I'll have a word with Miss Weston today; she might be able to throw some light on the phantom dog. Why was this other report added Hedley?'

Always happy to stop work, Dave leant back in his chair and took his mug of coffee between both hands. 'Seeing as it was ghost related, I thought it might be connected.'

'I'll mention it to Miss Weston.'

Dave twitched eagerly in his chair and waited impatiently for the word to go. Lucas had returned to studying the reports and didn't notice the Constable's eagerness. Lisa, though, was enjoying his impatience. She waited another minute before clearing her throat. Lucas looked up suddenly, his eyes swiftly going from one Constable to the other.

'Ants in your pants Hedley?' A scowl descended upon Dave's features, as he never did have much of a sense of humour. He was about to fall into a major sulk when Lucas finally relented. 'Go on then, find Miss Weston and ask her to help us with our inquiries.'

Dave Hedley couldn't help but look like an excited school boy as he jumped to his feet and dragged on his jacket. Lisa reached over to take a set of car keys down from off the wall and threw them across to Dave.

'Try and keep both hands on the wheel Romeo,' teased Lisa and Dave poked his tongue out but the Sergeant didn't see the humour.

'Don't even look at Miss Weston the wrong way! That's an order!'

A look of surprise covered Dave's face; the Boss had never called his flirtations into question before. In fact he had sometimes encouraged the handsome Constable to use his charm to put people at ease or on side.

'Certainly Boss! All above board,' Dave spoke a little subdued, his manner a little hurt. Whatever thought had caused Lucas to seriously reprimand the Constable; suddenly dissipated.

'Sorry Hedley. I just don't want any complaints from the Council about our dealings with Jenny Weston.'

'Right Boss. Back soon.' The hurt look went, and Dave nodded amiably.

Thoughtfully Lisa chewed on her pencil as she waited until Dave had left the office, before turning to seriously scrutinise her Boss. 'That wasn't like you Gov. There's more to this than you're telling us.'

Reluctantly, Lucas nodded. 'Kathleen May believes that young woman is in danger. If she's right we could be looking after a potential victim.'

'A victim of what, though Boss? Can we pre-empt the crime?' Lisa didn't even think to belittle the elderly witch's prediction; she had in fact great respect for the older woman's powers.

'I hope so Mac.' Lucas wearily scratched his head. 'The crime may very well be murder!'

The Three Stooges

Within five minutes of arriving at the Palace Ruins, Dean was completely bored, for although he enjoyed Jenny's company, his ideas of interest were usually self-centred. He perched upon a bit of broken stone wall, and absently smoked a couple of cigarettes. He didn't pay too much attention to what was going on around them. Dean's thoughts were solely revolved around the future hour or so of pleasure that may likely come his way.

Thus preoccupied, he didn't see the appearance of the ghost of Ian, or where he led Jenny to the possible sites for the secret door. Most importantly, he didn't see the three men who gathered in the protective shelter of the nearby trees and watched the whole proceedings with interest.

Simeon Masters, a lit cigarette ever present in his mouth, Nigel Baines and Lenny watched as Jenny made strategic measurements around a site that Ian had suggested.

'Know what I think?' Nigel was busy picking his teeth with a tooth pick.

'I saw your attempt at the Pub last night! You'd have better luck fucking the stones over there to get info!' Simeon snorted in disgust.

Nigel thumped him, but had to grudgingly acknowledge the fairness of the statement. 'I wasn't gunna say that any way, fag breath! We could let the Ice Princess find the book for us, then take it.'

Lenny nodded, stroking his chin thoughtfully. 'Yeah, but there'd be a hell of a stink, and the Boss don't want publicity. I mean how do we stop the girl from telling the world about the book before we're ready to off load it?'

'Simple. Moron!' Flicking his toothpick away, Nigel looked at him as if he was a complete idiot. 'We kill her!' Lenny wasn't happy, even Simeon was uneasy about the concept.

'That's heavy duty stuff man,' Lenny complained.

'The Boss wouldn't like it either,' added Simeon.

Nigel threw up his hands into the air in disgust. 'You're both a pair of pussies! I'm not afraid of the Boss! I say let the bitch do the hard work for us and screw the consequences.' He strode off, not waiting for a reply from his associates, which was just as well, as he would not have liked what they would have said anyway.

'It is a way out Simeon.'

Simeon shook his head, lighting a fresh cigarette. 'I don't stick to murder. That's not for amateurs like us.' Taking several drags of smoke, Simeon turned to watch Nigel's retreating back. 'We'll have to watch him Len! If he screws up it'll be all our heads on the chopping block.'

With a weary sigh, Lenny agreed. 'Why do you think the Boss is protective towards her?'

Shrugging his shoulders, Simeon didn't want to waste any energy thinking about unimportant matters. Looking back at Jenny, he gave a dirty little chuckle. 'Tell ya what though, if the Boss gets his leg over, Nigel will be spitting blood.' They turned away from the ruins and headed back to where their cars were parked on the other side of the park. Lenny paused for a moment to look back over his shoulder at the Ghost Healer.

'I'm getting a bad feeling about this one, Simeon. The vibes ain't good!'

Simeon urged him on with a slight push in the back. 'Maybe, but it's too late to turn back now. We must go on.'

Lenny shivered slightly, 'No matter what?' There was a note of fear that Simeon didn't like and he was forced to swallow hard.

'Yeah, no matter what.'

Out Of Luck

When Dave Hedley first went to the Dog and Bone, Jenny had still been asleep and there was no way that Cheryl was going to let the Constable disturb her. When Dave tried to catch up with her later at the Theobalds Ruins, Dean had taken Jenny out to lunch, and then dropped her back at the pub. Dean's secretary had left several messages on his mobile phone and there were half a dozen people he had to call or see so he did not accompany Jenny and Carmen to the Institution.

Zachariah Taylor

In a room that was dimly lit, painted symbols for protection lay over the window, and the walls thickly padded, a young man barely 20 suddenly sat upright in his bed, his body shaking uncontrollably. Not of fear, not entirely, but mostly of illness. He was a handsome man, a little too thin, very pale, but a personality none the less. His eyes rested thoughtfully on a woman who sat, with her shoes off, in a comfortable easy chair; her head bent slightly as she quietly knitted. She was barely over 40, but life had not treated her kindly and she looked much older. Worry, heartache and trauma had permanently etched lines upon her face.

'They are coming!' The despair in his voice caused his mother to look up sharply. Her eyes quickly scanned the room, but it remained perfectly sealed, it was impossible for anything living or dead to enter the room without their permission.

'Yes, my dear. The nurse said Jenny phoned earlier to say she was bringing a novice to see you.' Mary Taylor put down her knitting and rose to her feet to take Zachariah's hand between her own. 'That is all right, isn't it?'

His moods could swing so suddenly that he could agree to something one moment, and dislike it seconds later. Zach nodded his head frantically. 'Yes, yes. They must come. The chosen one, she must come. I need to see her, you know I do Mum. Please I must see her!' His fingers clung to hers almost painfully.

I know only too well what he has in mind, it disturbs me, as it would any loving parent, but I realise that it is probably for the best. She released his hands and returned to her chair, as she contemplated the future, she twisted absently her wedding ring. Sighing, Mary wondered, *why do I continued to wear it? My husband had left as soon as Zach had to be institutionalised, nearly 15 years ago. He hadn't been able to handle the crisis that had descended upon us. Zachariah wants peace, and I pray that either Jenny or Carmen can give it to him.*

Zach's Story

When Jenny entered, with Carmen well behind her, Zach appeared to be sleeping. Something he did not do a lot of, as his mind rarely let him rest. Jenny hesitated, her gaze swept from the young man in the bed, across to his mother in her chair.

'Is this a bad time, Mary?' The older woman put aside her knitting as she rose to her feet, but it wasn't Mary who answered. Zach's eyes suddenly opened and he struggled to sit up. Mary moved towards him to prop up the pillows behind her son.

'Come, Jenny, come.' Smiling Jenny came forward, and bent down to kiss Zach upon the cheek.

'You seem much calmer today, Zach, are you up to reliving old wounds?' Jenny held out her hand for a very nervous

Carmen to join them by the bed. Zachariah's shaking increased, but he still appeared in control.

'Yes, yes! But we must make sure that we are alone, completely alone. We must not be disturbed.'

Instinctively Mary went across to the door, and shut it firmly, locking it and ensured that the salt and magical herbs that were ever present in the room were scattered around the base of the door. This made it impossible for any ghosts to enter the room. Carmen shyly shook hands with Zach and he gestured towards a chair beside the bed. Zach took Jenny's hand and urged her to sit on the bed.

'Do you want to tell Carmen, or shall I?' Mary laid her hand upon her son's shoulder.

'No, no. I'll try to explain.'

Mary returned to her chair and the three women waited patiently for him to speak.

Leaning back on his pillows, Zach took a sip of water from the glass beside his bed before beginning his story, 'It wasn't until I was five years old, that I understood that some of the people I saw were in fact not visual to other people. For years Mum and Dad believed that I had imaginary friends, until one night, my power was strong enough for others to also see the ghosts.' Zach turned his head to smile at his mother. 'Mum kept her head, but Dad freaked out. I don't remember how many Doctors or psychiatrists I saw. The problems began when the ghosts started following me around, growing in numbers every day, until I started to feel smothered.'

Zach's lips trembled as the memories of horrors and fright flooded back to him. Jenny rubbed her hand across his, offering him silent support. Unshed tears shone in Mary's eyes as her son's voice trembled in deep emotion.

'From the few ghosts I started off life with, by my sixth birthday I was surrounded by hundreds. More and more came, sucking me dry of energy. They kept feeding off me, wanting more and more of my life, to pretend that they were still living. You can't imagine what it was like to be six and suffer a nervous breakdown!'

'It didn't matter where we went, even when I came here, they still found me.' Zach's hands flew to his face, as he lost control of his emotions. Jenny took him in her arms, gently rocking him. Mary rose and opened a drawer to remove a bottle of medication, and extracting Zach from Jenny's arms to force him to take two tablets. Zach was gasping for breath as he collapsed back into his pillows. Jenny soaked a cloth in a bowl of water, which stood beside the bed and gently wiped Zach's brow.

It was Mary who continued, 'We were fighting a losing battle. I had no idea how to get rid of the ghosts, and they just kept coming. I was ready to pull my hair out; I was close to a nervous breakdown myself. Zach had attempted to kill himself twice, but the nurses managed to stop him. Frank, my husband, had walked out and I was ready to put Zach out of his misery. Then Jenny's mentor, Allen Stone walked in and took control. The ghosts were banished, he organised the protective seal around the room. No ghost can enter, and peace settled around us.' Mary paused, as she looked pityingly down at her son. 'Problem is that Zach can never leave this room; even if he was physically able to now.'

'I don't understand!' Carmen shook her head, trying to take in all that she was hearing.

Zach uttered a weary laugh. 'Allen was a miracle worker, but he came too late. The ghosts had robbed me of 80% of my life. I have a year at the most left before one of my ailments finally kills me.' He broke into an uncontrollable fit of coughing that once more saw his mother react swiftly to aid him.

Carmen could not stop the tears that fell, and gratefully took the tissue that Jenny handed her. 'Was there nothing they could do?' Her words were barely a whisper.

Jenny shook her head. 'Zach was granted too much power too young. Normally a Healer is at least past their teens before they achieve that level of power. Unfortunately, Allen was informed too late about Zach to protect him.'

His coughing subsided; he reached out to grasp Carmen's hand. 'It is the Healer's Power within me that has meant I have lived this long. It won't let me die until the energy in the power is completely depleted. So I suffer a slow, painful death. The nurses here won't let me kill myself and I won't have Mum prosecuted for murder by helping me. You can do it though. If you are the chosen one, Carmen, you can drain the healer's energy from me and let me be at peace.'

I Just Want Peace

Carmen snatched her hand away in horror, springing to her feet to pace the small room. 'I don't know anything about the power, or how it works! I can't be responsible for someone's death!'

'But you won't be responsible,' Zach struggled to sit upright. 'You take away my healer's power, I'll still be alive, but it means that I'll be able to pass on quickly to freedom. Carmen, you'll not be taking my life, but giving it to me.'

'I don't understand!' She sat down again beside the bed.

'Look around you child.' Mary waved an expressive hand around her. 'What sort of life is this, for anyone? Once he has crossed the river, Zach will be free. To have the life denied him in this realm.'

'But your son will die? Do you really want that?' Carmen raised a hand to her head.

Mary looked down at her son, and the love in her eyes could not be disguised. 'I want him to be happy, my dear, and... I've been given my own death sentence. The Doctors don't think I'll live another six months. I'm worried what would happen to Zach's care if I die first.'

Carmen turned to Jenny in appeal. 'Is there nothing you can do?'

Jenny shook her head. 'I'm like most Spirit Healers, Carmen. I can only give energy, I can't take it. Very few Healers can, which is why you may be able to live to an extreme old age, and most of us will die young. If you can't do this right now, we'll understand, but consider all that Zach has gone through, and will continue to suffer.'

Still in a lot of doubt, Carmen glanced nervously across at Zach. 'What would I have to do?'

Jenny moved off the bed. 'Think back to your fairy tales, Carmen, you release the Prince with a kiss.'

'Is that what you really want?' Carmen wanted to make sure that there would be no regrets.

'Yes, oh yes! To be free!' Zach managed to nod his head.

Looking up at Mary, who also nodded, Carmen added, 'Jenny what exactly do I need to do?'

A weary smile touched Jenny's lips. 'A kiss is just a kiss. Just close your eyes and give a young man the thrill of a lifetime.' Jenny gestured for Carmen to take her place; Mary hesitated beside the bed.

'Would you feel more comfortable if we were not here Carmen?' asked the mother.

Suddenly laughing, Carmen shook her head, 'No, not really.' She sank onto the bed, and placed her hand over Zach's. 'Are you sure this is what you want?'

'Even if it doesn't work, can I really turn down the opportunity of being kissed by a pretty girl?' An impish grin lit up his entire features.

A blush crept across Carmen's cheeks as she gave an embarrassed laugh. 'Cheeky boy!' Gently she lowered her head until their lips met. The kiss was soft and tender, but didn't last long.

Zach sighed, 'That was nice.' There was an obvious 'But' to his statement. It was Jenny, though, who provided it tactfully.

'A little more depth may be needed.'

'Pretend it is Evelyn that you're kissing.' A twinkle entered Zach's eyes.

Carmen looked accusingly across at Jenny. 'You know of Evelyn? How?'

Mary chuckled in spite of the rawness of her current emotions. 'Zach is telepathic. He probably sensed that you had feelings of guilt due to a boyfriend.'

'Oh!' Carmen took a deep breath and smiled sheepishly.

She placed a hand on either side of Zach's face and this time when she kissed him, she did not hold back. His arms moved up slowly to encircle Carmen's waist. She was virtually lying against him, but the weakened nature of Zach condition meant that he couldn't take advantage of the situation, only enjoy it. A gentle glow began to spread around them, growing as their life forces blended and mixed slowly, but gradually the glow around Zach began to diminish. At the same time Carmen's glow increased. By the time she drew away again, Zach's glow had completely vanished. His eyes were closed, but a satisfied smile lingered upon his lips.

'Thank you.' His voice was barely audible and Mary moved in close to the bed. With his energy gone, it would not be long now before he died.

'Zach? Are you all right?'

Opening his eyes, Zach sighed. 'Yes Mum,' He reached out for her hand and tried to squeeze it as tears fell freely down his mother's cheeks. 'I... want... to thank... you for sticking by... me... through everything. I'm... sorry... for all the trouble... you have suffered.' All three women were now crying, but Zach was still smiling.

'Don't say that Zach. I would never have deserted you. You meant everything!'

Jenny glanced briefly across to the door. 'Would you rather we left?' She asked quietly.

Mary reached out to her son with her free hand. 'No, my dear, you have been as much a part of Zach's family as anyone.'

The young man's eyes closed and he appeared to be sleeping, but the shallowness of his breathing and the constant twitching of his body, meant that he was not.

Lord Death Is Coming

Jenny gently laid her hand upon Mary's drooping shoulder. 'Lord Death will be coming soon. If you don't want to see his Lordship take Zach, you should leave now.'

Mary shook her head. 'No, Jenny, I want to see this out.' Even though she sounded resolute, she was a little frightened, and slipped her hand into Jenny's for comfort. Despite herself, she began to cry, as she watched her only child die. 'Oh Jenny, I'm so confused! I love Zach so much. I don't want to lose him, and yet, I don't want his pain to continue. Am I being selfish?'

'It has been just the two of you for so long, parting is hard. It is better though that he slips away peacefully now, than screaming in agony and despair.' Gently Jenny rubbed in a rhythmic motion across Mary's hand. 'He may not be with you physically, Mary, but he will always be with you here.' Her other hand lay briefly on the other woman's heart. Although reconciled, tears continued to fall and Mary managed a faint smile for an anxious Carmen but she was staring at the wall opposite the doorway.

'Jenny,' she spoke barely above a whisper, 'who is that man over there?'

Looking up quickly, Jenny inclined her head respectfully as the male figure materialised. 'This is Lord Death, Carmen. If you take on this profession, you will deal a lot with him.' Releasing Mary's hand, Jenny moved around the bed to drop into a curtsy before the man. 'My Lord, may I present my latest pupil, Carmen Roberts.'

Her jaw dropped a little, but still Carmen managed to curtsy as she stared at Death himself. Smiling, his Lordship reached out to take Carmen's hand, and shook it lightly, a twinkle in his eyes.

'Does she speak?' He addressed Jenny.

I am so thankful that for Carmen's first meeting, he has appeared in a human, flesh-covered form. He does so like the skeletal look! Jenny mused.

'Of course she does, you've just shocked the words right out of her. I was just the same when I first met you.'

His Lordship laughed a deep rich sound that vibrated through them all.

'My Lord, this is Mary, Zach's mother.'

Death looked professionally from mother to son, and his features softened into pity as his gaze returned to Mary. 'You've both suffered, and yet there is still some doubt in you, my dear. Do you wish me to stay my hand?'

Resolved, Mary shook her head. 'No! His life after this must be better mustn't it?'

His Lordship inclined his head in agreement. 'Indeed it will be, that I can promise you.' He placed his hand over Zach's heart, hovering over him, not touching him, as Death's eyes continued to rest upon Mary. 'Do you have any final words for your son, he can hear you.'

Rising from her chair, Mary kissed Zach's cheek, already cool. 'I love you, Zach, no matter what happened, nothing ever changed that. We'll be together again soon. I love you!' Tears chocked the last few words, but Mary was thinking clearly as she placed her hand over His Lordship's and pressed it down onto Zach's body. For a moment she felt the beating of his heart through the supernatural being's hand, and then, suddenly, nothing.

Lord Death drew his hand away and Mary collapsed back into her chair, now sobbing uncontrollably. Carmen rushed to her side, placing her arms around the older woman, as Jenny wiped the tears out of her own eyes.

'You had to bring the child here? Now?' asked His Lordship quietly, so as not to distress the mourning mother.

'It had to be my Lord. Only Carmen could give Zach release, and she needed to see the down side to our gift before she makes her decision.'

Death nodded slowly, 'She will have great power that one, but will she be able to handle it?'

'I think so.' Jenny's eyes rested thoughtfully for a moment on Carmen. 'Her ideals are a little unformed, and she is very insecure, but I have hope for her.'

Falling silent, Jenny watched as Zach's spirit rose from his inert body, and slipping off the bed, came towards Jenny and His Lordship. As Zach took Lord Death's hand, Mary gave a gasp as she could see her son's ghost. He looked round, smiled happily and waved his free hand. At last he was free of pain, and Mary forced herself to smile and wave back as Zach and Death disappeared.

While Carmen continued to comfort Mary, Jenny slipped outside the room to notify the nurses of Zach's passing. As the nurses busied themselves with the usual things they had to do, Jenny stepped outside to use her mobile phone. *I've a friend who does a lot of counselling, of the living people variety, and is especially good with people who have lost a loved one.*

Although she had been prepared for her son's death, Mary may need help coping, and I don't feel that I can devote enough quality time to Mary, while I still have the King James business to deal with. Until her friend could get there, Jenny was prepared to stay, but Mary did not want that. She thanked them both for all they had done, but she wanted to be alone for a while. So with both of them lost in thought, Carmen and Jenny headed back to Waltham Cross.

Sean Dresses Up

Sean checked his appearance in the rear view mirror of his second hand Volkswagen, as he sat in the Dog and Bone car park. He wasn't a terribly vain man, but as Jenny had promised to have a drink with him, he wanted everything to be just right. Finally getting out of the car, Sean made a final check on the knife-edge pleats of his trousers, before locking up and heading into the pub.

Less than a minute later he was back out the door, flat on his backside, and blood pouring from his nose. Glancing down at the blood staining his once pristine shirt, Sean picked himself up and now very angry, re-entered the pub. This time, though, he ducked and weaved, as he contemplated the chaos around him.

Chairs were being hurled about as punches were being thrown and glasses were smashed left and right. The place was in total anarchy as a right royal row was brewing towards total destruction. Sean's nose wasn't the only bleeding going on, but it didn't deter the violence. Cheryl was behind the bar, a hand over one ear, as she pressed the telephone to the other, and tried to make herself heard over the noise, as she called the police.

The door to the Restaurant was closed and bolted, but there were many curious faces pressed against the glass watching the fighting from the other side. More than one restaurant patron even had their mobile phone out and was filming the chaos in the pub.

Sean made his way through the chairs towards the bar. Someone knocked into him, and Sean threw him across the room, and when someone else tried to hit him, they ended up crashing through a table. Cheryl reached out instinctively towards him as a broken glass flew passed his ear.

'Oh Sean, this is a nightmare! I've called Bobby, but he can't get here immediately.'

Nodding solemnly, Sean scratched his chin. 'I'll see what I can do.' Before he could even turn around, two fighting men careered into him. Grunting in displeasure, Sean grabbed hold of the two men and banged their heads together, knocking them out. Sean tossed them into a corner of the bar. Disregarding Cheryl's plea for him to be careful, Sean waded into the fracas.

As he was charged at by an angry fighter, Sean stopped him before he could lay a finger on him, with a punishing knock out fist to the face. He quickly joined the first two in the corner of the room. Sean dealt with another who was trying to kick a man who had fallen in the fight, by knocking his legs out from under him, and smacking his head against the wall. Both were added to the growing pile of unconscious bodies in the corner.

Frankie Mann, a man small in stature, was creating most of the ruckus with a power and endurance that appeared beyond his capabilities. Sean, though, was a big man; powerful in build and strength, due to the extensive manual labour he did every day. There should have been no contest, but no sooner had Sean grabbed hold of Frankie's shirt, than the little man flung him halfway across the room and into the wall. Sean wasn't knocked out, but he was winded and couldn't immediately rise to his feet.

Just A Training Exercise

It seemed like there was no way to stop Frankie single handed, so Sean was very surprised when Jenny entered the pub, with Carmen close behind, and she actually confronted Frankie. *How can someone so petite succeed where I've failed?* mused Sean.

'You're a tiresome creature! Are you going to make this hard for me?' A diabolical laugh came from Frankie, which sent a chill down Sean's back, but Carmen looked only disgusted. With the arrival of the two women, the fighting seemed to peter out.

'Jenny, why does he ooze green slimy stuff from his shirt?' asked Carmen.

A chuckle came from her mentor. 'He is possessed. Apart from his violent behaviour, he appears normal to other people.' Jenny sighed as she tugged thoughtfully on one ear. 'Could you deal with this one, I don't feel up to the energy drain of a possession?'

'What do I need to do?' Carmen looked more than a little worried.

'I'll talk you through it.' Smiling, Jenny squeezed her hand.

With an angry roar, Frankie rushed at them, causing Carmen to forget herself and scream. Jenny completely composed, reached out and grabbed Frankie by the nose and began to pull. The green ooze that Carmen had seen was drawn out of Frankie's body.

'Grab hold, Carmen and pull hard.'

A little loath to touch something slimy, Carmen reluctantly obeyed, and was surprised when Jenny relinquished control, that she needed little effort to draw out the greenish tinged being. Once fully emerged, Frankie's real body collapsed to the floor, leaving in his place a semi-transparent greenish apparition. It tried to struggle, but Carmen had no difficulty holding it.

'To avoid facing judgement and retribution, a spirit has a rare opportunity if they possess a living person, casting out that person's soul. The violence displayed by the person is often a reflection of the owner's soul trying to evict the invader.'

'Are you going to deal with me or talk me to death?' The apparition snorted.

'Oh please!' Jenny laughed scornfully, 'You're nothing more than a training exercise, so shut up and do as you're told!'

The apparition tried to have a go at Jenny, but Carmen grabbed hold of his shirt and pushed him into a chair that hadn't been smashed and was still standing upright.

'No counselling this thing, Jenny. How do you get rid of him?'

'We just have to stop him trying to possess anyone else, until his transport arrives.' Picking up a chair and calmly sitting down, Jenny shook her head.

Reinforcements Arrive

The sound of a siren outside caused more than just Jenny's eyes to turn towards the exterior door. Several police officers burst into the pub, expecting a major brawl, headed by Bobby Michaels, and were surprised, not in the least disappointed to find the fighting over. Cheryl came out from behind the bar, determined that justice would be done.

'Arrest them all, Bobby, just look at my establishment! Someone will pay for this damage!'

Bobby's eyes widened in surprise as Sean, normally a quiet, peaceful man, picked himself off the floor, blood still dripping from his nose, and limped across to stand by Jenny.

'Everyone?' asked a bemused Bobby.

Cheryl tut-tutted in annoyance. 'Well obviously not Sean, he was trying to help me, and not my daughter or Jenny.' Bobby gestured for his colleagues to arrest all involved in the fighting.

For a moment, the Constable's eyes rested upon the ghoul before he turned to Jenny, 'An acquaintance, Miss Weston, or a nasty?'

The green apparition snorted, 'What a simpleton! I'd have had better luck in the city!'

'Shut up!' Carmen smacked the ghoul across the back of its head. Much to her horror, the head actually fell off and rolled towards Bobby, who jumped back pretty quick smart. 'Gross!' Carmen was not impressed by this decapitation.

Smiling kindly at Bobby, Jenny bent down to pick the head up and nonchalantly placed it on a table. 'It started this chaos, Constable, but it will be disposed of shortly. A higher court than ours will deal with him.'

'Enough of the talk already!' A scowl appeared on the dismembered head, 'I ain't getting any younger!'

Carmen gave a squeak of horror as the body reached out for the head and held onto it in its lap. 'Ugh! Double Gross! Isn't there some way to shut him up?'

Introducing Cherberus

Jenny didn't immediately reply as her head was slightly tilted as if she was listening for something. Carmen could not hear anything, but Jenny must have, because she smiled.

'Not long now.' As if her words were a cue, a strong gust of wind blew the doors open and a humungous dog loped into the pub. He ran straight up to Jenny, licked her cheek, and after accepting an affectionate scratch behind his ears from Jenny, bounded over to Carmen. The young witch was decidedly nervous by the size of the dog and extremely cautious as she held her hand out to be sniffed. This, the dog did, pressing his wet nose into her hand, before also licking her cheek.

'It's been a while Cherby, it's not like you to let one get away from you.'

The dog had returned to Jenny's side, and Carmen nearly fainted when she heard the dog speak. 'Can't be everywhere at once Jen, you know that!'

Carmen looked wildly around the room, but no one else looked surprised, as they heard not words, but barking. Only Jenny and Carmen it seemed, could understand him.

'How do you want him?'

The dog sat down and had a quick scratch behind his ear. 'Bit peckish at the moment Jen,'

Jenny laughed, 'Carmen, throw Cherby the head.'

Still surprised, Carmen prised the head out of the body's hands and threw it like a ball towards the dog. The huge jaws opened up and the head went down whole. The body rose, no longer in control, and walking towards the dog, followed the head down its throat. The dog licked his chops when the entire being was gone; he grinned, burped and then winked at the two girls.

'Catch ya later!' He bounded out of the pub and vanished into the night.

Those who couldn't walk out of the Dog and Bone under their own steam were assisted into an ambulance. Carmen helped her brother Peter to pick up some of the chairs and tables that had survived in one piece. Bobby was more concerned about getting the full story from Cheryl, so she was reluctantly led to her office.

'We'll close up Mum, we can't trade any more tonight.' Carmen reassured her mother. Sean tucked his shirt back into his trousers, but the pristine neatness that he had entered the pub with was gone.

'Jenny, what exactly did you call that dog?' Sean's words were a little muffled as he held a handkerchief against his nose to stem the blood flow.

'Cherby? Well Cherberus is a little bit of a mouthful to say.'

Pausing to sit down opposite Jenny, Carmen was frowning. 'Why does that sound familiar?'

'As in the three headed dog which guards the entrance of Hades.' Sean, though, had the benefit of a public school education.

'That's right.' Jenny nodded. 'Only the three heads is a bit of an exaggeration. Cherby is in fact three dogs with a linked consciousness. One dog guards the gates of hell, one rounds up escapees such as the ghoul you've just seen and the third patrols the judgement area to try and keep down the number of ghosts trying to escape their sentence.'

Carmen's frown lifted but she also had a question. 'I thought exorcism was more a priest's domain than yours?'

Again Jenny agreed, 'Mainly because an exorcism is so draining. For you that isn't a problem. Also the spirit hadn't actually taken full possession of the body, which meant a proper exorcism wasn't necessary.'

Finding that his nose was no longer bleeding, Sean fished his car keys out of his trouser pocket. 'I'd best head off home and get myself cleaned up. Blood will be difficult to remove if I don't soak this shirt straightaway.'

Taking Sean's hand, Jenny rose to her feet, and smiling she kissed him on the cheek. 'You're a good man Sean Hanson. A lot more damage could've happened if you hadn't stepped in.'

Sean coughed, helpless to stop his cheeks changing colour. Carmen kissed his other cheek.

'I'm ever so grateful that you were here to help Mum out.' The two girls escorted Sean out to his car, and having thanked him again, they watched him drive off.

Just Going For A Walk

A chilling breeze blew through them causing Carmen to shiver and wrap her jacket closer around her. 'Would you like some dinner, Jenny?' The question had to be asked twice before it broke through the deep contemplation of the older girl.

'Sorry Carmen. I was lost in thought. No thanks, not for the moment. I think I'll just go for a little walk.'

'You'll be all right?' Carmen frowned in concern. *It's already getting dark, and it is hardly the weather for being outdoors.*

Jenny smiled and nodded. 'Go on inside, I won't go far. I just need time to think.'

'Have I done something wrong?' Carmen continued to look concerned.

There was a definite shake of the other's head. 'No, I'd tell you if you had. I just need to consider my options on how to proceed with the Theobalds problem. Go inside now. Cheryl will need you.'

Remembering her mother, Carmen nipped back into the pub, but she did pause just once to glance back at Jenny's retreating figure and she tried to suppress the dreaded feeling that she was never going to see her again.

Carmen Is Worried

Leaning back in his chair in Cheryl's office, a look of bewilderment sat on Bobby's face as he shook his head, not for the first time. 'So this whole shebang was started by Ned accidentally spilling Frankie's beer? Didn't anyone try to break up the argument?'

Sitting opposite, Cheryl sipped a nip of brandy. 'Marcus tried to quieten them down, but only ended up with a broken arm. I thrust him next door before locking the door between us, and the Restaurant, and the patrons took care of him. That's when I got on the phone to you.'

'That other business... what do you make of that?' Sighing, Bobby scratched his head.

'I don't understand it. My daughter has this incredible power and it frightens me! What else exists out there that I hadn't thought possible?'

'I have no idea, Cheryl. Until I witnessed myself what happened last night in Cedars Park, I didn't believe in ghosts and paranormal activities. I've enough trouble dealing with criminals who are mortal without worrying about matters beyond my control.'

Bursting into the room without knocking, Carmen hastily apologised for interrupting, and firmly grasped Bobby's arm. 'Jenny has gone for a walk alone, and I'm afraid for her. Is there anything you can do?'

Carefully detaching her hand from his arm, Bobby straightened his sleeve. 'I'll need to phone the Boss first.'

'We'll check on Marcus and get him to hospital if he hasn't already gone.' Taking hold of Carmen's arm, Cheryl led her out of the room, closing the door behind them.

Carmen protested, 'Isn't he going to do anything?'

'More than likely dear, but I'm sure he has procedures that he has to follow.' Stepping through the double doors into the Restaurant, the women were mobbed by information hungry patrons.

Carmen left Cheryl to deal with the questions as she sat down opposite Marcus, whose arm had been bandaged and was now supported in a sling, by Olivia, the evening waitress.

'Do I need to take Marcus to Emergency, Olivia?'

Clearing away the odds and ends she had used in the First Aid kit, Olivia nodded. 'The bone has to be set and the arm plastered. My first aid skills aren't enough.'

Carmen still had the keys to her mother's car, so slipping one arm around Marcus; she assisted him outside, pausing only to add to Olivia, 'Keep an eye on Mum please. She'll need to contact the insurance company.'

Olivia shoved them out the door. 'Don't worry. This isn't the first bar fight that I've seen, and it probably won't be the last!'

Carmen had just driven away when Bobby entered the Restaurant. He drew Cheryl to one side. 'Keep people out of the bar until your insurance assessor speaks to you. I'll contact you in the morning.'

Cheryl agreed willingly. 'Are you going to find Jenny?'

Donning his hat, Bobby headed for the door. 'I'll head for the ruins. Try not to worry.' He smiled reassuringly, but as soon as he was out of the Restaurant door, his smile vanished. Bobby had every reason to be concerned; his orders were to find Jenny immediately, if not sooner, so as soon as he was out of sight of the Restaurant, and having no vehicle, he ran like hell to the Cedars Park. *I pray that the Boss is right about where I will find Jenny and that I'll make it in time.*

The First Attack

The possibility of being in danger was the furthest thing from Jenny's thoughts as her feet unconsciously took her to Theobalds Palace. *Time is a precious commodity, there being so little of it. With my presence and Carmen's growing awareness of her powers, there will be an increase in paranormal activity and there is only so much the people of Waltham Cross will be able to put up with. First thing in the morning, the Council will supply me with a metal detector and a strong hefty lad to dig up the grass when I find the secret entrance.*

Absently Jenny bent down at one of the sites she had previously staked earlier, and laid her hand over the ground. *It isn't possible to sense the presence of Sir Rupert, if he is a lingering spirit, so far underground. What I'm hoping to feel is the pulsing warmth of wood from the door, in comparison to the coolness of stone.* A breeze picked up suddenly, so cold and so intense, that Jenny stood up quickly to wrap her overcoat tighter around her.

This sudden movement actually saved Jenny from having her head caved in from a blow from behind. She quite easily out-manoeuvred her attacker's next strike by sidestepping away.

'I'm sure you've more to offer than that!' Jenny moved swiftly again, this time, he only managed to catch a glancing blow to her arm. *I'm not trying to get myself killed, but to force my masked attacker to speak, and betray him, or at least to buy me time by getting him talking. There is little I can do against such a much bigger and stronger adversary.*

Jenny attempted to run for it, but he grabbed hold of both her arms and thrust her hard against a waist-high stone. Jenny heard her spine crack under the pressure, and just vaguely as she was thrown over the stone and to the ground, she wondered, *Is my back broken?* As he knelt over her, and his hands wrapped around her throat, she actually laughed.

He paused in shock, his lips parted as if to speak, but Jenny only laughed harder.

'I don't fear death,' she said, 'Do you really think that you'll find the book without me?'

He considered her words before finally shaking his head. 'We'll manage!' His fingers tightened and no matter how much Jenny clawed at his hands and tried to struggle, his grip didn't loosen. On the point of blacking out Jenny saw a familiar figure appear, and knew the end was near. His Lordship, in his favourite guise of a hooded skeleton, reached out to touch the Assassin's shoulder.

'She dies, you die!' His words were quietly spoken.

In shock the Assassin released Jenny and he swore colourfully, 'what the devil are you?'

His Lordship grinned, very charmingly, which made it all the more frightening, 'Your worst nightmare, son!'

Reinforcements Arrive Again

'Oy! You there! Don't move!' The yell came in bursts of laboured breathes as Bobby Michaels ran at full pelt through the Park. The Assassin took one look at the police uniform and scarpered off in the opposite direction. Bobby zoomed after him, but he had already vanished from sight. 'Damn and blast it!'

Switching on his torch, Bobby trained the light upon the ground where His Lordship was tenderly feeling for a pulse at

Jenny's throat. 'Is she all right?' Bobby's light illuminated his Lordship's skeletal fingers, and as his torch travelled up the cloak covered skeleton to his Lordship's face, the police officer instinctively took a step back in fright, 'Sweet Jesus!'

Lord Death, though, had eyes only for Jenny. 'The pulse is very weak; she'll need medical attention.' His Lordship looked up to find that Bobby had turned into a stunned mullet. *Understandable of course*, thought Death, *but I have no time to be patient*. 'Hurry man! This one has much work to do before it is her time to come to me!'

Without being consciously aware of it, Bobby reached for his radio and requested an ambulance. Kneeling down he took off his coat and laid it over Jenny who was beginning to return to consciousness. Her eyes flew open and her mouth contorted as she tried to scream, but no sound came out. When she tried to move, Bobby gently restrained her, speaking quietly and reassuringly as she gasped for breath.

Not until the flashing lights and whirring siren of the ambulance arriving at the ruins, did his Lordship move from Jenny's side. Before Bobby's stunned gaze, Lord Death simply melted away into the darkness, but there was no time for him to consider what he had experienced as the paramedics were racing towards him and business returned to a normalcy that he understood.

At The Hospital

In the ambulance Jenny slipped into unconsciousness again and remained in that state throughout the preliminary examination by the hospital Doctor, x-rays of her back and finally admission into the hospital for observation. It wasn't until several hours had lapsed before she returned to the land of the living.

Carmen sat in a chair beside the bed; both her hands wrapped around one of Jenny's, and her head bent as if in prayer. Lucas Greenaway stood staring out of the window. He was furious with himself for not having prevented this attack.

When Jenny gave a choked cry that announced her return to consciousness, two concerned pairs of eyes were immediately cast upon her face. Carmen released her hand to pour a glass of water and assisted Jenny to sit up a fraction and sip the cool liquid. When Jenny tried to speak it came out as barely a whisper, and was obviously painful.

'Don't try to talk, Jenny. You're safe now, and Sergeant Lucas will catch the bastard who did this! You must rest.'

Jenny smiled weakly, before turning her gaze upon the big police officer. Again she tried to speak, but only ended up coughing; when this subsided, and another sip of water, Jenny tried again to communicate. She motioned with her fingers a writing gesture, and getting the hint, Lucas passed his notebook across. She wrote one quick sentence and showed it to Lucas.

'Medium build, muscular, large hands, wedding ring, couldn't see his face, old spice, uneducated drawl, but that could be faked.'

Lucas looked up, 'Old Spice?'

'It's cologne, Sarg.' Carmen giggled.

'Oh! Anything else you can think of, let me know when you're up to it Jenny.' Lucas shook his head. 'No more now, you need your rest.' Looking up he saw the intern Doctor enter the room, 'Right Doc?'

The young man quickly agreed with the Senior Sergeant. 'Oh yes, exactly. I'm still investigating what mix up happened with the two sets of x-rays, but it has me beat!' The Doctor scratched his head and went into a thoughtful muse.

Carmen was impatient for an explanation and interrupted the Doctor's thoughts. 'What was wrong with the x-rays?'

'According to the first x-rays, Miss Weston's vertebrae were broken. She should be paralysed from the waist down.' Before he could allow his thoughts to wander, Carmen interjected, 'But?'

'Well, then another Doctor asked if he could take a look at Miss Weston, you know, I don't remember his name, but he appeared to be a senior surgeon. Anyway I had another patient to see, so I left him, and when I got back, his hands were on her back, and I could've sworn his hands glowed. It was only for a second, but I wasn't mistaken. He asked for a second x-ray to be done, and being my senior, I saw no reason to argue. You could have knocked me down with a feather when the new x-ray showed no break at all!' Looking from Carmen to Lucas, the young Doctor searched for answers.

'What did he look like, this Doctor?' Carmen leant forward eagerly.

Unconsciously colour rose across his cheeks, as he laughed embarrassed. 'You know, when I first saw him standing in the doorway, I actually thought he was an angel!'

Carmen glanced across at Jenny, who merely nodded her head.

'Well just notch up another medical miracle! Probably just a mistake down in the x-ray department, you know how busy they are,' said Carmen.

'Do you think so?' The Doctor was concerned about being blamed for incompetence, but Carmen's manner was reassuring.

She shrugged her shoulders as if it really didn't matter. 'Who knows? Anyway no need to tell anyone, right Sarg?'

Picking up her cue, Lucas nodded. 'Just make your patient better.' With a final pat on the back, Carmen propelled him out of the room, and closed the door behind him.

The Powers That Be

For a moment Lucas and Carmen just looked at each other, neither sure about speaking first.

Finally Lucas asked, 'Well?'

Sighing, Carmen sank into her chair again. 'I think the Doctor hit it smack bang on the head when he described the other Doctor as an angel. It ties in with what Bobby told me about Lord Death being at Jenny's side in the ruins.'

'Bobby? When did you speak to him?' Frowning, Lucas began to pace. 'I haven't had a report yet from him.'

'I was already here with Marcus as he was getting his broken arm set. I saw Bobby when he arrived with Jenny in the ambulance. He was pretty freaked out.'

Lucas shook his head in disbelief. 'What on earth is going on?'

'A very good question Sergeant!' The words were barely a squeak, but certainly more audible than when Jenny had first come round.

'Don't try and talk.' Lucas handed her his notebook again, and his pen. 'Do you know what is going on?'

Jenny nodded, and wrote furiously. 'I believe it has to do with King James' Bible. More depends on me finding it than we first realised.'

Lucas handed back the pad, having read this aloud, 'about you tonight, how?'

Again Jenny wrote. 'The Powers that Be interceded. Carmen is right, the Doctor was an Angel. This mission must obviously need to succeed, and to do so I must be fit.'

Lucas looked up puzzled, 'The Powers that Be? Do you mean God?' Jenny nodded. The policeman shook his head. 'This is too much for me to take in at the moment. I think I need to sleep on it.' He hesitated in taking his notebook from Jenny. 'Is there anything I can get you before I go?' Jenny pointed at

Carmen and the door. Lucas smiled. 'That's all right; I'll make sure she gets home safely.'

'Are you sure, Jenny?' The younger woman hesitated. Jenny nodded and smiled, pressing Carmen's hand.

She reluctantly followed Lucas out and was surprised to find a police officer outside the door. Her surprise was obvious in her face, which caused a faint smile to appear on Lucas' face.

'The Powers that Be aren't the only ones who want Jenny Weston alive and well.'

Carmen paused, her hand laid upon his arm, her face so serious that his smile vanished. 'Do you believe?' She asked.

He scanned her face as he considered the question. 'I think I do, Carmen. I saw the two x-rays and Jenny's spine was definitely broken in the first. I don't understand, but I think I believe.' They continued toward the hospital exit.

'Good! I need to know that someone will stand by us no matter how crazy this gets.'

Lucas placed his arm around her shoulders and gave a mock laugh. 'Just wait till you have teenage children, my dear, then you'll know crazy!'

A silence settled upon the hospital room as Jenny fell into a deep, pain free sleep, supported by drugs. The police officer outside the room, settled into a boring wait on his watching brief. A glow began to spread through Jenny's room to accumulate into a single form beside her bed. Tommy's expression was a mixture of sadness and anger as he ran a tender finger across the blackish blue bruising that covered her throat. Brushing his hand against her hair, Tommy sat quietly beside her bed, wondering, *if anything is worth all this pain?*

SATURDAY

The Stooges Quake

If anyone in Waltham Cross didn't know about the events at the Dog and Bone pub that night they certainly were aware by the time breakfast was over the following day. It took an even shorter period of time for the news of the attack upon Jenny to circulate and become the topic upon everyone's lips.

Three men, though, when they heard the news, fairly shook in their shoes. They had been summoned to the warehouse to meet before work, and they were quaking as they waited. A cigarette was permanently positioned in Simeon's mouth as Nigel Baines chomped his way through a Mars bar and a packet of chips for his breakfast. Lenny gazed off into the distance.

As the sound of a familiar firm tread echoed through the abandoned warehouse, Lenny brought his thoughts back to the reason they had been called and a cold sweat swept over him in fear. The three men sat in silence as they waited for the explosion. It was a welcome anticlimax when it did not occur.

'I presume one of you can explain last night to me?' The Boss's words were softly and calmly spoken, but none of the men were fooled as his tone was as cold as ice. Glancing anxiously at each other, they shrugged their shoulders as they each shook their heads.

'This has nothing to do with us Boss.' Simeon found his voice, as the other two appeared to be stuck dumb.

'Really?' The Boss didn't sound convinced, a hard edge crept into his voice and Lenny rushed into speech.

'Actually, it was only yesterday that we decided it would be easier to have the Spirit Healer do the work of finding the book for us. Isn't that what you suggested Nigel?'

Nigel slid down uncomfortably in his chair as he remembered the rest of the conversation. 'Yeah!' He tried to sound tough and defiant. The Boss stared at him for a minute before finally nodding.

'Then it is as I feared, there is someone trying to queer our pitch. So find these interlopers and deal with them. Warn them off, threaten them, eradicate them, but get rid of them. Get one thing clear gentlemen I want that book found before the elfin does!' The Boss didn't wait for an answer, turning on his heels and strode out again.

A significant look was exchanged between the three men as they heaved a collective sigh. They all knew that they were innocent, but that fact would not stop the Boss from damning them anyway. Collecting up their rubbish, they hurried out so that they wouldn't be late for their real jobs.

I Want Out Of Here

Only for half a day did Jenny permit the Doctors to keep her in the hospital. *There is so much to do, and if the attack upon me is any indication, little time to do it.* When Lucas entered the ward after lunch, he found Jenny out of bed, fully dressed and determined to go home with or without the Doctor's approval. Her ability to argue with the Doctor was hampered by the squeakiness and soreness of her throat, but the expressiveness of her hands made up for any limitations.

'But Miss Weston, it is essential that we understand what that Doctor did between the first and second lot of x-rays being taken!' As the Doctor rattled on, Jenny turned silently to Lucas in appeal.

'It's all right Doc, any change in her condition and I'll seek medical assistance immediately.'

The Doctor's resolution wavered under the policeman's calm and persuasive personality. 'If possible, restrict your movements, no running, climbing ladders, brawls.'

'Most of my investigations are not of the violent nature.' Jenny stiffened in indignation.

Lucas passed a hand over his mouth to hide his smile at her funny little croak. 'All right Wild Cat! Let's check you out of this place. I've got a job for you.'

Brightening, Jenny linked her arm through the police officer's, prepared to take on any extra jobs if it got her out of the hospital.

Tell Me About The Phantom Dog

Seated in the Sergeant's office, a cup of tea at her elbow, Jenny quickly read through the various reports of the gigantic dog attacking the burglars. Lucas had been forced to close the venetian blinds in his office as Dave and Lisa couldn't help but gawk at the Spirit Healer. Putting the reports down, Jenny permitted herself a little chuckle.

'Cherby is so protective!'

'Cherby?'

'Hum, yes, Cherberus.'

Lucas' eyes widened in surprise, his Greek mythology was a tad rusty, but he recognised the name. 'Why would the Hound from Hell be interested in mortal burglars?'

Jenny took a sip of tea, sighed in appreciation before answering, 'Me, I suppose. The Healers and Cherberus have a very close relationship. You see coming home from the ruins and finding they've been robbed would have tainted their experience, and reflected badly upon me. Any break-ins that were successful, then you would find that the residents were not in the Cedars Park.'

Lucas wrote something down. 'I'll have that checked. What do you make of the other report?'

Carefully Jenny re-read the report, but this time she was frowning when she put the papers down. 'This is more diabolical, Sergeant Greenaway. To do all this, they must be deeply disturbed. Is the house vacant at the moment?' Lucas nodded. 'I would like Carmen to be with me when I go to the house. A murderous ghost is something best not met alone.'

Again Lucas inclined his head. 'I'll pick up you and Carmen about three thirty. In the meantime, I'll take you back to the Dog and Bone now so that you can rest.'

'I'll have to ask Penny how she puts up with such a tyrant.' Pulling a face, Jenny willingly, if not a little stiffly rose to her feet.

A twinkle entered the Sergeant's eyes as he escorted her to the door, opening it before replying, 'Ah, but many things are forgivable if you're a fantastic lover.'

Lisa smothered a giggle as Dave's jaw dropped almost to the floor. *I can't even imagine the Boss naked, let alone having sex, nor do I want to try.*

A sardonic eyebrow was raised as Lucas glanced at the stunned expression on Dave's face. 'Don't I give you enough to keep you busy Constable?'

Snapping out of his horror, Dave virtually jumped out of his seat, 'Of course Sir! Just lapsed for a moment.'

Taking a set of car keys, the Sergeant led Jenny out of the Police Station. 'Don't forget the inventory list of the lost property room, Hedley.' Behind the Sergeant's retreating back, Dave pulled a disgusted face. *That's all I need, more work.*

Jenny's Present

The stairs up to the guest rooms in the Dog and Bone were a little more than Jenny had bargained for as she was extremely stiff and sore, and wasn't sorry for the assistance of the arm that Lucas Greenaway offered. In the end, after half a dozen steps when Jenny appeared to be struggling in extreme pain, Lucas swept her up into his arms and ignoring her protest, easily carried her up the remaining steps.

'Whatever would Penny say if she saw you now?'

Lucas laughed as he deposited her on the landing outside her door. 'She'd warn me about straining any important muscles! Now then you'd better rest until I come back to collect you.'

Jenny agreed meekly, opening her door and so raw were her memories of the previous night's attack that when a figure approached her from within, she screamed and stepped back against Lucas. His solid build was very comforting, especially as the Sergeant had reached for his extendable baton, and had it ready to use it.

'Whoa there!' Dean Schofields raised his hands as he backed up.

Lucas put his baton away, and placing a supportive arm around Jenny, assisted her into the room and onto the bed.

'Sorry. I hadn't thought my presence would be so disturbing.' Dean lowered his head and was permitted a kiss as he placed a tiny furry bundle into Jenny's hands.

Lucas chuckled as a stunned Jenny lifted her hands to stare into the bright blue eyes of a kitten, barely a week old. Glancing around the room, her eyes fell upon a basket which contained the kitten's siblings, all five of them, and their mother. The kittens were active and lively, trying to climb out of the basket, but their mother, a fine boned ginger, looked half dead.

'Oh Dean, what have you been up to?'

Dean opened his mouth but when he appeared lost for words, Lucas chipped in. 'I think Mr. Schofields is playing the Good Samaritan. This was Jack Mack's cat, he refused to have her sterilised so when Mitzy became pregnant, he tried to drown her and the kittens. A couple of kids found them starving and freezing, but still alive, and took them to Doctor Martin, the vet.'

Mitzy And Her Kittens

Slipping off the bed, Jenny sank to the floor beside the basket and placed the kitten back with its mother. When she reached out to pat the mother, Dean uttered a warning. 'I wouldn't Jen. She's been through a lot, and can be quite aggressive.' He raised his arm to show where he had been scratched just bringing them from the Vet hospital.

'That's all right. I know her pain.'

Although Mitzy hissed threateningly, Jenny continued to slowly lower her hand towards the cat's nose. Warily sniffing the open palm, Mitzy hesitantly nudged it with her nose, and receiving no violence, rubbed her face against the hand. All the time, Jenny was talking softly to the young mother in gentle, soothing tones that relaxed the cat's suspicions.

'Dean Schofields, you're such a wicked man!'

The multi-millionaire looked stunned at this sudden attack, even though her words weren't said angrily, but sadly. Jenny gently caressed her hand over Mitzy's head, allowing her to dictate where she was touched.

'You know I can't resist cats! What am I going to tell Cheryl Roberts? I'm sure this isn't allowed.'

Having watched the mistreated cat respond to Jenny's love, Lucas wasn't sure who needed whom the more. 'Don't worry about Cheryl,' the policeman said, 'I'll square the kittens with her. In the meantime, I'll help you find homes for these little ones when they're ready to leave their mother.'

'Thank you Lucas for all you have done.'

He nodded amicably, a mischievous twinkle in his eyes. 'Try and stay out of trouble 'till I return.'

Dean saw him out before throwing back the bed covers and easing Jenny on to the bed to lie down, taking off her shoes before covering her over. 'You gave us one hell of a scare, young lady!'

Smothering a yawn, Jenny agreed, 'I'm a little scared Dean, someone actually tried to kill me! They consider this book so valuable that they are prepared to damn their souls for all eternity for it.'

Leaning over, Dean pressed a brief kiss against Jenny's lips, and would have risen, had she not retained a strong grasp upon his hand. She drew him back down for a much deeper kiss before releasing him.

'We won't let that happen Jen.' Dean ensured that the feline family were all right before letting himself out of the room, and ran lightly down the stairs to catch up with Lucas. Jenny winced a little as she rearranged herself in bed, but it wasn't long after she was comfortable, that she was fast asleep, and Mitzy, snuggling into her kittens, began to purr.

The House's History

Standing beside Jenny, Carmen couldn't stop shaking as they looked at a house of evil and pain. Lucas had driven them to St. Stephens near St. Albans on the M25 and had filled them in on the history of the house. It had been built in the late 1850's, and had been the relatively happy home of the Davidson family until the last of the sons was killed during the Second World War.

The widow took in war orphans, but the loss of her sons, the breakdown of her marriage and the moving away of her daughters had seriously affected her. The children in her care were often subjected to harsh and unjust punishment.

Carmen had shuddered as Lucas had described how for some misdemeanours, the children were forced to spend up to a whole day locked in the cupboard under the stairs without food or water. How they worked from dawn to dusk in the vegetable garden, no matter the weather, and the use of starvation and beating to break their spirits.

The widow's reign of terror came to an end when she took a tumble head first down the stairs. The police looked into the possibility of one or more of the children being involved in her death, but as a neighbour had been in the garden with the kids and sworn that all were outside when they heard the widow fall, nothing could be proven. Although the widow wasn't known to walk as a spirit, occasionally sobbing could be heard from the cupboard under the stairs.

The house had been sold and the family that moved in had a troubled son. His temper tantrums were legendary and when he needed to cool off, he would be sent, or would send himself up to the attic where he had toys and other distractions. This was how his parents had managed until the birth of a sister, all pink and golden curls, and well behaved.

Needless to say with the parents' attention focussed largely upon the baby, the boy's behaviour became worse. Then one day, the mother's sister arrived for lunch to find both the mother and father dead, with their throats cut, and the baby girl absolutely butchered. Of the boy, there was no sign. When the police tried the attic door, it refused to open, and the boy was listed as a runaway, and never seen again.

Sold again, the house became the property of the recent owners, the Masons. With the exception of the sobbing under the stairs, which was heard occasionally by the children, there was nothing to disturb their peace. Not until the children of the house had grown into teenagers, and wanted more personal space. Father, Troy Mason, took the door off its hinges to get into the attic to find that a wardrobe had fallen and blocked the entrance. With the assistance of a mate and a few tools, the wardrobe was lifted and the contents revealed.

They had known of the murders when they had bought the house, but they were not prepared for what they had found in the attic. Amongst the toys lay the skeleton of the boy, the blooded knife still in his hand, and his own body covered with stab wounds.

The police were contacted, and the room finally cleared out, but none of the children wanted the room after that. Not that it mattered with the opening of the attic; the serious haunting had begun throughout the entire house. The children were attacked, the two girls molested, Troy and his wife often had to duck flying books or knives. That had started a week ago, and after only two days of abuse the family fled the house.

Father Brian, the local Catholic Priest who had attempted an exorcism, had to be carried out of the house in a state of petrified terror. It was at this moment that Constable Hedley had heard of the case and passed on the information to Lucas Greenaway.

Shane's Rage

As Carmen reached across to take her hand, Jenny smiled reassuringly at her. Jenny's own hand wasn't quite steady, which was actually a comfort to Carmen. Both taking a deep breath, they followed Lucas inside who had obtained the house keys. An extra little swagger was added to the Sergeant's stride in his own nervousness. He dealt comfortably with crime in the mortal world; these paranormal activities were beyond his expertise.

'Is this something you have to do alone?' He tried to make the suggestion light and unconcerned. Jenny smiled at his failure to sound casual.

'It doesn't matter how many others are around. If this ghost is as violent as you say, there may be a fair bit of ducking and weaving, so we'll understand if you don't wish to come.'

Lucas stiffened in masculine indignation. *As if they could possibly think that I don't have the balls to stand and face anything two girls could?* 'It is about time you showed me just what you do!' All three took a deep breath and entered cautiously into the house, and closed the door behind them.

A shiver ran down Carmen's spine as they moved through the hall and into the kitchen. *It is so quiet,* and Carmen shook her head, as she corrected herself, *no, it is actually silent.* Not a sound could be heard. Not from outside; the breeze in the trees or the cars that drove passed the house. Not from inside; the sound of the ticking of a clock, or the humming of an electrical appliance like the fridge. Nothing could be heard except their breathing and the pounding of their own heartbeats. Lucas was as freaked out as Carmen so when she took his hand, he held onto it tightly. Jenny was the only one who appeared outwardly calm, as she seemed to be searching for something.

Suddenly she called out, 'Lucas! Duck!'

The policeman didn't even pause to think, just obeyed, as Jenny's hand reached out to where his head had been and caught a rather large carving knife that was flying through the air. Straightening, Lucas stared at the knife in disbelief. *I could very well be dead now!* 'Bloody Hell!'

Shaking her head as she placed the knife down on the table, Jenny said, 'That wasn't very nice Shane. Obviously your time of imprisonment in the attic hasn't improved your manners!'

A sudden sharp burst of wind rushed through the house blowing curtains and loose rugs about, and sending smaller items crashing to the ground. Carmen lifted her hands to keep her hair from being ripped off her head as her dress swirled around her.

In spite of her previous fear, Carmen suddenly laughed. 'What a temper tantrum! Talk about a spoilt brat!'

The wind stopped as suddenly as it started as the face of a boy appeared out of nowhere. His features were distorted in anger and childishness.

'I'm not a brat! I'm not! You just don't understand! They never understand!' As he ranted, Shane became more solid in appearance. It was enough of a sight to make both Lucas and Carmen recoil in horror. Across the boy's torso, arms and face stood out the self-inflicted stab wounds.

'You must learn to control your temper young man.' Jenny spoke calmly, not in the least put off by his appearance. She didn't bother to look at Shane as he fumed, but walked across to the window over the sink and stared out into the vegetable garden. Carmen and Lucas exchanged a questioning look and Carmen merely shrugged her shoulders. They remained silent, waiting, but Carmen couldn't contain a gasp of horror as Shane picked up the knife off the table and hurled it at Jenny. The Healer swung round and nimbly caught the knife by the handle.

'I'll kill you! I'll kill you all!' Shane sprang across the room, grabbed up another knife from a collection on the wall. Carmen cried out in horror but yet again Jenny caught the knife before it reached her.

Shane continued to gape. 'You should be dead! Why can't you dead?'

Jenny put the knife back in the holder on the wall. 'You can't kill me Shane. Nothing can kill me. I am eternal. Even after death I shall still live on; where as you're trapped for eternity in this half-life. Trapped in a half existence where your hate will continue to boil and rage inside of you.'

His hands pressed against his ears, Shane spun round like a whirly gig. 'Stop it! Stop it! Stop it! Why aren't you dead? You have to die; they all had to die! I'm not naughty! I had to kill them, they were evil!'

Glancing across at Carmen, Jenny saw the look of horror on her face. 'He's mad, Jenny. Surely beyond redemption?' Carmen whispered.

Her mentor nodded. 'This will take a higher power than yours or mine. Shane needs treatment, but I doubt he will ever pass over the River.'

'No! No!' Shane began throwing things again, not directly at them, but it was still necessary for the trio to duck and weave to avoid the projectiles.

'What now then?' Lucas asked, just barely out manoeuvring a flying saucepan. Carmen wasn't as lucky as a knife nicked her ear. Blood poured from the cut and stained her white top. Putting her hand to her ear, she brought it away covered with her life force. She wasn't horrified, she was bloody angry. Grabbing hold of Shane's arm, Carmen dragged out a chair and sitting down, pulled the boy across her knee.

'You should have been disciplined years ago! Such behaviour should not have gone unchecked.' As she spoke, Carmen spanked his backside.

'Ow! Beast! Don't! I hate them! They never cared for me! Ow! They never wanted me! It was always her! Pink and golden! Ow! Oh! Oh! Yes! Harder!' As Shane appeared to be enjoying his punishment, Carmen thrust him away from her in disgust.

Cherby Returns

The front door flew open in a blast of wind that was so ferocious that it made Shane's attempts appeared little more than a fart. For the first time Lucas felt real fear as the biggest, most savage dog he had ever seen bounded into the room. Instinctively despite his fear, the policeman positioned himself in front of the two women. Shane stared open mouthed at the huge animal. Cherberus went from Jenny to Carmen for a pat before investigating Lucas. Jenny smiled as he almost jumped out of his skin as Cerberus licked his hand.

'What do you think?' asked Jenny.

The dog grinned. '40, maybe 50 years! If he keeps off the fried food, it'll be healthier.'

Lucas could only hear barking, but Carmen understood, but was confused by what the dog meant.

'What's that supposed to mean?' she asked.

'Cherberus can tell how much time a person has left.' Jenny turned to Lucas to add, 'He says you have at least another 50 years to live, but cut down on the fried food.'

Nodding solemnly, Lucas said thoughtfully, 'I can live with that!'

Cherberus had already left his side and was sniffing around Shane, who stood ridged in fright. 'There's no way he's ready to cross over. Judging by the state of his mind, he may never be able to leave Purgatory,' stated the hound as he began to circle the ghost and Carmen could feel the fear radiating from Shane.

Jenny smiled reassuringly at both of her companions. 'Perhaps we'd better step outside for a moment.'

Leading them out into the sunshine, Lucas wandered over to look at the roses and when the first of Shane's horrific screams reached them, Jenny placed her hands over Carmen's ears as the cry pierced through them both. *I'm accustomed to the cry of the damned, but the first time can be unsettling to a novice.* When the screams had stopped, Jenny found a band aid in her handbag and tended to Carmen's bleeding ear.

It was several minutes before Cherberus joined them, licking his lips, satisfied. 'There's another ghost in there, Jen, not my line though. Also there is something amongst Shane's belongings that needs to be dealt with. It personifies evil and has to be destroyed.' The big dog loped off, vanishing before their eyes. Jenny explained to Lucas what Cherberus had informed them. Lucas sighed as he turned back to the women.

'Another ghost? This one isn't going to be as difficult as the last?'

They headed back inside, cautious in case of any further flying objects.

'No, I presume it's the child under the stairs,' said Jenny and understanding this was her practical lesson, Carmen headed straight for the closet.

The Girl Under The Stairs

Lucas was more reluctant to get involved with another counselling session. 'I'll organise to have the belongings of Shane delivered here that are stored at the station.' He headed outside to use his mobile as Carmen stepped into the opening of the closet. Jenny stood back and watched, very tired after such a struggle of wills with Shane and was prepared to allow the younger woman to test her newly fledged powers.

'Hello? Is anybody there?' Silence followed Carmen's questions for several minutes, and then suddenly there was a sob. 'Come, now, this isn't a very comfortable position to talk in, and if you won't talk to me, I can't possibly help you?'

There followed another silence, and just when Carmen was about to give up, there was a faintly whispered, 'Please help me!'

As Carmen backed out of the cupboard, she gestured for the child to follow. Slowly the girl shaking and crying began to develop a physical form as it crawled out of the cupboard, and when Carmen smiled, the girl fell into her arms. Gently stroking the child's hair, Carmen looked across at Jenny in inquiry. 'What now?'

The older woman sank into a chair a short distance away and smiled mischievously. 'Follow your heart. I'll help you if you need it.'

Exhaling slowly, Carmen bent her head back towards the child who, although she had stopped crying, was still shaking.

'Do you want to tell me why you're still in the cupboard?' The child, a girl of 10, determinedly shook her head. Carmen continued to hold her, stroking her hair. 'Come now, the Widow's dead and buried and cannot harm you.' Silence answered Carmen, and lasted for so long that she looked round to Jenny for guidance. Jenny placed her index finger on her lips and shook her head.

'She... She can't touch me?' whispered the child.

Carmen nodded, 'No one can touch you. You need to move on to the life that you deserve.'

'Will... will it be better than this one?'

Carefully considering her answer, it was a moment before Carmen finally spoke, 'I can't see any reason why you wouldn't have a pleasant after life. Why are you trapped here?'

The young girl swallowed hard. 'My name is Cecilia; we'd been working in the veggie garden, even though it was pouring with rain. I fell and broke my arm. Donna, one of the older girls brought me in and cleaned me up a little. The widow threw me into the cupboard.' Cecilia started crying again. 'I hadn't meant to fall over; I wasn't trying to get out of my chores! Honest!'

Carmen shivered in sympathy. 'How long were you kept in the cupboard?'

'I don't remember how long I stayed there. I only remember being cold and coughing. Donna tried to let me out, but only got a beating for her trouble.' Cecilia frowned in thought, wiping her tears away on the back of her sleeve. 'Then one day I crawled out of the cupboard on my own. It's locked on the outside, you see, and yet I could somehow get out.'

Continuing to stroke the girl's hair, Carmen glanced across at Jenny who nodded in agreement. 'You were already dead,' Carmen explained.

'A man, a nice man, came to me, held out his hand, and asked me to come with him. Men frighten me though, so I backed away and crawled back into the cupboard.'

Carmen looked across to her mentor. 'Oh why did his Lordship not take her away?'

Rising to her feet, Jenny laid a gentle hand upon Cecilia's head, 'He can't take those not willing to go. This time, though, it may be different.'

'He will come then?' Carmen's eyes lit up with hope.

'Oh yes. Your work with this little one is almost done.' Jenny glanced across to where Lucas stood looking stunned. 'You may not see our next visitor, Sergeant.' Lucas had quietly joined them while Carmen had been talking to Cecilia.

Lord Death Is Adaptable

Jenny had barely ceased to speak, when a bright glowing light began to grow not far from where Carmen knelt with the child. When a man appeared, Cecilia clung more tightly to Carmen, even though he appeared good looking and gentle. Jenny curtsied before assisting Carmen and Cecilia to their feet.

'Your present appearance although pleasing, my lord, won't convince this child to come with you.'

He shrank in size and took on a more feminine contour as a young woman emerged. Even without Cecilia's cry of 'Donna! Donna! Oh Donna!' Jenny knew whom his Lordship would transform into. The child ghost ran out from behind Carmen and went willingly into the image of her friend's arms.

'It is time to go home, little Cecy. Will you come?'

The child nodded enthusiastically, but there was a certain air of hesitation. 'I won't have to see **her** will I?'

They all understood that 'her' meant the widow. Donna's image shook her head. 'No you won't. The widow is serving time in Purgatory before she'll earn her after life.'

All doubts fled from the child, but she turned away from Donna for a moment, to hug Carmen warmly.

'Thank you!' Cecilia took the hand that Donna extended, and with a huge smile upon her face, they both faded away.

It was several minutes before anyone moved or spoke. Lucas Greenaway sank into a chair. 'So, a gentle ghost and a violent ghost, all in one session. That isn't normal is it?'

Carmen moved towards Jenny, who instinctively opened her arms to take her pupil into her embrace.

'No session could be held up as being normal. Each will be different, as each ghost will be different.' Jenny gave Carmen a reassuring hug before releasing her.

Lucas was curious, 'how could you catch those knives that were thrown at you?'

'That comes from the connection you make with the spirit.' Jenny smiled mischievously. 'Because I entered first it was my energy that Shane locked onto. As they draw upon your energy, they become almost a part of you, so that you can almost hear their thoughts and know exactly what they are planning to do.'

Toys No Child Should Possess

There was a discrete knock on the front door, which Lucas rose to answer. He returned a minute later with a full large plastic rubbish bag.

Jenny had a quick glance inside the bag before she stated,. 'I think we'd best do this outside, we might be making a mess. I think we've done enough damage inside with Shane.'

Lucas courteously opened the glass back door for the ladies and waited until they had passed through before dragging the bag out into the afternoon sun. Upon a patch of grass, Lucas pulled out the items from the bag. They knelt down beside the assorted belongings and looked warily through the toys that were in bits, pulled apart or mutilated.

There was a shred of blanket and several books that were risqué, definitely unsuitable for a child of any age. What caught their attention, though, was a suspiciously sweet looking doll's house. A closer scrutiny brought a gasp from all three.

Upon the veranda, at the front of the doll's house, sat a couple on a swing seat; it looked fairly innocent, but looking carefully at the detail of the figures, brushed away any illusions of innocence. One arm of the male figure lay around the female figure's shoulders, but his other hand was well entrenched in her bodice, fondling her bosom. Also at first glance it appeared as if was kissing her neck, but turning the figures around, there were spots of blood on her neck and the male figure had huge fangs. Carmen gave an exclamation of disgust as she raised questioning eyes to her mentor.

'This isn't going to get any better is it?' Carmen asked.

Shaking her head, Jenny took a deep breath before turning the doll's house around and opened the doors. The outside dolls were hardly graphic enough to prepare them for the inside. The furniture was exquisitely made, its detail and craftsmanship was first rate. It was the figures themselves that sent a cold chill down the spines of Lucas and Carmen. In the kitchen, a male doll stood in front of the cooker, holding down another man so that his face, contorted in agony, was pressed against the hot plate and his out stretched hand lay on the table as a cook chopped the man's fingers into little pieces.

Beside the kitchen was a narrow staircase, and from one of the balustrades, an elderly servant had hanged himself. Beside the staircase was the bathroom. In the bath, a naked female doll lay, a variety of stab wounds covered the body and a knife was still embedded in the chest. A young boy was thrust head first down the toilet, and was being held down by a girl, the same age, while the boy also had his pants pulled down and a man was spanking him with a paddle.

The master bedroom contained only two beds, but at least half a dozen naked to semi naked figures in various positions of a sexual nature. With male and female dolls intertwined, the graphic detail of sodomy and debauchery was more accurate than a child should have been able to reproduce. In the baby's room, the Granny was sucking the cock of the butler, while the baby defecated on the floor.

Finally the parlour and this was the worst of all. Body parts were strewn all over the room, a headless corpse seated in a chair, in front of the television. A dog was depicted chewing on the torn end of a loose arm.

Jenny, anticipating Carmen's next reaction, directed her to a flowerbed nearby, and held her hair out of the way as she threw up. Lucas walked away, his gaze raised to the sky as he attempted to forget what they had just seen. It was several minutes before he could trust himself to speak.

'That never came out of the mind of a child! No wonder your doggy believed it was a personification of evil. How do we destroy it?'

'Fire and a little purification spell. You don't have to take part, but you'll probably enjoy it.'

Destroying Evil

It wasn't long before a good fire was burning happily away in the middle of the back lawn. Lucas continued to tend the fire as Carmen threw the broken toys and the blanket upon the flames. The perverted books had already gone into the making of the initial fire. Jenny circled them, speaking in what Lucas thought was Latin and throwing what looked like glitter into the fire. Each sprinkle set off sparks in the flames.

With the fire burning fiercely, Lucas, with some glee, took an axe to the doll's house itself. He took out a lot of his revulsion in the destruction of the building and it took Carmen's hand on his shoulder to prevent him from turning the house into toothpicks. Together they threw the wood splinters into the flames and jumped back as an ungodly scream erupted from the fire.

Suddenly the flames burst skywards with a ferociousness that lasted several minutes before it died down completely. Jenny moved slowly across to a garden chair and sank wearily into it. A look of concern crossed Carmen's face as she knelt beside her mentor. With his hands thrust deep into his trouser pockets, Lucas continued to stare at the ashes. He pulled his foot back to kick the fire remains away, but Jenny raised her hand and called out, 'No!'

Lucas moved his foot away as he glanced at Jenny in surprise. 'What's up?'

'The purification spell has not been completed yet.' Jenny looked up to the sky as if waiting for a sign. 'Step back and let it take its own course.'

Stepping back quickly, Lucas was glad to follow Jenny's advice as a sudden burst of wind descended upon them, developing into a mini tornado over the ashes. The fire remains whipped up and were carried off, leaving no trace of the once diabolical artefacts, except for the ring of scorched grass.

'Well! I think I've had more than enough for one day.' Carmen tried to sound more nonchalant than she felt and didn't quite succeed. With her assistance, Jenny slowly rose to her feet.

'Yes, don't be surprised if you have nightmares.'

'Thanks for being so cheerful!' Lucas grinned ruefully. 'Come on ladies, I'll take you back to the Dog and Bone.'

Lucas locked up the house as they left; Carmen linked her arm through Jenny's offering support if she needed it. Once they were seated again in the car, and heading back to Waltham, Carmen finally spoke, 'What will happen to the Priest who attempted the exorcism?'

'Once Shane was taken away by Cherby any remnants of him will be destroyed.' Jenny smiled.

'Oh good!' drawled Lucas, 'I was so not looking forward to driving out any more demons today!'

Leaning back into the seat, closing her eyes and sighing, Jenny agreed. *An early night is definitely in the plans, as I doubt that I could handle too much more.*

Have I Failed My Own Children?

The wonderful aromas of Penny's cooking greeted Lucas as he wearily stepped in through the front door of his home. Tim, wandering through from the living room took one look at his father's face, and a look of concern covered his.

'Wanna beer dad?'

'You bet!' The policeman's expression softened as he looked at his son.

As Tim got a bottle out of the fridge, and a glass, Lucas kissed his wife on the cheek before wandering into the living room to collapse onto the lounge. Tim followed, pouring a glass of beer and handing the glass to his father, before placing the bottle on the coffee table.

'Bad day? Do you want to talk about it?' asked Tim.

Flashes of images from that afternoon passed before Lucas and he grimaced. 'No, I don't want to burden anyone else with what I've seen today. How's school going?'

Every day, ordinary things are all that I want to think about. I hope and pray that I've never shown any favouritism between Jayne and Tim, or ever done anything that could turn them into Shane.

'I'm up for a spot on the cricket team this year. Miss Pollock thinks that I might be in the running for the mathematics medal if I apply myself a little more.' Tim paused, his eyes resting thoughtfully upon his father, and although Lucas was listening, he couldn't completely banish away the images of Shane.

'Dad, what is it about today that worries you?'

Lucas hesitated, his finger running absently around the rim of his glass. 'I always wonder if I'm doing what is right by you and Jayne. This kid murdered his baby sister and parents because they paid more attention to the baby. Are you jealous of your sister?'

Tim laughed. 'Of course I am!' At his father's startled expression he added, 'It's more envy than actually burning jealousy. I envy Jayne's creativity, and artistic talent, but I also know she's envious of how easy I find maths and sports. It's nothing we'd kill each other over! Neither you nor Mum favour either of us over the other. Actually we're pretty disappointing compared to other copper's children! We've never done drugs, or got arrested, I've tried cigarettes, but it made me sick, so I never tried again. Does that answer your dilemma?'

A rueful grin touched Lucas' face as his eyes twinkled. 'What about girls?'

Tim pulled a face, as he couldn't stop the colour rushing across his cheeks. 'I'm no Romeo. Tina and I have some fun, but no pressure, no hassles.' A sudden thought made it easy for Tim to quickly change the subject. 'The coach mentioned you'd been pretty unstoppable on the footy field. If we have time before dinner, can you show me some of your moves?'

Taking a sip of beer before rising to his feet, Lucas said, feeling slightly more cheerful, 'You're on!'

He was heading for the door when Tim stopped him by standing quickly and laying a hand on his father's arm. 'I do appreciate all that you and Mum do for us.' Without any hesitation, Tim hugged his father and allowed himself to become wrapped in a bear's embrace. Lucas pulled away first and with his arm around his son's shoulders, they headed for the kitchen.

'Let's go and beg 5 minutes from your Mum to kick the footy.'

Jayne was sitting at the kitchen table, having helped Penny with preparing dinner, and they were now discussing their day's events. Penny immediately said they had at least half an hour before dinner would be ready, mentally readjusting her cooking times and temperatures to make that actually possible.

'Come on Jayne, I'm going to need your help out-manoeuvring the Sarg,' said Tim.

Jayne jumped up and followed them out into the backyard. Penny turned the stove and the oven down, so that dinner would neither burn nor dry out. When satisfied, she went out to stand in the doorway of the back door, to watch indulgently as her children joined forces against their formidable father.

Seizing an opportunity Penny ran forward in her slippers and apron, and surprising them took possession of the ball and kicked it straight between her husband's goal posts (Two sticks stuck in the ground). Husband and children stared at her, stunned, before pouncing on her, sending them all tumbling in the grass in a scrum or hug. As they rolled about on the grass, all laughing, Lucas felt his heart lighten and once more thanked God for the happiness in his life.

Peter Lends A Hand

The Restaurant was full and the pub was filling up when Carmen followed Jenny into the Dog and Bone, which had been restored to almost its former glory with spare tables and chairs to replace those broken the night before. Carmen was just as surprised as her mother to see her brother, Peter helping out. She affectionately ruffled his hair and whispered something to him before bending down to kiss Evelyn. Carmen blushed, sitting down beside her love as the crowd broke into cheer at their display of affection.

Peter threw his cleaning cloth across the bar to Marcus, who seemed to be managing with one arm in a sling, before placing a supportive hand under Jenny's elbow and offered to see her up the stairs as Carmen had asked him to do. Jenny wasn't going to say no, and linked her arm though Peter's. Following his sister's instructions, he checked Jenny's room thoroughly, before leaving her alone.

'Thanks Peter. I'll be fine. I might have a soak in the bath before having an early night.'

He nodded amicably as his hands sunk into his jeans pockets in a typical male gesture. 'No problem. Just make sure you lock the bathroom door.'

A Nice Hot Bath

Closing the door, Jenny eased herself down onto the floor beside Mitzy's basket and spent some time talking and stroking the young mother. As Mitzy's purrs seemed to vibrate through her whole being, Jenny felt the tension slowly draining out of her. Picking up a towel, a bottle of vanilla body wash, and her towelling bathrobe, she headed down the corridor to where there were three bathrooms. One female, with three toilets and three shower cubicles, one male, the same figuration as the female and the third was much smaller and contained a luxurious bathtub.

It was into this smaller bathroom that Jenny entered, locked the key in the door behind her and poured in the body wash as she ran hot, steamy water into the tub.

Once this was at the right depth and temperature, Jenny checked again that the door was locked before slipping out of her clothing and easing herself with a sigh into the foamy water. She felt safe, enclosed in warm water, with no hiding place in the room, the window too small for man, woman or child to fit through and the door locked, with the key on the inside, she had every reason to feel secure.

The Second Attack

Even so, this security was false. Slowly and quietly the key in the door eased out of the lock and ell with a tiny tinkle onto the floor. There was no bolt or chain on the door, so when another key was inserted into the lock, the door opened without hindrance. A big man dressed in dark clothes and wearing a balaclava silently entered the bathroom and closing the door, locked it behind him. The click of the door was audible enough to finally attract Jenny's attention.

'I suppose you've come to finish what you started?' She was too exhausted to be able to contemplate any sort of real fight as the intruder locked the door behind him.

'You can't be allowed to succeed.'

Sadly Jenny shook her head. 'If I don't find it, others will.'

'We'll make sure that the Holy Book remains lost.' The big man moved closer.

Her eyes opened wide in surprise. 'You don't want the book found at all? How strange!' Although she could only see his eyes, she knew that he was smiling.

'That's because you don't really know what's in it. We've been protecting its secrets for centuries and don't intend stopping now. You've been our biggest threat, that's why you must die.'

His large hands wrapped around Jenny's shoulders and with one swift shove, pushed her head under the water. Although she struggled against the superior strength, her hands clawing at his arms, she was powerless to save herself. As darkness closed in, Jenny finally knew for herself the peace of death.

Carmen To The Rescue

Downstairs in the bar, Carmen had a soft drink with Evelyn as she told him a little about what had happened that afternoon. She didn't go into too much detail, as like Lucas, Carmen didn't wish to burden her loved ones with too much horror. She started suddenly when Tommy materialised before her. It took her several deep breaths before she was able to speak.

'Bloody Hell! You scared me! Can't you let me know when you're going to appear? A warning bell or something?'

Normally Tommy would have grinned at her question, but he grabbed her arm in deadly earnest. 'The Mistress needs your help now, or she will die!'

Carmen didn't wait to hear any more as she glanced first at Evelyn, then across at her brother and decided on the latter for strength. 'Peter, I need your help!' Her expression was so serious that he didn't even argue, but ran up the stairs after her.

Evelyn also rose to his feet and as a precaution he called out to Marcus to phone the police. Reaching the bathroom door upstairs, the siblings heard splashing from within, so putting his shoulder to the door, Peter, a sturdy lad, attempted to break it down.

'Kick at the keyhole!' Evelyn ordered as he hurried towards them, as fast as his crutches would allow. Peter didn't hesitate, aiming a high kick at the door. This time there was a little more give in the door. As Peter kicked again; Evelyn rammed one of his crutches at the door, their combined efforts causing the lock to give way.

Carmen charged in without any fear of danger to herself and seeing the big man holding Jenny under the water, she immediately went for him. 'You bastard! If she dies, I'll kill you myself!' Carmen pounded her fists into his back but was sent flying by one sweep of his powerful arm. Evelyn threw one of his crutches to Peter, who hit the masked man over the head with it while Evelyn used his other support to hit the man behind the knees. Their dual attack forced him to release Jenny as he crumpled to his knees. The two boys struck him again, this time Peter broke the crutch over the attacker's head, but they had momentarily knocked him out.

Carmen grabbed hold of Jenny by the shoulders and supported her head out of the water as she checked for vital signs. With horror in her voice she turned to Evelyn. 'She's not breathing!'

'Get her out of the water!' ordered Peter.

Evelyn shook his head, leaning upon his good crutch. 'There's no time. Is there a pulse?'

Carmen had checked, but checked again and sighed in relief. 'Yes! Just!'

Peter dragged the attacker's body out of the way as Evelyn sank to his knees and tilting Jenny's head back in approved St. John style, began CPR. Carmen held tightly on to Jenny's hand, rubbing it between her own, willing her to live.

'Come on Jenny! You can't go yet!' begged Carmen checking Jenny's pulse again; just to make sure her heart hadn't stopped. Tears began to fill in Carmen's eyes and she was beginning to lose hope when Jenny's fingers suddenly tightened around hers and her body heaved as she breathed once more on her own.

Plunging his arm into the water, Evelyn supported Jenny around the shoulders as he positioned her so that her head was over the side of the bath as she purged her lungs of water.

The Accident

Peter was so absorbed in watching Evelyn resuscitate Jenny, that he didn't notice the attacker stirring and was therefore taken completely by surprise when the big man got to his feet and sent Peter flying across the room. Evelyn still had hold of Jenny and didn't dare move. Carmen wasn't prepared to try and tackle the big man, letting him pass her before springing to her feet and running after him down the passageway. Bobby Michaels was just at the top of the stairs so Carmen called out, 'Bobby, stop him, he tried to kill Jenny!'

Bobby moved forward to grab the attacker, but was knocked off balance as the big man charged at him. On his way down to the floor, Bobby managed to grasp hold of the attacker's jacket. Twisting and turning to release himself, the big man lost his footing on the top step, and when he wrenched himself free, he toppled down the stairs.

Carmen cried out, but there was nothing she or Bobby could do to help him. Lucas had been bounding up the stairs and managed to jump out of the way as the attacker came crashing down the stairs towards him. He had seen Bobby try to tackle the masked man and fairly sprinted down to where the attacker finally came to rest.

Lucas checked for a pulse, but wasn't surprised when he couldn't find one. Jumping to his feet, Bobby had run down the stairs to join his Boss, his distress written over his face, which had gone white with horror.

'I'm sorry Boss, it happened so quickly.'

'It was an accident Bobby. Is Miss Weston all right?'

Bobby glanced questioningly up at Carmen who was still standing at the top of the stairs.

'Evelyn had to resuscitate her. Can I go back and check up on her?'

Lucas nodded, stepping nonchalantly over the dead body. 'Find out who that is, Bobby, then call for the Medical Officer. We want all this to be on the level.'

'Right Boss,' Bobby pulled off the balaclava and whistled in disbelief, 'Bloody Hell! It's Chad Nelson, Judge Nelson's brother. What on earth is going on?'

Lucas shook his head. 'Maybe Miss Weston has some answers.' He left the Constable in charge before he took the stairs two at a time.

Getting Answers

With only one crutch useable, Peter assisted Evelyn out of the bathroom, as Lucas leant Carmen a hand in getting Jenny out of the tub. Jenny clung to Lucas for stability as another coughing bout came over her, and Carmen knowing that he had a good hold on her, dashed across the room to pick up Jenny's bathrobe, before wrapping it around her mentor's shoulders. Lucas, ensuring that she was completely covered up, swept Jenny up into his arms and carried her down the passageway to her room.

Carmen dashed on ahead with Jenny's door key and had it open for them so that he could deposit Jenny gently upon her bed. Lucas and Carmen helped Jenny into her nightie, and finally into bed. Peter tapped quietly upon the open door and seeing that Jenny was decent, brought in a glass of brandy from which she took a grateful sip.

'The identity of Jenny's attacker has got round the Pub already. Don't be surprised if it's round the village in an hour.' Peter departed as the Sergeant swore.

'Damnation! We'll have the Judge down on us before we can scratch ourselves! I'll have the Doc check up on you when he comes to look at the body.'

Jenny finally found her voice, 'Body? Then he's dead?'

Lucas nodded. 'Yes. I must go.' Already they could hear an excessive amount of noise rising from downstairs.

'I don't like this, Jenny.' Carmen grabbed a towel and gently dried her mentor's hair. 'Why is this book worth killing for? It can't just be money.'

Jenny's laugh suddenly turned into a coughing fit. 'Money is always a good reason for murder, Carmen. But this time there is more to it.' She explained her conversation with her attacker.

'So there's one group of people who want to find the Bible, and another group who don't want it found. This is getting crazy.'

Jenny nodded. 'And it isn't over yet, not by a long shot.'

Doctor Shepherd

As foretold, the news of Jenny's assault and the identity of her attacker had spread through the village like wild fire. So neither Jenny or Carmen were surprised when Doctor Shepherd, all dressed up in a dinner suit and bow tie, already knew most of the details by the time he entered Jenny's room to check on her. His examination was quick, but the prognosis was good.

'I'm sorry you were called away from your lodge meeting, Doctor Shepherd. Are you the current or past Master?' Jenny's question caused him to nearly jump out of his skin.

'Have we met before?' He suddenly became very cautious. A twinkle entered Jenny's eyes.

'No, Doctor, but I know a little about Freemasonry. The ring you wear is only worn by Master Masons. You wear a dress suit and upon your lapel is a small square and compass which denotes Masonry.'

'A regular Sherlock Holmes aren't you?' The Doctor chuckled in delight. 'As to your question, I passed through the chair last year. Actually I'm glad you know about our organisation as it makes what I have to say easier.' Shepherd pulled up a chair and lowered his voice. 'Our brothers are concerned about you and some have influence in various sectors in society, and if there is anything you need, we'd see what we could do.'

'Nothing illegal I hope?' Carmen's eyes opened wide in amazement.

Doctor Shepherd smiled indulgently. 'No, no, we have strict moral beliefs. We could, though, try to discover who and why this organisation wants to keep the Bible hidden.'

'That would be a great help, thank you,' Jenny agreed. 'I'm not ready for yet another near death experience just yet.'

Rising to his feet, the Doctor straightened his jacket before picking up his medical bag. 'All I can suggest is that you rest, and don't go anywhere without a body guard.'

Carmen saw him to the door, locking it, before returning to sit beside Jenny. 'Are you all right to leave alone?'

A smile graced Jenny's lips. 'Head down to your young man and don't worry about me.' Reassuringly she took Carmen's hand.

'Would you like some dinner?'

'A little later, I'll be fine after a rest. I need to get my hair dry. Go and make sure that Evelyn is all right. Such physical exertion may have been too much for him.'

'I couldn't stand it if anything happened to you.' Carmen returned the pressure of her mentor's fingers before rising to her feet.

'Death is inevitable Carmen,' Jenny shook her head. 'No one cheats his Lordship. You must have courage.'

Sighing, Carmen slowly nodded her head. 'I know, but it doesn't mean I won't still grieve.' Without waiting for an answer, Carmen let herself out and hurried downstairs. *What I need right now is a dose of reality.*

A Breath Of Fresh Air

When Lucas descended again to the ground floor, the forensic team was already examining the scene, so he stepped over the body and around them. The noise had escalated even though Bobby was valiantly trying to keep everything under control. He looked up relieved as Lucas joined him. It wasn't to come from the Senior Sergeant though, as Cheryl stood on a chair and blew upon a whistle very hard. A silence followed as all eyes turned towards her.

'Knock it off! You're giving me a headache!' She commanded as Lucas held up his hand to assist Cheryl down. 'Do you need this lot out of here, Lucas? Being a crime scene and all?'

He shook his head. 'No need to close the pub. We'll need to take statements from anyone who may have witnessed the fall. A little less noise though would be appreciated.'

Cheryl glared at the assembled crowd. 'You hear that? Any more nonsense and you'll be arrested!'

Whether in fear of spending the night in a cell, or being banished from their favourite watering hole, the crowd went back to their drinks. Although they continued to discuss the accident they had witnessed; the noise level was reduced enough for Lucas to be able to think. *I blame myself for not believing that anyone would seriously wish to harm Jenny, or that she would be in danger within the pub.*

The forensic team had little to do, and were soon wrapping the body of Chad Nelson up in a body bag, and carrying it out of the pub with a nod to Lucas. Statements from the patrons were being taken by the other Constables who had been called in, so turning to head back up the stairs; Lucas collided with Carmen as she bounded down them. He grabbed hold of her to stop them both from falling, and was startled to discover that she was crying. Retaining a grip on Carmen's arm, he led her down the stairs towards the bar.

'Do you want some fresh air?'

Carmen nodded, grabbing her coat from the stand by the door leading to the Restaurant, and led the way out the back.

Here were tables and chairs set up for al fresco dining, which was very popular in summer but at present everyone was inside.

'I honestly don't know if I'm up to this sort of life.' Carmen's voice trembled with raw emotion.

Recognising the signs of what was going to happen; Lucas wrapped her into a bear hug, as Carmen started to sob uncontrollably. 'That's it, kiddo. Let it all out. Release the pain.'

They stood like this for some time until Carmen's tears stopped, and she was once more in control of herself. Accepting a handkerchief that the Sergeant offered, Carmen wiped her eyes and blew her nose thoroughly. This completed; they sat down at a table together.

'Okay! I'm back! What do you need to know?'

Stretching his feet out in front of him, Lucas contemplated what was most important. 'Let's start with the bathroom incident.' Carmen went through everything Jenny had told her as well as what Doctor Shepherd had said.

A whoosh of expelled air escaped from Lucas as he leant back into his chair, and covered his eyes with one of his large hands. 'Why did it have to be my County?' Carmen waited patiently as he considered the situation. After a couple of minutes, he sat up straight and placing his elbows on the table as he prepared to get down to business. 'How long do you think it'll take to find this book?'

Carmen shook her head and blew her nose again. 'Jenny has an idea where to start looking but…' Her words trailed as Lucas snorted in disgust. 'But we have to stop people trying to harm the one person who may be able to bring this to an end,' She added.

Lucas sighed. 'Yes, now we'll deal with what we're going to do next.'

Judge Nelson

Agreeing, Carmen opened her mouth to speak, but a demanding voice from the doorway over rode her.

'Greenaway! What the blazes is this about Chad being killed?' Jarrett Nelson was a renowned Judge, a 25 years membership with Rotary, and a family man with a solid marriage of 30 years. What he lacked in height, he made up for in presence. He was an authority to be reckoned with, but he was a fair man. Right now, though his brother was dead, and his patience was very thin. 'What are you doing about catching my brother's killer?'

Lucas rose slowly to his feet, and gently pushed Jarrett Nelson down into a chair. 'Chad was caught trying to drown Jenny Weston in the bath, and in an attempt to get away, he struggled with one of my officers at the top of the stairs, and slipping, Chad fell down the stairs and broke his neck. It was an accident, Jarrett.' The Judge suddenly went deathly pale, and made a gurgling sound as he began to shake. 'While I'm dealing with the Judge, do you want to return to Evelyn?' added Lucas.

Shaking her head, Carmen settled back in her chair. 'No thanks, I want to know what Judge Nelson has to say about King James' Bible.'

'What has Chad got to do with the search for the Bible?' His confusion looked genuine, but Lucas wasn't immediately convinced of his non-involvement.

'What I'm about to say will either come as a complete surprise to you, or if you're in with your brother, then you'll know all this anyway,' Lucas paused to see how this would be taken before continuing. The Judge continued to look confused, and the look didn't alter considerably as Lucas explained.

A silence followed which neither Lucas nor Carmen broke, allowing Judge Nelson time to assimilate the information.

'I knew our family went back to before the Orange Invasion, but I didn't know we had any ties with King James. What is this organisation Chad is supposed to belong to?' Carmen's eyes met Lucas' in understanding. *If the Judge is in on the murder plan, he is managing to hide his involvement very well,* she thought.

'We have a few inquiries out at the moment. Is there nothing you can tell us about Chad's most recent activities?' This was where Lucas mentally held his breath. *Can I really determine if the Judge is lying to me?*

'I have a vague remembrance of him telling me that he was working on the family annuals. Transferring old archived diaries on to the computer, I think.'

The policeman's eyes lit up. 'Is there any chance of seeing these diaries?' His excitement was caught by the other two.

'Certainly, Lucas, but I don't see the connection.'

Carmen had a sudden flash of inspiration. 'Perhaps there was more of a connection with King James than you previously thought.'

'I'll get Allan, Chad's son, to find the computer disks or floppies or whatever they call them, for you.' The Judge rose slowly to his feet.

The angry firebrand that had arrived was a tired old man as he departed. It would be some time before the truth finally sank in, and in the meantime he had to break the sad news to the rest of the family. It depressed Carmen and as she slouched in her seat, Lucas smiled indulgently.

'Take yourself off to your fella my girl, and we'll talk tomorrow about finding this blasted book.' Lucas dragged her on to her feet and propelled her back into the pub. He deposited Carmen in a chair beside Evelyn before trotting up the stairs to where Constable Lisa McGraw was seated on a chair outside Jenny's bedroom.

'Have you had dinner yet, Lisa?'

The Constable grinned ruefully up at him. 'Not yet, I'm not worried though, it got me out of Dad's Shepherd's Pie.' Lisa pulled a disgusted face at the thought.

'You just don't like all that potato! I'll see if Olivia or Carmen can arrange something on a tray for you.' Lucas laughed, relieved to release some of his pent up emotion.

'Please be kind enough to send up the menu!' She assumed a snooty tone, which brought a smile to the big bear's face.

Lucas nodded. 'While I'm here do you want to pop off to the loo?' Jumping to her feet, Lisa took him up on his offer, and disappeared down the corridor.

Lisa To Babysit

With a sigh, Lucas sank onto the chair in the passageway, outside Jenny's room. *I've never had a day like this before and hope I won't have any more. How Jenny survives this every day seems a miracle to me.* The rumbling of his stomach now reminded him of the absence of his own meal, and hoped to hurry home soon.

This contingency seemed to fade away as he heard feet pounding up the stairs and he prepared himself against a possible attack. *I'm only half expecting trouble, as Carmen would've called out a warning before the person had even reached the first step, so the sudden appearance of Dean Schofields running up the stairs in a highly agitated state, isn't a complete surprise.*

'What is this about another attack?'

Lucas grabbed Dean by the shoulders and forcefully stopped him from bursting into Jenny's room. 'The attacker tried to drown her, but he fell down the stairs and broke his neck. Now quieten down or you'll disturb Jenny.'

'Sorry. Can I see her?' A boyish, guilty expression crossed the millionaire's features.

Lucas smiled ruefully. 'I doubt she would've slept through all that noise.' He turned to knock upon the door, and only when he received an answer did he open it.

Lisa was coming back down the corridor as Dean slipped into the room. She looked surprised at her Boss. 'Is that wise Gov?' She asked as the door closed behind Dean.

A mischievous twinkle entered Lucas' eyes. 'Probably not, but not for the reasons you mean.'

'You're a protective papa, aren't you?' laughed Lisa. 'Don't you believe in medicinal sex?'

For a minute Lucas considered this question. 'That wasn't an offer was it, Mac?'

When Lisa's eyes widened in shock, he smiled wickedly. 'Don't panic, I was joking.' He shook his head as he became more serious. 'Anyway keep an ear open for trouble Lisa, and don't hesitate to break in if you hear any problems.'

Lisa grinned. 'Right you are Gov!'

Dean's Declaration

Lisa settled back down in her chair and was surprised when Lucas opened the bedroom door without knocking, and stuck his head in. Dean was kneeling beside the bed, his hands enclosed around Jenny's as he brushed his lips against her forehead.

'Is everything all right Jenny?' The concern was very obvious in the policeman's voice and he didn't try to hide it.

'Yes thank you Lucas.' She smiled in reply.

Lucas' concern eased a little. 'Lisa will be outside if you need her. Night.' He closed the door behind him and with a reassuring pat on Lisa's shoulder; he trotted downstairs, organising dinner for his Constable, before heading home to his own belated meal.

Dean released the crushing hold he had upon her hands, and dragged the armchair closer to the bed. 'Is this bloody job really worth what it's putting you through?'

'This is not just a job, this is my life!' Sighing, Jenny closed her eyes and lay back on her pillow.

He snorted in disgust. 'If you're not careful my girl, this will be your death!'

'Most assuredly it will be!' Her calm acceptance of this prospect momentarily stunned him into silence.

'What the bloody hell are you talking about?'

'You never used to be this dense, Dean!' Jenny was unable to contain a weary sigh. 'Yes, this job will kill me, but it is what I was born to do.'

As she spoke, Dean was shaking his head. 'No! It still doesn't make it right that you are taken before your time.'

In a spurt of anger, Jenny suddenly sat up and grabbed Dean by the lapels of his jacket. 'Who are you to say when my time will be? Twice already his Lordship has intervened to prevent my death!'

A frown descended upon Dean's brow. 'Why?'

'I beg your pardon?' Jenny released him; her eyes opened wide in surprise.

'Why is he preventing your premature demise?'

'Obviously the Powers that Be, want to make sure that this job is completed.'

Dean sprang to his feet and paced up and down the room. 'So if you successfully complete this job, then his Lordship will withdraw his protection?'

'When my time comes then so be it. Why are you so hot under the collar about this anyway?'

In his frustration Dean thumped his fists against the wall, 'Because I love you, damn it!'

The door burst open as Lisa dashed into the room, her baton extended. For a moment both women stared at Dean in surprise. Jenny was the first to recover and managed a smile at the alert police officer.

'It's all right, Constable McGraw. Mr Schofields is just a little upset.'

Taking a look at Dean's furious features Lisa was hesitant to leave, but at that moment Mitzy jumped out of her basket and leapt on to Jenny's bed in front of her and hissed at Dean. Bursting into laughter, Lisa relaxed her defences.

'I don't think I could protect you better than 20 claws and sharp teeth. I'll be outside.' Lisa withdrew with a small smile upon her lips as she wondered if Dean would dare hazard getting scratched.

Having calmed down considerably, Dean sat back down and stared moodily at Mitzy. Her tail was fluffed up, her fur raised and her eyes glared back, daring Dean to make a move towards Jenny. Mitzy settled down on the edge of the bed beside Jenny and started to knead her claws into the blanket. She was purring, but continued to watch Dean warily.

'Damn it all Jen. I've just admitted my true feelings to you!'

'Dean, before you go any further, stop now so that you don't say anything you may regret.' Jenny lowered her eyes in remorse.

Surprise was etched upon his face. 'Jen, I…'

She held up her hand to stop him. 'No Dean. Don't! You know how I feel about you. Why do we have to go over this again? I like you as a friend, enjoyed our time together as lovers, and thrilled by the adventures we had in rescuing your mother from the relic hunters in Asia. My life was always going to be short and we agreed that it would be live life for the moment. No commitments, no regrets.'

Dean buried his head in his hands and if she had the strength she would have wrapped her arms around him.

'Dean, don't do this! Neither of us need this!'

Slowly he raised his head, there was no sign of tears, but he was obviously upset. 'Tell me this, then, would I have ever been the one for you?'

A silence followed as Jenny seriously considered the question. 'I honestly don't know.' Tenderly she brushed her fingers through his hair; until Dean caught her fingers between his own and raised her palm to his lips. 'If we were soul mates, destined to be together forever, then nothing would have stood in the way of us being together. But I have never felt that connection with you... or anyone.'

'I hate it when you're right!'

Jenny burst out laughing. 'I have made mistakes you know.'

Nodding, Dean kissed her hand again before placing it back on the bed as he rose to his feet. 'Maybe, but unfortunately this is not one of them.'

'Don't do anything silly.'

The Millionaire's eyebrows rose mockingly. 'That's rich coming from you!' Blowing her a kiss, he left without waiting for a reply. Jenny heard him mange to bid Lisa good night, before she turned off the bedside light, and her fingers buried in the softness of Mitzy's fur, Jenny dropped off to sleep. Not a deep or nightmare free sleep, but sleep none the less.

Let's Make The Most Of This

Simeon Masters was thinking deeply as he sat watching the drama of Chad Nelson's death that was unfolding in the pub. Moving outside, he got through three cigarettes before he finally acted. Nigel Baines was seated in the Restaurant with his girlfriend, Paula, and he was surprised when Simeon came through from the bar, and sat down at their table. They had agreed not to interact in public more than was normal for nodding acquaintances.

'Well Simeon, this is a nice surprise.'

Simeon nodded amicably at Paula before speaking, 'This is important. While the bimbo is upstairs sleeping, tonight will be a good time to get a head start on the ruins, without being disturbed.'

Nigel looked like he was about to explode, but after several deep breaths his colour lessened. 'You know how to bloody well ruin a date don't you? Go get Lenny and I'll meet you in Cedars Park in about 20 minutes.'

Paula protested, but Nigel wasn't moved, 'Later baby! This is business.' Simeon got up and just walked out of the Restaurant knowing full well that Nigel would be there when he and Lenny arrived at the park.

A Quiet Moment Alone

In the privacy of their own lounge room above the restaurant, Carmen and Evelyn sat on a couch; Carmen's head lay in his lap. For a long time they didn't speak at all, words were not necessary, as they needed time to recover from the evening's events. Peter didn't speak when he returned from the chemists with a hired pair of crutches. He just left them leaning against the wall near to hand for Evelyn before leaving again.

'I don't like this Eve. It's hard to know whom to trust.'

'Do you include me in the suspect list?'

Carmen shook her head. 'No of course not, but I can't honestly rely upon you for physical defence. Don't get upset at that, but you're not 100% fit. And I don't want to see you get hurt.'

'Understood.'

'I'm not causing you any pain, am I?'

Pressing a gentle kiss upon her brow, Evelyn chuckled. 'You're not hurting me. Well not in the way you think.'

She tried to sit up, but he held her down. 'Evelyn please let me up if I'm hurting you.'

Evelyn refused to obey, silencing her by sealing her mouth with his own in a passionate kiss. For a moment Carmen willingly succumbed to this embrace, but the thought of him in pain, made her push against him.

'Eve.'

With a wicked laugh that Carmen hadn't heard before, he lowered his head to whisper the nature of his pain into her ear. A deep flush swept across her cheeks as she quickly sat up so that her head no longer rubbed innocently against the front of his trousers.

'You could have warned me!'

Evelyn chuckled, 'What makes you think I wanted you to stop?'

Surprised, Carmen began to laugh. 'Perhaps you should go home now, Mr Sauce!'

Rising shakily to his feet with the aid of his new crutches, Evelyn became serious once more. 'Will you be safe enough, do you think?'

'I don't see why not.' Carmen helped him to adjust the length of his new crutches. 'I have no ability to find King James' Bible. I might drive you home though.'

Evelyn nodded, following her out of the room and slowly down into the bar room. 'Good idea. You will be careful won't you Carmen?' At the look of concern upon his face, she turned and kissed him. It could have developed into something deeper if the packed saloon had not broken into applause, and the couple embarrassedly hurried out of the pub. The scene she had just witnessed brought a smile to the lips of Cheryl Roberts. *At long last my daughter is acting like a normal teenager.* She wondered, absently, *how long will it would last?*

The Stooges Search

'Damn and blast it! Hell and damnation!'

Simeon shone his torch over to where Nigel sat on the ground clutching his knee as he continued to swear. 'What on earth is wrong with you?' Simeon whispered angrily. A flow of colourful language followed.

'I smashed my frigging knee into that bloody bench! Why the hell does this have to be done in the dark?'

Simeon rolled his eyes towards the star laden sky for inspiration and patience. Lenny grinned from where he was using the metal detector, as Simeon struggled to control his temper.

'This may be the only chance we get to search these grounds. Now watch where you put your bloody feet.' He roughly hauled Nigel up and their torches continued to dance across the ground as they searched for the secret opening. Nigel muttered under his breath, but although he limped, he continued to scour the ruins. In the darkness it was easy to believe that they were all alone.

This though was far from being the case. Eyes were watching their progress; eyes that belonged to not only the dead but also the living. No one made a move yet to deter them, they simply continued to watch. As the area they were searching wasn't where King James suggested, Ian McGregor was prepared not to become involved. Although he too couldn't see the other watchers, he was aware of them. Ian was also aware of another presence, but this one didn't worry him. Instead he turned and bowed politely.

'Sire! Ya shouldn't be seeing this! There be nuttin' we can do 'til Miss Weston is ready for us.'

King James shook his head sadly. 'This desecration is not right, Ian.'

The Deadly Chase

A bullet whizzed through the ruins and instinctively Ian placed himself in front of the King, forgetting that bullets couldn't hurt either of them. Simeon, Nigel and Lenny hit the ground, but as footsteps ran out of the darkness towards them, and more bullets began flying; they were back on their feet in an instant and running towards the ornamental pond.

A gunman raced after them, decked out in all black with a balaclava obscuring his or her features and carrying a hand gun. Ian was about to follow when there was a shout from the direction of the car park.

Constable Natalie Laurence leapt over a low stone wall and was well on the heels of the gunman, but she couldn't stop them firing and hitting one of the fortune hunters. Natalie was a tall, athletic woman, her features, more handsome than pretty, but although she would call a spade a spade, she had a kind heart.

The wounded man plunged head first into the pond, and after several seconds of attempts to haul himself up the bank, he suddenly disappeared completely under the water. It was as if there had been someone or something in the water, which had grabbed him by the legs and pulled him under.

Natalie paused for a moment to see if she could spot him emerge again. The gunman continued to chase one of the other men as they separated. Natalie scanned the water with her torch as she radioed for back up. Letting her colleagues know that there was a gunman on the loose, and would soon be heading for the village centre. She also asked for assistance finding the wounded man in the pond.

Bobby Michaels answered her call immediately and being still at the Dog and Bone, he made his way down the main street intending to cut off the gunman's retreat.

Unexpected Assistance

To Natalie's surprise, she received additional back up from Dave Hedley as it was supposed to be his evening off. He came running across the Park from the opposite side of the pond. He was dressed in civvies, but attached to his belt was a police radio. For an athletic young man, he appeared quite out of breath. As Natalie didn't know how far Dave had run, and she had other important matters to concern her, she didn't even pause to question him.

Stripping off his shoes and police radio, Dave Hedley dived into the chilly water, ignoring the cry of protest from his colleague. Natalie trained her light upon the spot of water she had seen the wounded man fall in. Several times Dave ducked under the water, using his hands to feel around in the inky blackness for any signs of a body.

Bobby came running up from the village, very out of breath. 'I saw the two men you said were being chased, but no black clad gunman. I recognised Nigel Baines and Simeon Masters,' said Bobby trying to regain his breath.

'It was Lenny Carter who went into the water,' Natalie added.

'Man, you have more balls than brains!' Bobby's eyebrows rose as he watched as Dave resurface again. 'If he hasn't been swept away by now, the weeds will have dragged him down. Get out of that water!'

Dave grinned as he swam up to the edge of the pond and attempted to haul himself out but an unknown force pulled him under. Bobby reacted immediately, kneeling down on the bank and reaching in to grasp hold of Dave's arms and heaved him out. With the experience of Chad Nelson's attempt to murder Jenny at the Dog and Bone still in his mind, Bobby shook his head.

'The gunman was probably trying to stop anyone finding that book period!' As they drove back to the village, he filled in his colleagues on the latest attack on Jenny Weston.

Dinner Delayed... Again

Lucas stood in front of the microwave, sipping a beer as he waited for his dinner to warm up. 'Done your homework kitten?' The Sergeant's tone was light, but there was no doubt that he was serious.

Jayne smiled as she planted herself on the edge of the table, 'As soon as I got home, Dad. Do you want me to go elsewhere?'

Lucas reached across and lightly patted her on the backside. 'Not really, but you know how your Ma feels about you sitting on the table!'

'How can you be so calm, having just come from a murder?' Jayne slid into a chair, her eyes firmly fixed upon her father's face.

His eyebrows rose in surprise. 'It was an accident. If Chad hadn't struggled with Bobby, he probably would never have fallen. I'm more concerned over these attacks upon Miss Weston.'

The microwave beeped, so, using oven mitts, Lucas removed his dinner and laid it upon a place mat on the table. The sudden ringing of the doorbell from the hallway interrupted their conversation. Although Tim immediately answered it, Lucas was already heading for the door.

'Dad, its Bobby,' Tim went back to the lounge room and Lucas went straight out to speak to the Constable. While he listened to Bobby's story about Lenny drowning in the pond, he didn't think he was going to get his dinner any time soon.

'Dave, Natalie and I split up to take one house each to save time.' Bobby was interrupted at this point by his Sergeant.

'Dave? He's not on duty!'

Shrugging his shoulders, Bobby indicated that he had little considered the question. 'He showed up when Natalie called for help, and it seemed natural that he was with us. Anyway, I went to Simeon Master's and he was there, a bit out of breath, but alive. Natalie went to Lenny Carter's and he hadn't returned home, so it seems he's definitely our man in the water.'

Lucas was frowning, 'But what about Nigel Baines?'

'Didn't I say?' Bobby started, looking a bit upset. 'Although he had apparently made it home, Dave found him dead. Either the gunman had got him, but he managed to get home, or the gunman followed him and killed him there. Dave didn't give me any details, just that Nigel was dead.'

'An autopsy will hopefully be able to tell us which.' Lucas stopped pacing, grabbed up his car keys and headed out with Bobby to investigate the damage.

A Bloody Ending

There is something that worries me about what Bobby had reported, but I'm damned if I can put my finger on what it is. Pushing these problems aside for the moment, Lucas drove over to Nigel Baines' house to find the forensic team already on site and Dave Hedley standing out the front smoking a cigarette. His shirt and trousers were generously covered in blood. Lucas' face showed surprise as he approached the Constable. 'I thought you'd given up smoking, Dave?' The tone was light as Lucas saw Dave's hands were shaking.

'Once you've been in there Boss, you might take up smoking too!'

About to enter the house, Dave's words made Lucas hesitate. 'I thought Bobby told me that Nigel was shot?'

'No, Boss, I only told Bobby that Nigel was dead, not how he died.'

Taking a deep breath, Lucas stepped inside the house. A tarp lay over the body in the middle of the kitchen floor, but this didn't cover the extensive blood that spread across the linoleum. Lucas prepared himself for a gruesome sight as Jim Kennedy, head of the forensic team, approached.

'I'm not surprised your boy out there threw up, Lucas. This one's enough to turn anyone's stomach.' As Jim spoke he pulled back the tarp just enough for Lucas to see underneath. Nigel's head had been completely severed from his body and half his left arm had been chopped off. The axe used was still embedded in Nigel's chest. Lucas swallowed hard as he motioned for Jim to replace the cover.

'What on earth is happening to our village?' *I can very well understand Dave's need for a cigarette.*

Jim shook his head, the plastic of his special overalls rustling. 'It may get worse, Lucas, forensics is coming up with zilch in the way of evidence. It doesn't help that Dave slipped and fell in the blood. Any evidence we collect would probably convict him.'

'Silly bugger, I though he knew to be more careful of a crime scene?' Lucas huffed in disgust.

Jim chuckled as he scratched his chin. 'Don't be too hard, according to the boy he actually caught sight of the killer fleeing out the back door. He chased after him, but slipped in the pool of blood and ended up face down on top of the body.'

The only answer he got to that was a grunt. 'Let me know as soon as you can about what you find here.'

Lucas left the forensic team to get on with their job, and pausing in the front doorway, he addressed Dave, 'Get yourself home, but first strip off your clothes for the forensics to bag up. I'll understand if you're not in tomorrow morning.'

Dave, used to getting the sharp end of the Sergeant's tongue, was surprised by this show of compassion. 'No worries Boss, we've seen worse! I'll see you tomorrow!' Dave stubbed out his cigarette and after allowing the forensic team to take his clothes and slip him into a plastic jumpsuit like they wore; before he headed back to the village. Watching Dave's retreating back, Lucas once more thought, *there is something I heard or seen that is out of place, but I can't put my finger on what exactly it was.* Sighing, Lucas shook his head as he tried to throw off the feeling as he slowly made his way home.

Sean's Service

After an hour and a half of sentry duty, the pangs of hunger were beginning to distract Lisa McGraw's concentration. The stomach grumbles became so noticeable that Lisa began to wish that she had eaten her dad's Shepherd's Pie. Her attention immediately snapped back to her duty as footsteps lumbered up the stairs. Lisa's hand lingered on her baton, but she couldn't help giving a cry of gratitude as Sean Hanson struggled to carry two trays of food up the stairs.

'You're a lifesaver!' Lisa knocked on Jenny's door and upon getting a reply; she opened the door before taking one of the trays from Sean. 'I'm hungry enough to eat a horse, how about you Jenny?'

Lisa noticed that Mitzy had returned to her basket and her kittens, but upon their entrance, the cat had risen up, her back arched as she stared at the intruders.

Lisa grinned in response, 'Still on duty, Mitzy?' She kept a close eye on Sean as he waited until Jenny was sitting up in bed before he placed the second tray across her lap.

'Olivia is run off her feet in the restaurant so I offered to bring dinner up to you.' Sean couldn't keep his eyes off Jenny, as he finally realised how close she had come to death.

'Thank you Sean. How is everything downstairs?' Jenny removed the cover off her plate, and breathed in deeply with pleasure. Lisa pulled up a chair to the desk to tackle her own meal.

'I've never seen the Dog and Bone so busy. Chad's accident and the attempts upon your life are all anyone can talk about. Here let me.'

Jenny had been having trouble undoing the top of the bottle of Iced Tea, so Sean took the bottle from her. Undoing the top, he poured it into a glass for her.

'I know that you're now surrounded by protectors, Jenny, but I want you to know that I'm here for you if you ever need me!' Although his heart was in the right place, Sean's protectiveness was oppressive, causing Jenny to choke on a bit of potato. Lisa quickly came to her rescue as it appeared Sean had a lot more to say.

'We'll do everything we can Sean, but I think Jenny needs some alone time to recover from her latest ordeal.' Sean was quick to pick up the hint and rose awkwardly to his feet.

'Thank you Sean.' Jenny smiled as she reached up to press his hand. 'We'll have that drink sometime soon.' Sean smiled like a besotted puppy dog and left the room, a happy man.

Lisa waited until she could be sure that he had descended the stairs before she allowed her eyes to meet Jenny's. They both burst out laughing which Mitzy thought it better to ignore such silliness, and turned her back on them as she settled down in her basket.

Everyone's Kid Sister

'There's something I must know,' Lisa said, slightly incoherently due to a mouthful of food. Jenny waited patiently for the rest of the question. 'How do you do it? I mean I can understand Dean Schofields being a long-time admirer, but you're here five minutes and you've already captured a dozen hearts.'

Giving an embarrassed laugh, Jenny couldn't stop her cheeks from flushing. 'One admirer hardly makes a dozen.'

'I'd say your conquests are wider than you realise. There's talk about you throughout the village, and most of it's praiseworthy.'

'Spare my blushes.' Jenny's hands flew to cover her cheeks. 'Perhaps we should start a fan club.'

Although Lisa laughed at Jenny's self-mockery, she said seriously, 'Don't even suggest it; someone might just take you up on it.'

Jenny shook her head and chewed another mouthful of dinner. 'In answer to your original question, I don't know. Men like Nigel Baines try it on with anything or anyone. Perhaps it's the unusualness of my job that attracts them, someone just passing through. I would assume you get more sincere offers than I do.'

Choking in laughter, Lisa waited until the tears stopped trickling down her face before she could speak, 'You've got to be joking! I'm everyone's kid sister! I'm a handy stand in for innocent dates and functions. The only indecent advances I get are pecks on the cheek.'

Jenny didn't join in the laughter. 'You're still young Lisa, there is plenty of time. One of those kisses on the cheek may lead to something more substantial.' Lisa shook her head but Jenny smiled at the other's doubt but they continued to eat their dinner in silence.

Sighing, Lisa picked up Jenny's tray and put both trays on the ground outside the door. 'Are you going to try and sleep?'

The Spirit Healer, throwing off the bed covers and getting up slightly shaky, had other ideas. 'Not right away. I want to get some work done.' From the desk, Jenny collected a map of the Palace grounds and a notepad she had been working on. *I need to do some brainwork before attempting physical action in the morning. Time is short, shorter than anyone actually realises.*

SUNDAY

Finding Lenny

At first light, Lucas Greenaway stood solemnly at the edge of the ornamental pond in Cedars Park as police divers dragged out the body of Lenny Carter. As forensic officers prepared the black plastic body bag and assisted to heave the body out on to the grass, Lucas turned away, not needing to give any instructions, as these men knew their job.

'What are you doing about Simeon?' asked Jim Kennedy, the head of forensics.

Hesitating, Lucas debated about how much to reveal. 'I dropped round there last night, but Simeon had already legged it. His missus didn't know where he was, so it makes it difficult to protect someone I can't find.'

A Little More Information

Practically dancing down the stairs that morning, Carmen was surprised at how truly happy she felt for the first time in years. Hesitating by the doors that led from the saloon into the restaurant, Carmen suddenly turned and went back to the Function Room. The light was on, and for a moment Carmen feared a burglar, but seeing Jenny, she let out a sigh of relief. 'You know it's funny. I had a feeling that you'd be here.'

Carmen sat down opposite her mentor, who had been absently flicking through a book.

'In time you'll be able to hone that sensation that tells you that another of our kind is nearby,' Jenny paused, her whole attitude so serious that Carmen began to think that something was very wrong. Jenny finally continued, 'In a day or two I must ask you if you wish to choose the path of the Healer, or if you want the voices suppressed.'

Carmen opened her mouth to answer, but Jenny held up one hand for silence. 'No, don't answer yet. Your future as a Spirit Healer will certainly be much longer than anyone I have known, but you must consider the disadvantages of longevity. We know so little about what the effects of these other powers will be.'

Carmen listened patiently, but when Jenny had finished, she only smiled. 'But if I never try, I'll never know will I? I'll continue to think about my options, but my Grandad used to say, "you only live once, so do it right and leave with no regrets." So Yolo!

Nodding, Jenny placed her book into Carmen's hands. 'During my time as a Healer I've put together a working manual for others. It's not really instructions, but more a guide. Each Healer finds their own style, but you can learn much from the experiences of others before you. It is suggested that you keep a diary. Some are compiling a group book electronically. In this book you'll find names, addresses, contact numbers of other healers as well as other types of spiritual workers who can assist you.'

'Other types of spirit workers?' queried Carmen.

'Not everyone in our field can actually see or give energy to ghosts. Some people can hear them, some can channel messages from those passed over the river of unrest that have something they want to tell relatives mourning them or to answer a question that those left behind may have. There are also a number of charlatans out there that you want to avoid becoming associated with. We keep a detailed list of these people as they have a tendency to change their names as they move around to find new marks and escape from the law. Don't ever feel that you are alone when you go solo, there will always be someone you can reach out to.'

As Jenny rose stiffly to her feet, Carmen jumped up and impulsively embraced her. Carmen blushed like a schoolgirl and suddenly became tongue-tied. She heard Penny Greenaway in the kitchen, and excused herself to Jenny, in the need to set up for the breakfast crowd that would soon be arriving.

The Doc Reports For Duty

The Restaurant was packed for breakfast so it was several moments before Doctor Andrew Shepherd spotted where Jenny was sitting. Although the other patrons were curious about her, they kept their distance, so that the Spirit Healer could eat her breakfast in peace. The Doctor slid into a seat opposite and upon Carmen approaching him for an order, he said, 'Just a coffee thanks.' She headed off again and Doctor Shepherd looked curiously around the Restaurant. 'I had expected to see a bodyguard somewhere. Lucas is slipping!'

'Not at all. Lucas is on his way and Penny is licenced to kill with her fry pan.' Mischief made Jenny's eyes twinkle, 'Have you discovered something already?'

A look of pride covered the Doctor's features. 'I have actually. There is a secret organisation that is definitely against the discovery of the Bible. The organisation goes back to the time of King James. It is apparently a family secret handed down from father to son.'

Pausing beside the table as she put the coffee cup down, Carmen asked, 'Then surely Judge Nelson would be aware of what Chad was doing?'

Doctor Shepherd nodded. 'You'd expect so.' He took a sip of coffee, grateful that it wasn't over brewed. 'What I understand, though, is that the father passed on the knowledge of their secret to his sons, only upon their majority. Captain Nelson died before Chad and Jarrett were 21. Old man Nelson, their grandfather was already institutionalised, and their uncles had died during the Vietnam War. That's why the Judge was in the dark about the Society.'

'The question is, though, why do they want to stop the book being found?' Jenny asked the question, as Carmen went back to serving breakfast.

'I think I know that too.' Doctor Shepherd looked pleased with himself. 'Our own Annuals speak of a possible rebellion against James, but it was only rumours, and nothing was ever substantiated as the King died before they could rebel.'

Taking a moment to chew thoughtfully upon a piece of bacon, Jenny didn't immediately answer. 'Why would they be fearful of a Bible?'

'There I can only guess.' Doctor Shepherd shook his head. 'There must be a list of conspirators that would taint their family as traitors.'

Frowning, Jenny took another mouthful of her excellent breakfast. 'But why should such a list be in the King's possession?'

'I don't know.'

The Nelson Journals

'Perhaps this might help!' The Judge's voice from behind them made them jump. Doctor Shepherd reached defensively for his walking stick. Judge Nelson smiled apologetically as he sat down at their table. He gently placed an ancient book beside Jenny's elbow. 'Sorry, I didn't mean to sneak up on you. I've been through the family journals and this one dates back to King James. More importantly, it's indecipherable.'

'Bad handwriting or faded ink?' asked the Doctor.

The Judge gave a dry laugh. 'No, no. It's in code.' He rose again to his feet. 'I have quite a bit to do with Chad's funeral arrangements; can you let Lucas know about finding this book?'

'Aren't you even just a little bit curious to know what it says?' Jenny was a little surprised.

The Judge paused, his face covered by a look of confusion. 'I don't approve of murder, or my brother's actions. I'd rather not be forced to fulfil a family pledge that I abhor. Good morning.' He headed out of the Restaurant, without a single glance back.

There was a moment of silence as the Doctor scratched his head thoughtfully. 'Perhaps to some ignorance is bliss.'

'I know.' Smiling, Jenny shook her head. 'Oh, here's the man we want to see.' Looking up, she saw Lucas Greenaway enter the Restaurant. Doctor Shepherd half rose from his seat.

'Do you want me to go? It's just that I may be able to help with cracking the code.'

Jenny waved him back into his chair. 'Please stay, all assistance is appreciated.'

Shepherd resumed his seat as Lucas joined them. He collapsed into a chair and Carmen immediately came across with a cup of coffee. The other two waited patiently in silence as the Senior Sergeant emptied the cup.

'Ah! I needed that! What a morning!' He didn't go into any details, feeling that the Spirit Healer had enough to deal with, without any additional concerns. Jenny quickly filled the policeman in on the Doctor's investigations and the book left behind by Judge Nelson.

'Isn't anything going to be easy?' Lucas groaned as he flicked through the diary.

Clearing his throat, Doc. Shepherd said, 'I may be able to help. A friend of mine was a code breaker. He's retired of course, but he was unsurpassed in his field.'

'Won't he be well... old?' Lucas looked considerably doubtful.

Edging towards 60 himself; Shepherd smiled ruefully. '86 actually, but his brain is still as sharp.'

Jenny interjected, 'Would he be willing to help? I mean, there is a time limit hanging over us.'

'It'll add to the challenge. Bugsy likes a challenge.'

Jenny passed the ancient tome across to the Doctor and with a brief nod; he tucked it under his arm and left the Restaurant after paying for his coffee.

Mitzy Ventures Out

Lucas signalled to Carmen for another coffee and commandeered a slice of toast from Jenny's plate. His eyes opened wide as he choked on his mouthful of toast.

'Bloody Hell! That's not going to be good for business!' Through the Restaurant Mitzy strolled nonchalantly with a dead mouse in her mouth. The cat stopped in front of Jenny and dropped the offering at her feet.

'Aren't you a clever girl? Where did you find this little appetiser?' Jenny praised the feline. Mitzy gave a pretty little meow, and began to purr as Jenny scratched her head.

'You'll have to keep that animal out before the Restaurant loses all its customers,' protested Lucas.

Jenny didn't even look up at the police officer as she continued to talk to Mitzy, 'Come on darling, how about we take your mouse outside.' When Jenny got to her feet, Mitzy picked up the mouse and willingly followed her out of the Restaurant.

When Cheryl burst into the room from the saloon, greatly excited, Lucas slid down a little in his chair. The Innkeeper had obviously seen Mitzy and her offering.

'Where is that cat?' She demanded.

Lucas tried to look invisible, which was impossible for a man his size. Carmen told her Mum that Jenny had taken Mitzy out. Lucas waited for the explosion, but it didn't come.

'That darling cat! For months I've had problems with mice because the place behind has been empty for a while. Mitzy is here a couple of days and is already catching vermin! I should've got a cat ages ago!' Cheryl rushed out after Jenny, determined to secure Mitzy as a permanent resident. Lucas left a tip beside his payment for the two cups of coffee before he slipped out of the Restaurant. He still had to find Simeon Masters, before he too became a corpse.

The Huntress

Having found Jenny's bedroom door open and her kittens fed, but unable to get out of their basket, Mitzy had enjoyed a snoop around the pub. As pleased as Punch with finding a mouse, Mitzy had gone looking for Jenny, and was just as pleased by her human's response to her present. When Cheryl followed them out to the courtyard, Mitzy instinctively cringed; her mistrust of humans was still deeply embedded in her. Jenny encouraged Mitzy to come to where she sat, with soft, soothing words, promising that Cheryl wasn't a threat.

'Oh Jenny, would you consider letting me buy Mitzy, or at least one of her kittens? What a darling! I've had a problem getting rid of pests.'

As Mitzy jumped onto Jenny's lap to have her ears scratched, Jenny laughed at Cheryl's rush of speech. 'If Mitzy is happy here, then I'm quite satisfied to leave her in your care. As I travel around so much I can't have pets.' Cheryl sat down beside them, and gently offered her hand to the cat to smell. Mitzy hesitated, sniffed and then licked Cheryl's fingers. With this show of acceptance, Cheryl scratched Mitzy under the chin and was rewarded by a brief purr.

Jenny smiled, but had one concern. 'Because of Mitzy's past, Doctor Martin, the Vet, has offered to sterilise her for half price. I ask that you take him up on his offer.'

Receiving another lick, Cheryl willingly agreed. 'How soon before the kittens can be found homes?'

'About twelve weeks, but it isn't too soon for you to offer them. It's just that they must be weaned from their mother.' Mitzy placed one paw on Cheryl's knee but didn't move from the security of Jenny's lap.

When the side gate squeaked, both women jumped. Mitzy pressed herself closer to Jenny, but there was nothing to worry about as Lucas entered the courtyard.

'Jenny, you won't be able to go up to Cedars this morning as the park is still a crime scene. I'll let you know when you can have access.'

'Thanks Senior Sergeant. Sorry to be causing you so much trouble.' With a soothing hand, Jenny settled the raised fur on Mitzy's back.

Lucas dismissed her apology, 'Keeps life from getting dull.' With a wave he was gone again, Cheryl returned inside to her duties as a Publican. With little to do until the police cleared the area, Jenny leant back in her chair, and stroked Mitzy until she was purring in an ecstatic trill. Sighing, Jenny closed her eyes and contemplated her next move.

What happened next was nothing Jenny had planned; it was nothing any mortal had planned. It had begun to rain. Not just a little drizzle, but a heavy down pour. Jenny followed Cheryl back into the saloon.

'Can I get you a drink Jenny?' Cheryl gestured towards the bar, but Jenny shook her head.

'No thank you Cheryl. I still feel so tired; perhaps I should capture some extra sleep while I can.'

The Last Of The Stooges

It wasn't long before the police found Simeon Masters. Unfortunately he was no longer in the land of the living. The assassin had strangled Simeon with a length of rope, probably only a couple of hours before he was found. Leaving a couple of Constables to cordon off the crime scene and wait for the Forensic team Lucas left very tight lipped. *Someone is constantly one step ahead of the police and appears to have access to inside information.*

At the moment, Lucas was heading to an interview with the Detective Inspector for the area; the murders would be taken out of his hands and investigated by C.I.D. *What I need to do now is to get a line on who the 'Boss' man is, as he too will be a target. The major problem is all who knew who he is, were now dead.*

Sir Edward Dent

Leaning back in his chair, Andrew Shepherd savoured the exceptionally fragrant coffee that he rolled around this tongue, breathing in the aromatic flavour as well as tasting it. He enjoyed his drink in silence as his old friend Bugsy sat opposite, studying the Nelson family diary. They were seated in a quiet room in an exclusive club in London.

With the exception of a slight stoop from years of working bent over a table, and a head of receding white hair, Bugsy hardly looked older than 65. Bugsy to his friends, to polite society he was Sir Edward Dent. The nickname had come about as Sir Edward had devised an interesting cipher involving the Latin names for insects.

Glancing up from the book, Bugsy looked over the top of his glasses in amusement, 'My God! You've got a cracker here Andy! How long have I got?'

'Not long.' Doctor Shepherd shook his head at his friend's boyish enthusiasm. 'A young woman's life is in danger. The names of the others in the organisation are most important. We need to know who to watch out for.'

Bugsy glanced back down at the book, silent for a moment. 'Can I call in a couple of mates of mine? Many hands and all that.'

Shepherd hesitated. 'You understand the need for secrecy?' At the utterance of his own words, the Doctor laughed. 'Sorry! I forgot to whom I was talking. I'll be in London till this evening, if you need longer than that let me know.'

As Shepherd finished his drink and rose, Sir Edward smiled; a twinkle in his eyes. 'Do you think me that good that I could crack this in a couple of hours Andy?'

'If you can't, you're not the man I thought you were! I'll pick you up at 7 tonight for dinner.' The Doctor only received a half-hearted answer as the legendary code breaker already had his nose back in the book, his mind lost to all else but the intricate puzzle.

What Is Wrong With This Picture?

Even though his eyes rested upon the television screen, Evelyn's thoughts were so deep that he didn't really see what was showing. It wasn't surprising then; that Kathleen May entered the living room to find her grown up grandson apparently watching Postman Pat. Slightly startled, Kathleen looked from the television to Evelyn, and realising that he probably wasn't even in the house, she turned the television off.

'Eve,' Kathleen gently touched his shoulder in her attempt to bring his thoughts back to the present.

'Oh, hi Gran, Sorry, did you want me for something?' He looked like he had come out of a deep sleep.

Kathleen sat down on the couch beside him. 'What were you thinking about Eve?'

'It's about last night. Something happened that shouldn't have.' It was difficult for him to put into words exactly what he meant.

'Do you mean the murders?' She prompted.

Evelyn shook his head. 'No, well I mean they were wrong, but in character. What I think I mean is someone did something last night that they wouldn't do. That is out of character for them, but I just can't recall what exactly it was.'

Although Kathleen nodded her head in understanding, they remained silent for a while, as they both considered Evelyn's words. 'The problem is,' she finally said, 'the more you try to force yourself to remember, the more it may elude you. I think you need to take a break, go out and get some fresh air. See that lovely young lady of yours. Then go and see Lucas Greenaway, and go over everything that happened last night with him.'

Accepting his grandmother's advice, Evelyn had only one question, 'Why not go and see him now?'

Kathleen shook her head, a grim smile upon her lips. 'No, my dear, Lucas has his hands full at the moment briefing the Detectives. Now is not a good time.'

Handing Over To The Detectives

If the Senior Sergeant had heard the old woman's words, he would have laughed, for they were most definitely an understatement. Broad minded as he was, Lucas was having a hard time trying to explain some of the paranormal activities that had taken place over the past couple of days. Detective Inspector Kevin Harris and Detective Sergeant Tony Gregg both stared at Lucas in disbelief. They had heard about some of the goings on, but this was the first time that they had all the details.

Lucas felt a fool telling the story, but was relieved when neither Detective laughed. Then again, three murders, and two attempted murders were no laughing matter. It was, therefore with an uneasy mind, that Lucas left the Detectives to undertake their own investigations, for the last thing he wanted to be looking at was early retirement on psychiatric grounds.

The Erotic Dream

Lying down in her room, Jenny felt a strange floating sensation, not quite awake, and yet not asleep either. She allowed her subconscious to lead her into a dreamlike world. *The bed I'm lying on is a grand affair, four posters with a luxurious quilt, downy pillows and there are numerous candles to softly illuminate the room. At any other time I would've been interested in exploring my new surroundings, but I find I can't take my eyes off the delicious example of man that is lying beside me.*

Without having ever seen him before, I instinctively know this is Sir Rupert Steele, with long dark wavy hair, a handsome face with dark eyes that seems to burn into my soul, and a body, hard and muscular from being a soldier. This body is barely covered by only a shirt that is half-open.

My own nakedness doesn't concern me as Sir Rupert lovingly cups my face in one hand and lowers his head to kiss me gently and yet thoroughly. Wrapping my arms around his neck, I draw Sir Rupert harder against me, so that the kiss intensifies. I can feel his erection press against my thigh, but he makes no move to hurry our joining.

I utter a whimper of pleasure as Sir Rupert trails one hand down my throat towards my breasts. As his hand cups one, Sir Rupert takes the nipple of the other breast into his mouth and teases me lightly with his tongue. So aware of his own mounting desire for me, Sir Rupert is awake to the fact that I respond every time his fingers move to the top of my inner thighs. He wants so much to allow his fingers to travel higher to give me full satisfaction, but he is determined to take it slowly.

Almost purring with desire, I move so that I can press his erection against my aching pubic bone, and I can gain satisfaction without penetration. Sir Rupert smiles at my impatience, and as I climax, he raises his head to kiss me once more on the lips.

'Thou art mine one and only true love!' He whispers. 'I would wait for thee forever!'

As his final word repeated in her ears like an echo, Jenny suddenly sat up, once more back at the pub; her eyes open wide and she was breathing hard. The sudden movement caused a stab of pain in her lower back. *Never had my dreams, if that was what it had been, had ever felt so real.*

The Detectives

The Dog and Bone was having a busy afternoon. The rain wasn't a deterrent against a crowd. Cheryl was grateful for Carmen's assistance when she completed her duties in the Restaurant that afternoon. *What I don't need is two Detectives annoying me with questions that I neither have the time to answer or the answers to give them.* Despite this, Sergeant Tony Gregg continued to fire questions at the two women.

'Need I remind you ladies that three men are dead?'

From behind the counter, Carmen slammed down a pint of beer. 'How dare you? Why aren't you doing something about finding this organisation that is responsible for these murders? Stop hounding us and do something constructive!' Carmen's outburst caused a round of applause from the patrons.

'Shut up!' Tony glared at the crowd.

'Don't start throwing orders around in my pub! We've answered your questions, so I suggest you leave!' Cheryl finally lost her temper.

Inspector Kevin Harris looked as bored as if he was ordering a pizza. He hadn't yet said a word, allowing his Sergeant to do all the bullying; he was good at it. 'One final question then; where is Jenny Weston?'

'Jenny does not need to be brow beaten by the likes of you!' Cheryl, an amicable woman in most situations, suddenly turned mulish.

Tony took a step forward as if to threaten Cheryl with arrest, when Jenny almost floated down the stairs. She seemed to sparkle and all eyes in the pub turned to her as Kevin stepped in front of her to impede her progress.

'Miss Weston?'

'Detectives?' The unnatural light in her eyes disappeared as Jenny was forced to return to the real world, 'Perhaps you should ask Cheryl to borrow her conference room, unless you wish me to come down to the station with you?' Her cool efficiency surprised Tony, who had expected her to be afraid of their presence. Cheryl graciously agreed and Jenny led the two men to the empty room.

Dean To The Rescue

After half an hour of questions, cross-questions and accusations from Tony Gregg, Jenny was beginning to feel like she had personally led the three men to their deaths. Kevin Harris had tried to soften the Sergeant's questioning style but it only left Jenny with the feeling that they were playing "good cop, bad cop". All the pleasure of her erotic dream had vanished and Jenny was beginning to feel depressed. If Dean Schofields hadn't stormed in, Jenny could have easily burst into tears.

'All right Gentlemen, that's enough. If you've any further questions then I want my lawyer present. I won't have you badgering Jenny, she's not strong enough.' At that moment, with his hands on his hips, exuding authority, Jenny had never been gladder to see anyone.

'Mr Schofields...' started Tony, but Dean cut him off.

'I'm not interested in what you have to say. You want to question me, make an appointment with my secretary. Right now, Jenny should be resting, and I mean to see that she gets it immediately.' Ignoring any attempts by the Detectives to protest, Dean scooped Jenny up into his arms and carried her out of the room. The police officers were left gaping; they were left with no alternative but to pursue inquires elsewhere.

Not until Dean had carried Jenny upstairs and into her room, did he finally put her down. Then they both fell onto the bed in gales of laughter.

'Oh Dean, how did you know I needed help?' Jenny wiped away the tears of laughter as Mitzy jumped up onto the bed between them. The cat had accepted Dean, but she was still wary of him.

'Cheryl called me as soon as Sergeant Plod started demanding to know where you were.'

After giving Mitzy a scratch behind the ears, Jenny shooed her back to her kittens. 'I'm ever so grateful Dean.' To show her appreciation, Jenny wrapped her arms around his neck, and gave him a friendly kiss on the cheek. When Dean tried to deepen the intimate contact by placing his hands around her waist, Jenny drew away in pain as he accidentally touched her damaged back. Releasing her, Dean looked angry, not with Jenny, but at the pain she was enduring during this job.

'Do you have to go immediately?' Jenny kicked off her shoes as she lay down on the bed and drew Dean down beside her.

'What do you have in mind?' His eyebrows rose suggestively.

Jenny smiled apologetically, 'Not that, I'm afraid.'

Sighing in defeat, Dean positioned them on their sides, Jenny's back pressed against his chest as he wrapped his arms protectively around her. 'Sleep then, my Princess. I'll be here to watch over you.' Gently he nuzzled her neck, but instigated no other intimate contact. Within ten minutes, Jenny was fast asleep.

Lucas And Evelyn

There was a pile of papers sitting in front of Lucas waiting for his attention, but he saw none of them. He was mentally going through the events of the past few days. At first, when Evelyn struggled into the police station, Lucas didn't want to be disturbed.

It was late afternoon and he was far from working out what the answer could be to what was eluding him. Evelyn, though was insistent, he wasn't going anywhere until he saw the Senior Sergeant. Lucas finally agreed, and cursed himself for his own churlishness as Evelyn was evidently in pain as he leant heavily on his crutches for support.

'Sorry Sarg, but Gran figured that since I was probably doing the same thing as you, which is thinking through this business; she decided that two heads were probably better than one.' Having eased into a chair, it took Evelyn several minutes to regain his breath.

'I've seen something, or heard something vital, but I can't for the life of me work out the connection,' stated Lucas.

Evelyn nodded. 'I agree. Someone did something they wouldn't normally do. That's why we need to compare notes.'

Getting to his feet Lucas shut the door to his office, 'Right! How about you start with what happened at the Pub.'

Closing his eyes, Evelyn recapped the events. 'Peter comes home from work, and instead of going off for an evening with his mates, he stays and helps out. He isn't 18 yet, so he shouldn't be a part of this organisation, but his actions are definitely out of character. He does, though, break down the bathroom door and helps me to tackle Nelson; a plus on his side. While Carmen and I are reviving Jenny, Peter does let Nelson escape. The accident down the stairs is clear-cut. Bobby tried to grab him, not push him. The Judge storms in, he doesn't know about the organisation, but any doubts about that are cleared about the majority clause. You assign Lisa for protection duty, all normal. Dean Schofields bursts on the scene, concern for Jenny. Him I can't make out, what is real and what is not? I think he truly cares for her, but there is something else under the surface. Who have I missed? Oh yes. Sean Hanson, another suitor, takes dinner up to Jenny and Lisa in appropriate puppy dog manner. Faithful, but predictable and yet... too predictable? With the exception of Peter, and my doubts about Dean, there's nothing there that doesn't ring true.'

Lucas had been jotting down notes as Evelyn had been speaking, and didn't reply until he looked up from his notebook. 'Let's consider what happened in the park then. How much do you know?'

'Most of it third hand.' Evelyn shrugged his shoulders.

'We know that Lenny, Nigel and Simeon were at the ruins, probably looking for the entrance of the secret chamber. That's in character. Natalie Laurence was doing a drive by check like I've asked my officers. That is in character. She chases the gunman, who is chasing the trio. Natalie stops when Lenny hits the water, radios for backup. Dave comes in answer to Natalie's call and dives in to try and rescue Lenny. Bobby joins them, and has to help Dave out as he feels something pulling him down. My officers split up to take one household each. Simeon was home but out of breath, Lenny was missing and Nigel was found hacked into pieces.'

Stretching with a sigh, Lucas looked inquiringly at Evelyn. 'Well what have I missed?'

Evelyn frowned. 'Who was officially on duty last night?'

'Natalie was, and Bobby was on call.'

'Not Dave?'

'No,' Lucas shook his head. 'He supposedly had a date.'

'Yet he had a police radio on him, answered Natalie's call, and joined them in the search. Is that in character?' They both already knew the answer to that question, but it needed to be said out loud.

'No, it's not.'

'He came from the direction they were all running to, didn't he? Not from behind Natalie?'

'That's correct. Surely we're making too much out of a coincidence?' *I do not like the idea that one of my officers could be a serial killer.*

'Is it also a coincidence that Dave just happened to go to the house where Nigel was murdered? Who suggested which Officer went to which house?' Glancing through his notes of the evening's events, and finding the answer Lucas swore. 'Well?' demanded Evelyn.

'It was Dave who suggested that they split up and who to visit.'

They were silent for a moment, until finally in frustration, Lucas slammed his hand down onto the desk. 'It can't be true! I mean, sure the boy is egotistical and self-centred, but a killer?'

'What if it is true?' Evelyn's thoughts hadn't strayed from the main objective.

'We must warn Jenny. Come on!' Jumping to his feet, Lucas assisted Evelyn out of his chair.

'You'd get there quicker without me!'

Ignoring the protest, Lucas did everything he could to get Evelyn out of the station and into his car. 'You're going to explain your theory to Jenny and see if she can believe it any more that I can.'

Evelyn allowed himself to be hustled along. 'The problem is you believe it more than you want to admit.' The truth of this retort silenced the big man. *It is like a knife in my heart, and I have no hands to pull it out.*

Lisa And Dave

After several hours of sleep, Lisa was bouncing with energy. Entering the pub, the police officer checked the faces of the patrons to make sure she knew who was around. With a cheery hello to the regulars, Lisa moved through to the restaurant, again scanning the patrons as she bought herself an apple. Checking with Cheryl that Jenny was in her room, Lisa trotted up the stairs and knocked on her door. She wasn't surprised when Dean opened the door, and stood back to allow her to enter. Jenny was awake, but still lying down. She smiled as Lisa popped her head round the door.

'Just checking up on you Jenny, I'll be back in a couple of minutes. I've just got to pop off to the loo.'

As Lisa disappeared down the corridor, Dean turned to look inquiringly at Jenny. She smiled sympathetically. 'When you've got to go, you've got to go!'

Checking his watch, Dean nodded. 'And I've got to go. If those detectives start pestering you again, get in touch with my secretary, she'll get my lawyer to you ASAP.' Kissing Jenny on the tip of her nose, Dean was about to leave the room when he walked into Dave Hedley.

'Hi! Just checking on our resident celebrity,' said Dave.

Dean glanced back at Jenny and shrugged. 'One police officer, or two, what more protection do you need?'

'I'll be fine, Dean. Go and run your Media Empire.' Smiling, Jenny waved her hand and the two men swapped places. As Dean headed down the stairs, Dave shut the door and locked it behind him.

Another Attack

Having extracted Evelyn from the car, Lucas ran on ahead into the Dog and Bone and straight into Doctor Andrew Shepherd.

'Senior Sergeant, I've got to talk to you.'

Lucas held up his hand. 'Just give me a minute Doc.' He glanced across to the bar, 'Cheryl, who's with Jenny?'

It was Carmen who answered, 'Lisa is up there, and Dave went up about a minute ago.'

'Shit!' swore Evelyn, showing that he had heard as he had slowly followed in Lucas' wake. Lucas was about to streak up the stairs, but Doctor Shepherd laid a hand on his arm to stop him.

'Dave Hedley? The Hedley name is on the list!' That was all Lucas needed to know. He was up those stairs quicker than any man half his age. Carmen was half a dozen steps behind him, and the Doctor not far behind her.

Lucas reached the bedroom door, as Lisa was coming up the corridor. She took one look at her Boss' face filled with horror and broke into a run. Lucas tried the door handle, already knowing that it would be locked. Stepping back he put his foot to the door. On the second kick, the door burst open. The two police officers, the Doctor and Carmen hurried into the room and they stood there with their mouths open.

Dave was kneeling astride Jenny's body on her bed. In one hand was a jagged edged dagger. The other covered Jenny's mouth to muffle her screams. Jenny used both hands to keep the blade away from her chest. Lucas grabbed Dave from behind and thrust his knife arm behind his back. The knife was torn out of Dave's hand and thrown across to Lisa.

'You, of all people, I would never have suspected!' When Dave only laughed, all pity left Lucas as he read him his rights. Doctor Shepherd pushed passed as Jenny managed to sit up.

The Doctor examined Jenny for any injuries, as Lisa and Lucas led Dave away in handcuffs. Satisfied that Jenny hadn't suffered any further harm, Shepherd sat down on the chair beside the bed.

'You're not having much luck are you?'

'I've never been so wanted! Your friend managed to break the code?' Removing a sheet of paper from his jacket pocket, he handed it over to Jenny.

'Some of them are prominent families. Now, though, we have some idea whom to look out for. How about some tea? I'm sure we could find a table downstairs,' suggested Shepherd. Jenny took the hand that the Doctor held out and getting to her feet, she linked her arm through his and after slipping on her shoes allowed him to escort her down to the Restaurant.

Who Can We Trust?

Having used a great deal of energy just getting into the Dog and Bone, Evelyn didn't attempt to follow Lucas up the stairs to Jenny's bedroom. He could be of no use to the Senior Sergeant and was better off out of the way. Seated at a table, not far from the bar, Evelyn watched with interest as Lucas and Lisa led Dave away. His interest turned to concern as a very pale Carmen came down the stairs and joined him. He reached out his hand to her, and sliding onto the seat beside him, she willingly took it.

She briefly detailed what had taken place. 'I just don't know who we can trust anymore!'

'You need a break from this for a while. Why don't we go out to the pictures?'

Some of the colour came back to Carmen's cheeks as she smiled impishly. 'I'd rather stay in for a movie.'

He looked puzzled, so Carmen continued in a lowered voice. 'Theatre seats aren't that comfortable for you. Besides which, we'd probably be thrown out of the pictures if we did what I have in mind!'

'Carmen…' His cautious tone made her giggle.

'Settle down Romeo, I didn't mean that! I was thinking of some of those exercises your Gran wants you to do.'

Relieved, and yet disappointed, Evelyn managed to hide both emotions. 'You're a slave driver, aren't you? Are you still needed here?' Looking around the pub, Carmen noticed that Cheryl had everything well under control. Even so, she approached the bar to check that her mother could manage until Marcus arrived, before she assisted Evelyn out of the pub.

It's Out Of Our Hands

Upon entering the custody area, Lucas walked straight into DS Tony Gregg.

'The Inspector will take over,' stated Tony.

'I don't think so.' Lucas retained the hold he had upon Dave's arm, and didn't hand him over to Tony.

The Detective's jaw dropped in surprise. 'Are you disobeying a command from a superior officer?'

There was a significant pause as Lucas simply looked at Tony. Lisa felt her heart race as she watched the power struggle between the two Sergeants.

'There's nothing to disobey, Tony. This case is out of both our hands. CIB will be here in roughly half an hour.'

The Detective goggled in disbelief. 'You've already contacted them?'

'It was the right thing to do. If Inspector Harris wishes to run up against the Complaint Investigation Branch then he's more than welcome to take over.' Lucas gestured for Lisa to lead Dave to the desk to enter his details before he would be placed in a cell.

Tony shook his head. 'This is not the end of this, Greenaway.' The Detective stormed out of the custody area.

Lucas grinned at Lisa as she looked anxiously at her Boss. 'Don't worry Mac. You're not in the line of fire. Get him into a cell, before you head back to the Dog and Bone.'

'About that list of names...'

Lucas drew it out of his pocket and handed it across to the Constable. 'Have it photocopied, and send one copy to Inspector Harris, and take one to Cheryl.'

Standing in Dave's way, Lucas locked eyes with the Constable and remained standing almost nose to nose. 'I trusted you. At times I didn't like you, but I did trust you.' As Lucas turned away, Dave grinned. The Sergeant clenched his fists to control his emotions. 'May you burn in Hell!' Lucas said through gritted teeth and strode away before he forgot himself and did something he would later regret.

Lisa Scores A Win

Although Tony continued to rant about Lucas putting a spoke in their wheel out of spite, Kevin was a little relieved to have the case taken from him. *When one of our own turns bad or corrupt, it is a blow to the face, but when a cop turns killer, we're in for a serious public back lash upon the entire force.* Lisa, entering the Detective's office upstairs several minutes later, did so cautiously. Tony snarled at her, but Kevin smiled wearily, and gestured for her to approach. Lisa ignored Tony's grumbling as she handed the photocopy of the list of names across to the Inspector.

'Doctor Shepherd's friend is still working on the body of the text, but he felt that we needed the names immediately.'

Kevin thanked her. He only briefly perused the list before once more looking up at the Constable. 'Is the Doc still in Waltham?' He enquired.

'No Sir. He's gone back to London to have dinner with Sir Edward Dent.'

'What do you think of Miss Weston, Lisa?' Kevin stroked his chin thoughtfully. He ignored his Sergeant's impatience.

She hesitated as she considered her answer. 'What exactly do you want to know, Sir? I mean, personally, I think she's a nice lady. Her talent must make life lonely as she has to move around a lot, but it doesn't affect her attitude, she's very positive.' Tony's impatience grew as Kevin leant back in his chair.

'Do you think she's lonely enough to do anything to draw attention to herself?' He asked.

This drew a gasp of surprise from Lisa. 'No! Of course not! Not the way you mean. I honestly believe that the quicker and quieter a job is completed, the better Jenny likes it.'

Kevin nodded. 'Who do you think the Boss is?' When Lisa screwed up her nose and appeared hesitant to answer, he knew she was considering evidence. 'All right then. Educated guess,' he added.

Lisa's features relaxed into a grin. 'Well I'd put money on Dean Schofields. I mean he was born here, and would know all the stories about the Bible. He has the money to pay off three men to look for the book. He's sticking pretty close to Jenny, but that could be for other reasons. Also our trio made no move against her. If Dean was the Boss, and he's as much in love with Jenny as it appears, then he would have stressed that nothing happen to her.'

'A well-reasoned argument.'

Tony chipped in snidely, 'But no proof!'

Lisa shook her head. Her dislike for the Sergeant was growing with every second spent in his company. 'No Sir, but the Inspector did ask for an educated guess, not a concrete case!' She glanced back at Kevin Harris. 'Will there be anything else Sir?'

With a twinkle of appreciation in his eyes, Kevin shook his head. 'No, that will be all, thank you Lisa.'

The Inspector chuckled as Tony threw himself into a chair opposite when Lisa had left the office. 'Well that was a spit in the eye for you, Tony! I don't see you getting far, pulling rank on that one.'

Tony snorted, 'Insubordinate Bitch!'

'You're only peeved because she scored one off you!' Chuckling, Kevin shook his head. 'She's a smart cookie. Everyone sees Mac as a kid sister, but there is something sparkling about her.'

Jumping to his feet, Tony slammed his hand against the desk. 'Then why don't you marry the girl?'

Slamming out of the room, Tony didn't receive the reprimand that he rightly deserved. Picking up the list of names, the Inspector glanced over it carefully before putting it down again. For a moment his thoughts dwelt upon the case, before his musings changed back to the Constable.

I had never really considered Lisa McGraw as anything other than a fellow police officer. Now I'm interested in discovering the woman behind the uniform. Straightening his tie, the Inspector wondered, *How does Lisa feel about dating a colleague?*

Tony would have gagged on the idea, but it wasn't that far-fetched an idea. Lisa was 32 years old and Kevin Harris was only 38. In a mild, commonplace way, Kevin was considered handsome. Although his hair was a little thin, it was still dark and still all there. Unlike Tony, whom the Inspector gleefully knew was going bald on top and was desperately trying to hide the fact. Deciding to give Tony the fun job of tracking down descendants of the names on the list, the Inspector wondered what time Lisa had dinner.

I'm Off Duty

Walking into the Dog and Bone later that evening, as all heads turned to stare at him, Kevin Harris definitely felt personae non-grata. The bar was full, the restaurant just as well patronised and in concern for her star resident, Cheryl purposefully approached him.

'Inspector, if you intend questioning Miss Weston, then I...'

Kevin held up his hand to cut her off. 'No, no, Mrs. Roberts; I'm off duty. I simply came in for a drink and some dinner.' His calm manner was effective upon Cheryl.

'You won't start any trouble?' She was still a little doubtful.

The Inspector couldn't help smiling; it seemed a very odd question to ask a police officer. 'No trouble, I promise. I presume you've seen The List?'

'Oh yes. I'm sorry if I was rude just now, but Sergeant Gregg does have the habit of antagonising everyone.'

'The guilt of association, I suppose.' Sighing, he shook his head. 'If I could have a pint, I might go and find a table in the restaurant before I cause a riot.' His gentle self-mockery caused Cheryl to relax further and even manage a smile.

'Not a problem. You go through and I'll have your beer brought to you.'

Strolling through the adjoining double doors, Kevin found himself facing a similar welcome. Although there were a couple of empty tables, he couldn't help but allow his gaze to linger upon the table where Jenny and Lisa sat. Jenny, watching him, noticed that he seemed to focus his attention upon Lisa and she smiled in delight.

'Inspector, why don't you join us?' Jenny's offer surprised her companion. Watching Lisa's reaction, Kevin was interested to see her blush, as he sat down between them.

'Here to check up on us Sir?' There was restraint in Lisa's voice, a little nervousness too.

'Oh no, I am human Lisa, contrary to popular belief, and I do need feeding sometimes.'

'So you're not the one brow beating Jenny this afternoon?' Lisa demanded.

'No, no. I leave that to my Sergeant. He enjoys being heavy handed.'

Olivia came across taking their orders, and as she flitted off again, Mitzy strolled into the restaurant. She headed straight for Jenny, wrapped herself round the legs of the chair a couple of times before jumping up onto her lap. As Jenny stroked Mitzy's head, Lisa looked concerned at Kevin Harris, but he only reached across to scratch Mitzy under the chin.

'Now then miss,' Jenny said to the purring feline, 'You know you shouldn't be in here. I suppose you've been catching mice again like a good little hunter?' A meow that was slightly distorted by a yawn answered her.

With thoughts of Health Inspectors raiding the restaurant, Lisa quickly sprang to her feet and held out her arms for Mitzy. 'I'll take her upstairs and give her some dinner, shall I?'

The cat wasn't happy about leaving Jenny's lap, but didn't fight against being picked up by Lisa. Jenny felt an imp of mischievousness stir inside her. 'Perhaps Inspector Harris would like to see the kittens?' His eyes met hers for a moment and a look of understanding passed between them.

'I would indeed,' Kevin agreed, 'If you don't mind Lisa?'

Not seeing how she could refuse, Lisa smiled, 'Of course not.'

Kevin followed Lisa and Mitzy out of the restaurant, accepting the plate of scraps that Olivia handed him, explaining at his surprised look that they were for Mitzy's dinner, not his.

Kevin Meets The Kittens

Mitzy, once set down in Jenny's bedroom, went across to her basket to check on her kittens before heading for the plate of food Kevin placed on the floor. Lisa perched on the edge of the bed, watching as her superior officer sat down on the floor beside the basket and very gently picked up one of the little balls of fur. The look of delight on his face as he tenderly handled the tabby coloured kitten surprised Lisa and she found herself voicing her thoughts before she could stop herself.

'I didn't know you liked cats Sir.'

A little awkwardly, with one hand Kevin pulled his wallet out of his back pocket, opened it up before handing it across to Lisa. Inside was a picture of a magnificent Russian Blue Cat.

'That's Nicholai! He was a grand boy! A real smoocher. He died about six months ago,' he explained.

'I'm sorry.' Her words were heartfelt and not just an automatic response.

Kevin smiled. 'Oh don't be, he'd had a good long life, but I do miss him.'

Getting off the bed, Lisa sat down on the floor beside the Inspector, and absently began stroking one of the kittens. 'Had you thought of getting another?'

For a moment he looked into the ball of fur where bright blue eyes stared up at him. 'Not until this moment. I find kittens hard to resist. Is Miss Weston planning to keep them or sell them?'

Lisa shook her head. 'Mitzy is staying with Mrs Roberts, but I think they'll try to give the kittens away to good homes as soon as they are able to leave their mother. Doc Martin, the Vet, has promised a discount for sterilisation!'

'Good idea.' Kevin nodded solemnly. 'I wonder if two kittens would be better than one. That way one on its own wouldn't get lonely or bored while I'm at work.' At Lisa's look of surprise, he smiled. 'What's wrong? Am I showing that human side again?'

Blushing Lisa looked away. 'I suppose I just never really knew you, Sir.'

Chuckling as his kitten tried to climb up his arm, he added, 'When we're not at work, you can call me by my first name.'

'Oh no, that would never do! I mean, I do like you, but what if I forgot myself at the station?' Lisa was horrified by the thought.

Kevin smiled. 'Then it would illustrate that you were human too! Seriously though, I would like to get to know you better, but if you insist on calling me Sir or Inspector, then there would always be this barrier of work between us.'

Still doubtful, Lisa reluctantly agreed. Then a thought struck her. 'I don't think I know your first name.' She was so embarrassed by this, that he couldn't help smiling.

'Kevin.'

Frowning, Lisa repeated it, before lapsing into silence for a moment. 'It suits you. Shall we return to the restaurant Sir? I mean... Oh dear, this is going to be harder than I thought.'

Kevin laughed, putting the kitten back into the basket as they both struggled to their feet. 'It will come with practice.' Gallantly, he held the door open for her and waited until she had locked it once more behind them; before they ambled happily back down the stairs.

Lisa And Kevin On Duty

After dinner Jenny was seated at a table in the pub, finally having the drink she had promised with Sean Hanson. Out the front of the pub, getting a breath of fresh air, Kevin stood with Lisa. The evening was cool but pleasant and as the two police officers chatted together about matters outside of work, Lisa began to wonder, *where is this all leading?*

'Kevin, there is something I need to know, and it may come out as being rude or insulting.'

The Inspector looked interested. 'Go on.'

'Your attention is very flattering and I could become quite fond of you, but I need to know now what is behind your sudden interest. Is it some sort of dare or bet with someone at work? I know I'm not the sort of girl men want to flirt with, but I do need to know the truth!'

There was no immediate reply, and as they stood leaning against the wall, Lisa couldn't quite see the expression on her superior's face. She wondered if she had overstepped the mark. There was little need to worry, for when Kevin spoke; it was in a calm thoughtful voice.

'There is no bet or dare. My motivation is curiosity. Your show of spirit with Sergeant Gregg intrigued me into wanting to find out a little more about the woman behind the uniform. You sell yourself short by thinking that all men see you as a sister figure.'

Glad for the dim lighting, Lisa knew that her cheeks were blazing bright red. *The only other person to tell me that I underestimate myself has been my mother, and I had put that down to a mother's affectionate love.*

'I don't know what to say. I'm confused!'

'When this madness is over, I want you to have dinner with me. No strings attached. I just want to get to know you. I won't even kiss you if you don't want me to.' Tenderly Kevin took one of her hands between his own.

Considering this point, Lisa decided to take a gamble. 'And what if I do want you to kiss me, would you?'

'You don't seem to realise how inviting those lips are.' Smiling, he gently ran a forefinger over her lips.

'Oh!' There is a first time for everything and Lisa McGraw was lost for words. She wondered, *why is he hesitating and doesn't kiss me?* Lisa realised eventually that Kevin was waiting for her to ask him. 'Would you...' Lisa began, but she caught sight of someone she recognised about to enter the pub, 'Hey you! Stay where you are!' She called out and Kevin, turning, put his hand on the young man's shoulder.

'I'm of legal age, Inspector!' protested Cameron Alston.

Kevin turned him away from the doorway. 'That'd make a change Cameron but that's not why you've been stopped. Your name is on a list and until further notice you and your brethren or brothers or whatever you call yourselves will be kept out of the Dog and Bone.'

Cameron was a big lad and he tried to stand over the Inspector, who wasn't especially tall. It didn't work as Kevin wasn't one to be intimidated. 'Get off with you Cameron before I arrest you for insolence!'

Lisa watched amazed as the human she had only moment before been speaking to was now suddenly a cold and hard police officer.

Cameron snorted in disgust. 'You can't do that Inspector Harris! You've nothing on me!'

Kevin looked bored at the boy. 'Aren't you glad that the old ways of the police interrogation are outlawed?' The steel in his voice was unmistakable, causing the lad to swallow hard and retreat. When Kevin turned back to Lisa, the hard cold look on his face, seen by the street light, caused her to gasp in fear.

'My God! I hope I never get on your bad side!'

The Inspector's expression softened. 'You don't have to worry about that Lisa. I'm sure you'll get used to the two sides that make up my professional and personal life.'

'It may take some time.'

'You can have time.' Kevin smiled. 'There is something professional I need to ask you.'

Slowly Lisa drew back so that personal contact between them was broken. 'What would that be Inspector?'

'About Sean Hanson...' Kevin leant against the pub wall.

A laugh escaped from Lisa. 'I've already run a check on Sean by the list, and the police database. I've also checked on Dean Schofields and Marcus Lipitor, the bar tender. All have a clean record.'

He couldn't resist smiling at her thoroughness. 'You appear to have everything under control. Will you be staying here tonight?'

'Oh yes. We've arranged that I'll be in the arm chair in Jenny's bedroom.'

The Inspector checked his watch. 'Good. You have a mobile phone don't you?' Lisa nodded, checking her mobile to make sure the battery was well charged. 'Take care of yourself Lisa. I'll be at the office for an hour or so. I want to speak to CIB when they arrive to interrogate Dave.' With a tender caress along her cheek, Kevin left the Dog and Bone to return to duty.

Carmen's Future

Looking up as Lisa floated back into the pub, Jenny smiled indulgently. Sean Hanson followed her gaze and shook his head.

'Is that girl going to be able to do her job if her feet aren't on the ground?'

Jenny glanced cautiously to where Lisa had joined Cheryl at the bar, to see if she had heard Sean's words before looking back at him. 'I trust Lisa with my life. Her professionalism won't be compromised by her emotions.' The sternness of her tone made Sean beg her pardon.

He tried to change the subject so as to wipe the displeasure from Jenny's face, but the pub door flew open as Carmen danced in. She came straight across the room to hug Jenny before mischievously popping onto her lap.

'Oh Jenny, I feel so unreal! I can't believe how happy I am!' Giving Jenny another rib breaking hug, Carmen slid off her lap onto the chair beside her.

Jenny laughed at her exuberance. 'What decisions have you come to?'

'This is what I'm supposed to be! This is my purpose! No more darkness for me, only light!' Seeing Sean glaring at her, Carmen looked at Jenny in concern. 'Am I intruding on an intimate moment?'

Sean continued to glare at Carmen, but Jenny smiled as she shook her head. 'Not at all, you enjoyed your evening with Evelyn then?' A twinkle entered Jenny's eyes as colour rushed across Carmen's cheeks at the memory.

'Yes, thank you. What happens now about me?'

Shrugging, Jenny said, 'That depends upon you. A University course in Counselling may be what you want. Flying completely by the seat of your pants is not always a sensible option. It helps if you understand something about psychology.'

'Problem is I can't afford to stop working to go to Uni.' Carmen looked doubtful and a little worried.

'That's been arranged. You've only to decide if it is what you want and the money will be made available.' Jenny patted her hand reassuringly.

Not completely convinced, Carmen continued to question her mentor, 'How? Why?'

Remaining silent, Jenny hesitated about revealing the whole truth. After a minute, Carmen should have realised it was a touchy question, but with the insistence of youth, she was determined to get an answer.

Jenny finally relented, 'Why, because you may have a long and rewarding life as a Spirit Healer, and to make it also successful, some training is essential,' Jenny paused momentarily before continuing, 'As for how, well, I talked Dean into supplying the money necessary to see you through college. I feel it's that important, and that sum would cause little inconvenience to him.'

Jenny waited for Carmen's protest and was mildly surprised when the teenager agreed with her. 'It's a great idea! I didn't like the thought of being a drain on Mum while I'm studying.'

In an attempt to draw Jenny back into a more intimate conversation, Sean was again frustrated as Lisa joined their table. The arrival of Carmen seemed to indicate to Lisa that their private time was at an end. Jenny attempted to hide a smile at Sean's obvious annoyance, and the way Carmen and Lisa ignored his displeasure.

'I think you need a breath of fresh air. You shouldn't be trapped inside all the time,' suggested Lisa, placing her hand over Jenny's. Sean felt himself being drawn away from Jenny as her minders appeared to take command.

'Actually it is getting rather late; I think I'll head up to bed. You don't mind, do you Sean?'

'Not at all Jenny,' He rose swiftly to his feet, and drained off the remainder of his pint, 'I've an early start in the morning anyway.' Sean turned towards Lisa and added, 'Take care of her.'

She smiled at his solemn nature, 'Of course! Jenny will be alive in the morning, I promise!' Sean didn't seem to be at all pleased by Lisa's flippant manner, and left the pub rather tight lipped.

'Now you've upset him Lisa,' Carmen couldn't help but grin at Sean's unamused attitude. 'Your roses won't bloom this year if you upset the holy grail of gardeners.'

This reminder of Sean's occupation brought a frown to Lisa's happy countenance. 'Doesn't it strike you as odd, someone of his obvious education being a gardener?'

'He seems amiable enough, but doesn't appear to be a genius,' Carmen shook her head. 'Perhaps horticulture is his passion. It's no longer the occupation of the uneducated.'

'Do you have any doubts about Sean being what he says he is?' Jenny stretched, placing her hand over her mouth as she yawned.

A mischievous gleam lit up Lisa's eyes. 'I've done a thorough check on everyone, even the dog at the Vicarage. Sean has no police record, not even a speeding fine.'

'No police record could also mean that he's clever enough to stay under the radar,' Jenny mused as she smothered another yawn.

Lisa sat up a little straighter. 'Do you have any serious doubts about Sean?'

'Just a niggling feeling that Sean was more interested in my progress with the Bible rather than me.' Wearily Jenny shrugged.

Laughing Carmen said, 'You mistrust Simple Simon rather than your High Flying Millionaire?'

Lisa didn't agree. 'Oh no, Carmen... I don't trust anyone!'

Night Vigil

Later that evening a small sigh escaped from Lisa as she looked around Jenny's bedroom by the aid of a lamp beside her on its lowest setting. It was enough for her to read by, but not bright enough to disturb Jenny in the bed. Lisa was curled up in the armchair in the room, with a romance novel to keep her awake. For a while Mitzy lay beside Jenny, but moved to sit on Lisa's lap. She set up a contented purr as Lisa absently stroked her.

The Dog and Bone finally quieten down as guests turned in, and patrons headed home to their own beds. The night settled down around them, and although Lisa occasionally yawned, her book was interesting enough to keep her awake and focussed.

The hero was just tearing off the bodice of the heroine, when the lamp beside Lisa suddenly went out. Her first reaction was annoyance at having been disturbed during an exciting part. Her next reaction was one of fear that saw the adrenalin kick in.

Easing Mitzy off her lap and back into her basket, Lisa rose silently to her feet and moved across to the window making sure that she didn't create an easy target by being visible. Every sense was straining to full capacity in the darkness as she waited for an attack to come, if it was coming. She had her baton and heavy torch, and pepper spray, and was quite ready to use any of them.

As if she had found the total darkness disturbing, Jenny stirred, and opening her eyes to find there was no light, she cautiously raised himself on one elbow. 'Lisa?' she whispered.

'I'm here,' Lisa whispered back. 'It might be a power failure only but I doubt it as the street lights are still lit and the property next door still has its lights on.'

'What do we do?' Jenny felt a shiver of fear run through her.

Lisa shrugged her shoulders. 'We wait!'

When one of the floorboards on the stairs creaked, Lisa's hand tightened around her baton, and she swallowed hard, praying her pounding heart beat couldn't be heard by anyone else.

Finding that the door was locked, the intruders didn't bother with subtleties such as picking the lock, they, as there were two of them, put their shoulders to the door and broke it open. One intruder fired his gun at the figure in the bed, while the other was prepared to do battle with the police officer.

That attack didn't come, causing the first intruder to throw back the bed covers to discover only a pile of pillows where he thought there had been a sleeping body. The room was completely empty. Too late they realised they had been set up, and turning to quickly depart, they walked straight into the custody of two of Lisa's colleagues.

As they were led down to a waiting police car, one of the police officers contacted Lisa on her radio. 'Plan A successful. We'll put Plan B into operation.'

Lisa sighed with relief, 'Happy Hunting.' Turning to Jenny, she gloated, 'Now didn't I tell you changing rooms would be a good idea?'

Jenny laughed at her. 'None of us were actually against the idea, especially after Lucas had to break the door down to save me from Dave. Do you think we'd be able to get some sleep now?'

Lisa yawned and stretched her whole body. 'Plan B will ensure that they won't get into the pub. Are you all right?'

The Spirit Healer had pushed back the bedding and risen to her feet. 'I feel guilty, using up so much police resources to protect me. This is not what my work is about! I'm supposed to be helping others.' She paced up and down the room.

'It's only for a couple of days,' reasoned Lisa. 'If they're prepared to kill you, this book must be pretty important. Think of the fact that you'll be helping to release about four or five ghosts who are trapped on earth, because of this book.'

Sighing, Jenny sat down on the edge of the bed. 'That is the main reason I continue.' *There is still five hours to sunrise, and anything could happen in the darkness.*

MONDAY

Business As Usual

There was only one further attempt to reach Jenny that night, but as Lisa's colleagues kept a watch outside the pub, no one was able to enter. With a couple of solid hours of sleep, Jenny finally woke at eight and was alarmed that Lisa was no longer in the room. Carmen had been standing outside the bedroom, and looked in as Jenny stirred, smiling reassuringly.

'It's all right; Lisa's just having a shower. We're planning to head downstairs to breakfast in about 20 minutes, will that be long enough for you to wash and dress?'

Jenny sprang out of bed. 'Is the power back on yet?' She pulled on a dressing gown, and gathered together the toiletries and clothing she would need.

Carmen nodded, 'They only turned it off at the mains rather than frying the whole system.'

'Back in ten minutes.'

In fact she was back in eight and a half minutes, all spruced up and ready to be escorted by the two ladies down to the restaurant. The meal was uneventful, so when Lucas arrived, Jenny was ready for him. Lisa went home for a couple of hours of sleep. Although it was no longer raining, it was really quite crisp outside, so they wrapped up warmly before heading out to the ruins.

Jenny got down to business quickly, kneeling down alternately at the two spots indicated by the ghost maid Mandy and her swain Ian. Deciding which location she preferred, Jenny agreed with Lucas that the digging could commence immediately.

Even though she knew the Sergeant would dearly love to get out of the cold, Jenny felt drawn towards the water. Unconsciously her feet led her to the ornamental pond's edge, and she stared into it, her reflection unseen by her. Lucas could see that she wanted to think, so he stood slightly back from her, constantly scanning the area around them for any signs of trouble.

The Boss

Glancing over his right shoulder, Lucas saw no one around, so he glanced to his left, and behind him, where there was also no one, before glancing back to the left. He took a step backwards in surprise. *Seconds ago no one had been in sight; now there is someone standing right beside me!* Lucas had only the chance to cry out a warning to Jenny before he was whacked across the head with a heavy piece of wood. Jenny turned as Lucas fell unconscious to the ground. Recognising the assailant, her eyebrows rose in surprise.

'You're the last person I'd expected to be the Boss! You won't kill him will you?' Jenny spoke quite calmly as the Boss slowly approached her.

'I won't kill him.' He appeared to hesitate which caused Jenny to smile.

'It's all right, I won't struggle. I don't have the strength.'

To her surprise the Boss dragged her into his arms and kissed her, hard and long, literally taking her breath away. He picked Jenny up, as if she was as light as a child, and effortlessly threw her into the pond. The water was quite deep near the edge and extremely cold, and she surfaced only once. Like Lenny and Dave, Jenny felt something beneath her pulling her under. The Boss waited several minutes to make sure that she didn't reappear. Then he turned and walked away, without a single backward glance.

Officer Down

Walking up from the car park of Cedars Park, Sean quickly thrust work problems to the back of his thoughts as he saw Lucas laid out on the ground beside the pond, and no sight of Jenny. Frantically, he glanced around for any sign of her before kneeling down beside the unconscious policeman. Checking his wound, Sean was relieved that Lucas was breathing, and his heart was still beating. He had lost quite a bit of blood from the crack to his head, which Sean attempted to slow by placing a clean handkerchief over the indent to Lucas' skull.

His own mobile was dead, and Lucas was only carrying a police radio. *I have no idea how to use one of these, but I can't afford to leave Lucas to run back to the pay phone.* So Sean dragged Lucas' radio out of his coat pocket and pressed the button down.

'I've got an officer down! I repeat a police officer injured and in need of serious assistance. Cedars Park,' releasing the button, Sean almost held his breath in fear.

'This is an official channel, please use proper police procedure!' stated a stern female voice.

With this reply, Sean's fear turned to anger. 'Shit lady! I have a Senior Sergeant bleeding to death on me, and the woman he's supposed to be protecting has disappeared! I'm sorry I don't know your bloody procedures, but I'm only a civilian!'

The female voice was replaced by a male voice, of obviously higher authority. 'Restate your position please.'

'Cedars Park, Broxbourne. Hurry please. We must find her before it's too late!'

'Can you do anything to stop the bleeding?'

Sean glanced down to see that his handkerchief was already soaked through, 'Yeah, but not for long,' he tossed the radio down on the grass beside him, before once again thrusting his free hand into Lucas' pockets. Finding a handkerchief and a couple of tissues, Sean placed these over the top of his own handkerchief and applied a little pressure with the palm of his hand.

It seemed like forever to Sean, but it was only a couple of minutes before an ambulance and three police cars pulled up at the ruins. Despite freezing himself, Sean had taken off his coat and laid it over Lucas. For only a brief moment before the paramedics arrived, Lucas regained consciousness.

'He wasn't there!' He managed to say, grasping hold of Sean's arm, before lapsing once more into unconsciousness. Once placed on a stretcher, the Paramedics wrapped a blanket around Lucas, handing Sean back his jacket.

As the ambulance pulled away, the police officers surrounded Sean to discover what had happened. There was Natalie, Lisa, who hadn't yet gone to bed, Bobby, Kevin Harris and Tony Gregg. It was the Inspector who momentarily silenced all questions and sitting Sean down on the grass, poured a drop of brandy from a flask down his throat.

'Get your breath back, my boy, and then tell us everything.' Kevin's tone, so bored, so calm, had its desired effect upon Sean. Once he had collected himself, Sean was able to calmly explain what he had found. Bobby searched the grass for any evidence to Jenny's whereabouts. His findings were given with as much professionalism as he could muster.

'There are no indications of a struggle. No blood, except for the Sergeant's, so she wasn't killed immediately. The grass is considerably damp along the edge of the pond.'

Kevin drew his Sergeant out of Sean's earshot. 'I want the pond searched and a rounding up of all people named in that organisation's list.'

'Do you want me to put the whole police force on this job, Sir?' Tony Gregg floundered.

The bored look on the Inspector's face was replaced by one of determination, 'If necessary! I'm off to find a magistrate for a search warrant.'

Tony shook his head. 'You'd never get one to agree to a warrant on such flimsy evidence.'

Smiling devilishly, Kevin frightened Tony even more than when he frowned. 'No? I should think that Judge Nelson will be only too happy to comply.' He turned to Lisa, his expression softening. 'Get Mr Hanson back to the Pub and see that he's looked after.'

'Of course Sir.'

Tony was already heading back to the car, but Kevin paused to add, 'Keep me informed as to Lucas' progress.'

Lisa nodded. 'Of course,' she was pleased to see that his human side did appear in his professional life. As she and her colleagues assisted Sean to his feet, he managed to pull himself together.

'I'm all right. I've got to get on with my work!' He strode away, not even listening to Lisa's attempts to get him to go with her.

Where Is She?

Having heard the sirens of the ambulance and police cars as they tore passed, heading for Cedars Park, Carmen had pulled on her jacket, enlisted her mother's assistance in the restaurant. She was about to go out to see what was going on, when Lisa walked through the door. Carmen took one look at the expression on Lisa's features and had to grab hold of the back of a chair to steady herself.

'Oh God! No! Not Jenny! What's happened?'

Lisa swallowed hard on the lump that had formed in her throat. As calmly as possible she repeated what she knew. The whole restaurant had fallen silent, so naturally several people jumped, startled when from the kitchen came the sound of a plate breaking. Penny emerged rather pale and shaking.

Lisa took hold of one of Penny's hands. 'He regained consciousness and was quite lucid.'

'How was he injured?'

Lisa explained about the head wound and was shocked when Penny smiled weakly.

'That's all right then,' Penny said and added when she saw her look of horror, 'Lucas has a skull of iron, any other sort of injury and I may have been more concerned.' Lisa opened her mouth to tell Penny how much blood her husband had lost, but catching a glimpse of Evelyn who shook his head, she shut her mouth again.

Pulling away from Lisa, Penny picked up her handbag and car keys from under the counter. 'I'm sorry to leave you in a rush, Cheryl, but I need to go to the hospital.'

The Innkeeper waved away her apology. 'I wouldn't expect you to do anything else! Let us know when there is any news.'

So Lisa leant Cheryl a hand while Carmen disappeared with Evelyn into the empty Conference Room. Evelyn sank onto the sofa, whereas Carmen paced the room.

'She must be alive! How can we know for sure?' As her words were little more than mutterings to herself, Evelyn didn't even attempt to answer. Suddenly Carmen ceased pacing, and her eyes opened wider in surprise. 'Tommy!'

Closing her eyes, and taking a deep breath, Carmen silently screamed out his name again. Within seconds, Tommy materialised looking rather shaken and disorientated.

'Talk about breakin' the speed of light! What's so urgent?'

Carmen repeated what she knew. Tommy chewed on a fingernail thoughtfully but he didn't say anything. 'I thought you were keeping a close eye on Jenny?' accused Carmen.

Tommy shook his head. 'I was told to back off this morning.'

'By whom?' Evelyn demanded.

Tommy hesitated, 'By his Lordship. He said my Mistress had something to do and that I wasn't allowed to get in the way.'

'She's alive then?' Carmen grabbed his arm in a painful grip. 'He wouldn't let her die yet, surely?'

'Not unless it was her time, or the only way she could complete this mission was as a ghost.'

'But why...'

Tommy cut Carmen off before she could finish her question. 'Look, in your own lingo, his Lordship is one dude you don't mess with! If he tells you to do something, you just do it. No asking questions or debating the issue.'

Evelyn asked the question that was burning on Carmen's lips but couldn't come out. 'Will he tell you if Jenny is alive or dead?'

The ghost teenager shrugged his shoulders, 'When he's ready. Don't you understand? He Is Death! Even the other Angels are wary how they tread around him. We'll be told what is going on when the time is right.' Tommy began to fade from their presence.

'That's not good enough!' Carmen yelled.

Innocent to the irony Tommy replied, 'That's life!' before vanishing completely.

He Wasn't There!

Sitting perfectly still in the emergency waiting room, Penny could have been a statue. When the Doctor finally approached Penny, he thought he must have the wrong person. 'Mrs Greenaway, if you'd like to come through, your husband is now conscious.'

'With words without bark on them, Doc, how is he?' Penny rose calmly to her feet to follow.

The Emergency Department Doctor scratched his head, looking doubtfully at Penny. 'He'll suffer from mild concussion, and headaches for a couple of weeks. He shouldn't drive for a while, and I've written out a prescription for painkillers.'

'He always was lucky.'

Entering the Emergency Area Penny found that Lucas' head was completely bandaged and his rosy cheeks were unnaturally pale. When Lucas smiled ruefully at her, Penny let out a sigh of relief and moved forward to take her husband's hand.

'He wasn't there Pen! When I'd looked around a second before, and it was only seconds, he wasn't there!'

Penny brushed her hand against the side of his face. 'It's all right darling, there was nothing you could have done!'

'Jenny!' The Sergeant's eyes misted over. 'Is she all right? They won't tell me anything!'

'They're still looking for her. There's nothing you can blame yourself for.'

Groaning, Lucas closed his eyes. 'I've failed. I was supposed to protect her!'

There was nothing Penny could say to this, so she was silent. The Doctor came quietly up beside Penny.

'You can take him home Mrs. Greenaway. Any deterioration of his condition, see your G.P. Lucas will need to take a couple of days off, preferably with his feet up, or in bed.'

Penny nodded. 'Thank you Doctor.' She waited patiently as Lucas regained control of his emotions. There was nothing she could say or do to ease his feelings of guilt.

The Search Must Desist

Entering the Restaurant, having seen Evelyn out through the pub, Carmen found her mother arguing with two Local Government Councillors.

'You must be joking?' Cheryl was saying, and seeing her daughter arrive, added, 'Perhaps Carmen can understand what you're trying to say, because I certainly don't.'

One Councillor swallowed nervously as he repeated, 'The Borough of Broxbourne Council has decided to withdraw its permission for the search for Kings James' Bible to continue. Digging within Cedars Park is prohibited and any further search must cease. Too many lives have been lost.'

Silence followed this little speech and if the patrons were expecting an explosion, they were to be disappointed.

'Oh really?' Although there was a dangerous edge to Carmen's voice, it wasn't raised. 'We shall see about that!' She turned away from the Councillors towards her mother. 'I have to sort this matter out.'

Cheryl, a little doubtful about what her daughter could do, wasn't prepared to stand in the way of a determined female. 'We'll be all right. You go give them hell! You must finish this for Jenny!'

The Councillors started protesting that there was nothing she could do. Sighing, Carmen just looked at them causing them to fall silent.

'You've delivered your message, now clear off. When I want to see you, I will notify you of the fact!'

Ignoring their blustering, Carmen grabbed her coat and her handbag from behind the till. 'I won't be long Mum. Sorry to dump this on you.'

Cheryl wrapped her daughter up in a quick embrace, 'Nonsense! I'm very proud of you dear! Go and sort this mess out.' The patrons cheered Carmen as she left, the Councillors were quick to leave with so much support against them.

I Need Help

Several reports lay on Kevin Harris' desk, but he didn't see any of them as he stared blankly out into space. The pond had been dragged, Judge Nelson had sanctioned the warrants, and Tony Gregg was leading one of the teams that were searching through the homes and businesses of suspects from the list of the organisation members. It was quite providential that just as the Inspector was thinking about going to find Carmen at the restaurant, she stormed into the police station demanding to see him.

Kevin sat back on his seat opposite Carmen and said quite calmly, 'You know she's alive don't you?'

'Yes! She has to be.' It came out like a sigh of relief, that someone else thought it was possible. Carmen explained why she felt Jenny was alive. Kevin listened carefully, and only when Carmen had finished did he speak.

'Only one small flaw in that theory. You're putting a whole lot of faith into something even you can't see.'

Carmen looked horrified at the thought, but instead of arguing with him, she considered the matter for several minutes before finally shaking her head. 'There was no reason to take her away to kill her. The killing would have to be public as a warning to others who might try to find the Bible.'

Slowing nodding, Kevin smiled. 'Good girl! Keep your convictions. Hold on tight to them. What now then? We're checking all possible suspects of the organisation.' This brought back to Carmen her reason for being there. She told the Inspector about the visit from the Council.

'So you think there is something I can do to change the Council's mind? I looked into whether Cedars is actually Council property or belonged to the hotel Theobalds Park, which is owned by the De Vere Group, and they might be easier to influence but it is Council land,' stated Kevin.

Fatalistically, Carmen shrugged. 'If Jenny is dead, which I pray to God she's not, then retrieving the Bible is finishing what she started. If she has found some other way into the secret chamber, then it's a rescue mission.'

Kevin looked up in interest at this last statement. 'Do you think that there is another way in, through the pond?'

'Well, you'd have to check up with the official reports, but Natalie said that when Lenny and Dave both tried to haul themselves out of the pond, it looked like something was sucking them down. Isn't it possible that there is something that draws water into the secret chamber?' Carmen was frowning in thought.

Both Kevin's eyebrows rose. 'Possible but is it probable? That's academic at the moment, what we need is to find someone who can put the fear of God into the Broxbourne Council.'

Jumping excitedly to her feet, Carmen knocked her chair over as she cried out in delight, 'Fear of God! How could I have been so stupid? I must find Doctor Shepherd. He's a Mason, and he said that they have contacts with people in power!' Carmen would have run out the door, but placing his hand on her arm, Kevin managed to stop her charging off.

'Wait a minute, I'll get my jacket and come with you.' Although Carmen agreed, she could hardly keep still while the Inspector grabbed his overcoat and car keys.

Higher Power

Kevin was still getting out of the car, and locking it, when Carmen burst into Doctor Shepherd's waiting room. Once inside she was a little at a loss to know what to do. She faltered slightly and the words of help trembled unsaid on her lips. All the patients were staring at Carmen, and she felt the urge to retreat.

Inspector Harris, entering the waiting room, blocked the doorway.

'What is it Carmen?' asked Doctor Shepherd, 'Do you have an emergency?'

Carmen shook her head. 'We need your help, Doc.'

'Go into my office, Carmen, Inspector.' He ushered them through to his office.

As quickly and as carefully as possible, Carmen explained what had happened, and what she thought had happened to Jenny. Catching her breath, she hesitated before asking the Doctor to use his Masonic connections to get the Council to change their mind. Doctor Shepherd smiled and she exhaled in relief.

'I can't promise instant results but I should be able to get back to you before this evening.' They rose swiftly to their feet, and followed the Doctor out of the consulting room.

'Thank you Doctor Shepherd! It's such a relief that you didn't dismiss me as being mad!'

'I advise you to keep calm, Carmen. You'll need all your strength over the next couple of days. Good day to you Inspector.' Shepherd showed them out before returning to his patients.

Kevin's Brilliant Idea

Having dropped Carmen off at the Dog and Bone, Kevin Harris returned to the Police Station to find Tony wearing a long face.

'Cheer up, Tony, it might never happen! I take it you didn't have any luck then?'

Tony snorted in disgust. 'You knew it was going to be a dud job, Sir. I suppose you've had a miraculous break through?' The snide tone was not lost on the Inspector as he hung up his coat.

'I'd watch that tone, my lad, there is only so much insubordination that I'll wear before I throw the book at you. Besides what's the point of having a flunkey, if you do the dirty work yourself? It's called delegation. You'll learn that word if you want to consider promotion.'

Having shuffled the papers back into order, Kevin picked up the telephone to relay a request to the forensic team. They were still at the crime scene at Cedars Park, and it was easy enough for them to carry out the experiment the Inspector asked to be conducted. Half an hour later, Kevin received a phone call from Jim Kennedy, in charge of the forensic team. The answer he received brought a smile to his lips, and out of his seat. Tony looked like a sulky puppy as he watched Kevin draw on his overcoat again.

'Come on Tony! If you're not there, who will I show how clever my experiment was?' Tony continued to scowl, but willingly followed his superior out of the office.

The forensic team was packing up when the Detectives arrived at the ruins. Jim Kennedy stood at the edge of the pond chomping on a green apple, 'Ingenious idea, Inspector! What put you on to the pond?'

'Apart from this grass area being very wet when Lucas was found knocked out, Carmen Roberts is convinced that Jenny Weston went into the pond. Do we get a demonstration?'

Jim Kennedy signalled to a young man on his team. 'Stanley, show the Inspector your apple trick.'

The young man, reaching for the bag of apples at Jim Kennedy's feet, became quite animated, 'Amazing Sir! They're just sucked straight down. One of the apples bobbed up once, but that may be how we put it into the water.' Stanley threw an apple in close to the edge, accidentally splashing droplets of water upon Tony's shoes. Stanley cringed, expecting to get his head bitten off, but apart from glaring at the young man, Tony didn't say a word.

Kevin took no notice of this side play as all his attention was focussed on the apple. It bobbed gently on the water's surface before suddenly being dragged under. When it didn't reappear, Kevin smiled satisfied. 'If that doesn't help convince the Council, nothing will!'

Glancing down at the bag of apples, Kevin said, 'See that you're reimbursed for the apples Jim. Stanley, I want you to put the rest of the bag into the pond.' This was received in stunned silence. Kevin's eyes twinkled. 'We don't want Jenny to starve while we're trying to rescue her, now do we?' They all agreed that they didn't want that.

'Perhaps we should flush a steak and chips down the pond or perhaps she'd prefer caviar and champagne?' Tony's sarcasm brought a dangerous light to Kevin's eyes.

'That sort of attitude is neither necessary nor helpful, Sergeant.' The reprimand was a mild one in front of others, but Tony took it hard. He turned on his heels and stormed off. Stanley grimaced to his boss, as he threw the apples into the pond.

'Problems with the cub, Kevin?' Jim moved aside with the Inspector.

'I may have to officially reprimand him, and that will go on Tony's record. I tried to warn him, but he seems to be on a self-destruction course. I don't know what's wrong with him.'

Thoughtfully, Jim stroked his chin. 'He's hardly a boy. You've given him enough warnings; if he can't take the hint, then that's his look out.'

'Thanks for the experiment Jim. I just hope we're on the right track.'

'Only time will tell.' The two colleagues headed back to the car park.

Kevin shook his head, 'unfortunately time isn't something we have a lot of!'

Criminal Investigation Branch

Chief Inspector Graham Browne of the Criminal Investigation Branch leant back in his chair in the interrogation room, his eyes continued to rest upon Dave Hedley, who wore a supercilious grin. The silence continued for several minutes, but Dave wasn't intimidated, he knew all the tricks. He simply waited.

'So you're not going to say anything in your defence, Dave?' Graham finally asked.

'I've got nothing to say. You've no evidence to hold me with!' Dave shook his head.

Graham flicked through the papers in front of him, which documented Dave's alleged activities. 'How else would you describe kneeling over a young woman with a dagger pressed against her breast then? The fact your DNA was found all over the murder scene of Nigel Baines' house?'

'My presence at Baines was a part of my duty; my DNA is explained by the fact that I was chasing the killer when I slipped in Baines' blood.' Dave's grin widened. 'As for the woman, I never actually harmed her.'

'You think you know all the answers don't you? What has your organisation done with Miss Weston?'

Looking blank, Dave shrugged his shoulders. 'What organisation? Has something happened to the ghost girl?'

Graham waited several seconds before asking, 'Don't you care about anything?'

'Oh yes!' Dave's eye sparkled with enthusiasm. 'I believe in loyalty to my name. I believe in our oath, our past and our destiny. I believe in silence.'

Again Graham Browne remained silent, hoping to provoke Dave into further rash speech. Dave, though, had control of his emotions once more, and was quite happy to play the waiting game. After five minutes, his Sergeant, Paul Masters, was getting restless and looked cautiously at his superior. The Chief Inspector was a patient man, but even his endurance had its limits.

'You'll be charged with attempted murder, and bail will be refused. If you believe in God, I suggest you start praying. It'd take a miracle to save you from prison.'

Dave only grinned. 'I believe in miracles!'

'Well I don't!' Graham's lip curled. 'Take him back to his cell, Paul. Maybe some quiet reflection will bring him to his senses!'

Inside The Secret Chamber

When Jenny Weston regained consciousness, she was soaking wet, lying on her stomach, on a cold, hard stone floor, with a blanket thrown over her. Managing to raise herself, Jenny found that she had miraculously not broken any bones. Finally getting to her feet, it took several minutes for Jenny to overcome dizziness from a knock to the head.

There was no natural light; the only illumination came from a burning wall torch and there was a pool of water with a waterfall coming out of the wall. Opposite her was the four poster bed that had appeared in her dream. Just seeing the bed was enough to cause butterflies of excitement to flutter in her stomach.

There was a large wardrobe, which contained an assortment of male and female attire from the 1600's. There was a doorway that led to a bathroom that was quite modern for its day. Back in the main room, the only other pieces of furniture were an exquisite desk with elaborately carved drawers, and a bookcase full of books and nick knacks. In front of the desk, on the floor, sat the skeleton of Sir Rupert Steele; his hand still lying upon the hilt of his sword as he remained on guard.

Respectfully, Jenny dropped to her knees in front of the skeleton. After 390 years there was only the bare skeleton and his clothing. 'I'm Jenny Weston. I must thank you, Sir Rupert for pulling me out of the water.' She paused, feeling no presence in the room of the dead soldier, although she knew that he couldn't be far away.

'King James the First of England, and the Sixth of Scotland, asked me to help in releasing you from your guard duty. He gave me the password of your sister's name, Isadore. There is much you need to know about what happened when you came down here.' Again she hesitated in a hope that Sir Rupert would appear.

When she got no reply, Jenny could only continue to talk to the skeleton. 'When King James asked you in 1625 to guard his Bible, he was suffering from a severe illness called Porphyria. Upon the day you came down here, King James fell ill with a fever; he collapsed in convulsions and ended up having a stroke. He died 22 days later, completely mad, and impossible to understand.'

Finding her legs going to sleep, Jenny pulled them from under her and sat down with her legs stretched out in front of her. 'Once you've handed the Bible over to the King, there'll be no reason for either of you to remain earthbound.' Jenny passed a hand over her forehead as her temples continued to throb. 'I'm sorry, but my head hurts, and I'm feeling quite cold. If you'll excuse me, I'll lie down for a little while.'

Rising painfully to her feet, she headed for the bed, and lifted cautiously the huge doona by a corner to check that rodents or insects didn't infest the bedding. Throwing back the blanket, Jenny glanced at the skeleton. 'I hope you're not the prudish type, Sir Rupert. I need to remove my wet clothes to get warm.' Despite her warning, she kept her back to the skeleton as she stripped out of her attire before slipping under the bed cover. Silently, the clothes on the floor rose up off the ground and travelled across the room to lie over the back of the chair.

Sir Rupert Steele

After a couple of hours of deep, restful sleep, Jenny had warmed up considerably, and thrown off the doona. She lay upon her stomach, which allowed the cool air to dance across her bare back. The gentle breeze became a little colder as fingers of ice trailed lightly across her skin. As the coolness moved down her right arm, she rolled over so that the ice-cold fingers slid accidentally across her naked breast. The fingers flew away from her skin as if they had been burnt. As Jenny didn't stir or waken, the temptation was too great to resist and the icy touch returned to caress against the supple softness of her skin.

The coolness caused Jenny to finally stir, and as she opened her eyes, although she couldn't see him, she could feel his presence. 'Sir Rupert?' Her voice was slurred in sleep. The hand vanished from her skin as she felt the ghost about to disappear. 'No, don't go! Your reaction is completely understandable.' Self-consciously she drew the doona back over her naked form. 'If I had been alone for over 390 years, I'd want to know what it was like to touch another human being. Please show yourself.' Jenny waited, until a faint outline of the Knight began to emerge. She sat up in bed.

'Fair lady, it was not mine intent to intrude upon thine slumber. It is true what thee said, that the temptation was great. It does not though; excuse the liberties which I have taken. Thou art solid to my touch, and yet should I not pass through thee?'

The closer Sir Rupert came to the bed, the more solid his form became. His tall crowned hat was sitting on the desk, so the ghost's head was bare to reveal shoulder length jet-black hair tied back with a ribbon. He was attired as expected for the period, with gathered breeches to the knee, a fitted doublet tunic with wide collar; deep cuffs and lace edged gauntlets were also on the desk.

He wore knee high boots but appeared to be free of the ornaments of lace, ribbons, rosettes and frilly garters that the highly fashionable wore back then. Sir Rupert was a soldier, and although he needed to be presentable to be in King James' court, he didn't see any need to be decked out like a fop. His eyes were as dark as depicted in her dream, and he was indeed handsome.

'In normal situations you would be able to pass through me, but I'm not normal.' Considering her words carefully, Jenny explained about her work as a Spirit Healer. During the explanation, Sir Rupert sat down on the bed beside her. He picked up one of her hands and placed his palm against hers, before entwining his fingers through hers.

'It is difficult to believe, I can almost feel mine own heart beat again.' Slightly embarrassed, Sir Rupert disentangled their hands and laid hers back down on top of the doona. Jenny couldn't help smiling.

'It's a side effect to sharing energy. It is usually not so perceptive to the Spirit.'

Jenny stirred restlessly, and glanced briefly towards the bathroom, and she wondered how to voice her need. Modesty prevented her from just getting up. As if following her chain of thought, Sir Rupert got up off the bed and went across to the wardrobe. He removed a turquoise embroidered silk dressing gown and brought it across to lie on the bed.

'I won't intrude upon thy privacy!' With a small bow Sir Rupert vanished. Jenny was touched by this show of gallantry, slipping into the luxurious robe before getting out of bed to answer her pressing need.

The First Supplies

Returning to the main chamber, she found Sir Rupert kneeling down at the pool's edge. Hearing her approach, he looked around and held up an apple. 'It would appear as if someone above is trying to send thee a message.'

Jenny took the apple and bit into it. 'It seems as if Carmen is on the right track. I wish I could get a message to her.' Thoughtfully she took another bite of the apple.

'It is possible, my lady, this pool returns to the pond above. A man's body came here the way thee did, but when I attempted to drag him out, he was already deceased. Leaving him in the water meant that he would be dragged back to the surface. This did occur?'

Jenny nodded. Another apple came down the waterfall, soon to be followed by another. These Sir Rupert scooped out of the water. Ten minutes later more than a dozen apples dropped down. These too were scooped out and placed into a bowl that Jenny found on a shelf of the bookcase.

'Well I'm not going to starve while I'm here.' Seeing a look of pain cross Sir Rupert's face, Jenny immediately apologised, 'I'm so sorry, Sir Rupert, it must have been a shocking way to die, not knowing what was going on above you, and no one knowing you were here. I meant no disrespect to you.'

'I know thee meant no harm, for a moment it was just a painful memory, for how long have I been down here?' A smile dispersed his grave look.

Jenny didn't immediately answer as she did the mathematics in her head. 'Over 390 years. That's a long time to be alone.'

Sir Rupert nodded towards the bookcase. 'I spent a lot of time reading and while the paper lasted, writing.'

I Should Get Dressed

Chomping upon her apple, Jenny caught the scrutinising glance that the Knight cast her. The silk robe did little to conceal her voluptuous figure. 'Perhaps I should get dressed.' Colour flushed across her cheeks as she moved across to where her dress lay over the chair. Touching it, she found that it was still wet. Sighing, Jenny looked across to the wardrobe.

'Not on mine account!' The Knight's eyes twinkled wickedly.

Turning suddenly, Jenny stared at him in disbelief. 'You men don't ever change! That's the sort of remark I'd expect from a male of my time!' Sir Rupert grinned, which caused Jenny to frown deep in thought. 'No, come to think of it, it is something a male of any century could say! Come and tell me what I'll be wearing.'

There was a great deal of laughter and amusement as Sir Rupert instructed Jenny in the various pieces of ladies apparel. For a brief moment, she was surprised at how knowledgeable he was about feminine under garments, but considering his handsome countenance, his impressive physic and his favoured position in King James' court, would have meant that he could have had any woman he wanted. Having laid out an assortment of garments upon the bed, Sir Rupert surprised her again by vanishing.

Slipping out of the robe, Jenny picked up the knee length bloomers and pulled them on. Next she held the corset against herself, but the tight restrictive nature of the garment would cause too much pain to her already damaged back. The dress of brocade, she slipped into, was an incredible weight. The skirt fell to the ground with pleats from the waist. There should have been padded hip rolls to spread out the skirts more, but these Jenny also omitted. The bodice of the dress was extremely tight, with long sleeves that ended in lace edged cuffs, and a pearl trim down the front. There was no Elizabethan ruff around the neck, but a rather large collar laced at the edges.

There were laces to be tightened at the back, and as Jenny struggled to do them up, Sir Rupert reappeared. Gently he eased the laces tighter until she could barely breathe. He tied off the laces before turning Jenny around. Tenderly, Sir Rupert ran his fingers through her loose curls.

'Except for thy hair, thee look perfect.' His glance travelled down her briefly, 'Well almost,' His fingers hesitated at the neckline of her bodice. 'Thou art displaying a little more bosom than would be allowed. If I may be so bold as to rearrange thee?' Blushing, Jenny nodded and Sir Rupert adjusted the bodice to cover a little more of Jenny's curvaceous cleavage. He took a step back to survey the results.

'Better.'

'But not perfect?'

Sir Rupert shook his head, 'Thee have more fill than the woman for which this was made.'

Amused, Jenny asked, 'Do you mean I'm fat?'

He hastened to reassure, 'Nay! Without the restrictive corset thou art more real, more natural. There is little joy in bedding a half starved stick, I can assure thee!'

'I see!' Jenny tried hard not to laugh.

Realising what he had said Sir Rupert quickly apologised. 'I didn't mean... I wasn't implying that it was mine intention... I meant no disrespect.'

Jenny eased the tension by laughing. 'Don't worry Sir Rupert; I'm sure there'll be several faux pas as this is your first day of having someone to talk to in a long time.'

Putting the corset back into the wardrobe, Jenny made the bed before attempting to sit down upon it. *With so much material in the skirt, that is easier said than done. I had thought I'd had enough problems with the ball gown I'd worn to meet the King.* It was finally achieved with a great deal of laughter and some assistance from

Sir Rupert. Once she was settled, he sat down on the bed beside her.

What Is Thy Mission?

'Will thee tell me about thy mission? Thine injuries that thou has sustained are recent and of a serious nature. Are they related to thy quest?'

Jenny told him about her search for the secret door. She detailed the various attempts upon her life, as well as the people who had been her staunch supporters.

Sir Rupert looked amazed. 'What is it about this book that brings people to violence?'

'Money is a big motivation. The actual Bible belonging to the King who initiated the conception of the first bible to be translated into English would be worth millions. Also if there was a list of people who were working against the King, their descendants would be branded as traitors. Not that I see the relevance of that after 300 years.'

Nodding, Sir Rupert added, 'His Highness spoke to me about fearing he was surrounded by enemies. His son, Prince Charles and the Duke of Buckingham were believed to be plotting against the King. It is quite possible that there could be a list of people the King suspected.'

Looking around the room, Jenny pondered, 'Where did the King put the Bible?'

Sir Rupert shrugged. 'I have no knowledge of its whereabouts. I wasn't present when it was hidden. Is it important?'

It was Jenny's turn to shrug. 'Not exactly, but it would speed up the process of you completing your duty so that you can cross over, if we had the book at hand when the door is finally opened by King James.'

'Doeth thou consider it possible that the door will still be found from above?' His eyes scanned the room.

This Jenny had no doubts about, 'Of course! Carmen is a very competent girl. She'll be doing everything she can to find me.'

'Should we attempt to open the door from our side?'

Jenny shook her head. 'No, the Palace was reduced to rubble and if we opened the door from here, we could end up buried by the layers of dirt that covered it. Besides I have a feeling that it can only be opened from the outside.'

The Search For The Book Begins

Sliding off the bed, Sir Rupert held out his hand to Jenny. 'Shall we begin our search for the King's Bible?'

Taking his hand, she joined him on her feet. 'If you'll start with the shelves, I'll try the desk.' When Jenny tried to move towards the desk, Sir Rupert refused to release her hand.

'I'm very glad thou art here Jennifer Weston. Very glad indeed.'

Surprising herself, Jenny found herself blushing. 'I'm glad too, Sir Rupert. More than perhaps you can imagine.'

'I think I can imagine!' He raised her hand to his lips, his eyes locked with hers. 'In all mine life I had never met a woman that I had wanted to wake up every morning with. I understand why now, because it would be centuries before she would even be born.'

Jenny's breath caught in a gasp. 'Are you trying to flirt with me, Sir Rupert?' she demanded.

'I speak only the truth.' He smiled as he released her hand.

Jenny still looked doubtful. 'Perhaps, but maybe you only feel that way as I am the first living person you have seen in a very long time.'

'Time will tell, Jennifer.' Slowly he shook his head. 'Thee was sent for a reason and it is not just about a book.'

Jenny hesitated, *as I too feel that this mission has become more than a search for an ancient tome. It has become personal with that waking dream, with the need to find my soul mate.* Finding no argument to use, she turned her attention to the elaborate desk, as Sir Rupert searched the bookshelves, giving her the opportunity to think.

A *Progress Report*

Entering the restaurant at teatime, Doctor Shepherd found it completely full. Carmen was assisting Olivia at waiting on tables, while Cheryl was in charge of the kitchen as Penny was still at home with Lucas. Having tea was Kevin and the Chief Inspector Graham Browne and Kevin indicated that the Doctor should join them.

'How are your investigations going Doc?' Kevin offered a cup of tea, which Shepherd gratefully accepted.

'I've put the word out. Contacts with contacts will see how much they can achieve. I told them how urgent this is.'

Graham Browne glanced from the Doctor to Kevin. 'Is this legal, Kevin? Nothing underhanded?'

Kevin grinned. 'Doctor Shepherd has friends who may be able to persuade the Council to change their minds about digging up the ruins; legal and honest friends, who just happen to also be influential.'

Graham laughed, 'All right. I won't ask any more questions.'

Finding a minute to herself, Carmen came across to the table, her eyes resting anxiously upon the Doctor. 'I know it's too soon for news, but has anything happened?'

Shepherd took one of her hands and patted it reassuringly. 'I've contacted as many worthy brothers that I thought would have higher contacts. Bugsy, too, will do what he can in his own circle of colleagues. You just have to be patient, little one.'

'I know Doc,' Carmen managed to smile. 'Oops, gotta go, table six is ready to pay their bill.' She hurried away to her duty.

Finishing his tea, the Doctor was about to rise when Graham Browne asked, 'Bugsy?'

'Sir Edward Dent, specialist in code breaking.' The Doctor's aging eyes twinkled.

Kevin sat up straighter, but didn't stop Doctor Shepherd from leaving. Quietly to the Chief Inspector, Kevin said, 'Sir Edward Dent is known to be a regular guest at parties held by the Rich, Famous and the Aristocracy. We're talking high circles.'

'We're also talking about delicate toes. Tread carefully, my boy.' Slowly Graham nodded.

Scratching his head thoughtfully, Kevin said, 'Always do Sir.'

About Dave

As if an omen, Kevin's mobile phone rang. 'Yes?' His face went completely blank as he listened. When he said, 'Thank you, I'll let him know.' The words were barely audible. Hanging up it took Kevin a minute to control himself before he could speak, 'Dave Hedley has just been found dead in his cell. Half an hour ago he received a visit alone with his lawyer.'

'Damn!' Graham slapped his thigh in anger. 'So he'll remain silent now!' Pulling out his wallet, Kevin paid for the tea as Graham rose and added, 'I'd better get back to the station. Are you coming Kevin?' At that moment though, Lisa McGraw entered the restaurant and came towards them.

'Eh, no Sir, I'll catch up with you later,' stated Kevin.

Graham took one look at the young Constable and chuckled. 'Good luck Kevin.'

Inspector Harris ignored his superior's joke, as Lisa was looking considerably troubled. She wished Graham a 'Good Afternoon,' as he left and missed the twinkle in his eyes. She slid onto the seat beside Kevin. 'Have you heard?' Her voice was barely a whisper.

'About Dave? Yes I just heard. I know you worked closely with Dave, are you all right?' Kevin reached out to lay his hand over hers.

'We were never the best of friends. I'm sorry he committed suicide though, it's the coward's way out of facing justice.'

Kevin didn't agree. 'You haven't been paying attention to Jenny Weston. Dave will be facing the ultimate judge. He will be punished.'

'I certainly hope so.' Slightly embarrassed, Lisa cleared her throat. 'I was going to check on Sergeant Greenaway and I wondered if you wanted to come with me?'

'I want to ask Lucas if he can remember anything about the attack.'

Talk Of The Village

As they stood up Lisa was looking worried again. 'You're not going to interrogate him or harass him are you?' She knew she was on thin ice, speaking like that to a superior officer.

'What a low opinion you have of me!' Kevin looked hurt by her accusation.

Lisa protested that she had meant no disrespect, as they stepped out of the restaurant. She was about to go into major grovelling, when Kevin started laughing. So indignant at being teased, Lisa turned to walk away from him. Not prepared to allow her to storm off, Kevin grasped Lisa around the waist and turned her around to face him.

'Now then Miss Flounce, you must know I was joking.'

'I'm just not used to these professional/personal changes that can take place in an instant.' Taking advantage of Lisa's closeness, he kissed her.

'Do you want to make us the talk of the village?' She protested.

Glancing around at the curious looks that they were receiving brought a rueful grin to Kevin's face as he released her. 'Bit late for that, I think!'

'I should've listened to my mother.' Lisa blushed even more as she realised that people were staring at them. Impatiently she tugged on Kevin's arm to get him to start walking again.

'And what did she say?'

'Never get involved with a colleague!'

Shaking his head, Kevin smiled at her. 'Then we're just going to have to prove your mother wrong!'

There was no arguing with him, and to be honest, Lisa didn't want to try. *We'll have to face the music like any other office romance. I'm a little frightened and yet excited too.*

Kathleen's Guidance

When the restaurant had quietened down a little, Carmen walked down to Kathleen May's cottage. Kathleen made a pot of tea and would have left her with Evelyn, except that Carmen asked her to join them and offer her wisdom and advice. They all agreed that Kevin's experiment was a good indication that Jenny could still be alive. Lucas knew the area where Jenny had decided was the best place to dig, but they were hampered by the Council's refusal to let them excavate.

'Doctor Shepherd urges me to be patient, but there must be something I can do Granny May, and is there nothing that the Craft can do to aid us?'

They allowed a silence to descend to allow Kathleen the opportunity to think. 'You can keep your Mentor alive. A bag of apples won't last her long. Send more food through the pond, fruit and cooked food that don't require reheating. It might also be possible to get a message to Jenny, and for her to reply.'

'The old message in the bottle huh?' Evelyn couldn't help smiling. 'The only problem is that the Council has closed Cedars Park to all visitors. They've even put security guards on to keep people away.'

Carmen shook her head. 'No, the police will be able to overrule any security. I'll have a word with Lisa and the Inspector. They believe in what we're doing.'

She jumped to her feet. 'I've got some food shopping to do. Is there anything else we need to consider?'

Kathleen finally voiced their greatest fear. 'It may be prudent to realise that you don't know for certain that Jenny is alive.' She quickly continued before Carmen could protest, 'I know you have your convictions, and we all want to believe that it is true, but you must prepare yourself for disagreeable news.' The older woman was surprised when Carmen didn't argue with her.

'I am prepared for the worst, Gran. In the back of my mind I accept that death is a possibility. At the moment, though, I want to focus on the belief that Jenny is alive, and we can save her. Only when we have tried everything, then I'll accept the worst.'

'Bravo!' Evelyn surprised them by clapping.

Carmen looked at him suspiciously. 'Are you taking the Mickey?' She demanded.

'Far from it, I'm very proud of you. None of us want to throw doubt on your theory, but we don't want to see you absolutely crushed if anything goes wrong.'

'With such faith, we can't fail!' Carmen kissed him passionately. 'Is there anything I can get you from the shops?'

Kathleen shook her head, but Evelyn said, 'Some bananas would be nice. I feel like a banana smoothie.'

To this Kathleen added, 'If that's the case, we'll need more milk.' Lovingly she ruffled her grandson's hair.

'It's good for mending bones, Gran!' Carmen left them to amicably bicker, as she headed for the Supermarket before it closed.

Lucas' Visitors

Penny had gone upstairs to make sure her husband was up to seeing visitors, before she allowed Lisa and Kevin to come in. Lucas, sitting up in bed, still had a bandage wrapped around his head, but some of the colour had returned to his cheeks. Lisa wasn't at all happy to see the dark rings under her Boss' eyes or how tired he looked. She whispered urgently to Kevin that they must not stay too long or upset the Sergeant.

'Again with the aspersions? What do I have to do to improve my image with you?'

Although this time Lisa knew Kevin was only teasing, she was embarrassed that Lucas would have heard them and was greatly amused.

'Penny and I used to have little disagreements like that when we first went out. Must be the big, heavy handed copper image that one gets as a teenager, that makes them think we still interrogate using cattle prods and thumbscrews. I expected better of you Mac, you've been in the job long enough.'

Lisa's embarrassment increased. 'I didn't! That is to say… But that's not why we're here.' Lisa tried valiantly to get the conversation back on the right track.

'Nor to tell me that you two are an item?' Lucas' eyes gleamed with mischief.

They looked at Lucas stunned, which caused him to throw his head back and laugh. Something he wished he hadn't done as his head hurt doing so. 'You can't honestly expect to get away with smooching in public without it becoming common knowledge within seconds! Word gets around pretty quick in a village; you should know that by now.'

'This is not the way I wanted Mother finding out! Besides which nothing is going on!' Sinking onto the edge of the bed, Lisa groaned in disbelief.

'Yet!' Kevin added mischievously.

Lisa cast him a speaking glance, but Lucas changed the subject. 'I know why you're here, and to be honest with you, I don't know.' He went through what had happened at the pond's edge once more. Lisa wasn't at all surprised at Lucas' next question. 'Is there any news about Jenny?'

She looked to Kevin to answer. He explained Carmen's theory, seeking help from Doctor Shepherd and his own experiment with the apples.

'An entrance through the water huh? It gives us something to cling to anyway.' Lucas reached out and touched Lisa's arm. 'Keep me informed no matter what the news.'

Lisa nodded. 'Of course Boss.'

Dean's Anguish

All three jumped, a little startled as an angry cry of 'Greenaway!' came from outside. In that yell Lisa recognised Dean Schofields' voice, and rose quickly.

'Don't worry, I'll deal with this,' she said.

Lucas didn't argue, as Lisa and Kevin trotted down the stairs to confront the, beside himself with rage, ex-lover. Dean tried to force his way into the house, but Lisa firmly shut them out as she took a hard grip upon Dean's arm. They could smell the alcohol radiating from his pores.

'You can't blame the Sergeant for what happened, and making a scene will only get you arrested. You don't want that, now do you?'

Collapsing onto the kerb, Dean began to sob. Seeing that they would soon have a worse scene, Lisa slapped Dean once across the face. He caught his breath, remained silent for several minutes as he pulled himself together.

'You were supposed to look after her!' There was a note of hysteria still.

'Not another word now until you're in control.' When he opened his mouth, she held up a warning finger. 'No! Not a word!'

Kevin had to bite his lip to stop himself from laughing at Lisa's stern school teacher manner. 'Do you think he's on the level?' He asked quietly.

Lisa nodded. 'If he's acting, then it's a world class performance. I still picked him as the Boss. I don't know now.'

Dean showed that he had acute hearing, 'The Boss? Why would I want to hurt Jenny?'

Lisa wasn't disturbed by his rising anger. 'The Boss wants to find the Bible, but harming Jenny wasn't part of the plan. She was getting too close to the secret room, so the best thing to do was get her out of the way, which would also be a way of protecting her from the organisation. You wouldn't have Jenny stashed away for safe keeping?'

'I'd never harm Jenny!'

Kevin wondered why Dean was being such a blockhead. 'We're not accusing you of harming Jenny, but of hiding her away for protection.'

Dean looked like he wanted to pull his hair out. 'I wouldn't be here screaming my head off if I had her somewhere safe! Now would I?' Lisa didn't immediately answer. 'Well would I?' Dean demanded.

Kevin scratched his chin thoughtfully. 'Good performance if it is one. Most men aren't capable of bursting into tears without a very good reason. Don't kill me, but it is something women do better.'

'Stop talking about me as if I wasn't here. Why would I want this bloody book?'

Lisa looked at him in surprise. 'That book is worth millions!'

Laughing harshly, Dean had to wipe the tears from his eyes. 'Do you know how many millions I make every year? Does that clear me of kidnapping Jenny?'

Kevin shook his head. 'No. Give us time we'll think of something else. Don't go harassing Sergeant Greenaway, or we will nick you. Now how about you move along?'

Dean reluctantly got to his feet and allowed himself to be led back to the village square, where a diplomatic Kevin bought him a cup of coffee, actually several cups of strong coffee to try and sober him up.

Moonlight Deliveries

It was through Lisa that Carmen finally got hold of Kevin as night was beginning to fall. They met in the pub and her plan was quickly explained. He supported the idea, but it was the underhanded manner, in which it was to be undertaken, which bothered him. It didn't take much persuasion from Carmen to get Kevin and Lisa to go with her to the palace ruins as soon as it was dark.

They didn't park in the car park, but a little along the road, and they each carried a fully laden shopping bag. They spotted the Security Guard standing quite visibly in the middle of the park, they didn't attempt to hide or run when the security guard eventually spotted them. They waited for him to run across to them; waving a torch and yelling, 'Stop!'

John Anderson, the security guard was no more than 19, and his attempts to appear threatening were indeed laughable. 'The Park's closed. You'll have to leave.'

Both Lisa and Kevin pulled out their identification cards for the guard to flash his torch over.

'Sorry Inspector, but I have my orders not to let anyone enter.'

Kevin took command as per Carmen's plan. 'We have no intentions of damaging anything in the Park. I suppose you've heard about my experiment today?'

'The apples?' John laughed, 'What a stroke of genius! So you really think Miss Weston is alive under our very feet?'

'We do, but she won't be for long if we can't get food to her. To do that, we have to get to the pond.'

John took the shopping bags from Lisa and Carmen. 'You won't cost me my job will you Inspector Harris?'

Smiling, Kevin shook his head as they all continued towards the water's edge. 'This will be our secret.'

Finding the right spot, they tied a knot with the plastic bag handles so that they were almost completely airtight. Kevin removed a banana from one bag before it was tied and used it to correctly gauge the best spot to have the bags placed in the water. They waited until each bag was sucked under before turning to walk back towards their car.

'You'll be leaving now then Sir?' The young guard asked nervously.

Kevin reassured him upon this point. 'Do you want to make yourself more useful?'

'Of course!' John's eyes lit up in delight; his duty so far that evening had been pretty dead quiet, no pun intended.

'Amongst the food is a sealed bottle with note paper and a pen inside. If you see anything pop up in the pond, even if it only a banana skin, haul it out and give me a call.' Kevin handed the guard one of his business cards.

'I'll keep my eyes peeled Sir!' The lad slipped it into his pocket.

Kevin patted him on the shoulder. 'Good man!' John saw them off the park before returning to his patrol of the ruins.

The Desk

Sitting down at the desk, with a little awkwardness due to her bulky dress, Jenny began to work methodically through the drawers. The top right hand drawer was mainly full of odds and ends. Sir Rupert started at the bottom of the bookshelves, pulling out each book to flick through it before putting it back and pulling out another. In the second drawer, Jenny found loose paper that turned out to belong to Sir Rupert. Being private notes Jenny didn't look too closely at them but continued to the bottom drawer. This she found to be locked.

'I suppose it means it's the drawer I want,' she mused aloud.

'There should be keys in the top drawer.' Chuckling, Sir Rupert came across to join her. 'If not we can break it open.'

Looking up horrified, Jenny could only stare at him, 'Absolutely not! This desk is an antique!'

Opening the top drawer again, they hunted through the odds and ends in search for a key. Not surprisingly their search came up empty.

Shutting the drawer again, Jenny tried to remember all the mystery books she had read. *If the key is here at all, it will be hidden.* Running her hand under the desk, she found nothing, so Jenny opened the second drawer again to feel the inside. This too proved to be empty on the underside. Not to be beaten, Jenny felt under the first drawer, this too proved futile.

'I wonder if King James had it on him?'

'We could tear this room apart, but we have yet only begun to search.' Surprising Jenny, Sir Rupert dropped to one knee beside her and ran his hand under her seat. With a satisfied grin, he raised his hand with a key between his fingers.

'Would this perhaps be what mine lady is seeking?'

Laughing, Jenny placed both hands on either side of Sir Rupert's face and kissed him upon the lips.

'You're amazing!' Realising what she had done, she blushed as she released him. 'Oh Sir Rupert, I'm…'

He interrupted her, 'If thou art about to apologise, please don't. I regret it not.'

Tenderly he caressed his finger down Jenny's cheek. Sighing she closed her eyes and was prepared to give in to the pleasure that came from a simple touch. Without another thought, Jenny slipped naturally into Sir Rupert's embrace, and placed her hands upon his shoulders. He lowered his head until their lips met in a kiss so soft, so gentle, that it felt almost unreal. It was necessary for a second kiss but it was the third kiss though that unleased their pent up desires.

Picking Jenny up, Sir Rupert sat her upon the desk and pressed her hard against him. This time when their lips met, there was no holding back on their need for each other. She laced her fingers through his hair, determined to get as close as they possibly could. Jenny threw her head back as Sir Rupert trailed kisses down her throat and she purred like a contented kitten. Her fingers tightened around his shoulders as despite her full skirt, she managed to wrap her legs around his hips.

'To think that I have waited this long for this much pleasure!' Sir Rupert was ready to tear the dress off her very back, when Jenny suddenly pushed against his shoulders.

'No! We mustn't, not like this. It can't just be a convenience after a long time of being alone.'

A true gentleman, Sir Rupert immediately released her. 'I am sorry that is the impression I gave thee. I meant no disrespect. I had thought that there was something deeper between us. If I have moved too fast for thee, then I apologise. I only wished to show thee how much I love thee.'

In disbelief, she shook her head. 'How can you know that you love me? We've only just met. The attraction between us is great, but is that actually love?'

'I had no doubts the moment I first saw thee.' His eyes were filled with tenderness. 'It wasn't the need felt due to loneliness, but the fact that I had at last found the woman of my dreams. If thee don't feel the same, then I'll understand.'

She laughed. 'I thought I was being ridiculous, feeling that at last I had found my soul mate. I didn't want to appear too fast or easy. I don't jump into the arms of every man I meet.'

Sir Rupert couldn't help chuckling. 'I'm afraid that at that particular moment I wasn't thinking at all. I can wait until thou art ready.'

Delighted at such chivalry, Jenny kissed him briefly. 'Perhaps we should continue looking for the King's Bible. Keep our minds and bodies busy so that we've not got time on our hands to give in to temptation.'

'Better try the bottom drawer.' Sir Rupert held up the key. Jenny reached for it, but as their finger touched, they found it difficult to draw apart.

'This is incredible! I've never felt this burning need with anyone!' Slowly exhaling Jenny took the key and opened the bottom drawer. Squatting down they worked through the papers within.

Most of them were a rough copy of the Daemonologie which the King had written in 1597, as well as some of the psalms he had been trying to revise himself for the King James Bible. "The Daemonologie" or to give the book it's full title "Daemonologie In Forme of A Dialogie"; was written by King James in support and approval of Witch Hunting. *I wonder if all those years ago my own gifts would have labelled me as a witch and therefore been persecuted?* mused Jenny There was though, no book itself, but this didn't dishearten her completely.

'Thou art displeased with thy search?' His concern caused Jenny to smile softly.

'We have yet begun to search Sir Rupert. I'm sure there are several hidden nooks or secret cupboards yet to be discovered.'

With a little help from Sir Rupert, Jenny pulled the desk out to check behind it. Finding nothing, they moved the desk back.

The Bookcase

He returned to searching the shelves as she did a thorough search of the bathroom. Returning to the main chamber, Jenny found Sir Rupert attempting to reach up unsuccessfully to the top shelf of the bookcase. Glancing from the chair to Sir Rupert's muscular physic, Jenny thought, *I'd rather rely upon Sir Rupert's strength than a nearly 400 year old chair.*

'Think you can hold me up long enough to check the top shelf?'

Sir Rupert replied without hesitation, 'Of course!'

Taking hold of the top shelf and placing one foot upon the second bottom shelf, Jenny heaved herself up with Sir Rupert's assistance. With his hands about her waist, she was virtually seated upon his shoulder for support.

It didn't take her long to sort through the books, and from her position, she could see a box pushed back on the very top of the bookshelf. It was just out of her reach. 'How are you doing Sir Rupert? I want to go up another shelf.'

He tightened his grasp around her waist. 'Up thee go then! Thou art not a weight at all!' Effortlessly he lifted Jenny up so that her feet rested on the next shelf up. This extra height made it possible for her to grasp hold of the box. It was quite a large wooden box, about 24 by 18 inches. There was, though, no way Jenny could climb down the shelves and carry the box as well, so it was necessary for Sir Rupert to lift her straight down.

With her feet on the ground, he took the box from her and carried it across to the desk. It had quite an elaborate lid, with intricate carvings and no obvious locking device, but it was locked. When Sir Rupert laid his hands over the box several of the intricate symbols carved onto the box began to glow and emit a strange heat. Removing his hands, the glow subsided and any attempt by Sir Rupert to slide his hand into the box was also hindered.

'This has to be it!' There was a smile on Jenny's lips as she looked up at Sir Rupert. 'Now all we have to do is find out how to open it.'

He looked the box over closely before returning her smile. 'Well, I'm not going anywhere.'

News From Above

At that moment four plastic bags full of food came hurtling down the waterfall and interrupted them. Sir Rupert reached in to drag them out and Jenny knelt down beside him to open them up. She sent a silent prayer of thanks to her benefactors above ground as she looked at the wide assortment of fruit, packaged foods that didn't require cooking, as well as a glass water bottle, that contained not water, but paper and pen. Releasing the stopper on the bottle, the pen fell out, but the paper took some manipulating to extract it.

While Jenny was struggling with this, Sir Rupert noted that they had also sent down a decent sized kitchen knife and a few toiletries. Jenny gave a triumphant cry as she drew the paper out of the bottle, and eagerly unrolled it. There were five pages, four were blank, and the top one held a brief message from Carmen.

'Dear Jenny, We're working on a plan to get you out, but the Council won't let us dig up the ruins. Have a plan for that too, but it may take several days. Don't panic, we are on top of everything. Lucas is all right, only concussion. Try and see if you can get a message back to us. We will see you soon! Carmen.'

Relief flooded through Jenny as she read aloud the message. *They haven't given me up for dead.* Sir Rupert looked thoughtful as she rolled the letter up again. 'Doeth thou think this Council will create difficulties?'

'Not if I know Carmen! She'll find a way.' In contrast to his solemness Jenny appeared quite cheerful. 'Now where to put all this food?' The desk was quite covered by the carved box, and the shelves were full. 'Bathroom?' She suggested, and when he nodded, they carried the bags into the other room and placed them for the time being in the empty bath.

Returning to the main chamber, Sir Rupert asked, 'Shall thee attempt to send a reply to thy protégé?'

Jenny nodded, picking up one blank sheet of paper and the pen. 'Something simple I think,' she absently chewed on the lid of the Biro before writing.

'Dear Carmen, all is well, food much appreciated. Look forward to seeing you soon. Jenny.'

Allowing Sir Rupert to read it, she asked. 'What do you think?'

'Ingenious!' He was more interested in the pen. 'The ink is actually inside the quill!'

Jenny rolled up her note, stuck it into the water bottle, and put the stopper back in. She threw the bottle into the pool and when it didn't reappear, she was satisfied.

Can I Actually Eat?

'Well then, I think we deserve something to eat. Come on, let's go and sort out what Carmen has sent us, and then we can take a look at that box.' They headed back into the bathroom, but Sir Rupert hesitated for a brief moment with a question.

'But can I …?'

Jenny smiled up at him reassuringly, 'Most definitely! You can eat. While we're together you'll be as close to being alive again as you'll ever get.'

This caused him to stop and think. 'Does that mean that I put a severe strain upon thy energy?'

Jenny looked surprised at him as she hadn't felt in the least drained by his presence. *In fact for the first time in years I feel full of life and energy.* 'Strangely enough, I don't think you are. That has never happened before, but I'm not knocking it. Don't worry. I'll let you know when I get tired.'

'Good!' A look of tenderness entered Sir Rupert's eyes. 'It would grieve me if I was the cause of any pain to thee.' Jenny wished that her cheeks were not glowing red hot and after muttering something unintelligible, they focused their attention on choosing something they wanted to eat before returning to the main room.

The Ornate Box

Sir Rupert ate very little, feeling no actual hunger for food, but he ensured that Jenny was sufficiently fed. They used one of the plastic bags as a rubbish bin, tidied up their feast before turning their attention to the locked box. She offered the chair to Sir Rupert, but like a true gentleman he declined, and when she had sat down at the desk, they looked more closely at the carved container. Running her fingers over the top of the lid, Jenny found that some of the images actually moved.

'If we arrange these icons in a particular way, we may just unlock it. What exactly are these pictures?'

Sir Rupert leant over the back of the chair to glance over Jenny's shoulder. There wasn't enough light to see the actual details, so he used the lit torch to light the other one over the table. With the extra illumination it was easier to make out the carvings.

Standing behind her chair, he was a little too close for her concentration. He didn't seem to be aware of the effect he was having on her.

'They're not pictures, but elaborate letters.' He stated. 'There is a space here so that the letters can be moved so that they could make a word.'

Absently Jenny nodded. 'Hum! The question is what sort of word or words would hold the most significant meaning to King James?'

'Let me think about that for a moment,' Sir Rupert thoughtfully stroked his chin. 'What letters do we have?'

Jenny picked up the pen and paper sent by Carmen, and together they worked out the letters 'A, A, B, C, C, E, F, I, I, I, I, P, and T.'

A	A	B	C	C	E	F	I
I	I	I	P	T			

Looking it over, Jenny shook her head. 'Well that's a lot of help! Is it even in English?'

'It could even be Latin.' Sir Rupert added, thoughtfully. 'I mean His Highness was translating the Psalms into English. So Latin must also be considered.'

Jenny covered her mouth to smother a yawn. 'Oh, excuse me! I suddenly feel very tired.' She yawned again. Sir Rupert lifted Jenny to her feet and guided her towards the bed.

'Thou shalt rest, or thou shalt not be of any use in solving this puzzle.' He threw the doona back and began to undo the laces at the back of her dress. She was glad to be able to breath more freely again. The dress had been quite constrictive.

As Sir Rupert drew the dress down off her shoulders, he couldn't resist pressing his lips against her bare skin. Purring, Jenny threw her head back as his lips travelled up her throat.

'Oh God! This could lead to dangerous grounds!'

Her words caused Sir Rupert to pause. 'I'm sorry I didn't mean to pressure thee.'

Jenny turned, as she allowed the dress to fall to the ground and wrapped he arms around his neck. 'It's not that, Sir Rupert. It's just that…' Her words faded away as she suddenly collapsed. He supported her, and eased her down on to the bed.

'It's just that thou art exhausted?'

'I'm sorry…' Jenny smiled weakly.

'Hush! Thee must sleep.' He laid a forefinger against her lips. 'We have plenty of time. I'll start work on the box.' Briefly, Sir Rupert touched his lips to her forehead. Laying the doona over her, he brushed his hand over her hair before stepping away from the bed. As sleep came to Jenny, he picked up her dress and hung it up in the wardrobe before he sat down at the desk. For a moment, he studied the pen. When his curiosity was satisfied, he turned his attention to the code.

TUESDAY

She's Alive!

The next morning Kevin and Lisa had just ordered tea in the restaurant, when John Anderson, the young security guard hurried in, all excited. He came across to their table and sat down without being asked.

'Just before I came off duty this morning, I checked the pond as you asked and I found this.' Triumphantly he handed a sealed water bottle with a piece of paper inside across to the Inspector who turned around and called out to Carmen to join them. As she hurried over, Kevin pulled out the stopper and removed the piece of paper. He handed it to Carmen unopened and she almost tore it apart and read it out aloud. Seeing Jenny's signature, Carmen surprised the entire Restaurant by screaming in delight.

'She's alive! There is a God! She's alive!'

Cheryl came running from the Saloon at Carmen's screams. 'What is it?' She grabbed hold of her daughter's arms as she danced merrily around the room.

'Jenny's alive, mum! We have the proof!' Carmen waved the piece of paper under her mother's nose. Kevin attempted to bring Carmen back to earth by reminding her that they still had to get Council approval before they could start digging. She waved aside this problem, feeling that the letter should be proof enough of Jenny's whereabouts.

Unfortunately for Carmen, when she presented the letter and the story of its discovery to the Broxbourne Council, they still refused to allow her to continue Jenny's work. They told her blankly that they thought Carmen had faked the whole thing and would not budge an inch, even when John, the security guard, backed up her story. Carmen left the Council Chambers fuming, even more determined to bring the Council to its knees.

Kathleen and Evelyn May were more impressed by Carmen's news. She went there straight after leaving the Council. Carmen could only stay a few moments before she needed to get back to the restaurant.

Reprimanding Tony

After the disastrous visit to the Council, Inspector Harris sat in his office, his feet on the desk, his head leaning back as he contemplated the ceiling, in particular the damp spot in one corner. To the casual observer, Kevin was day dreaming. In fact he was planning, organising the future events that they needed to initiate to ensure Jenny's safe return.

The other thing he was contemplating was what to do about Tony Gregg. *The Sergeant is a loose cannon ball, which is waiting to explode. I want to defuse the bomb, before it disembowelled us all.* Tony entered the office and dropped a file in front of the Inspector. He was about to leave again, but Kevin decided it was time to take the bull by the horns.

'Sit down Tony, and shut the door.' Grinning, despite himself, Tony sat down on a chair and leaning back on it, flicked the door so that it shut behind him. Kevin nodded his approval.

'Glad to see you haven't completely lost your sense of humour. You're going to need it in a minute.' Kevin cleared his throat before continuing, 'You've been like a bear with a sore head for days now.' He ripped the top sheet off a note pad on his desk, and handed it across to Tony. With considerable reluctance he took the list and read through it.

> *Does not like women*
> *Does not believe in supernatural*
> *Does not approve of Inspector's methods*
> *Not enough sex*
> ~~*Too much sex*~~
> *Not enough sleep*
> *Health concerns*
> *Family concerns*
> *Death wish/career suicide*
> *Relationship Problems*
> *PMT/Pregnant*

Taking a pen out of his breast pocket of his shirt, Tony made a few notes before handing it back to the Inspector.

> *Does not like women   They have their uses.*
> *Does not believe in supernatural.   Don't.*
> *Does not approve of Inspector's methods.   No comment.*
> *Not enough sex   Never enough.*
> ~~*Too much sex*~~
> *Not enough sleep No*
> *Health concerns No*
> *Family concerns No*
> *Death wish/career suicide   Is that a threat?*
> *Relationship problems What relationship?*
> *PMT/Pregnant   Huh?*
> *The problem is this ghost girl case is a waste of time!*

Glancing over his notes, Kevin nodded, before tearing up the paper and throwing it into the bin. 'You had only to say, Sergeant. There are plenty of other cases that need investigating. If that's all you have to deal with, then deal with it. You're a good cop; don't make it necessary for me to mark your record.'

Hastily Tony rose to his feet, he was glad to get out of a serious reprimand, but he did just have to ask one question. 'Gov. I've gotta know, why did you cross out too much sex?'

'Can you have too much of a good thing?' One of the Inspector's eyebrows rose as his eyes twinkled.

'You've got a point there Gov!' Tony laughed. With an amicable nod, he left the office in a much better mood than when he had entered.

Can We Have A Drink?

The Dog and Bone was as busy as always when Kevin wandered down to the pub that evening. It had already grown dark, but it was still easy enough for him to see Lisa standing outside the favourite drinking hole, reprimanding a couple of youths who had tried to purchase alcohol at the bar, being underage. Upon seeing the Inspector, the two lads stopped giving Lisa cheeky back chat and took themselves off in a hurry.

Watching them disappear, Kevin shook his head. 'There was a time we could've boxed their ears and given them a kick in the pants. Now we can't even swear at them!' Smiling, he took in the attractive outfit Lisa was wearing. She blushed under his appreciative gaze and self-consciously glanced around to see if there was anyone about.

'They're just full of mouth these kids, but usually don't mean any harm. We're lucky here.'

Kevin inclined his head to one side. 'Such faith and innocence is always refreshing.'

'Don't tease! If I didn't look on the bright side in this job, I'd probably crack up. Are you coming in?' She gestured towards the door but Kevin captured her hand in his.

'In a minute, I was wondering if you'd like to have a drink after the meeting? Just you and me?'

There was a pause before Lisa spoke, 'Are we talking a drink or a **Drink**?'

Kevin chuckled at the distinction of the one word. 'One drink in a pub, not this one, or even a cup of coffee in a café, we talk, I drop you off at your home, make sure you get in safely, and then I go off to my own home.' In a show of good will, he released the hand he had been holding.

'I'm sorry.' Lisa gave a nervous laugh. 'I just wanted to be crystal clear about your intentions. I'm new to all this.'

'That's all right. There's no hurry. Well, what about that drink, without strings?'

'Yes, I'd like that.'

'Come on, time for the meeting.' He offered Lisa his arm, and she readily took it.

Rescue Team Meet

Seated at a table in the pub, Lisa and Kevin found Evelyn and Carmen, heads bent close together as they talked intimately. Their hands were entwined and they shared the occasional kiss. They were oblivious to anyone around them. Kevin's face took on a look of weary boredom.

'Oh please! Will someone get these kids a room?' Lisa giggled as Evelyn poked his tongue out at the police officers.

'Jealousy is such an ugly emotion!' drawled Evelyn.

Attempting to smother a yawn, Kevin said, 'Well break it up, as we have plenty to get through.'

Leading the way through the pub, expecting them to follow, Kevin paused for a moment beside Doctor Shepherd. The Doctor had looked up anxiously as the Detectives approached, and had raised a hand in salutation.

'Anything wrong, Doc?'

The older man sighed. 'I have had verbal confirmation from several contacts, and letters, emails and phone calls should start arriving at the Council's Chambers tomorrow. Sorry that it's taking a while, Inspector.'

Kevin laid a hand on the Doctor's shoulder. 'No need to apologise. Now that we know for certain that Jenny is alive and well, we're less panic stricken.'

'I'm glad.' This time the Doctor smiled in relief. 'Do let me know if there is anything else I can do to assist at any time?' By this time, the others had caught up with Kevin who reassured the Doctor, and they headed into the conference room which seemed to have become their temporary war office.

The Boss Revealed

Tommy was perched on the top of the couch backrest. He had been waiting for Carmen. When the other members of the rescue team entered the room, Tommy began to fade away. The only one to show surprise was Kevin, who simply raised his eyebrows.

'Tommy, don't go on our account,' said Carmen. 'You're quite one of the family.' The ghost became more solid at her words.

Kevin closed the door behind them for privacy and they pulled up a couple of the chairs closer to the lounge. He had tried the Council again before the close of business, but had once again had access refused. The guard would be kept on at the Park and their 'No' was going to stay 'No'. This didn't depress those gathered, as they were more confident that the Doctor's higher connections would be more influential.

'So we have two concerns,' stated Evelyn, 'The organisation as a threat to Carmen and the secretive Boss. His hidden agenda worries me more that the organisation's.'

Frowning, Lisa shook her head. 'Why is that? I mean, the Boss has been the least violent. As far as we know he wants the book found, and isn't prepared to kill to keep it hidden.'

'True,' agreed Kevin, 'but an open attack is easier to prepare for, compared to the unknown. What does this man want? Who is he? How could he suddenly appear without Sergeant Greenaway seeing him approach?'

Seated, almost over Evelyn's shoulder, Tommy suddenly giggled. 'You know this mystery man stuff; it is the sort of thing his Lordship would get up to. The Boss Man has always been protective of the Mistress. Even if he did want the book, he definitely wouldn't let anyone hurt her.' Four pairs of eyes stared at Tommy in disbelief, as collectively their jaws dropped.

'Who is his Lordship?' Kevin was the first to recover.

Tommy looked surprised at the question. 'Why, Lord Death, of course.'

'You also called him the Boss Man,' added Lisa. 'Are you suggesting that he's "The Boss" who had hired Lennie, Nigel and Simeon?'

Tommy was taken aback by the reaction to his statement. 'I'm not suggesting anything, Miss. But if as that Sergeant said, the man who hit him appeared out of nowhere, with no cover to sneak up from; then I know of no one who could do that, but a ghost or his Lordship. Why he'd want the book I can't say.' The room remained silent as they waited for Tommy to continue, 'So if he dropped the Mistress in the pond, he must definitely have a job for the Mistress to do down there.'

Considerably worried. Carmen looked around at the faces of the others before fixing upon Kevin. 'What if we rescue Jenny too soon? How will we know when Jenny has completed this task his Lordship has for her?'

Lord Death Explains

'Perhaps I can assist you in that matter,' said a deep, attractive masculine voice from a corner of the room. Evelyn and Carmen jumped in surprise, wheeling around as Tommy fell off the back of the lounge. The others looked at them in surprise as they had heard nothing. Tommy staggered to his feet, as

Carmen rose to curtsy. Evelyn was still looking around for where the voice came from.

'Where is he?' demanded Evelyn.

'Where's who?' asked Kevin.

'You can't see him?' Carmen looked from where Lord Death had materialised to the others.

A handsome smile spread across his Lordship's human features. 'No they can't Carmen.'

'I can't see him, but I can hear him, why is that?' Evelyn was frowning in confusion.

His Lordship came towards them. 'When you had that car crash Evelyn, you had a near death experience. That makes you receptive to my presence.'

'Is this your Boss, Tommy? Wouldn't it be easier if we could all hear and see him?' asked Kevin.

Tommy looked across at his Lordship, but it was Lisa who spoke first, 'Whoa there! Let's discuss this. I mean, this is **Death** himself! How dangerous is it to actually see Lord Death?'

Carmen glanced nervously across at his Lordship to see how he would take this. Surprising her, he laughed. 'It won't necessarily kill you.'

The crowd held their breath, as his Lordship became visible to all. No one was struck dead, and indeed, his attractive features pleasantly surprised Lisa.

'I presume you wish to know why I want to find King James' Bible,' added his Lordship.

This was too much for Evelyn, who was far from being sanguine about meeting Death. 'No kidding! We want to swap knitting patterns!'

Calmly his Lordship shook a warning finger, 'Now, now! Be nice to the supernatural being with powers to take a life. Please be seated and I'll tell you a little story about the balance of the Universe.' Not until they were seated, did Lord Death speak again. 'There is a fine line between insanity and genius. If you have been paying attention over the last couple of days, you would have realised that King James suffered from a serious mental disorder. He made a list of men he believed to be plotting against him. This wasn't paranoia as there really was a plot. The King also stumbled across the greatest secret of the Universe. How to live forever,' He paused to allow them to assimilate what he had just told them.

'Bloody hell!' whispered Evelyn.

'I can see why that would worry you,' Lisa added.

Carmen shook her head. 'What is this about the balance of the Universe?'

His Lordship inclined his head. 'Life as you know it would cease to exist. Throughout all life there is a continuum, an ebb and flow of existence. There is life, there is death, and there is re-birth. That is the cycle that applies to the plants, the stars, vegetation, humans and creatures alike. Break this cycle and you destroy the natural ebb and flow. Catastrophic events would follow. Consider what would occur if man achieved immortality. The possibilities are endless and all diabolical.'

Lord Death continued, 'While the secret was locked away in James' cellar, all was well, but as soon as I knew a Spirit Healer, in particular Jenny Weston, was coming to Waltham Cross, it was essential for me to act quickly. I employed the use of three men whom I assumed had some semblance of intellect and cunning, but I was gravely mistaken. I had also thought that the brotherhood of traitors, you call 'The Organisation' was long gone.'

A moment of silence followed, and Lord Death waited patiently for the inevitable questions.

Lisa was the first to speak up, 'was it you who hit Sergeant Greenaway?'

Regretfully he nodded. 'I'm sorry for the necessity, but I ensured that I only knocked him out, rather than cause serious injury.'

'I'm sure the Sergeant will be grateful to hear that!' drawled Kevin.

Carmen shushed him. 'But why was it necessary to throw Jenny in the pond?' There was a stir of excitement as it appeared as if they were about to finally get an answer to this problem.

His Lordship took a turn around the room before he answered. It was as if he was debating how much to tell them. 'One of Jenny's tasks is to release King James and the other ghosts by finding the Bible, but there is another, more personal task she must fulfil.' When he hesitated again, the others were prepared to pounce on him, to get him to continue, 'Everyone has the right to find their true soul mate before they die. It is just a shame that Jenny's soul mate has been dead for more than 390 years. I needed to give Jenny time to realise some happiness before she released him from his imprisonment.'

Lisa was looking puzzled. 'But how will we know when the time is right?'

'I'll let you know. In the meantime, keep on at the Council to allow you to dig.'

He began to fade away, but Kevin had a question, 'Are we going to live through this?'

Pausing, his Lordship looked around at the assembled group. 'No one in this room is going to die.' He finally admitted. This didn't satisfy all the concerns that they may have had.

'Then others will die before this is all over? I'm sorry if I sound sceptical but the three men supposedly working for you are now dead!' demanded Kevin.

Although Lord Death would have preferred not to have to answer, it was obvious that they wanted the truth. 'Yes, others will die. As for those three, another reason I chose them was because their time was drawing near anyway.' This time his Lordship vanished before any more questions could be asked. His words had left the group feeling more than a little depressed.

It is nice to know that we will live, mused Carmen, *but it is a concern that more deaths will occur.*

We Mortals Need Food

Evelyn placed a hand over his rumbling stomach. 'My inner man needs feeding. Are you Detectives going to join us?' Lisa assisted Carmen in getting Evelyn to his feet. Both police officers exchanged guilty expressions, and Lisa knew that her cheeks would be burning.

'No thank you,' managed Kevin in an even voice. 'We've got a bit of work to do back at the station.'

When the door had closed behind them, Carmen looked at Evelyn. 'Do you believe that story they spun?'

'Of course not!' He laughed, 'I must talk to the Inspector about the art of being subtle.' Carmen didn't think that this was actually a good idea, and they argued the point as they entered the restaurant in search of sustenance.

Outside, Lisa and Kevin paused to decide where they wanted to go. Kevin was prepared to be led, so Lisa made up her mind alone.

'I feel like Chinese. If you could get a bottle of wine, I'll get the take-away and we can go to your house.' Kevin was instantly taken aback, and found himself wordless. Lisa blushed at the implication of her words. 'I mean, Mum and Dad are at home, and at your place we can talk without being disturbed. I didn't mean anything improper.'

Kevin found himself laughing. 'It's all right. You just surprised me for a moment. I'll meet you back at my house. You know the directions don't you?' Lisa nodded, and they parted to undertake their own tasks. They were being watched as they left the Dog and Bone. Even so, there would be no attempts to take Carmen's life; they knew that she was being protected.

I Would Like To Explain

A world away, and yet, physically not that far away from her rescuers, Jenny was having quite a different sort of day. She had woken that morning, revitalised and even refreshed, which wasn't at all usual.

Wrapping the dressing gown about her, Jenny stretched as she looked appreciatively at Sir Rupert's back as he still sat working industriously at the desk. Although he could feel neither cold nor heat, the Knight had removed his tunic, and rolled up his shirtsleeves to reveal powerful forearms.

When a yawn escaped from her, Sir Rupert suddenly realised that she was awake, and turned in his chair to look up at her. A smile that wasn't only sexy, but also contained more than a hint of tenderness appeared upon his face. Immediately, the Knight rose to his feet.

'Good morrow to thee! Thy slumber was deep and restful?'

Sheepishly, Jenny nodded. 'I must apologise for last night, Sir Rupert.'

'There is no need for apologies, Jennifer. Thee must take care of thyself. Exhaustion will help neither of us.'

Determined to clear any misunderstandings, Jenny laid her hand upon the Knight's arm. 'That's not quite what I meant, Sir Rupert. I feel like I made a fool of myself last night.' She held up her hand for silence as Sir Rupert was about to interrupt.

'No, please let me finish. I don't want to give you the impression that I fall into the arms of every man I meet, or that I'm the sort of woman who likes to tease men and then not follow through. It's just that during my life as a Spirit Healer, I never allowed myself to become too emotionally attached to anyone especially not a ghost. Life was going to be too short to look for a soul mate, and yet, even before I had met you, I knew that you were essential to me.' She broke off in confusion and Sir Rupert smiled.

'I do understand, Jennifer. Just as I tried to explain that I didn't mean to treat thee as a convenient interlude. Now that we have resolved our misunderstandings, where does that leave us?'

'I think now that we know where we stand; I say whatever happens, happens. Agreed?' Sighing deeply, Jenny brought up a smile.

Sir Rupert took her hand into his, 'Agreed! Now, bathe and breakfast mine lady. Then we can discuss the puzzle.'

'Choose something nice for me to wear.' Tightening her grasp upon his hand, she drew him close to briefly kiss him. As Jenny headed for the bathroom, Sir Rupert straightened up the bedding before opening the wardrobe. A rueful smile appeared as he pulled out a costume and laid it upon the bed. *I am interested to know what her reaction is going to be when she sees my choice. I hope that I have not under-estimated her sense of humour.*

Hardly Appropriate

The Knight had returned to studying the puzzle, when a clean, relaxed and humming Jenny reappeared. She had also had a bite to eat, and used the corner of the towel she was wearing to remove a trace of toothpaste from her mouth. Sir Rupert didn't look up from attempting to move the letters on the top of the box. He wanted desperately to turn to watch Jenny's reaction to the garment on the bed but didn't dare. Gasping in surprise, Jenny looked suspiciously at him, but he resisted the urge to turn around.

Giggling, she slipped off the towel, laid it across the bed, before easing herself into the dress. It was the lightest of materials, transparent, with a hint of pearl in the colour. In the style of the Ancient Greeks, the tunic with no sleeves, ankle length and fell gracefully to reveal all of Jenny's contours. It was also very good at not concealing anything else. For modesty's sake she may as well have been naked.

'Now this will not do Sir Rupert. You may not be able to feel hot or cold, but more than five minutes in this and I'll freeze!' As Jenny tied the matching sash about her waist, Sir Rupert finally turned around in his seat. He could not conceal a grin as he slowly took in her attire.

'I'm sorry, Jennifer, but I do not think thee would actually remain in that dress for more than five minutes. Any man would have thee out of it and into that bed as soon as they saw thee!'

Chuckling, Jenny slipped one arm around his shoulder and sat down on his lap. 'And was that your intention Sir Rupert?' Her voice became very husky.

The closeness of such desirable flesh caused him to squirm uncomfortably as he began to experience the imprudence of having a virtually naked woman so close. It had been meant as a joke, but the sight of Jenny's naked curves and the temptation of her luxurious breasts were causing a stirring in the Knight's loins that had not occurred in a very, very long time.

'I regret my actions now, my lady. Although I would not have missed such a sight for all the world!'

Under her thigh, Jenny could feel his rising desire, but she was not one to torment and rose reluctantly to her feet. 'Perhaps we should find something a little more suitable, and warmer.'

Sir Rupert took one long last look at her before sighing and returning to the wardrobe to find something more suitable. It was with regret that he handed a dress from his own era across to Jenny. *Although being a gentleman can sometimes be a pain in the posterior, I am every inch a gentleman.* He sighed with the repressed desire to turn around and watch Jenny dress.

He couldn't concentrate, so instead he closed his eyes, and listening to the sounds behind him, he could see Jenny's actions in his mind's eye. The sound of the Grecian gown fluttering to the ground signifying that she was completely naked caused Sir Rupert to groan softly. He could see Jenny standing there naked, as she picked up the dress off the bed. In his mind's eye, he could see her slip the dress over her head and ease it down to cover her desirable body. He stirred restlessly as he listened to Jenny tighten the laces and adjusted herself within the bodice.

Not unaware of what he was feeling she sympathetically wrapped her arms, around his neck from behind him. 'Try not to think about it Sir Rupert.' She pressed her cheek against his, as he sighed; breathing in the clean scent she exuded.

'Easier said than done, mine lady!' Although he attempted to be light hearted, his voice wavered slightly.

'True! Do you think you can stand doing up the laces on my dress?' She moved around his chair so that she presented her back to him. Managing to control himself while tightening the dress laces, Sir Rupert found his gentlemanly convictions waning as Jenny turned and kissed him.

He gave in to his desires, wrapping his arms around her waist and drawing her on to his lap. Their kiss deepened and intensified as Jenny placed her arms around his neck. They couldn't get close enough; their hands couldn't feel enough with so much clothing between them.

Resisting Temptation

'We should be... concentrating... on the box!' Jenny managed to say between kisses.

'Hum, just one more!' Sir Rupert made the kiss last as long as possible, before he lifted her off his lap. He rose to his feet so that she could take the chair.

She read through the sheets of possible alternatives to the letters on the box, and tried to focus upon the anagrams. 'This one looks like pacific. I don't know if that is any help.'

'Hum! Perhaps, His Majesty had a special motto. Now what was it?'

Jenny mused, *I want to tell the Knight that the more he tries to force himself to remember, the more likely the memory will be elusive.* 'If there was a 'y', this could be pacify,' she muttered quietly to herself as she glanced back at the possible anagrams. She gave a little squeak of surprise, when half hearing her words, Sir Rupert reached over her shoulder, and almost snatched the papers out of her hands.

'Pacify, pacifier, pacifici! Yes, peacemaker! What was the saying?'

Jenny sat silently, not daring to move. She didn't wish to break into his flow of thought.

'Peace makers! Blessed be the Peacemakers! I'm almost certain that was the saying. Translated into Latin though is what pacifici?' He closely scrutinised the letters available and gave an exclamation of joy, 'Of course! Beati Pacifici! Blessed are the Peacemakers! Why could I not see it before? Thou art surely an inspiration!' In his delight, Sir Rupert bent over the back of the chair to kiss Jenny. She enjoyed the embrace, but speedily rose to her feet, so that he could reach the box.

For a moment, Jenny stood at his shoulder, watching as his nimble fingers manoeuvred the letters around to get the 'B' into the first position. Checking the two words he had hastily jotted down upon solving the problem, Sir Rupert started to move the 'E' into position. Determined not to break his concentration, Jenny went across to the bookshelves to see what other treasurers she could find.

Thou Art So Beautiful

Solving the code was only half the puzzle, actually getting the letter into their correct position was just as challenging as each little icon glowed with heat and seemed to be trying to repel his touch. So an hour later Sir Rupert was able to remember that she actually existed. Turning in the chair, he smiled as he gazed upon Jenny seated upon the floor at the bookcase, with a book open in front of her. The skirt of her dress billowed around her, as Jenny read with interest the tome upon her lap. As if feeling his eyes upon her, she looked up and colour flushed across her face.

'How long have you been looking at me?' She wasn't angry, just embarrassed. Smiling he rose to his feet and moved across to squat down beside her. Tenderly he cupped her face in his hand and brushed his thumbs against her cheek.

'I cannot believe just how beautiful thou art. Without any attempts to lure or attract, thee radiate sensuality.'

Briefly Sir Rupert kissed her upon the lips. An impish smile lit up Jenny's face.

'So alluring that you've been able to ignore me for so long?'

'If I have ignored thee, I apologise, but had I not focussed my attention upon the puzzle, we would not be any closer to opening the box.' Sir Rupert paused as a slow engaging smile began to appear. 'It would have definitely been more pleasurable, but the box would have been low upon mine priorities.' His eyes twinkled and his smile grew as Jenny gave a gasp of surprise.

'My, my! Do you think that I could be persuaded into an hour of pleasure, while a tantalising treasure chest lay only a few feet away?'

'Mine darling Jennifer, thee should not say an hour, but hours! One hour would hardly be enough to even begin to discover how many ways I can find to satisfy thee over and over again.'

Jenny stopped breathing; her heart began to race out of control. She had to consciously force herself to begin breathing again as she waved her hand in front of her face, like a fan, to cool her heated cheeks. 'If I didn't believe that you have just unlocked the box, I'd be demanding that you prove your boast.'

With a look of dejection, Sir Rupert sighed. 'The woman of mine dreams has more interest in a puzzle box than me!' He rose, assisting Jenny to struggle to her feet. The skirt of the dress was the major hindrance, but once the book she had been reading was once more back on the shelf, they approached the desk.

Sir Rupert had seated himself in the chair, as she stood on one side of the desk, leaning against it, her arms crossed at her stomach to support her. Unconscious of it, this made the neck of her dress droop to reveal more than a hint of what lay beneath. Her eyes rested thoughtfully upon Sir Rupert's face. He turned his head so that their eyes met, and he couldn't help but notice the delicious swell of breasts that were visible.

'Admit it! You're just as curious as I am about what is in that box!'

Sir Rupert managed to drag his gaze back up to Jenny's face with a rueful grin. 'Frankly nay, I am not! Thou art so tempting that it is like a burning sensation in mine stomach. I feel that if I do not know the pleasure of thy touch, the fire will consume me. Though if I am not to have thy complete attention during such an intimate moment, then it is best to get the distraction out of the way!'

Cracking The Code

B	E	Q	J	S			
P	Q	C	S	F	S	C	S

Returning his attention to the carved box, Sir Rupert made certain that all the letters were in their correct places before attempting to lift the lid. It refused to budge an inch and continued to emit a hot glow whenever he touched the box. He looked up, startled, at Jenny. She didn't share his alarm.

'I think there may be a spell on the box to stop anyone but mortal access. I'll try pressing on each letter in sequence,' she suggested. A tiny click could be heard as each letter was pressed, and they both held their breath as Jenny pressed the last letter, and tried to raise the lid.

This time, although a little stiff, the lid was raised and almost as one, they exhaled a sigh of relief. Jenny lifted the lid off completely and laid it down gently. She reached inside and removed a large book. Her eyes sparkled with tears as she opened King James' own copy of the first edition of the Bible in English. Sir Rupert was amused at how reverently Jenny handled the book. 'Is it that important, Jennifer?'

'Oh yes!' Her answer was little more than a whisper. Clearing her throat, she continued, 'In 1631, the psalms were rewritten, and it is the revised psalms that are used to this day. This book actually contains the psalms as King James originally translated.'

Her fingers trailed across the images upon the cover. The figures, the ornamentations, the colours, they were as brilliant and as spell binding as the day they had been created. Sir Rupert watched indulgently as Jenny carefully opened the book and caressed her hand over the page.

'Thou art really pleased with thy treasure?'

Closing the Bible, Jenny laid it down upon the table before slipping onto Sir Rupert's lap. She hugged him tightly. The happiness she felt was too much to put into words. She pulled away, only enough so that their lips could meet. The kiss was so gentle, so tender that she felt like they could kiss forever. Sir Rupert framed her face between his hands. His eyes twinkled with mischief.

'If that is how thee react to one treasure, what will thee do when thou discover that there is something else in the box?'

Jenny swivelled around upon his lap, so that she could peer into the box. It appeared empty, but putting her hand inside, Jenny found that a cloth of black silk covered another book, and removing it, she leant back against Sir Rupert's chest as she opened it. He couldn't comprehend what caused her to gasp in surprise.

'It is another Bible.' The understatement of this remark caused Jenny to chuckle.

'No, Rupert, not just another Bible! This is the 42 line Bible, better known as the Gutenberg Bible. This is the first Bible ever printed. Published by Johannes Gutenberg, who developed the printing press in 1455; this was about 20 years before the first printing press in England! This is like the Holy Grail of Printing!'

'It is special then?' His flippant tone caused Jenny to open her mouth to explain just how special the book was, when she caught the laughter in his eyes. She put the Gutenberg Bible back into the box before attempting to get off his lap.

Desire Unleashed

Sir Rupert wrapped his hands around her waist and held her down but her wriggling on his lap, only increased his excitement.

'Contain thyself Jennifer!' The obvious plea in his voice caused Jenny to stop moving and looked at him in surprise.

'Am I causing you discomfort?' Her eyes were wide open in an imitation of innocent concern.

'Aye!' He managed to get out. Sir Rupert gritted his teeth together as Jenny manoeuvred her huge skirts so that she sat facing him, straddled across his legs. She whispered against his ear. 'Do you want me to go away?' Provocatively Jenny placed butterfly kisses against his throat, the line of his jaw and his ear.

'Aye! Nay! Damn thee woman! Thou art playing with mine mind.'

Jenny laughed. 'You destroy every resolution I made about getting involved with anyone!' She attempted to get off his lap, but Sir Rupert refused to let her go. 'I still need to find the list of names that James felt were traitors, and whatever Lord Death was looking for.' She attempted to turn back to the box, but the

Knight's grasp upon her waist was like a grip of iron. 'Sir Rupert, please, just another couple of minutes!' Her plea broke off in a sigh as he lowered his head to kiss the swell of breast exposed over the top of her bodice.

'Later!' His voice was so husky that it didn't sound like his at all. He kissed his way up her throat as his hands pulled her harder against him.

'Just two little pieces of paper.' Her words were hardly convincing even to herself. He kissed her chin, and then along her jaw.

'Later!'

Claiming her mouth, it was several minutes before Jenny could say anything at all. She looked quite dreamy as she managed to say, 'Much later!'

This was all the encouragement that Sir Rupert needed. This time when he kissed her there was absolutely no holding back, for either of them. Their mutual need was so intense, so desperate, that they didn't have time to undress, or even move from the chair. Jenny hadn't bothered to put on the pantaloons, having found they were too big. So as Sir Rupert slid one hand inside her bodice to cup and mould her breasts, Jenny tugged up her skirts before reaching down to undo Sir Rupert's trousers.

Her boldness surprised him. Not that he spent much time reflecting upon this, as she had released his penis and her loving caress was making him even harder. With incredible ease Sir Rupert lifted Jenny up and dragging in a shuddering breath, he slowly lowered her until she was impaled upon his penis.

'Sweet Mother of God!' He earnestly attempted to sit still, but there was a building itch of desire and she felt so good so intimately surrounding him. Jenny sought Sir Rupert's mouth in a soul searching kiss as she moved her hips.

Jenny was in charge due to her position and knowing that he wouldn't be able to contain himself for long, she made their sex hard and fast. Every thrust down, every twist of Jenny's hips brought them a heartbeat closer to each other. There was no need, or any time for words and when Sir Rupert felt that they both bordered upon climax, he drew her head down so that their mouths were locked together.

Their cries of ecstasy mingled as Jenny's body tightened around his. Drained, and breathing hard, Jenny collapsed against his chest, her head resting upon his shoulder and they were still so intimately joined.

When her heart rate had returned to a more normal speed, Jenny slowly lifted her head. Tenderly, Sir Rupert kissed her forehead and then her lips.

'Perhaps I can look for that list now?' Her voice was faint and far from convinced that really was what she actually wanted to do. Sir Rupert assisted Jenny to her feet, but didn't allow her the chance to turn towards the desk, as he swept her up into his arms and carried her across to the bed.

'Later!' He said, placing her on her feet to remove her dress, and help her under the doona. Sir Rupert picked up the dress and hung it over the back of the chair before removing his own clothing.

Everything I've Ever Wanted

She extended her hand towards him, the sparkle in her eyes an invitation he couldn't refuse. Slipping under the doona, Sir Rupert drew Jenny into his arms. She laid her head against his shoulder, and ran her fingers across the matt of hair on his chest. A look of tenderness was in his eyes as he lay perfectly still to allow her to explore his body.

When her fingers had enough of trailing across his chest, they journeyed down his taut stomach. After lingering for a moment, they dipped lower to wrap gently around his penis. Inhaling sharply, Sir Rupert's eyebrows rose in surprise. As her loving touch caused his desire to return quicker than he thought possible, all concerns about his ability to satisfy Jenny again so soon were swept away.

To ensure that this time their intimacy lasted a lot longer, Sir Rupert detached Jenny's hand and turning on to his side, it gave him the chance to do some exploring of his own. For quite some time, he traced a forefinger across the features of her face, as if he was memorising every detail. Under his intense gaze a delicate hue crept across Jenny's cheeks.

'Well?' She managed a shy smile.

'Thou art so lovely.' Gently he placed a kiss upon her nose. 'I never believed in attraction upon first meeting, but thee have captured me from the moment I saw thee.' Sir Rupert's fingers travelled down Jenny's throat towards her luscious breasts. One of his large hands expertly cupped and caressed each breast, sending a shiver of delight down Jenny's spine.

As the Knight lowered his head, Jenny closed her eyes, waiting for the feel of his lips against her tingling breasts. She uttered a gasp of surprise as Sir Rupert's lips didn't replace his hands, but caressed sensuously across her stomach before returning to claim her mouth once more.

Sir Rupert continued to caress Jenny's breasts as he gazed down into her passion filled eyes. She found that she couldn't move, so mesmerised by his expression. *Everything I have ever wanted, but have fought so hard to resist, is here; love, desire, tenderness, warmth, humour, compassion, and a connection... A soul mate.*

Then he kissed her, and although it wasn't savage, it was demanding, searching, and passionate and left them both a little breathless. Gently he caressed his finger down her bare spine, hesitating as he reached her lower back. Concerned, the Knight raised his head to look seriously at Jenny.

'Thy back? Will I hurt thee if we make love like this?' His concern was incredibly touching.

'I honestly don't know, Rupert.'

Grabbing one of the pillows not being used and lifting Jenny up from the hips, he placed it under her. The coolness of the linen was soothing and yet strange to have her hips slightly elevated. Jenny wasn't given much time to consider this as Sir Rupert lay again beside her, his hands tantalising every inch of her flesh.

Their lips once more met and supporting himself upon his elbows, Sir Rupert gently rolled on top of her, one of his knees urging Jenny's thighs apart. For a moment he laid perfectly still, his head resting against Jenny's shoulder as he prepared himself for this intimate joining.

'I would have waited for thee forever!'

Tears appeared in Jenny's eyes at his pain filled words. *So soon after finding each other, we will again be parted.* Sir Rupert raised one hand to brush her tears away, before kissing her. Mindful of her newly healed broken back, he was careful as he slowly sank deep into Jenny. Mistaking a gasp of pleasure for one of pain, Sir Rupert paused. 'Jennifer?'

Smiling, she shook her head. 'No, no, it's all right. For God's sake don't stop!' Lacing her finger through his hair, she drew his head down in a passion charged kiss.

Both having discharged their pent up sexual frustration in the chair moments earlier, this time they were determined to make it last as long as possible. Sir Rupert concentrated upon giving Jenny as much pleasure as possible, raining kisses across her face and breasts as he slowly thrust in and out of her.

She wanted their time together to last forever, but that wasn't possible. So when Jenny felt the wave of ecstasy reach its peak, she tightened her thighs around his hips and sought to match the increased speed of his thrusts. She came first but it was only seconds later that Sir Rupert also found his own release. He rolled so that Jenny lay beside him as they both fought to restore their jagged breathing. Absently, Sir Rupert caressed his fingers through her hair. It was quite a few minutes before either of them could speak.

'Doeth thou still desire to look for those papers?' His tone was half mocking, as Jenny reached down to draw the doona up to cover them both. She snuggled comfortably into the crook of his arm.

'Later!' She whispered, pinching his chin. Within ten minutes, Jenny was fast asleep, in the security of his embrace.

Rupert's Important Document

A little while later, when Jenny stirred, she found herself still in her lover's arms, her head against his chest. She sat up abruptly; she couldn't take her eyes off the papers in the Knight's hands.

'Are these the documents that everyone is seeking?'

Lowering the papers, Sir Rupert brushed his hand through her hair and pressed his lips against her brow. 'Not the first. That is very special. I want thee to see it.' He passed one sheet over and Jenny couldn't help gasping in surprise. Off the page stared back at her, was her own face. Her hairstyle was typical of his era, but every other detail was completely accurate.

'That's amazing! Did you do this while I was sleeping?'

Sir Rupert shook his head. 'This was drawn while I was on guard, before I… before I died.' The last three words were a little hard to actually say.

Tenderly she stroked his cheek and kissed him gently. 'You can't have known we would ever meet.'

'Nay, this is the image that haunted my dreams, of my perfect mate.'

'Obviously we were never meant to be happy in this life.'

Sir Rupert laid her head against his shoulder. 'There is a saying is there not? Better to have loved and lost, than to never have loved at all.'

'I just wish that we had more time together before you cross over.' Jenny nestled against him.

Trailing his lips across her brow, Sir Rupert made his way down her cheek. 'True, but better the little time we have than our meeting only in the time for thee to send me on. That would have been a tragedy.'

Jenny was being swept away by the logic of his words and the caress of his lips. 'You have an answer for everything, don't you?' She sighed as their lips met.

It was some time before Jenny could even think about speaking again. Although she could have easily succumbed to the desire that he stirred within her, she was burning with curiosity about the other papers. Reluctantly she drew away from Sir Rupert.

'Please Rupert; may I see the other papers?'

Wickedly, the Knight chuckled as he placed a provocative kiss against her neck, 'Of course! How am I impeding thee from doing so?' His eyes danced mockingly as Jenny couldn't help but react to his sensual touch.

'By driving me out of my mind with desire!' She retorted, managing to reach out to take the papers from his hand. A devilish gleam entered her eyes. 'I'll make it well worth your while.' She teased.

His hand, now free of the sheets of paper, slid seductively across her stomach, and up to cup one of Jenny's breasts under the doona. 'Doeth thee wish to play games, mine lady?'

Unable to contain a gasp as his fingers flamed her desire, Jenny managed to say, 'Only because you play dirty, my lord!'

Documents To Die For

Laughing, he released her breast, but still held her in his arms, so Jenny could finally concentrate enough to be able to examine the other documents.

Not that they mean much to me as the writing is too bad for deciphering. The first is obviously a list of names. Jenny turned her head to look at Sir Rupert, and wished she hadn't as they were suddenly nose to nose, and too close for rational thought.

'It is a list of names, though?' She managed to drag her eyes away from his tempting mouth.

Sir Rupert nodded. 'It would appear to be the list of traitors that the King thought he had.'

Laying that piece of paper down on the bed, Jenny turned to the next one. *This one, despite the difficulty of the handwriting, I can make out the general gist of its contents.* The colour drained from her face, causing Sir Rupert to tighten his hold upon her.

'No wonder Lord Death is so anxious that this paper should never be found!' Her words came out as little more than a whisper.

'It appears to be some sort of recipe.' Sir Rupert spoke lightly, to try and lessen the severity of Jenny's reaction.

'A very dangerous one! Immortality! That explains why it was imperative it was found by his Lordship, or destroyed.'

The Knight waited for a moment, one hand rising to caress against Jenny's hair, in the manner one would comfort a child. 'So what doeth thee intend to do about these papers?'

'There is only one thing to do!' A worried look left her eyes as she came to a decision.

Jenny's Only Option

With resolution, Jenny slipped out of the bed, and picking up her dressing gown, slipped it on. Not for modesty sake but out of Sir Rupert's arms it was cool in the chamber. Leaving the papers upon the bed, she disappeared into the bathroom and returned with a couple of small resealable plastic bags that had come down the waterfall containing food, and the bowl which they had put the apples into.

Watching, amused as Jenny placed these odds and ends on the floor, Sir Rupert got up and pulled his shirt and trousers on.

Taking a calming breath, Jenny picked up the list of traitors and touched the corner of the paper to the lit torch upon the wall. When it caught on fire, she placed it into the bowl until the paper was completely reduced to ashes. Standing beside Sir Rupert, she put her arms around his waist, her cheek resting against the soft fabric of his shirt, as they waited for the ashes to cool down enough to be handled. The ashes were then placed into one of the resealable bags before Jenny repeated the process with the incantation for immortality.

From the desk, Jenny picked up pen and paper, and quickly jotted down the contents of the two bags before slipping them inside with the ashes. Once sealed up, she uttered a sigh of relief.

'Now there should be no further reason for anyone to want to kill me!' She tucked the bags into the top drawer of the desk, and turned to look up doubtfully at the Knight. 'I did do the right thing, didn't I? I know they were historical documents and as such should have been sacred, but the content made them just far too dangerous.'

'Doubt not thy action.' Sir Rupert gathered her up in his arms. 'Thy heart and motives are pure. Thee have nothing to condemn thyself upon.' Although his words were a comfort, she did still feel a twinge of doubt and guilt.

Jenny ensured that both the King James' Bible and the Gutenberg Bible were once more carefully placed in the carved box before the lid was replaced. *Such important tomes need careful handling, which I feel more self-conscious about having just destroyed two ancient documents.* Sir Rupert washed the bowl and returned the apples to it. After such an exciting morning, Jenny was feeling quite hungry. She would have redressed, but an impish gleam in Sir Rupert's eyes changed her mind.

'I would only have to go to the trouble of taking it off again.' His words caused her heart to skip a beat. Thoughts of food could have easily been swept out of her brain, but Sir Rupert insisted that she eat. Mischievously adding, that Jenny would need all the strength she could get. She couldn't help laughing at his audacity.

A Pleasurable Way To Pass The Time

Although he only had an apple, Sir Rupert ensured that Jenny had quite a substantial meal. He cleaned up as she had a quick shower, but it wasn't long before he slid into the shower with her. They discovered together the joys of shower sex, and they had barely dried off before they fell back into bed. They lay in each other's arms for quite some time, just talking, although Sir Rupert was allowing his hands to caress over her skin.

He had so many questions about what had been occurring above ground for the last 390 years, and although Jenny could understand his curiosity, she limited what she told him. *Too much knowledge would overwhelm him, and he will never get to see these changes as he will cross over almost as soon as the doors to the hidden room are opened.*

Realizing that there was only one way in which to silence his questions, Jenny reached out to caress him intimately. It didn't take long for his thoughts to turn from inquiry to pleasure, and although his desire was obvious, Sir Rupert ensured that her satisfaction came first. Whenever it appeared as if her back was causing Jenny pain, he immediately altered their positions and was even prepared to stop, if she was in too much discomfort. Jenny thought, *I'm not about to let a little pain get in the way of so much pleasure. There is so little time, and so much yet to be learnt about each other.*

WEDNESDAY

A Summons From The Council

As Carmen went about her duties in the restaurant, she couldn't throw off the feeling of excitement and anticipation. She was as professional as ever, but her smile was just a tad mechanical and she spent little time in idle chatter. When the postman came past, Carmen fairly belted to the front door for the mail.

The only one she was really interested in was addressed to her and had a crest upon it. With shaking fingers Carmen carefully opened the envelope and hastened out of the restaurant to find her mother. Cheryl was doing a stock take behind the bar, when Carmen thrust the letter under her nose.

Cheryl slipped her reading glasses on to see what had excited Carmen into speechlessness. The letter was handwritten personally by the sender, rather than typed by a secretary, and the signature caused the colour to drain from Cheryl's cheeks.

'An Earl! The Earl of Elgin. You have reached high circles!'

Carmen found her voice. 'Do you think that the Council can stand against this sort of request?'

'I don't know how they can dear.' Cheryl looked at the signature again and exhaled slowly.

As if in answer, Kevin and Lisa entered the pub via the restaurant in uncontained excitement.

'The Council are jumping up and down like crickets!' exclaimed Lisa.

Carmen grasped hold of Lisa's outstretched hands. 'What's happening?' She looked from one police officer to the other for news.

'They want you down at Council Chambers to answer a few questions.' Kevin was so calm he could have been reading the telephone directory, not preparing for an event in history.

'Oh!' Carmen dithered in indecision. 'I can't leave the restaurant short-handed.'

Cheryl came out from behind the bar. 'Don't worry about that love. The stocktake can wait. This is important.'

'Thanks Mum.' Tugging off her serving apron, Carmen thrust her arms into a jacket as she eagerly followed Lisa and Kevin out of the Pub.

Mayor Stanley Jones

When Kevin, Lisa and Carmen entered the Chambers they were ushered straight into the Mayor's office. Behind the Mayor, who sat at his desk, stood four of the Councillors. Mayor Stanley Jones held in one hand nearly a dozen letters.

'Who the hell are you?' The Mayor's angry demand caused Carmen to take a step back, startled. She was extremely glad to have the two police officers standing supportively beside her.

'You asked for Carmen to come here. If it is your intent to insult her, we'll take our leave immediately.' Coldly, Kevin turned on his heels and would have opened the door had Mayor Jones not called him back.

'No need to get on your high horse, Inspector, I just want to know how the hell a teenage girl can have connections such as these!' The Mayor waved the letters in front of him. His insolence brought the light of battle to Carmen's eyes but Kevin wasn't going to let her lose her temper.

'Settle down Carmen. We'll just get what we came for, and be on our way.' Kevin's calmness soothed her.

'What if I refuse to let you dig?' demanded the Mayor.

Carmen tugged her arm out of Kevin's grasp and leant on the desk facing the Mayor; her eyes glaring straight into Jones'. 'With or without your permission I'll begin digging in Theobalds Palace ruins today.' Carmen snatched the letters out of his hand and having glanced down at the signatures, threw them one at a time at the desk.

'The Earl of ----, The Prince of-----, three Cabinet Ministers, a Foreign Prince, two Queens Councils, and at least three Knights. How much higher must I go? Do I have to get the word of God before you admit that you have been outranked?'

Lisa placed a gentle hand upon Carmen's shoulder. 'I'm sure no one wants to be responsible for Jenny dying in that hidden chamber.'

The Councillors immediately agreed and although Carmen backed off the desk, the anger in her eyes didn't die. For a moment the Mayor stroked his chin thoughtfully. 'Permission denied! Don't slam the door on your way out!' Even the Councillors looked at the Mayor in horror. Kevin's lips thinned in disapproval, and Lisa looked anxiously at Carmen, ready for her to explode.

That explosion didn't occur, as Carmen started to laugh. 'You have no idea what you're dealing with!'

The trio walked out of the Mayor's office, and not one word was said until they had left the Council Chambers, and reached Kevin's car in the car park.

'If you want to swear, Carmen, we'll understand.' His unemotional suggestion caused her to laugh again.

'Thank you, but that's not necessary.' She hesitated for a moment, leaning against the car as Kevin unlocked the doors for them. 'If you both want to draw back at this point, I'll understand. I'm so grateful for all your assistance, but where I go from here will not be entirely legal.'

Lisa slipped her arm around Carmen's shoulder. 'Now is that the Musketeer attitude?'

Kevin added, stepping round to the driver's door, 'All in or all out Carmen. Jenny's life depends upon us and I, for one, don't run away when the going gets tough.'

Carmen breathed a sigh of relief. 'Thank you. I just wanted to give you the opportunity to protect your careers.'

They drove back to the Dog and Bone in silence, mainly because Carmen was re-reading the letter she had received that morning from the Earl. *Before signing off, the writer had asked me to contact him if I had any other problems. I'm a little shy about speaking to such an important peer, but if it is one of the last options I have, then I will do anything to ensure Jenny's safe return.*

The Rescue Team Are Resolved

Doctor Shepherd was waiting for them when they returned to the restaurant, and a single glance at their faces was enough to answer his question, before he had even asked it. His dismay was quite evident, and Carmen immediately hugged him.

'Don't blame yourself Doc! I was blown away by the response from the Freemasons, they were just great!'

Kevin, more conscious the people in the restaurant were listening, steered them through into the conference room. As they sat down, Kevin took up his position on the windowsill.

'Mayor Jones has no intention of giving his permission to resume digging,' stated Lisa to the Doctor.

'Right then, we have to decide when we're going to do this. We'll need shovels and some powerful torches, if we're going to wait for nightfall. Anything else?' Kevin looked authoritatively around at the group.

'I don't want you or Lisa to get into trouble, Inspector.' Doubts once more rose for Carmen. 'How will this affect your careers?'

Kevin shrugged nonchalantly. 'It'll go on our records, at worst we could be thrown off the force.' He managed to sound as bored as if he was telling her the time.

'I can't let that happen!' Carmen said firmly.

'How were you planning on stopping us?' asked an authoritative voice from the doorway.

Don't Forget About Me

They all jumped. None of them had heard Lucas Greenaway enter the room. He smiled at their surprise. 'What? Did you think I was going to be left out of the Grand Finale?'

Lucas was warmly welcomed and Lisa urged him to sit down. 'Should you be up and about Sarg? That was quite a knock to the head you took.'

'My head's made of concrete. It would take a lot more to do any serious damage.' Lucas laughed.

'Back to Carmen's question,' Kevin attempted to return to the main topic of discussion. 'I personally feel that I should voluntarily turn in my badge, if I put my career ahead of rescuing an innocent person. I'm in this to the end.'

Lisa and Lucas both nodded and said almost simultaneously, 'I agree.'

Resigned to accept their stubbornness, Carmen shrugged her shoulders in defeat, 'Right then. I warned the Mayor that I'd be digging today, with or without his permission. I think we should go ahead with that plan.' There was general agreement to this proposal.

'I'll organise the shovels,' said Lucas.

'I'll be on hand in case Miss Weston requires medical treatment,' added Doctor Shepherd, intent upon not being left out.

Kevin turned to Carmen to add, 'you might want to get in touch with whatever spirits are involved. Do we have wait for word from Lord Death?'

'Yes, and there is something else I want to try before we meet at the ruins this afternoon.' Any more than this, they couldn't get out of her, so the group dispersed. Each returning to their usual jobs, but never far from their thoughts, was the task ahead.

You Are Insatiable

Jenny awoke that morning feeling like she had been dreaming the last twenty-four hours, so euphoric did she feel. *My state of nakedness and the slight ache of every muscle from making love nearly all the previous day is testimony to the fact that the dream had in fact been reality.*

Stretching indulgently like a cat, Jenny purred with satisfaction. Glancing curiously around the room, she was surprised that Sir Rupert was neither in the bed beside her, nor to be seen in the room.

'Rupert?' Throwing off the doona, she pulled on the dressing gown and was about to get out of the bed when it sank down beside her under an invisible weight.

Slowly Sir Rupert Steele materialised beside her. He picked up one of her hands and raised its palm to his lips. As their eyes met, they both involuntarily smiled and Jenny dragged in a hasty breath as her pulse quickened at his simple touch.

'Good morrow to thee. Thy sleep was indeed sound.' Tenderly he kissed her forehead. Brushing the back of her fingers against the line of his jaw, Jenny drew his head down so that their lips met in a more passionate kiss.

'Is it any wonder, Sir? Your energy and appetite are insatiable.'

'Is that good?' Sir Rupert looked at her doubtfully.

'Yes, very good,' She kissed him again before reluctantly pushing him gently away. 'I'm so hungry!' Jenny caught the glint of mischief in his eyes, and gave an embarrassed laugh, 'For food, my lord! I need a shower, and some sustenance. I feel today may be quite active.' The Knight chuckled wickedly, causing colour to flush across Jenny's cheeks. 'Don't you think of anything else, my lord?' Jenny managed to retort.

Kissing her, he chuckled again. 'Can I help if thee speak with double meanings? Go and bathe, mine lady, while I prepare thee some breakfast.' He playfully patted her on the backside and a mutinous look entered Jenny's eyes. He met it with a mocking smile, and for a moment Jenny wondered, *which of us would come off the better in a tussle of wills. Probably he would, but it would be entertaining to see where it led us.*

Deciding against confrontation, Jenny wagged a warning finger. 'Be careful, Rupert. You might just start something that you can't finish.'

He took possession of her finger and pressed it against his lips. 'Is that a challenge, mine lady?'

Laughing, Jenny said, 'If we had time, yes it would be a challenge, something for us to look forward to in our after life together.' She would have headed for the bathroom, but Sir Rupert more firmly gripped her hand to stop her.

'There is something I must know. Jennifer... Is there really an afterlife? Not just empty nothingness?'

There was no need for Jenny to even pause to consider this question. *I have been asked it many time by ghosts and mortals, afraid that in the end of life, there is only oblivion.* 'Yes, there is an afterlife, Rupert. For the wicked, they must atone for their sins in Purgatory, for the innocent; there is the afterlife of their choice. Some wish to be reborn, and return to this earth, otherwise, there is a place where you'll meet up with other members of your family, who have passed over before you.'

'I am glad.' Sir Rupert let out a sigh of relief. 'I had a long time to consider what would be waiting if I ever crossed over.' Relieved, he raised her hand to his lips before letting her go to shower, dress and eat. A big day was ahead of them.

Rescue Team Make Their Plans

By afternoon the rescue committee had gathered together in the conference room to finalise their plans. Evelyn had been very quiet since he had dropped into a chair, but the others had put it down to trying to manage his pain. Actually he had been thinking deeply about their problem.

'What we need is publicity,' Evelyn quietly stated. Everyone looked at him in surprise. He went on, not noticing their reaction, 'Television would be the most suitable media as it has immediate access to the public and if done right, access to millions of viewers through the internet.'

'You'll need someone with some sort of influence over the media to get them even interested,' frowned Lucas.

Lisa gave a cry of surprise, drawing all their attention towards her. 'Dean Schofields! What's the point of having a millionaire media mogul in the vicinity if he can't be useful?'

Lucas stroked his chin thoughtfully. 'Is he still in the area? The last I heard of him, you and Kevin had dragged him away from pounding my front door down.' Kevin and Lisa exchanged a questioning glance.

'The last time either of us saw Dean, was here in the restaurant, drowning in coffee in a feeble attempt to sober up,' answered Kevin.

'Right then,' said Lucas. 'He'll need to be tracked down and if necessary, completely sobered up.'

'What we also need is a physical crowd as well as access to a television audience,' added Evelyn.

'Lisa and I can go and find Dean Schofields,' offered Kevin.

'Carmen and I'll rout out as many of the villagers as possible. The digging will have to be delayed a little while, but the result should be worth it,' added Lucas.

'I must make one thing very clear,' Carmen stated firmly. 'Once we start digging, I don't want to stop, so even when night falls, I want to keep working.'

Agreeing, Kevin added, 'I'll organise spotlights to be set up.' This was an obvious indication that the time for words was over, and the time of action to begin. The meeting broke up as they each had their own tasks to perform.

Restless Waiting

Jenny and Rupert were faced with a day of waiting. *Without knowing why we know, we both realise that today is our last day together,* mused Jenny. Having bathed, eaten and dressed, she felt the strange urge to clean. This only took about an hour, during which time; Sir Rupert had seated himself at the desk reading a book, having had his offer to assist politely refused.

That was until Jenny removed the book from his hands to return it to the bookshelves. As she finally sank down upon the floor, her back leaning against the wall, Sir Rupert smiled indulgently. 'Feel better, mine love?'

'Not really. I feel exhausted now.' Grimacing, Jenny couldn't fail to see the funny side to her frantic activity.

Sympathetically, he held out his arms. 'Come hither, mine darling.' He took her hands and hoisted her up off the floor and into his arms. She jiggled around for several minutes more than was necessary, before she was finally comfortable upon his lap.

Sighing, she wrapped her arms around his neck and laid her head against his shoulder.

'Comfortable?' There was a slight edge to his voice that could not hide how much her wriggling had excited him. Provocatively, Jenny moved again.

'I could be more comfortable, but that would mean disturbing the bed covers!'

Although one of the Knight's eyebrows rose, his face did not display any emotion. 'We would not want that now, would we?' Sir Rupert's dead pan answer caught Jenny by surprise, causing her to raise her head to scrutinise him closely. Thrown off guard for a moment, she made a speedy recovery.

'Oh well, I suppose I could always have lunch.' Decorously she slid off his lap, her eyes sparkling as an idea came to her. 'Or indeed this is a perfect opportunity for me to examine a little closely King James' Bible.' She reached out to pull the treasure box, which held the two Bibles, closer to her.

The lid hadn't been replaced properly, but her hands did not get a chance to touch the box, as Sir Rupert swept Jenny up into his arms. There was a sparkle of appreciation in his eyes.

'Naughty puss! As if thee was going to sit demurely reading a book when thee could have been lying in mine arms?'

'Fie my Lord! What sort of brazen wench does thou take me for?' Jenny pushed against his chest trying to dislodge herself from his embrace.

'Now then Madam, enough of that!' He grinned at her mock protest, refusing to put her down, 'I know thy blood runs as heated as mine. Besides it was thy suggestion in the first place.' Gasping in horror, Jenny thumped Sir Rupert's chest and removed herself out of his arms.

'My dear Sir, I did no such thing! Can I help it if you read double meanings into my innocent statement?' She turned an insulted shoulder towards him.

My Perfect Love

Concerned at having actually insulted Jenny, Sir Rupert reached out to place a hand upon her shoulder. 'Jennifer?' The softly spoken was rewarded only by a miserable sniff, 'My love!' He placed both hands upon her shoulders and turned Jenny around to face him. Expecting to see tears glistening in her eyes, Sir Rupert was surprised to instead see her eyes sparkle with mischief.

'Impossible imp!' He growled softly, sweeping her into his arms and she made no protest, especially when he headed purposefully towards the bed. Laying her gently down, he removed his boots and his jacket before joining her. For quite some time, Sir Rupert just looked at Jenny, a blush sweeping across her as he took in every detail.

'It seems difficult to realise that thou art more perfect than my dreams had hoped for.' Almost reverently Sir Rupert traced a finger down her cheek and along the length of her body.

'I'm hardly perfect, Rupert!' Jenny laughed as she blushed. *I had never thought of myself as being a paragon of virtues.*

'Perhaps,' he agreed, 'but thou art all I have ever wanted from a life partner.'

'Oh!' Jenny suddenly felt shy and very small. 'We'll have to settle for afterlife partners.' Her humour returned, reaching up to place her hand behind Sir Rupert's head to urge him to lower his lips to meet hers. He did not resist, in fact he participated with considerable enthusiasm, but he did draw back momentarily.

'Does it not worry thee? Death?'

'No, not in the least.' Jenny shook her head. 'There is nothing to fear. You only get what you deserve.'

Sir Rupert grimaced. 'That's what I'm worried about!'

Unable to help being curious, Jenny traced two fingers up his arm. 'Is this something that I should know about? Or don't you think that I should ask about past lovers?'

Despite his best efforts to keep a straight face, Sir Rupert could not keep the colour from flooding across his features. 'I think that is a question best left unasked, Jennifer. I was thinking more along the lines of people I've killed in battle, rather than how many women I may have made love to.'

Jenny was tempted to ask how many women that it may have been, but thought better of the impulse. 'I don't foresee any problems ahead for you. I think 390 years of being a ghost is more than enough punishment for any misdemeanour that you may have committed.' Tenderly Jenny traced an index finger along his jaw line.

'Is there anything I can do to convince you that there is nothing for you to worry about?' The Knight thought seriously for a moment, before lowering his head to whisper into her ear. This caused her to laugh. 'I don't know how that can reassure you about the afterlife, but I'm certainly willing to please you.'

She was answered by a wicked chuckle. 'Then why art we wasting time with words?' Laughing again, Jenny wrapped her arms around his neck. Sir Rupert drew her closer against him, his lips caressing any bare flesh that he could find. 'Then it is time I became a man of action.' Jenny wriggled against him, one hand slipping under his shirt as they prepared to become as close as two people can possibly be.

Sobering Up Dean

Carmen and Lucas were spreading the word throughout the village via the village shops, the local radio station and through various means of grapevine, such as the school, the Mothers' Institution and the vicar's wife. Evelyn was in charge of electronically spreading the word through twitter, face book, blogs, chat rooms and email.

While the other two police officers were rooting out Dean Schofields from the hole he had dug for himself. Ivy Schofields, when she opened the front door of her home, was definitely not what Kevin had been expecting. Dean's mother was 50, at present her short hair was fluorescent pink; she wore a crop top, and ¾ length hot pants.

On other women it would have looked like mutton dressed up as lamb, but somehow it seemed to suit Ivy. Although her well-manicured hands were covered completely with clay, she still held a lit cigarette in one hand.

'Come in, come in! I hope you're here to see Dean. He needs a good swift kick up the backside!'

Meekly Lisa and Kevin followed her into the house, listening to her constant flow of conversation, that luckily required no answers, only a listener.

'Forgive my appearance; I've been working at my potter's wheel. I find getting your hands dirty to be very therapeutic. Can I offer either of you a drink, or is this an official call?' Lisa reassured Ivy upon this point. 'Come on Dean, time to come out and face the world!' Ivy banged on a closed door, taking a puff from her cigarette before turning to the officers. 'You may have to throw him into a cold shower.'

Ivy left them at the closed door, and although there had been a muffled groan given from within from Ivy's knocking, there had been no other sign or noise from the media millionaire.

When Kevin glanced down at her, Lisa could only shrug. 'I suppose we just go in.'

'Well, here goes!' He took a deep breath. The room they entered, with Lisa firmly planted behind Kevin, was in complete darkness. It was only when Kevin walked into the edge of the bed that they even realised that it was a bedroom. Lisa giggled as he swore.

Rubbing his bruised knee, Kevin swung round to flick on the lights. There was a strangled scream and a flurry of activity under the blanket. The room was a complete shambles, empty bottles of alcohol littered the floor, and there was the unpleasant smell of sweat, mustiness and whiskey.

Looking around in disgust, Lisa strode over to the window and drew back the curtains and opened the windows as wide as possible. Kevin took the corner of the blanket and violently pulled it off the huddled figure on the bed. Dean moaned and tried to put a pillow over his head, but Kevin flicked it off the bed out of the reach of Dean.

'Time to get a grip on yourself, Dean, Jenny needs your help.' Kevin left the room to find the kitchen for some water.

'Have you found her? Is she still alive?' A bleary eyed, unshaven Dean peered up suspiciously at Lisa as he tried to bring his maltreated brain into a functioning mode.

'We know where Jenny is, and that she's alive, but we need to work fast to bring her back.' Lisa had to repeat herself twice before it managed to sink into Dean's brain. Kevin re-entered the bedroom with a jug of water and a glass. When Kevin filled the glass, Dean reached out for it, but instead of handing it over, the Inspector threw the water into his face.

Gasping and spluttering, Dean brushed the water off his face, he was about to protest when Kevin tipped the remainder of the jug of water over his head; ice cold water. Dean gave a strangled cry, but Kevin wasn't about to relent. He dragged Dean up by his arms and pulled him off the bed, which by now was sopping wet.

'You have a role to play and it's imperative that you're sober and functioning.' Almost having to completely support Dean, Kevin helped him out into the corridor.

Coffee And Make It Strong

'See what you can do about making some coffee, please Lisa?' Kevin asked, opening a couple of doors until he found a bathroom. Lisa went in search of the kitchen and she was filling up the kettle when there was a scream of real pain. Lisa couldn't help smiling; *I bet the shower is as cold as Kevin can make it.* Lisa found a plunger beaker and added several teaspoons of coffee and another for good luck.

There were all sorts of protests and groans coming from the bathroom. Lisa listened to Kevin half drag Dean's naked and dripping wet body back down the hall to his bedroom. There were more complaints and moans as Kevin helped the millionaire to dress.

When Lisa was adding the boiling water to the coffee granules, Kevin brought a drowned looking Dean into the kitchen. He was assisted into a chair, before the Inspector moved across to take down a couple of mugs from a rack.

Lisa looked up questioningly at him as she inserted the plunger. Kevin smiled and began to roll down his shirt sleeves, which he had rolled up so as to shower Dean.

'Once we get that coffee into him, we'll have to get him to talk.' Kevin absently kissed Lisa upon the brow.

'Hum! It may be quicker if we get this into him intravenously!'

'I was quite prepared to just tip his head back and pour it down his throat.' Laughing, Kevin shook his head.

There came a growl from the head on the table. 'Hey! I'm right here you know!'

Kevin turned a bored glance at the body slumped on the table top. 'We don't have time for self-pity.'

He took a mug, filled it to the top with black coffee and pushed it in front of Dean. He eased the media mogul into a sitting-up position and put the coffee mug into his hands.

'Drink up Dean. You've got a lot of calls to make!' Dean groaned, but raised the mug to his lips. He had a long way to go to pull himself together.

The People Gather

It was only a couple of hours later that all Carmen's plans were ready, but the daylight was already beginning to dissipate. Kevin and Lucas organised the spotlights around the palace ruins as a remarkably sober Dean was coordinating the media contingency in a spot that was good viewing, but not a hindrance to Carmen. She was in conference with the ghosts Ian McGregor and Mandy.

To one side a small marquee had been erected, and inside upon two folding chairs sat Evelyn and Kathleen May to protect them from the cool night air. Bobby Michaels was there to assist Lisa and Natalie to keep the crowd that had begun to gather, under control.

Although John, the security guard initially protested at the invasion of Cedars Park, having seen half a dozen representatives of the police force as well as Judge Nelson, he quickly fell into line and helped with crowd control. He even cleared it with Inspector Harris before contacting the Broxbourne Council about the invasion. He was more concerned about what the police, rather than the Council, could do to him.

It wasn't only the local people who had responded to the call for support. People were coming up from London, from surrounding counties, and even a couple of buses from retirement villages pulled up. Folding chairs were set up; blankets spread across the ground, rugs and jumpers were in evidence in preparation for the coolness of night fall.

Cheryl had set up an urn and was busy handing out cups of tea and coffee. Later there would be sandwiches if the digging went past supper time.

A Review Of Events

Receiving a signal from Carmen, Dean Schofields summarised to the cameras and reporters, the events that had led up to this present moment. He touched briefly upon those who had already died, because of this treasure, but his main focus wasn't upon the historical tome that lay hidden beneath their feet, but the fact that a living person was trapped under the ruins, and the need for haste in rescuing her.

Questions such as, 'Why hasn't something been done sooner?' and 'How do you know she's still alive?' were asked and Dean easily and calmly answered them. He had been fully briefed even if it had taken gallons of strong coffee to finally get it firmly entrenched into his alcohol abused brain. Describing how Carmen and her friends had sent down food through the pond, and had received a message in the bottle to inform them of Jenny's wellbeing.

Very briefly, Dean touched upon the refusal of the Council to allow Carmen to dig up the hidden door. The idea of illegal activities about to take place caused the reporters' noses to twitch in anticipation as they asked the questions, 'Will there be a riot? Will there be mass arrests? Who has the right to arrest the police? Is this going to turn out to be the biggest story of the week?'

Carmen Vs The Mayor

Mayor Stanley Jones and several Councillors strode into the park, and although a couple of them hesitated at the sight of so many television cameras, the Mayor continued unfazed through the crowds. The media focused their attention on Mayor Jones immediately. Questions were fired at him left, right and centre, but he ignored them as he continued to march towards Carmen.

For a moment he stood there, his hands on his hips as he stared defiantly at Carmen.

Even though she knew he was there, Carmen deliberately continued to speak with Ian McGregor about how much grass and soil they would have to remove before they cleared the doorway. Being ignored, wasn't something that Mayor Jones dealt with very well, and the longer Carmen refused to look at him, the redder he got in the face. Silently applauding Carmen's tactics, a faint smile was visible on Kevin's face. *I wonder if the Mayor is about to rupture something.*

In frustration, the Mayor turned to Lucas and pointed an accusing finger at him. 'Sergeant Greenaway! I order you to arrest these people. Move those nosy bystanders out of the park, and throw out those bloody press hounds!'

'Sorry Mayor, but I can't do that.' Lucas calmly shook his head. 'Most of the time as police officers, we only get to help people after accidents or a death occurs. It isn't often that we can actually be so instrumental in preventing a death.'

A round of applause broke out from the crowd, who were more than a little displeased at being called nosy bystanders. The media were lapping it all up, news reporters frantically taking shorthand notes as the cameras rolled, capturing every hostile word and moment. The action was being beamed live to audiences around the country and the globe via live broadcast on the television and the internet.

Defiantly, Carmen picked up a spade, and thrust it firmly into the ground, putting her foot on to it to drive it in deeply. The crowd roared with approval and the Mayor tried to wrestle the spade from Carmen. Kevin and Lucas quickly stepped in to protect her, forcing Mayor Jones to move back.

While this was going on Evelyn had made his painful way through the crowd, which automatically parted to allow him to pass, and was deep in conversation with Lisa. Granny May was having a quiet little chuckle as Mayor Jones tried to actually physically remove Carmen himself and Kevin or Lucas immediately counteracted any action against Carmen.

'I could ask for your badges, Gentlemen! I'd hate to have you all dismissed,' threatened the Mayor.

Lucas patted his shirt and trouser pockets, and sadly shook his head. 'Sorry Mayor, I don't seem to have my police ID on me.' The crowd laughed which infuriating the Mayor further.

'Don't make me call your colleagues to have you arrested Sergeant.'

Lucas irritated him more by laughing, 'It'll be a novel experience; that is if you can actually get any officer to obey such an order.'

The crowd was quick to get in on the act.

'Leave them alone, Jonesy!'

'Let them get on with their job!'

'What about that poor girl trapped down below, are you really going to let her die?'

'Save the girl!'

'Shut up you mongrels!' snapped the Mayor. 'There'll be no digging so long as this land belongs to the Council!'

'You don't really want to get re-elected as Mayor, do you, Mr. Jones?' drawled Kevin quietly.

Perhaps This Might Persuade You

An expectant hush fell over the crowd as Evelyn interrupted the Mayor's assault. 'Excuse me Mayor, although technically Cedars Park and the ruins of Theobalds Palace may be Council property...'

The Mayor turned on him with a growl. 'Did anyone ask for your tuppence worth cripple boy?'

'How dare you!' This proved too much for Carmen.

The Mayor began to mouth off at Carmen, but Lucas interrupted, 'Perhaps we should hear what Evelyn has to say about Theobalds,' Lucas suggested, trying to calm the volatile situation.

'I don't need to hear any mumbo jumbo! In 1919 Admiral Sir Hedworth Meux gave the park to the people of Cheshunt and although de Vere group bought the manor house for a hotel, Cedars Park is still our property! We have every right to deny anyone we like from its grounds!' explained the Mayor.

'True Mr Jones but perhaps the email I've just received will change your attitude,' stated Evelyn, handing the iPad in his hand to Carmen.

'I don't have time for any more of your tricks!' The Mayor's hands returned to his hips.

Glancing over the message, Carmen shook her head. 'No, I think you really need to read this Mayor!' She handed the iPad across to Stanley Jones. 'One of the benefits of being polite to your peers is the fact that some have friends in high places,' said Carmen. 'This is an email from her Majesty, asking you to allow us to continue digging from Jenny's return.' The Mayor had to peruse it twice before he believed it. The email with the signature 'Elizabeth R II' silenced the Mayor.

The Earl Of Elgin

This phenomenon only lasted a few minutes before disbelief was written across Mayor Jones' face. 'You must think that I'm an idiot if I accept this as being real! You can't have got through to the Queen as quick as that!'

'Perhaps you'd like to email back and tell her Majesty that you will not comply or do you need more light so that you can read the email address where this was sent from,' suggested Evelyn. Mayor Jones tried to outstare Carmen, but failed to faze her.

The staring competition was interrupted by the arrival of a very impressive, very expensive Jag into the car park of Cedars

Park. An extremely well dressed middle aged gentleman peeled off his driving gloves as he strode confidently through the gathered crowd towards the main action.

'Carmen Roberts? Sorry if I've kept you waiting but I was delayed from leaving London,' His well-educated plummy tone of voice caused Mayor Jones' hackles to rise.

'Who the fuck are you?'

'Alastair Bruce.' The gentleman had extended his hand to Carmen but he looked across at the Mayor in mild interest.

'Is that supposed to mean something you fucking toff?' chortling to himself, Jones glanced back at Carmen to see her drop into a nervous curtsy.

'Lord Elgin! We're honoured you could join us,' Carmen managed.

Trying to not laugh, Kevin drawled, 'As in the Earl of Elgin, Mayor Jones, which you might have known if you'd bothered to read any of the letters that the Freemasons sent you!'

'Is this the fellow you've been having trouble with?' The look the Earl cast over the Mayor caused Kevin and Lucas to bite down on their own lips to keep from laughing.

'Yes my lord,' agreed Carmen.

Deep in thought the Earl stroked his chin, 'Did you receive the email from her Majesty's secretary?'

'Oh yes, my lord.'

'Hum! Let me guess that didn't impress him either?'

Carmen smiled, 'no, my lord.'

'Just as well I have a backup plan,' the Earl nodded towards where Dean had a laptop set up to the large screen which kept not only the internet viewers linked through the television cameras but would also display onto the huge screen for all in the Park to see when they finally entered the chamber.

'Evening Dean, how's your mother? May I borrow your laptop for a moment?'

'Mother's fine, she's taken up pottery.' Dean gestured towards the small table where his laptop sat, 'Please help yourself Lord Elgin.'

Her Royal Highness

Squatting down in front of the table, the Earl's fingers flew over the keyboard. 'Would your honour, the Lord Mayor please step over here?' When the image on the laptop appeared also on the large screen, Elgin straightened up again as Kevin pushed Mayor Jones forward.

A gasp of awe rose around the ruins as the image of Britain's' reigning monarch appeared. Gob smacked, the Mayor tore his eyes away from the Queen and sneered in disbelief as he watched those around him bow or curtsey.

'Bollocks! I'm not impressed by this charade! How much did you have to fork out for the actors from that reality show "I want to marry Prince Harry"? That doesn't even look remotely like the Queen, more like Matt Lucas in a bad wig!'

The lips of the elderly regal woman on the screen thinned in displeasure as a gasp of shock raced around those gathered. 'Silence Mr Jones! I find you rude, your actions intolerable and your attitude defies logic! If this was only about the ancient tome reported to be below your feet then perhaps your arrogance and abuse of your power could be justified. But a young woman, a living person is also trapped beneath Cedars Park and it is inconceivable as to why you are holding up the rescue efforts.'

Applause broke out at the Queen's reprimand and that just annoyed Jones even more.

'Look lady, I'm not buying your act so give it a rest!' Another gasp arose from the crowd at the Mayor's rudeness.

'Alastair minimise my screen for a moment so that everyone can see from where I am broadcasting. Perhaps if my appearance does not convince the Mayor then the web address will.'

Jones burst into laughter, 'Minimise screens? Web addresses? Now I know that you're not really the Queen!'

Before the Earl reduced the image of the Monarch, she glared frostily at the Mayor. 'I have grandchildren Mr Jones, I know about twitter, blogs and face book!'

As the web address became visible to not only the Mayor but also everyone else in the park, Jones choked and gagged, seeming to suddenly have difficulty breathing. For those who couldn't read it, Dean read it out aloud and an "ooh" arose as Dean said the words, 'Buckingham Palace.'

'Oh my God!' Stanley Jones swallowed hard on the bile that was attempting to choke him.

As the Earl maximised the screen again, he chuckled, 'Satisfied Mr Jones?'

'I... I...'

'You have impeded this rescue long enough, Mr Jones; I am removing you from your position as Lord Mayor,' stated the Queen. 'If we discover that the young lady trapped below has died then I promise you that you'll never again hold any position in any form of government.' At that moment ex-Mayor Jones fainted. 'Alastair? Have we lost the link?' asked the Queen.

Lucas, being closer, stepped in front of the camera on the laptop, 'No, your Majesty, the idiot just fainted.'

'Thank you Senior Sergeant, if Mr Jones continues to hinder your mission please arrest him. Good luck to all of you,' said the Queen.

'Thank you, your Majesty.' Lucas bowed to his regent before the screen went blank. Dean stepped forward to reconnect the internet feed with the television cameras. Cheryl arranged for another chair to be set up in the Marquee for the Earl beside Evelyn and Kathleen May.

Lisa couldn't stop laughing. 'I am never ever going to forget this day!' She felt the hairs on the back of her neck stand on end as a cold shiver ran through her.

Is It Time?

Turning, Carmen wasn't surprised to find Lord Death standing beside her. She swept down into a curtsy and looked up at his serious countenance questioningly. 'Is it all right to go ahead, my Lord?'

Solemnly Lord Death nodded. 'It is time Carmen. This evening you will discover that life is anything but predictable!'

'But we will succeed, won't we?' A feeling of dread swept over Carmen.

'I cannot tell you any more, Carmen. You must have faith!' Lord Death vanished before she could ask any more questions. With a hesitant smile she turned back to her fellow rescuers.

'Well we have the Boss's all clear. Now we dig!' Lucas immediately picked up a shovel and Kevin took possession of the one Carmen had already dug into the ground. A hushed silence fell over the crowd, as they were about to be part of history in the making.

Uncovering The Door

The mood was one of hushed excitement as the men dug through the hard earth and rubble. When Kevin hit something solid, a murmur ran through the crowd and the cameras zoomed in close to the action. Clearing away the last remnants of dirt, Kevin had discovered only the stone floor, but with another spadeful of earth removed, he found a corner of a wooden door.

It was the first physical sign that they were digging in the right area. Moments later, Lucas also found parts of the trapdoor, and it was now a case of clearing the area between them to reveal the entire door.

Excitement rose to a fever pitch as Lucas's shovel hit something with a twang of metal, and after a few more scrapings, revealed what appeared to be a brass door ring. The men cleared the remaining dirt away. The Press tried to surge forward, but were held back by a command from Dean, and the threat of losing their story if they stepped out of line.

The crowd were more obedient about keeping out of the way, as they had a perfect view of all the action from the big screen but their excitement was demonstrated by a rise in noise level.

Cheryl came across with a glass of beer for each of the diggers, as Carmen held up her hand for silence. The crowd immediately responded. It took a few minutes more for the Press to obey. Finally, when she was satisfied, Carmen turned to the ghost Ian McGregor. 'The King will come won't he, even with all these people here?' She couldn't hide the doubt she felt about what was going to happen next.

Ian grinned, 'Tis nearly the end. He'll come.' For a brief moment the ghost Scotsman disappeared, and when he reappeared, King James was with him.

Shaking nervously, Carmen sank into a low curtsy before the dead Monarch. 'Thank you for coming, your Majesty. I am Carmen Roberts.'

The King looked around at the surrounding people, intently staring at him as he and Ian were visible as they drew on Carmen's energy before transferring his gaze to Carmen, 'At last, at last! Sir Rupert will be free and I can finally rest.'

King James knelt down by the door and from his pocket he removed a brass key. A silence fell as the key was inserted into the lock, but a murmur of doubt rose as it refused to enter. Lucas knelt down beside the dead Monarch, removing a pocket knife from his trouser pocket, and flicking open the blade, he cleared the build-up of earth in the lock.

This time when the King inserted the key, it entered properly, although it did grate a little. There was a moan of sympathy as the King found it impossible to turn the key.

'Allow me,' offered Lucas. King James removed his hand to allow Lucas an attempt, but even his brute strength refused to budge the key. The whole locking device had completely rusted through. Disappointment ran through the crowd and Press alike.

Another Way In

Having foreseen all sorts of problems, Kevin had brought several different tools along. As people started wondering about what would happen now, Kevin picked up a sledge hammer from his kit, and passsed it across to Lucas.

'That should do the trick,' suggested Kevin.

Lisa raised a polite objection. 'We are dealing with a historical site gentlemen!'

'Too right!' Lucas grinned as he lifted the sledge hammer.

Raising her hand to stop his, Carmen added, 'Perhaps we could unscrew the hinges of the doors rather than destroy the whole entrance way.'

'Spoil sport!' Lucas glanced across to Kevin who was rummaging around in his tool kit. The Inspector raised a screwdriver and Lucas lowered his sledge hammer. Lisa held a torch steadily as Kevin knelt down to brush excess dirt from the edges of the doors so that he could examine the screws in the hinges. The screwdriver refused to grip on the metal, which crumbled away without turning the screw.

Kevin looked up and shook his head, 'No chance, we'd be here all night.'

'Okay Sarg, it was worth a try.' Carmen gave the go ahead.

They all stood back from the door as Lucas raised the sledge hammer once again. Another silence fell in the park as the hammer came smashing down upon the door. The cracking sound of timber attempting to resist resonated throughout the ruins. The sledge hammer was raised and then brought down again and again upon the same spot. Each blow weakening the timber. The wood splintered and the metal buckled. One final blow saw the door collapse completely.

After You, Your Majesty

Oohs and aahs erupted from the crowd as the overhead spotlights showed beneath the door a spiral staircase leading down into the secret chamber. Lucas helped Kevin to pull the door off and put it out of the way.

'Tis time your Majesty, shall ye descend alone?' The sensible tone used by the Scot recalled the King's wandering wits momentarily.

'No, oh no, no! Miss Roberts must come, and this fine specimen of a man.' The King reached out to lay his hand upon Lucas' sleeve. Lucas cast a quizzical look at Kevin, unable to keep his cheeks from flaming up. 'No one else, till all is ready,' added the Monarch.

Ian looked slightly disappointed, *finally my dream of finding James' Holy Bible is about to come true, and I'm not permitted to take part in its discovery.* King James sympathetically patted his head. 'You shall join us soon, Ian, but first it is essential to ensure that all is well before too many set eyes upon what may be below.'

'Of course, your Majesty.' Ian accepted this grudgingly and he could only solemnly watch as the King took Carmen's hand and led her and Lucas into the darkness below.

Why Do I Feel Afraid?

By the time the crowd and the Press had been gathered above, Jenny and Sir Rupert were once more fully attired, the bed covers straightened and they had had a light meal. All was in readiness for their rescue, but although Jenny had faith in her friends above, she couldn't shake off the feeling of nervousness.

It isn't that I'm about to be parted from Sir Rupert, I have accepted that. I don't like it but have accepted it. It isn't the possibility that out there could still be someone willing to kill to stop us completing this mission. As Jenny paced nervously, Sir Rupert took pity on her and sitting down on the chair, drew her onto his lap. With a sigh, Jenny laid her head against his shoulder.

'What troubles thee, mine love?' Softly he brushed his lips against her hair.

'I don't really know, Rupert. Naturally I'm sad that we'll soon be separated, but that doesn't explain why I feel so scared. It's almost as if something is going to end.'

His arms tightened around her, *I wish that we could make our last moments together last for a very long time. It isn't possible, I know this, but I just want to hold off the inevitable for just a little longer,* sighed Sir Rupert. 'Is there nothing that I can do to ease thy worry?'

Jenny smiled at his concern. 'Thank you darling, but I think half the battle would be won if I only knew what I'm so worried about!'

Sir Rupert raised her face so that he could look into her eyes. 'I must tell thee how much I love thee…'

Jenny interrupted him. 'Please Rupert, you don't have to. If I don't know how you feel after our time together then I must be pretty stupid.'

The room virtually shook with the pounding of the sledge hammer upon the door above. Jenny nearly fell off Sir Rupert's lap, and he instinctively reached for his sword. She laid her hand over his, when she had righted herself.

'It's all right. This should be our rescuers.' Jenny spoke a lot calmer than she felt. Releasing the hilt of his sword, Sir Rupert assisted Jenny to her feet, as she nervously made sure that her hair and dress were in order. This brought an amused smile to the Knight's lips.

'Ready mine love?'

Jenny inhaled deeply. 'No, not really, but we've got to go through with this!'

'That's mine brave girl!' He kissed her with such passion that they only looked up when the outer door was finally removed completely, and a bright, penetrating light shone down.

At Last! At Last!

Carmen had to fight to control her instinct to run down the stairs and into Jenny's arms. Protocol demanded that King James preceded her and Lucas. Tears began to fall uncontrollably as Carmen saw Jenny and Sir Rupert standing still locked in each other's arms, Jenny very much alive.

She waited until Jenny had curtsied, and Sir Rupert had bowed to the King, before running around the Monarch to launch herself at her mentor. Just seeing the tears in Carmen's eyes caused Jenny to start crying as they embraced.

'I thought I'd lost you!' Carmen sobbed.

'I'm so glad that you never gave up,' Jenny laughed.

'At last, at last! Rupert, my friend, can you ever forgive me?' Seeing Sir Rupert was a little too much for the King, who reached out to embrace the Knight.

'I have been given to understand that thee were not quite of thy right mind.'

'You're too good Rupert. Aren't you even a little angry?'

Turning his eyes to rest upon Jenny, Sir Rupert's expression softened. 'I believe that I've been well compensated!' Blushing, Jenny smiled as she took the hand that he held out to her.

'Now that you know that Jenny is alive, is it all right for Ian to come down?' asked Lucas, about to ascend up the steps again.

The King readily agreed, 'Yes, yes! Time we should be leaving.' Lucas trotted up the steps as Sir Rupert attempted to present the closed box containing the two bibles to the King, but the Monarch refused to take it.

'That no longer matters; it was your fate that worried me. My foolish fears meant your unnecessary and premature death.'

Sir Rupert placed the box back onto the desk, before offering the Monarch his hand. 'Then 'tis time thee ceased to punish thyself. Thee were not responsible for thy actions. It is time to let the past go.'

King James willingly took his hand between both of his, 'Too good! Much too good, my dear Rupert.'

A Ghostly Reunion

When Tommy and Ian materialised, Tommy, like Carmen, ran straight into Jenny's arms. 'I'm ever so glad to see you Mistress!' Tommy hid his face against her shoulder, ashamed of his own tears. Jenny forced him to look up and kissed his cheek, 'Darling faithful Tommy!'

He mumbled something incoherently as he glanced curiously across at Sir Rupert Steele. The Knight smiled kindly upon him, not in the least jealous of the lad being in his lady's embrace.

Ian, meanwhile, having located the carved box, was running trembling loving hands over its surface, 'To think that all of one's dreams lay within that one box!' His voice was filled with awe and he didn't even seem to notice the heat that the box emitted to keep anyone but a mortal at bay.

Dean's Disgust

Before Ian could attempt to open the box, down the steps flew Dean. Pushing Tommy and everyone else out of the way, he gathered Jenny up in a rough hug, crushing the wind out of her.

'Thank God, you're alive! I'll make you give up this madness even if I have to marry you to do it!'

Fighting for breath, Jenny managed to disengage herself from him and took a step closer to Sir Rupert. 'I'm sorry Dean, but that's not possible.' She tried to be gentle, considering his highly emotional state.

Dumbly, Dean looked from Jenny to Sir Rupert, whose hand lingered upon the hilt of his sword, ready to defend her if ever necessary.

'No! It's not possible! You and him?' Dean spat the words out in disgust.

'Dean, please, don't make a scene. I was never yours.' Jenny turned away as someone else came down the steps, but Dean seized her arm and dragged her towards him. Jenny had barely cried out before the point of a sword was pressed firmly against Dean's chest.

'Unhand mine lady, I have no grievance with thee, but I will have if thee hurt Jennifer.'

Dean tightened his grip upon Jenny. 'You can't hurt me!' He declared to the Knight. The sword was pressed further into Dean's skin to prove that it could do more than harm him, as blood was drawn.

'Release her now or I'll do more than hurt thee.' The look in Sir Rupert's eyes was enough to make Dean realise he was deadly serious, and he let go of Jenny's arm.

'Well done Rupert! Defend thine own!' King James broke into applause. Jenny and Sir Rupert exchanged embarrassed glances, as Carmen thumped Dean's arm.

'Behave yourself, or you can leave!' Carmen demanded. Dean glared down at her, but refrained from retorting as she would throw him out if he created a fuss.

The World Is Watching

One of the conditions for getting the media to cooperate was that Dean had to allow one cameraman into the chamber soon after it was open. He would then relay the action straight to the various television stations participating, as well as to a large screen up above for the spectators to also watch.

The lucky cameraman, Steve, had quietly entered the Chamber as Dean had grabbed Jenny, and he had set up his equipment without being noticed, until it was necessary for him to turn on additional lighting to make filming in the dimly lit room possible. Not at all liking the sudden burst of light, Sir Rupert started to once more raise his sword.

'It's all right, Rupert.' Jenny laid her hand over his to stop him.

The Knight looked dubiously at the camera. 'This is not a weapon?'

'Of course not you fool!' Dean gave an ugly bark of a laugh.

He received a clip across the back of his head from Carmen. 'He's hardly likely to know that, having been cut off down here for 390 years! Go on, get out!' When it looked like Dean wasn't going to obey, Ian McGregor and Tommy grabbed an arm each and marched Dean towards the steps.

The List Of Traitors

Making his way down the steps, Judge Nelson had to step aside as Dean stormed up past him. 'Miss Weston, I'm Jarrett Nelson, Chad Nelson's brother. I want to apologise for what he tried to do to you.'

'Thank you Judge.'

'Perhaps if you could give me this list they're desperate for, I can put a stop to any further attempts upon your life.'

'Of course,' Jenny turned to the desk, opened the top drawer and removed one of the sealed bags of ashes and handed it to the Judge. He looked puzzled, before breaking into a smile.

'I assume there are no copies?'

'None.'

'You didn't happen to notice who was on the list?' Jenny shook her head. Accepting this, he thanked her before ascending the steps.

Carmen blinked twice in surprise. 'I didn't think after all we've been through, that the organisation would simply ask for the list.'

Smiling, Jenny answered, 'The Judge wasn't actually a member, but it was a logical move to stop any further deaths occurring.'

The Recipe For Immortality

'Which bring us to the second important document...' Jenny looked around until she focussed upon the four poster bed. 'Well, my Lord, I presume you would like the formulae for immortality?'

A deep chuckle answered her, as Lord Death slowly materialised, in one of his less drastic and more pleasing male guises, where he sat upon the edge of the bed. Instinctively, Sir Rupert moved protectively towards Jenny, his eyes wary. She presented the second small bag of ashes to Lord Death with a curtsy. Taking the ashes, a gleam of amusement twinkled in his eyes as he gazed fondly at Jenny.

'You know what you have done, don't you?' His tone was light, not in the least annoyed.

'It is best this way. The circle of life must continue.'

'Were you not even slightly tempted by immortality?'

Smiling sadly, Jenny shook her head. 'When it is my time to cross over, I'll be ready. I know who will be waiting for me.' Tenderly she reached out for Sir Rupert's hand.

Sean Shows His True Colours

This interchange was interrupted by the sound of feet pounding down the steps. All eyes and the camera turned to see who descended. Carmen wasn't really surprised that it was Sean Hanson, who also wrapped Jenny up in his arms.

'Thank God! We thought you were dead!' Jenny struggled in his embrace as she found it difficult to breath. Sean was relentless in his hold.

'Sean ease up, Jenny's going blue!' ordered Carmen, pulling on his jacket sleeve. He released Jenny only long enough to spin her around so that he held her with her back pressed against him. With one arm holding Jenny, the other hand produced a pistol from the waistband of his trousers, which Sean pressed against her temple.

'Now then, let's cut the crap! I want that Bible.' Sean's whole appearance changed, his face hardened, his voice was no nonsense and cold, his eyes were filled with determination.

Sir Rupert tightened his grasp on the hilt of his sword, but Sean held Jenny as a shield between himself and the Knight. Significantly, Sean thumbed back the safety catch of his pistol.

'I have no compunction about pulling the trigger!' Although Sir Rupert removed his hand from the hilt of his sword, he didn't relax his defensive poise.

'If Sean wants the book, let him have it but if it is the list of traitors or formulae for immortality you want Sean, then you're too late. Both are destroyed,' Jenny explained.

There was a moment of silence before Sean slowly shook his head. 'You're lying! All that time I spent listening to King James droning on about immortality being just out of reach! I don't care about any list of traitors, but you can't have destroyed that formula!'

Lord Death held up the bag of ashes. 'She did, though. You'll have to settle for a couple of priceless books rather than live forever!'

In disbelief, Sean glanced around at Death. 'Who could destroy the chance for immortality?'

Surprising Sean, Jenny laughed. 'Mankind is not now, and probably never will be civilised enough to deal with eternal life. It wouldn't be used as a gift, but as a weapon. The world has too many weapons now; it can well do without this one.'

'You stupid bitch!' Sean's temper broke as he thrust her suddenly away from him. 'I didn't spend three years as a menial gardener to have some moralistic witch turn my dreams to dust!'

You Can't Die Now!

His gun swung up to point at Jenny and as Sean pulled the trigger, Sir Rupert's sword came slashing down upon his gun hand. Sean screamed, clutching a bloodied stump to his chest as his hand, still gripping the pistol, fell to the ground. Sir Rupert, seeing Jenny collapse as she clutched her chest, snarled as he swung his sword up and took Sean's head straight off his body.

Dropping his bloodied sword, Sir Rupert paid no attention to the blood that had sprayed everywhere as Sean's decapitated body fell. He had eyes only for Jenny as he knelt down beside her, cradling her in his arms.

As the realisation of what had just happened finally sank in; Carmen screamed. Her whole body shook in shock and Tommy could see she was close to hysteria.

'Get the Doc. Ian. Perhaps he can save the Mistress.' Tommy felt no conviction in his own words. Ian McGregor vanished as Carmen rushed to kneel opposite Sir Rupert, and took Jenny out of his arms.

'Jenny you can't leave me! There is so much yet for you to teach me!' Despite the blood that soaked through her clothes,

Carmen rocked Jenny in her arms but there came no response from her mentor. Tears were falling uncontrollably now. 'We're here to rescue you, you can't die now!'

Lucas came back down the steps with Doctor Shepherd and was momentarily overcome by the carnage before him. Shepherd managed to draw Carmen away from Jenny, and thrusting her at Lucas, recalled him to his duties. The Sergeant held the sobbing girl as the Doctor examined Jenny. It wasn't long before he raised his eyes to meet Lucas' and shook his head.

'I'm sorry. There's nothing I can do. The bullet went straight through her heart!'

Is There Nothing You Can Do?

Carmen broke away from Lucas as she screamed, 'No!' In desperation she turned to Lord Death, her blood stained hands grabbing at the lapels of his jacket. 'Please, please, my Lord! Is there nothing you can do? You've already prevented her death several times, can't you intercede now?' Her eyes begged him to act.

Reluctantly, his Lordship disentangled her hands, to hold them between his own. 'I'm sorry, Carmen, but I can't interfere when it is actually someone's time to go.' The ghosts of Lenny Carter, Nigel Baines, Simeon Masters, David Hedley and Chad Nelson appeared beside Lord Death ready to leave.

'Do you mean that no matter what we did, Jenny wasn't going to survive this mission?' Carmen stared at him in disbelief.

Lord Death sadly nodded. 'I couldn't warn you as you may have tried to prevent it.'

Several Why Questions

'Why?' sobbed Carmen.

Lord Death's eyebrows rose. 'The universal why or do you have a specific why in mind?'

'Why them?' Carmen nodded towards Nigel, Lenny and Simeon. 'Why did Jenny also have to die? Why did you need human agents to collect this immorality recipe?'

It was a moment before Death answered her, 'Even though we knew of the existence of King James' recipe, we had no idea where he'd hidden it except that it was somewhere in this chamber. When King James died he was... even more unintelligible than he is now.'

A giggle escaped from the Monarch, 'Nuttier than my Gran's fruit cake!'

Death cast an indulgent glance at King James before he continued, 'When I first appeared to collect Sir Rupert, it was too late for him to assist me and refusing to leave his guard duty I left him to protect the chamber and all its secrets. Over the ensuing centuries, treasure hunters have tried to find the hidden chamber which became even harder after the fire destroyed the palace above it.'

A frown descended upon Lucas' face as he tried to follow Death's story. 'You said to us in the Dog and Bone that it was Jenny's destiny to free Sir Rupert, so why did you hire the three stooges?' Lucas nodded towards the ghosts of Nigel, Simeon and Lenny. It didn't seem possible but Death actually blushed.

'I knew that who so ever discovered the recipe would have to die to keep the secret hidden. I had hoped that if my three employees found it before Jenny had to descend into the chamber, I could prevent her death now. My job description doesn't involve your human emotions and yet I have become fond of Jenny. I chose these three men because I knew that firstly they can be easily motivated by greed and secondly that their deaths were imminent anyway.'

'You knew that they were going to die like that?' Surprise was written all over Lucas' face.

Death shook his head. 'No, Lenny would be shanked, I believe you call it, in prison for his paedophile ways, Simeon's chain smoking was going to cause a massive stroke and Nigel sexual exploits were also going to be his down fall when one very jealous husband discovered that Nigel was having sex with his wife.'

Doctor Shepherd surprised even himself by asking, 'Why couldn't you find and destroy the immortality recipe yourself?'

Lord Death sighed. 'While it remains hidden, it was safe to just leave it there. Sir Rupert guarded the chamber from within, the destruction of the palace meant the doorway became hidden beneath soil and grass and the Brothers of Anarchy or as you called them The Organisation, also protected the chamber to protect their own secret.' Releasing Carmen's hands, Lord Death tenderly stroked a hand against her hair. 'Be a good girl and bring the box containing the bibles to me Carmen.'

Wiping her hand across her face to dash away her tears, Carmen accepted the handkerchief that the Doctor handed to her and blew her nose as she crossed the chamber to pick up the carved box. When Carmen presented the box to Death, he seemed to hesitate as if steeling himself for something unpleasant before finally taking the box.

The lid slammed shut as certain carved symbols began to glow red hot and the letters on the top of the box re-scrambled themselves. His lordship did not argue when Carmen ripped the box out of his hands. The magical glow immediately died down but had left an imprint upon Lord Death's flesh.

'Magical symbols and spells stop anything other than a mortal being able to touch the box or remove anything from inside it. It is a surprise that King James used magic to protect his treasures when his book "The Daemonologie" denounced witchcraft. Are there any other questions?' Death glanced around the room but received only silence.

Time To Go

Slowly Lord Death rose to his feet and addressed the room at large. 'We shall be departing now! If you please, your Majesty,' Lord Death bowed formally to King James, who acknowledged this condescension with a nod of his head.

'Yes, yes, it is time to go.' The King strode happily across the room to join Lord Death. Mandy the housemaid, materialised with Ian McGregor and they joined the King. Tommy affectionately hugged Carmen before he too joined the group. Sir Rupert still knelt upon the ground, Jenny's body before him.

'Come Rupert, your guard duty is at an end.' Lord Death held out his hand, but Sir Rupert didn't rise or look around.

'I didn't want this, but now that it has occurred, I won't leave without her.' The Knight spoke quietly and calmly.

Take Her Hand

Carmen began to cry again, and when Lucas offered his support, she didn't try to push him away, but clung to him.

'Take Jenny's hand then and rise.' Lord Death was patient as he smiled in understanding at the Knight.

As Sir Rupert obeyed, Carmen gave a cry of disbelief as Jenny opened her eyes and rose to her feet with Sir Rupert. For a brief moment, Carmen thought Jenny was alive, so real she looked, but as Jenny and Sir Rupert approached his Lordship, her mortal body still lay inert upon the floor.

Jenny turned, released the Knight's hand before laying her hands upon Carmen's shoulders. The younger woman immediately turned and wrapped her arms around Jenny.

'What am I supposed to do without you?'

Patiently as the girl sobbed, Jenny brushed her hand over her hair. 'Follow your heart and trust your friends. You must remember that every time you successfully counsel someone into crossing over, you'll have to say good-bye as well.'

'But I was supposed to rescue you!'

'You have, Carmen. It's just not the sort of release that you had expected.' Jenny held Carmen at arm's length to look into her face. 'You mustn't blame yourself for my passing. We cannot escape death; it is a part of our lives that we must all accept.' Gently she wiped Carmen's tears away, as she sniffed inelegantly.

Sean's Punishment

I have one request,' Carmen addressed Lord Death, 'I want to know what his punishment will be?' She pointed to where the three pieces of Sean Hanson's body lay.

With a devilish smile that sent a chill down Carmen's spine, Lord Death gestured towards the pile of body parts, and Sean's spirit rose to its feet. Jenny had to hold Carmen back from attacking the assassin's ghost.

'No Carmen, leave this to Cherberus,' As she spoke, the huge dog bounded down the steps.

Cherberus put his head on one side as he looked at Jenny. 'I'm sorry we won't be working together any more Jenny. I'll keep an eye on your protégé.'

'Thank you Cherby,' Jenny scratched his ear.

Cherberus turned to Sean Hanson, who was looking down disbelievingly at his dismembered mortal body. As the hound growled and approached Sean, Carmen had a question. 'Why does Sean not have to face Judgement?'

Lord Death looked down at her mockingly. 'My dear child, he committed a horrendous crime before my very eyes, his guilt is immediately noted upon his record and punishment is swiftly dealt in our world.'

Cerberus jumped, knocking Sean's ghost to the ground and as he screamed in terror, the huge hound tore the ghost to shreds, ensuring that every particle was taken in, before trotting over to sit at Lord Death's feet.

Finally Jenny released Carmen, who tried to continue to cling to her Mentor. 'It's time we left, Carmen,' she spoke gently, detaching Carmen's arms from around her.

'Thank you so much for all you have done for me. I shall never forget you!' Carmen permitted herself one more hug of Jenny before she moved to stand beside Sir Rupert, taking his hand.

Get Her Out Of Here

Lord Death and his collection of spirits began to fade from view. Carmen watched, tears once more falling, until the ghosts had vanished completely. Only then did she give in completely to grief, Lucas grabbing her before she could collapse to the ground in hysteria.

'Get her out of here Lucas.' Doctor Shepherd looked at her with a professional eye.

Lucas nodded, sweeping Carmen into his arms before carrying her up the steps to the fresh night air. Doctor Shepherd looked sadly around him at the additional two lives that this treasure had taken. Stepping over to the bed, he removed the doona and laid it carefully over Jenny's body.

Glancing across to the cameraman, whom everyone seemed to have forgotten, but had recorded the whole extraordinary scene, Doctor Shepherd addressed him, 'Time you packed up my boy. This is now a crime scene. There's nothing more to see.' Obediently, perhaps partly because he was still numb from what he had witnessed, the cameraman didn't argue, but picked up his equipment, and preceded the Doctor out of the room.

Stunned Silence

In the ruins above, the assembled crowd stood in a stunned silence; even the reporters were momentarily lost for words. Doctor Shepherd glanced across to where Evelyn was holding back his own tears as he tried to comfort his sobbing Grandmother. Judge Nelson led a shocked Earl into the pub so that Marcus could provide the stunned crowd with a stiff tonic.

'Get Carmen back to the pub, if necessary I can sedate her.' The calmness of the Doctor's voice was like a cold slap in the face for Evelyn.

'It really did happen, didn't it? Jenny really is dead!' In Evelyn's voice was the hope that what they had seen on the big screen had been untrue. Placing his hand on the younger man's shoulder, Doctor Shepherd nodded his head.

'Yes, I'm sorry.' Lucas carried the distraught Carmen to a car to drive her to the Dog and Bone and Evelyn and Kathleen May weren't far behind them.

Doctor Shepherd approached Kevin Harris, who was the only one who seemed to have control of himself, as he spoke authoritatively into his mobile phone. Lisa stood crying beside him. The Doctor waited until the Inspector had ended his phone call before speaking.

'Is there anything you need of me? Otherwise I'll see what I can do for Carmen.' Absently he handed Lisa a tissue, which she gratefully took.

'No thank you Doctor. God, what a mess!' Finally the control over his emotions broke and Kevin's voice trembled slightly. Bobby Michaels, Natalie Laurence and a couple of other police officers started to herd the stunned crowd out of the Park.

Officials Take Over

An ambulance silently entered the park and drove across the lawn between the departing people, to get closer to the ruins. Bobby had retrieved official barrier tape from the patrol car and was already cordoning off the area. It was an open and shut case, with them all actually witnessing the murder and Sir Rupert's swift retribution. There were still procedures to follow, though, and the need to keep prying eyes and shifty fingers out of the chamber.

Dean had lost his control and had to be led away by Cheryl, who although knew that she should be back at the pub, where Marcus would need a hand, she also knew she had to help another person suffering great emotional or physical pain. She saw him home, depositing him with his mother, rather than taking him to the pub. The last thing Dean needed was more alcohol.

It was not long before the forensic team arrived; their presence was a matter of routine rather than a desperate search for clues. The official wheels turned silently and efficiently as the bodies were removed from the secret chamber, and evidence was collected, or captured upon film.

Kevin got hold of the original recording of the events, and the media cars quickly dispersed with this news breaking story. The ambulance departed, and it was not long before forensic did too. Soon all that remained were members of the police force.

A tarp was placed over the entrance way weighed down by stones on the corners, and finally lots were drawn to see who would take first watch. The Security Guard would remain at the Council's expense, but also one police officer. In this case, Bobby had drawn the short straw. Lisa felt guilty about being relieved that it wasn't her that had to remain at the ruins, as she felt emotionally and physically drained.

She didn't reject Kevin's offer to see her home, and gratefully leant her head against his shoulder when he placed a protective arm around her waist. This was done in full view of their colleagues, but Lisa didn't care.

Her relationship with Kevin would be the talk of the station tomorrow, but she didn't care about that either. 'If only' scenarios were running through her brain, that only proved to make Lisa sadder. Kevin kept up a gentle flow of inconsequential talk that Lisa generally didn't hear, and only occasionally gave an incomprehensive answer.

Kevin would have left Lisa at the front door of her parent's home, but her mother ran out and dragged them both inside for a cup of tea. He wasn't quite prepared to meet Lisa's family, but they made him very welcome, and luckily for him, all they could think about was Jenny's murder.

THURSDAY

Reality Sets In

Breakfast the next morning was a subdued affair, with the newspapers and television being shunned in the restaurant and the saloon as they didn't want a vivid reminder of the events of the previous evening. Lucas' children, Tim and Jayne assisted in the restaurant as Carmen didn't feel that she could deal with customers.

Instead, Carmen steeled herself to go into Jenny's room to pack up her belongings. The delicate scent of Jenny's perfume lingered and Carmen dragged in an unsteady breath as her feelings threatened to overcome her. She moved around the bed to open the windows and took several deep breaths of fresh air before turning back to pack up Jenny's belongings.

It was a difficult job, every article of clothing, each book and personal item was a visual and an olfactory reminder of their late mistress. Having finished packing, Carmen placed the bag beside the door to take downstairs, before sitting down upon the bed and picking up the stuffed black leopard toy that had always accompanied Jenny. Hugging the leopard tightly against her chest, Carmen gave in finally to her tears.

For nearly ten minutes, she let her grief have its reign, before she used several tissues to blow her nose and dry her eyes. Putting the stuffed cat upon the packed bag, Carmen sat down on the floor beside Mitzy and her basket of kittens. The kittens were unnaturally subdued, and Mitzy, wore the concerned look that she had several days before when she had first arrived at the Inn. Carmen spoke softly to the nervous ginger, who settled a little under the reassuring stroke of Carmen's hand.

Relocating Mitzy And Her Kittens

There was a quiet knock at the door that caused Mitzy to look up expectantly, hoping that it would be Jenny about to enter the room. There was a look of disappointment upon the cat's face as Lisa and Kevin entered.

'Mitzy and her kittens will need a temporary new home.' Kevin knelt down and offered his hand to Mitzy to sniff.

'I thought Mitzy was going to stay here?' Carmen looked puzzled from one to the other.

'Eventually, yes, but we felt that you had enough on your plate without having to look after Mitzy too.' Lisa smiled.

'That is so thoughtful; I hope it's not too much to ask?'

'You weren't asking, we're telling you!' Kevin grinned as Mitzy licked his hand. 'They'll have the run of my house, without getting under anyone's feet.'

They picked up the bits and pieces that surrounded the care of the cats, bedding, kitty litter, food bowls, as well as the cats and took them downstairs to Kevin's car. Lisa sat in the back with the cats to keep the kittens under control, who wanted nothing more than to use their claws to crawl across the roof, or up Kevin's arm.

They couldn't use a carry case or box as Mitzy had a fear of small places due to the sack her previous owner had tried to drown her in. Lisa found great pleasure in watching Mitzy and the kittens explore Kevin's house. Mitzy was extremely cautious, but the kittens were into everything.

Carpe Diem

Kevin made a pot of tea as Lisa sat on the floor to play with the mischievous kittens. When he joined her in the lounge room, he placed the mugs of tea on the coffee table and sat back in his favourite chair to watch Lisa. The simple joy she displayed playing with the little bundles of fur brought a smile to his features. Looking up to catch Kevin watching, Lisa blushed and self-consciously reached for her cup of tea.

'What is it?'

'You'll probably hit me, but seeing you sitting on the floor playing brought the idea that you would make a very natural mother.' His smile spread to light up his eyes.

Laughing, Lisa put her cup down again. 'You're not propositioning me are you, Detective Inspector?'

This brought colour to his cheeks. 'I merely made an innocent observation that you'd be very good with children.'

'I'm sorry! I jumped to a conclusion!'

'More like leapt to a conclusion!' Kevin chuckled, picking up one kitten that was bravely attacking his shoe laces.

'Don't rub it in.' There was a pause as Lisa concentrated upon the kitten. 'Tell me just one thing...' She took a deep breath before continuing, 'When you visualised me as a mother, was it here in this room with your children?'

Kevin didn't immediately answer. 'We haven't progressed to even holding hands, let alone having children together.' His smile was mischievous. 'What's brought this change on?'

'It was Jenny's death actually. It made me realise that we never really know where or when it will be time for us to go.' Putting the kitten down, Lisa got up to sit in the chair beside him. 'I'm not trying to force you into anything, but I realise that I shouldn't allow any opportunities to slip by.'

'Carpe diem?' Kevin's eyebrows rose. 'Seize the day?'

'Something like that.'

'Then you won't mind if I do this then?' Smoothly he put his arms around her waist, and he kissed her. For a brief moment Lisa held back, but she soon placed her hands against the front of his shirt, not to push him away, but draw him nearer.

Mitzy, sliding unobtrusively into the room, looked condescendingly upon the entwining couple. *They are harmless though, and I'm prepared to forgive any foibles, as these humans are going to look after me and my children.*

Deciding though it was time for food, in an attempt to put a stop to it; she jumped up onto Lisa's lap and meowed in a demanding tone. She got their attention almost immediately, and as Kevin drew a little away from Lisa, Mitzy settled herself down, satisfied, upon Lisa's lap and began to purr.

The Shrine

The ruins became a focal point for the curious and the morbid. The door was still roped off and one police officer remained on guard at all times, even though the Council were forced to continue to ensure that there was a security guard within the park.

There was a moment of silence when Carmen was permitted into the roped off area with a bouquet of roses to lie over the boarded up door. It was definitely going to be a seven day wonder, drawing a crowd before the fascination would finally cease. The police just hoped that the seven days would go quickly.

FRIDAY

Requiem

More than a day had now passed since the startling events and most people were already returning to their normal routines. A small private ceremony was held for Jenny and Sir Rupert before the cremated ashes of the lovers were spread over the ruins of Theobalds Palace. The entire local police force was there in full dress uniform, and Jenny's parents, who had been overseas, managed to arrive in time for the ceremony.

Even without ever meeting them, Carmen immediately recognised Jenny's mother. She was an older version of Jenny, and it was necessary for Carmen to swallow very hard on the lump in her throat, before she could address the Westons.

In the ruins, the haunting music of "My Immortal" and "Bring me to life" from Evanescence's "Fallen" CD, which was a favourite of Jenny's, floated upon the breeze as Carmen sprinkled the ashes of Sir Rupert and Maggie and Harry Weston sprinkled their daughter's.

Except for the music, this rite was performed in silence. Several other Spirit Healers had travelled from various parts of the country to be present. Heads were bowed, and prayers were said, but when the music finally ended, the majority of the crowd, gently faded away.

It's So Unfair

Evelyn and Carmen stood alone in the ruins, except for the security guard, who kept a discrete distance away.

'If only…' Carmen broke off in a sob, and couldn't finish her sentence.

A gentle laugh came from behind them, causing the young lovers to jump startled. Turning, they watched as Lord Death materialized. 'Throughout life, child, there are a million 'if only'. Time cannot be reversed, but it is an excellent teacher.'

'But it's so unfair!'

His Lordship didn't disagree with her. 'Unfortunately many things in life are unfair. You don't know if turning left instead of right is the correct move until after you have made it, and can review your decision in hindsight.'

'Surely you didn't want this to happen?'

His Lordship shook his head. 'I have no say as to how and when people will die. I'm only the messenger boy.'

'But you prevented Jenny's death several times before the Bible was found!'

'You and I, my dear child, are merely the servants of the Powers That Be. Ours is not to question why…'

A shiver ran through Evelyn who completed the saying, 'Ours is but to do or die! Do any of us have control over our own destinies?'

'Of course you do. Yours is the decision whether you go left or right.'

'That's a great help!' drawled Evelyn.

His Lordship laughed. 'That's life!' He began to fade away and although Carmen had a hundred and one questions, she didn't stop his departure.

A Trust Fund

That afternoon was to be one of even more surprises. Dean Schofields set up a trust fund in Jenny's name, not only enough for Carmen to go to University, but enough for any Spirit Healer to do likewise - now and in the future. The Earl of Elgin arranged for the contents of the secret chamber to be relocated to the British Museum.

Jenny had made a will only the day before she had disappeared into the pond, and had left it in the care of Lucas. This he handed to Jenny's parents after the funeral service at the ruins. The contents were a complete surprise to Carmen as Jenny had left to Carmen all her books and research dealing with her time as a Spirit Healer, as well as any of her clothing that Carmen wanted.

Everything else was left to her parents to dispose of as they saw fit. Carmen was touched by the gesture, *I know that my new view on life is all due to Jenny. I will never forget the last week or so, and I will never forget Jenny.*

MONDAY

An Invitation

It seemed as if the past events were already becoming just a memory for so many people, so it was a surprise when Carmen received another letter with a crest on it.

'Mum, I have another letter from the Earl!' There wasn't one pair of eyes in the restaurant that were not turned with interest to look at Carmen who impatiently tore open the envelope.

There was a hushed silence as she removed a letter and what appeared to be an invitation or thank you card. 'Next week there'll be a special ceremony at the British Museum with a mock-up room of King James' secret chamber.'

There was a murmur of astonishment, but it was Cheryl who actually voiced their thoughts, 'These sorts of things usually take months to organise.'

Carmen waved the envelope in front of her mother, which bore the Earl's coat of arms, 'Friends in high places!'

'Is this ceremony open to all?' Penny, who was standing in the doorway of the kitchen, asked the question that was on all the customers' minds.

Carmen checked the letter before replying, 'Yes, anyone can attend, but apparently there is to be a special section for V.I.P.s.'

'Is that what the card is about?' asked Cheryl.

'I think that everyone in the rescue team will be getting a special invitation.' Carmen handed over the invitation card to her mother.

'It will give you some sense of closure to Jenny's death.' Cheryl put her arm around her daughter's shoulders. Carmen nodded, unable to trust herself to speak at the mention of Jenny's name. It still brought a lump to her throat.

The news of the Museum opening function spread quickly through the village, and had an uplifting effect upon their spirits. Arrangements were made for several busloads of villagers to travel to London to attend the occasion.

THE NEXT MONDAY

The British Museum

Nearly all of Waltham Cross closed down for the morning and there was a mass exodus to the British Museum in London. Great interest had risen all over Britain, in fact the world, in regard to the secret chamber of King James. As Carmen and Evelyn were escorted with the other rescue members by an usher towards chairs that were roped off, the museum began to fill with academics, scholars, archaeologists and peers of the realm. As well as most of Waltham Cross, there was also the curious, and of course the media.

There were two rows of seats, split in half by an aisle in the middle, and were reserved for V.I.P.'s. Carmen felt nervous sitting in the front row, with the rescue team, as around them were seated Earls, Dukes, Lords and Ladies as well as high ranking members of Parliament.

There was a buzz of talk as the Earl entered the museum and made his way across to the rescuers. They rose to their feet, Evelyn with some difficulty. The Earl placed his hand upon Evelyn's shoulder urging him back into his chair before he turned his attention to greet the others. He shook hands warmly with each of them.

The television cameras were strategically placed around the room, panning slowing the crowd, the VIP area, and the display. In the front row of seats on the other side of the aisle, there were about a dozen seats empty. Carmen was wondering what they were waiting for, when a burst of music suddenly made her jump.

Royal Entrance

It took more than half a minute for Carmen to realise that the music was 'God Save the Queen' and Lisa was impatiently tugging on her arm to drag her to her feet. Entering through the front doors and making her stately way to the seats reserved for her, was Her Majesty, Queen Elizabeth the Second. With her were Prince Phillip, Prince Charles, Camilla, Duchess of Cornwall, Prince William, Catherine, Duchess of Cambridge, toddler Prince George and little Princess Charlotte as well as Prince Harry, the sight of the handsome young Royals caused quite a stir amongst the young women in the crowd.

The Museum Director escorted the Royals to the front and after exchanging greeting with the Earl, they took their seats. Carmen felt that she would faint, never in her life had she thought she would be this close to royalty. Evelyn brought her back to reality as he swayed unsteadily on his feet. Standing still for long periods wasn't something he could do yet. Carmen reached out to steady Evelyn, supporting him as she eased him back into his chair.

Alastair Bruce, the Earl of Elgin, stepped forward and briefly outlined to the assembled what had occurred at Waltham Cross, leading up to this moment. His words so graphic and eloquent brought it all flooding back to Carmen, so that even before the ribbon was cut by the Queen to open the mock-up of the secret chamber, Carmen was already crying. Handing her a small packet of tissues, Evelyn noted that Lisa had already opened her packet and was trying to discreetly dry her eyes and blow her nose.

The Unveiling

There were ooh's and aah's as the curtain was drawn back, to reveal every detail of the secret chamber, right down to the water actually running down the wall into a pool. The reaction was not as astounded as it may have been, due to the fact that the chamber had already been seen by nearly all the world through the media when it had been first revealed. There was still awe, though, as this was as close as they would ever get to the real thing, and it was impressive.

Two mannequins were set up in the middle of the chamber, one dressed as Sir Rupert Steele, the other, Jenny Weston, both dressed in the attire they had been found in. Minus the blood and bullet wound in the middle of Jenny's chest. The sight of the mannequins was too much for Carmen and she broke down. She tried to contain her sobbing by covering her mouth with her tissue, but there was no concealing her sorrow. Evelyn wrapped his arms around Carmen and she buried her head into his shoulder.

Jenny's Return

The Earl was deeply concerned by Carmen's distress as he had a task for her to fulfil. Whilst debating what he could do to ease Carmen's sorrow, he was startled by the cool touch of a hand upon his arm. Looking round, Alastair Bruce had to swallow twice before he could trust his voice. 'Miss Weston, I presume?'

The ghostly figure inclined her head in agreement. 'Yes my lord. Just let me try to calm Carmen.'

'Of course, but why have you not yet passed over?'

'What, and miss my own tribute?' Jenny smiled. 'It's not every day you're immortalised in a museum!' Laughing, the Earl watched as Jenny's ghost glided over the floor towards the rescue team.

Kevin Harris was the first to see Jenny and his hold upon Lisa's hand tightened, causing her to look firstly at him, and then at what held his attention. Finally looking up Carmen burst out of her seat and launched herself into Jenny's arms as Jenny became visible to everyone as she drew more upon Carmen's energy. Carmen didn't care that hundreds of people, least of all members of the Royal family were watching, as she cried in sadness and joy.

Jenny allowed Carmen to cling to her for a moment before she gently put her at arm's length. 'Death is not the end; it is only a link in the continuing circle of life.'

'I need time to grieve.' Carmen dragged in a deep shuddering breath.

'I know,' Jenny drew her back into her arms. 'I was just as deeply affected when my mentor passed over. Right now, though, we need to finish this journey.' As Carmen nodded, Jenny took her hand as they stepped onto the mock set of the chamber.

Upon the desk, stood the carved box, which contained the two priceless bibles; the letters on top of the box had been altered. All attempts to open the box by the museum staff had failed, and Sir Rupert and Jenny hadn't left instructions upon how to break the code. The Earl needed Carmen to solve the puzzle so that its contents could be presented to the Queen. Carmen stared down at the box in dismay. She had never been very good at word puzzles.

With Jenny's assistance, Carmen quickly had the letters in order, and pressing the letters in sequence, she gave a sigh of relief when the lock clicked its release and she could lift the lid off.

Presenting The Bibles

Lifting the box carefully, as it was quite heavy, Carmen carried it out of the mock chamber and towards the Earl and the Queen. Cautiously, Carmen curtsied before her Majesty before offering the open box. The Queen reached inside and withdrew the King James Bible.

'Your friend and Mentor shall never be forgotten for the discovery of such a rare piece of our history,' stated Queen Elizabeth.

Without knowing why, Carmen said, 'There is another book inside the box, your Majesty.'

Passing King James' Bible to a waiting museum official, the Queen pushed aside the black silk and lifted out the second bible. The sight of this tome caused even the Earl to lose his poise as they found themselves looking at a rare copy of Gutenberg's bible.

The Museum Director fainted and cameras flashed, capturing this historic moment. Another official took the book and box from Carmen so that she could return to her seat, but the reigning monarch of England had an unusual request.

'I wonder if it is possible to actually thank Miss Weston and Sir Rupert Steele? Without either of them none of this could have been possible.'

Final Appearance

Glancing around the room for support, Carmen caught sight of Lord Death perched on the edge of the desk in the mock chamber, visible only to Carmen and as he nodded, Sir Rupert materialised beside Jenny. As they drew upon Carmen's energy, they both became visible to all eyes.

Excitement at seeing not one but two ghosts appear caused the room to burst into a fever pitch of wonder. The central characters ignored this fuss as Sir Rupert swept into an elegant bow, and Jenny curtsied before the Queen. It was obvious that her Majesty was a little thrown about actually meeting a ghost but her years of regal training mean that she kept her poise.

'Neither of you shall be forgotten for the service you have performed for your country. Your names shall always be linked to King James' Bible.'

'Thank you your Majesty.' Jenny linked her hand with Sir Rupert's as they turned back to where Carmen was waiting for them.

Lucas jumped to his feet, 'Three cheers for Sir Rupert Steele and Jenny Weston!' He called out to the crowd, who surprised him by readily responded. Jenny tried to wave down their cheering, but couldn't make herself immediately heard.

'Very touching, Senior Sergeant, but that should have been Sir Rupert and Lady Jennifer Steele.' She announced as soon as the room had quietened down.

With a squeal of delight, Carmen hugged first Jenny and then an astonished Sir Rupert.

'Is that possible?' Kevin Harris looked faintly sceptical.

It was Sir Rupert who replied, placing his arm around Jenny's waist. 'Whilst we stood before the Great Judge, our misdemeanours were apparently so small that He decided to perform a marriage ceremony instead.'

Jenny laughed, hugging her new husband. 'Besides which Rupert is an honourable man, no matter how much he loved me, he couldn't foresee us spending an eternity living in sin.' She became serious again, 'This will be final time that you will see us Carmen. I know you'll grieve, but you must try to remember that we're very happy.'

Tears were already beginning to form in Carmen's eyes as she nodded her head, but she tried to hold them back. The ghost lovers faded out of vision and as the crowd burst into applause, Lord Death also disappeared from Carmen's sight.

Group Hug!

As Carmen appeared about to give into her turmoil of emotions, Lucas dragged Evelyn and the other two police officers to their feet saying, 'Group hug!' They did too, much to Lucas surprise, all of them swept up in the emotion of the moment. The proceedings returned to some semblance of order, the rescuers sitting down once more, as the Royals made a stately exit. The crowd quickly dispersed and the media crews packed up their equipment to head off to the next story.

Life Goes On

Soon all that were left was the rescue team and the museum staff, who were busy tidying up the chairs.

'I think we deserve a pint.' Kevin looked from the mock chamber to his companions.

'I think we deserve lunch.' Lisa shook her head.

Kevin groaned. 'Not on my meagre salary you won't!'

'Let's discuss this outside.' Lucas linked his arm through each of theirs and directed their footsteps towards the doors. 'I think the Museum Director wants us out of here.'

Carmen turned to glance at where the Director was standing, glaring at them. A hint of mischief made her eyes sparkle. 'By the way,' she called out to the Director, 'Did you know you have several permanent ghosts here?'

Evelyn burst into laughter. 'Quick Sarg, get her out of here before we're all thrown out.' They filed out of the building, so glad to be alive, so happy that this mission was finally over, and so relieved that death is never the end - it is only a new chapter.

ABOUT THE AUTHOR

Anne-Marie Price was born and raised in Perth, Western Australia. She lives with her parents Margaret and Laurence and has two cats, Mickey and Jackson.

She has been a member of the Society of Women Writers WA since 2009 and has been their secretary since 2011.

Anne-Marie has had articles and flash fiction stories published in the SWW In Print Magazine as well as The Readers World Magazine.

In 1997, she obtained a Degree– Library And Information Studies, in 1998 a Diploma of Comprehensive Writing and in 2009 a Cert IV Training and Assessment to assist her ability to teach others the craft of writing.

Writing is in the blood of the Price family with Anne-Marie being the fourth generation of writers. Anne-Marie has been writing fiction since the age of ten and still uses pen and paper as a preference for a first draft.

Also By This Author

Hostage Of Diplomacy
2015
Contemporary Romance

www.ingramcontent.com/pod-product-compliance
Lightning Source LLC
Chambersburg PA
CBHW071053250626
47159CB00002B/461